DEAD
WATER

DEAD
WATER

Russ Snyder

DEAD WATER

iUniverse books may be ordered through booksellers or by contacting:

iUniverse
1663 Liberty Drive
Bloomington, IN 47403
www.iuniverse.com
1-800-Authors (1-800-288-4677)

ISBN: 978-1-4917-9560-6 (sc)
ISBN: 978-1-4917-9561-3 (hc)
ISBN: 978-1-4917-9562-0 (e)

Library of Congress Control Number: 2016906750

Print information available on the last page.

iUniverse rev. date: 6/10/2016

ACKNOWLEDGMENTS

I'd like to thank Alan Bower and Kevin Bezy from Author Solutions for all their help on this particular journey. Wherever it is that I am; I would not be here without Alan's help.

Also a tremendous shout-out to Traci Anderson of iUniverse. She showed patience, understanding, encouragement, and perhaps most of all, humor, in guiding me through the editing process. I would not have gotten through it without her.

I also must thank Margot Curtis Kinsman, Cheryl Lycans, Barbi Olson Coutts, and Bill Hawkins for all their encouragement and support while traveling this road of writing.

A huge shout-out, and thank-you, to Tracy Birdwell Sandlin for doing the photoshoot that produced my author's photograph for this book cover.

Lastly, but most important, I dedicate this work to 'Cattledog', the best friend I've ever had who I lost last November. Daff, you are *always* with me, in my heart and in spirit.

PROLOGUE

T-Minus 96 Hours

Rijah Ellhad strode confidently through the deep Alaskan woods. He was literally in the middle of nowhere, having parachuted into a small clearing earlier that morning, and now hiking toward his destination, a small unnamed lake chosen carefully for its remoteness. Dressed completely in hunter's camouflage, he traveled light, carrying a backpack with rations and water, a pair of high-quality binoculars, a small pouch attached to his belt, a hunting knife, and a Bushmaster AR-15 assault rifle, which featured a red-dot optical sight, a sound suppressor, and a high-intensity light mounted underneath. A foregrip accompanied the rear pistol grip. The sound suppressor was screwed onto the end of the barrel. He carried two forty-round magazines loaded alternately with fragmentation bullets and armor piercing. The gun was capable of firing either the .223- or NATO 5.56-caliber round.

He also carried a second waterproof pack affixed to the bottom of his backpack. This pack contained numerous specialty items that would be required for the completion of his mission. He paused for a quick drink of water. It was early summer, and the temperature was in the midsixties, with surprisingly few bugs. He continued his journey. It was nearing sundown when he arrived at the lake. He stopped and surveyed the area. He took out his binoculars and carefully scanned the entire shoreline. Not a sign of another person anywhere. He smiled. *Smaller than I thought.* He worked quickly. He removed his backpack and donned some of the gear from the smaller pack: a special hazmat pair of gloves and full head mask. He removed one more item from the pack, a small metal case. With some difficulty, he was able to unlatch the twin catches and open it. Very carefully, he removed a very small item that resembled a medical pill vial. He walked down to the lake. Carefully, he tossed it about fifteen feet out from the water's edge. He quickly turned and walked back to where he'd left the remainder of his gear. He rapidly gathered it up, strapped everything back into place, slung his AR-15 rifle back over his shoulder, and proceeded to walk back the way he had come. He'd been instructed to stay back a quarter mile from the lake. He doubled that distance to be safe. It was just getting dark when he found a spot to camp for the night, although his only camping gear consisted of a small heat-retention blanket.

He was used to sparse gear. In another life, he was a captain in the Iraqi Republican Guard, one of eight officers who made it out of Iraq before the fall of Saddam Hussein. It was a group that had sworn vengeance on America.

He'd been told to wait twelve hours before returning to the lake. He waited fourteen. Once again donning the hazmat gear, he walked down to observe. He took out a small digital camera and took half a dozen photos. He stared at the scene before him, barely believing his eyes. The fish floating on the lake were so thick he felt he could have walked across to the other side upon them. A chill went up his spine. He was prepared to see dead fish, but nothing like the scene before him. He took two more pictures and then left. He had a healthy hike ahead of him to where he would be picked up by helicopter. When he left, his chill went with him.

1.

Sitting behind his desk in the Oval Office, which was brightened by the natural light coming through the three large, perfectly clear, and bullet-resistant windows at his back, newly elected president Robert Williams had secretly changed one rule in the manner America was to fight terrorism. He had added a new element, one that only a handful of people knew about. This new tactic was highly illegal but one that the president felt was necessary. He put his country's safety above all else, including the law as currently written.

A white nondescript van coming out of Mexico, through Texas, had set off radiation-detection devices at the border. These had been installed at all major border crossings between the United States and both Canada and Mexico, the result of a botched attempt to set off a dirty nuclear device in Madison Square Garden that, through no more than sheer dumb luck, had failed.

The FBI had been shadowing the van by automobile and helicopter. It was being carefully watched, with no chance of it slipping away. Several high-resolution photographs had been taken of the driver. The result indicated the driver did not fit any profile thought to resemble a potential terrorist. The van's plates had been run. Surprisingly, it turned out to be not a rental but one belonging to an established business that had been operating for more than thirty years, a used medical equipment supply house.

President Williams met with his director of the FBI, Matt Sanderson, director of the NSA, Elliott Ragar, and Charles Rockford, director of Homeland Security.

Sanderson spoke first. "Mr. President, by all accounts, this van does not appear to be a threat. I think we should have the van stopped and checked out to be sure, but I'm not particularly concerned."

"Matt, what is your take on this?" asked the president.

"I think it's hauling used x-ray equipment. Bought cheap in Mexico and brought here to be sold. We've checked this company out thoroughly, and this seems to be routine for them."

"Anyone else have any thoughts?" the president asked.

The other two men in attendance merely shook their heads.

"Keep on it," directed the president. The three men got up from their chairs and left. The president pondered a moment and then decided to make a phone call. Using a secure line, he called Captain Richard Starr, retired, the unofficial leader of his "group." Under the umbrella of the new president's Department of the Presidential Office, or DPO, this unit was assigned the task of locating, identifying, and eliminating terrorist targets the president designated. This quartet had free rein on how that was accomplished. It consisted of four members: Starr, the nuts-and-bolts leader; Sergeant Marvin Styles, USMC "Force Recon Sniper," retired; Darlene Phillips, arguably the world's best computer hacker; and J. C. Christman, a TOPGUN flight instructor. President Williams had given this party everything they might require to carry out their missions. Starr and the president had been friends most of their lives. There was an unbreakable bond of trust between the two men. It was Starr, a former marine commander, whom the president had approached when the beginning of the idea to change strategy against the terrorists had emerged in his mind. Starr had commanded Styles for a long stint while both were in the marines. Those two, over the years, had developed a trusting friendship. Styles, though never admitting it, considered Starr his best friend. The phone call connected.

"Sir," Starr answered.

"Richard, I wanted to give you a heads-up. That van we've been tracking appears to be a nonthreat at this time. It's believed to be carrying used medical equipment, probably x-ray machines of some type, so your group can stand down for the moment. If anything changes, I'll get right back with you."

"Understood, sir." The call ended.

�֍   ✖   ✖

Starr came out of the communications room at the property he and Styles considered home and then sat down at the kitchen table across from Styles, who was just finishing a cup of coffee.

"Want some coffee?" Styles asked.

"No, thanks. Are you going exploring or something?" he asked, noting Styles's appearance; Styles was fully dressed in camo.

"No, I want to check on a few things over by the bluff," he replied, referring to the rearward side of the property. "Anything up?"

"The Man just called. That van they had under surveillance appears to be okay. It seems to be hauling medical equipment, so we can relax for a bit."

"Good to hear. Not the relaxation but the lack of threat," Styles replied.

"Yeah."

They were back at the Ranch, which consisted of three hundred acres located in eastern Tennessee. It featured the main house, two guest cabins for Christman and Phillips when they were required to be on-site, two barns, and an extensive training course for Styles, including two firing ranges. Styles also had a gym set up in one of the barns. He had a training routine that would make a world-class athlete hurt just to watch. They had been back for less than twelve hours since ending their mission in Saudi Arabia. Darlene Phillips had been dropped off outside of DC so she could return to her apartment, and Christman was in his cabin, probably sleeping. It had been a long and stressful flight, especially getting out of Saudi Arabia.

Starr went into the kitchen, coming back with a pizza that he had thrown into the oven twenty minutes earlier. He tossed it into the middle of the table, along with two plates.

"I swear, Starr, if I eat any more pizza, I don't know if I'll shoot you or me."

"Quit your bitching. It was fast, and I didn't feel like cooking. If you don't want it, don't eat it."

"Bite me," he said as he reached over and grabbed a slice. "Probably oughta call Phillips and tell her we're off the hook for now. We can wait till J. C. wakes up."

"Yeah," Starr agreed. He dialed Phillips, who answered immediately.

"What's going on?" she asked.

"We're standing down. The van doesn't appear to be a threat. Anything changes, I'll be in touch."

"Crap. I just packed two bags."

"Well, now you're ready for the next trip. See? Your time wasn't wasted."

"Thanks, Starr."

"Anytime. Later." He hung up.

Styles just chuckled. "It sounds like she was pretty set to go."

"Yeah, almost disappointed, I think. We got lucky when the president assigned her to us."

"You're right about that. Can't tell her, though." They grinned at each other.

Styles got up, went into the kitchen to pour another cup of coffee, and returned to see Starr toss two strips of pizza crust onto his paper towel that was being used as a napkin. "Didn't take you long to wolf those down," he remarked, receiving a burp in reply.

Starr commented, "That was a hell of a trip we just took."

Styles paused and then responded, "That's straight. I've been going over it in my head, and overall, I think we did a damned good job. We took out some primary targets, and, except for that incident with Phillips, didn't run into any real problems. J. C. did a good job getting our asses outta there."

"Yeah, he did," Starr concurred.

After a few moments of silence, Starr spoke again. "Did you

notice that after the president's phone call on the plane, Phillips went to the bathroom?"

"Yeah, I did."

"Think she made a phone call?"

"I'd bet my ass on it. I've got a real strong feeling that somewhere back there, one might find a corpse with no head."

2.

Somewhere in a secret location, Karyn Mason was enjoying a cup of hot chocolate. It was a homemade beverage that she brought in with her, as opposed to the packaged instant mix that she detested. It was exactly one thirty in the afternoon. A light on one of her screens lit up. She immediately put down her cup and focused all her attention on that screen. It was not a typical computer screen but a large, sixty-inch LED state-of-the-art monitor with crystal-clear resolution that allowed her sharp eyes to take in all the details sent back from the Keyhole satellite she was monitoring. She never ceased to be amazed at how clear of a picture she would be looking at, considering it was taken over ninety miles above the planet.

Karyn knew that any given point in time, there were an extraordinary number of satellites orbiting the earth for countless reasons, such as communications, weather tracking, and perhaps the most important, surveillance. The number of spy satellites is completely unknown. Multiple units are programmed for specific purposes. One might make numerous passes far above the earth and file what it sees. When any obvious difference is observed, it immediately turns its attention to whatever is different or out of the ordinary from what its previously filed programs have observed and recorded.

Within seconds, her fingers were moving quickly around one of her many keyboards. She brought up the area that had set off the alarm. No loud ringing bells or buzzers, just a simple red light. She found herself looking at a small lake, but it didn't look like a lake at all. She brought up the image on file to a similar monitor beside the one she was observing. That screen showed a pristine Alaskan lake, water that was a bright blue in color, the result from the reflection of a cloudless sky. She turned her attention back to the original screen. She zoomed in even closer. Finally, it dawned on her exactly what she was looking at, and she audibly gasped. Dead fish were floating on the surface. From shore to shore, it was nothing but a solid mass of dead fish. She could not see a single patch of water—just dead fish everywhere. She noticed birds also. Some were seen on top of the floating mass, others along the shore. She knew the computer program was recording the scene. There was a limited amount of time before the satellite would be out of range, and she would have to wait until the next orbit to continue her observations. She programmed the satellite to hold its position over the area on the next pass. She watched the screen until finally the image was no longer available.

She immediately called her supervisor. "Sir, this is Karyn. I've recorded something you need to see."

Martin Loren replied, "Be right down."

Thirty seconds later, Martin Loren, daytime supervisor at this facility, was approaching Karyn.

"Whatcha got for me, K?" he asked. He always referred to his personnel by the first letter of their first names.

"Major fish kill, sir. Worst I've ever seen or even heard about."

"Roll it."

Quickly she started the recorded image, leaving the original on the second screen. She offered no communication with her boss. She knew he wouldn't want any. She watched as he intently studied the picture.

"Again," he directed after the depiction was lost. He took control of the keyboard. Several times he paused the delineation and looked intently. After three complete viewings, he directed, "Send everything to my desk, *now.*" Four strides later, he was out of sight.

Within thirty seconds, everything had been shipped over to her boss. Her phone rang. Picking it up, she heard, "I've arranged another satellite to cover the same general area, but it won't be available for about six hours. I want you to start keeping an eye out on other lakes in the area for any similar signs. Be sure to brief your relief."

"Yes, sir." She began to set a program for the second satellite as soon as it was available. She would have it scan above and then below on alternating orbits while keeping the original satellite watching the lake in question.

From his office, Martin Loren called Clay Burrows, assistant director of the NSA.

"Yeah, Martin, what'd you see?" Burrows and Loren went way back together, with Burrows the reason that Loren was in his position.

"Clay, we've got a major—and I mean *major*—fish kill in Alaska. I've never seen anything like it. Hell, you could walk across the damned lake on top of them. There are birds, too, some on top of the floating mass, some on the shore. Don't know what it is, but it sure isn't right. I thought you'd better know."

"Damn straight, Martin. In today's world, you never know what might mean what. I'll be in touch." He hung up.

Instantly, Clay Burrows was on the phone to his boss, Elliott Ragar. "Elliott, you might want to get down to my office. Martin Loren is sending some satellite imagery over that I think you need to see."

"I'll be there in twenty minutes. Don't start the show without me."

Elliott Ragar had requested a meeting with the president. When asked what it concerned, Ragar had only replied, "Sir, it could be something major or nothing at all. However, as the old adage goes, a picture is worth a thousand words. This is a hundred times past that."

"All right, Elliott. One this afternoon would be good. How long do you anticipate this conference will last?"

"Impossible to say, sir. Probably would be a good idea to bring some of the others in." This suggestion surprised the president a bit. Ragar wasn't known for his sharing attitude. "All right. See you at one sharp." He hung up. He called his secretary, Alice Pritchard. The two went back almost twenty years and enjoyed a genuine friendship. The president appreciated her sharp, dry wit. "Get Sanderson, Rockford, Backersley, and Merritt here at one this afternoon. Sharp." He didn't wait for a reply.

"Wonder what this is about," he said aloud. He went back to what he'd been doing, preparing for a showdown with the Democrat leaders of the House and Senate over tax cuts in the impossible task of balancing the country's budget. *What a damned mess those clowns left me with. Two entire administrations' worth of screwups.* He looked out his window. "If I had my way, I'd have your bankers' heads on a pole in front of the Washington Monument," he said to himself, shaking his head in disgust. *I'd like to make greed an offense punishable by horrific death,* he thought. Thinking back to the bureaucrats, he wondered, *How can you not get it?*

His phone rang, interrupting his thought. "Yes, Alice."

"Sir, the meeting for this afternoon has been arranged. I'd appreciate it if you could ask Director Rockford not to be so damned rude. The man's an ass."

President Williams laughed out loud. "I'll take care of it, Alice. Thank you."

"Yes, sir."

Both hung up.

The president thought for a second and then called his secretary back. "Alice, ask Coverley Merritt to be here fifteen minutes early."

"Will do, sir."

Less than a minute later, Alice called President Williams back to inform him that Merritt would be there at 12:45 prompt.

"Thank you, Alice." He returned to his budget problems.

T-Minus 76 Hours

Rijah Ellhad heard the chopper approaching. He turned on his GPS tracker. This would bring the craft straight to him.

The wind had picked up considerably, and the area where he was to be picked up was precariously small and littered with large boulders. When the aircraft was twenty feet above the ground, a rope ladder was thrown out the now open side door.

Great! The lightweight ladder was swinging wildly about, the downward windblast from the helicopter's rotor blades only making the wind much worse. Swearing under his breath, Ellhad grabbed a rung, stepped onto the bottom one, and started a harrowing climb upward. To make matters worse, as soon as he was able to climb two rungs up, the pilot started moving the copter away.

"You stupid ass!" he yelled into the wind, but he was either not heard or ignored. The craft was picking up speed as it climbed upward. Ellhad was hanging on for his life. Agonizingly slow, he climbed toward the open door and safety. The chopper changed direction, which now made the rope ladder swing outward badly. Ellhad was nearly out of his mind with rage, and being loaded down with his rifle and gear only made the climb worse. He didn't dare let go to try to drop the extra weight for fear of falling.

Screaming at the top of his lungs was doing him no good. Gritting his teeth, he managed to make it up two more rungs before he had to stop to rest. Now the helicopter was flying along at close to one hundred miles an hour, and Ellhad found himself nearly horizontal as opposed to vertical. Looking up, he found himself three more rungs to the door. Every muscle in his body was on fire. He knew he had no chance to hang on for the entire ride. He *had* to make those final three rungs. With every ounce of his remaining strength, he started upward. At this point, he didn't really care if he fell or not. One rung, two rungs, and finally his hands were on the rung two inches below the floor of the aircraft. Two arms reached out and helped haul him the rest of the way and into the safety of the chopper.

He just lay there, breathing harder than he had ever before, glaring fire at the man who had helped him aboard. When he could finally speak, he snarled, "Why the fuck did he take off before I could climb up?"

"He was afraid of being seen."

"*Seen? Seen by fucking who?* What did you say?"

"I told him I thought you were going to fall."

Ellhad remained silent for the rest of the reasonably short journey. He changed out of his camo clothing and into jeans and hooded pullover sweatshirt.

Except for the pilot and copilot, he was alone. He noticed the copilot was armed with an AK-47, a Russian manufactured rifle. No words were spoken. Rijah Ellhad was ferried over to a small lake just outside of Bethel.

As the chopper touched down and the pilot shut it down, Ellhad grabbed the AK-47 from where the copilot had placed it and rammed the butt of the rifle twice into the pilot's mouth, knocking out several teeth. "Next time, keep the damn copter in place!"

He departed the helicopter and walked two hundred feet to a small dock where a floatplane was tied up. A man was waiting for him. He merely nodded at Ellhad. The door was open, and Ellhad climbed in. He took one of the six seats and strapped himself in. The pilot finished untying the dock lines and jumped aboard. He quickly made his way up to the cockpit, strapped himself into his own seat, and fired the big radial engine up. It coughed, sputtered, belched smoke, and finally set itself into a loud and shaking idle. After about a minute, it smoothed out nicely. This brought a small sense of relief to Ellhad. He was not afraid of flying but had never liked seaplanes. *Water. That's why they built boats.* Two minutes later, it was skimming quickly across the lake's surface, and then grudgingly, it let go of its grip on the pontoons of the plane. Looking out the window, he had to admit to himself that Alaska was indeed beautiful, as different from his homeland as night was from day. He already knew the plane's destination was just outside of Portland, Oregon. He rummaged through his pouch and found his earplugs. The plane was extremely loud. *Time for a nap.*

3.

At precisely 1:00 p.m., the meeting that President Robert Williams had called convened in the Roosevelt Room. Joining him were Elliott Ragar, Matt Sanderson, Bernard Backersley, Charles Rockford, and Coverley Merritt, who had arrived early. This did not go unnoticed by the other four as they entered the room. Everyone nodded at each other while taking their seats.

President Williams spoke. "Elliott, you requested this meeting — why don't you start?"

"Yes, sir. Gentleman, please take a look at the screen. These pictures were taken yesterday. They show a fish kill of unbelievable proportions. The lake is located in an extremely remote area of Alaska. We've obviously had fish kills before, all over the world. However, by all appearances, this was a complete devastation of the aquatic population. Birds are also seen, both on top of the floating mass as well as along the shoreline. I strongly believe this should be investigated."

Bernard Backersley, director of the CIA, asked him, "Wouldn't this normally be handled by the CDC?"

"Yes. However, these are not normal times."

President Williams stood. "Elliott, we have not had the chance to discuss this. Are you suggesting the possibility that this is not a natural occurrence? It's my understanding that fish kills are usually the result of something causing a lack of oxygen in the water — red tide, for example."

"That is correct, sir. However, in this circumstance, there wasn't any sign whatsoever of any dead fish on the previous orbit. Granted, that was at last light the previous day. Then the next morning, the entire lake was completely covered with dead fish. Whatever caused that fish kill did it overnight. In my opinion, that is *not* natural."

There was a slight murmuring among the group. "I'm inclined to agree, Elliott," replied the president. "After the Madison Square Garden incident, anything suspicious must be identified. I want you to put together a team to go up there and research the cause. Your call on who goes. Charles, I want you to send someone from your group; Coverley, you too." Charles Rockford was the director of Homeland Security, while Coverley Merritt headed up the president's newly formed Department of the Presidential Office, tasked to work with all other agencies on terrorism to keep the president informed in real time. This new approach had been resisted by the others until President Williams set them straight. *"Get on board or get out!"* Compliance had been achieved, but reluctantly. "I want this to be a priority. Get on it now." That statement signaled the end of the meeting. The president left via a private door, while the others started to rise to head for the main entrance.

"Charles, Coverley, how long will it take for you to put people in place?" asked Elliott Ragar.

"Forty-five minutes for me," replied Charles Rockford.

"Same," agreed Coverley Merritt.

"Good. I'll have your people picked up. I'm going personally. We'll take the NSA jet. I'll keep both of you informed personally every step of the way. I'm also going to bring some CDC personnel and let them take the first steps. We need to know what we're dealing with before we just go hiking in there."

"Sounds like a solid plan, Elliott," responded Merritt.

President Williams sat at his desk in the Oval Office, thinking. He was trying to decide if he should apprise former captain Richard Starr on the event unfolding in Alaska. *Better safe than sorry,* he thought. He grabbed a secure line and hit the speed dial.

"Yes, sir," Starr answered on the third ring.

"Richard, something odd is happening in Alaska. There's been a massive fish kill in a very small lake in a remote region. It was picked up by one of our surveillance satellites. It's not like anything we've seen before. The speed in which it happened is what has us concerned. I'm going to give you the GPS coordinates. Pull it up and study the entire area. I honestly don't know if it will involve your group; however, I'd like you to be prepared just in case. Something is very odd, and I don't like odd."

"Yes, sir," Starr replied. "Anything particular I should be looking for?"

"Just look it over. Talk it over among yourselves. I've got a team, including CDC, on their way. It might be nice to get an outside perspective."

"I'll send Christman to pick up Phillips. I'll be in touch."

"Thank you, Richard."

"Anything to try to help, sir."

Starr heard the president hang up. He went outside to the gym that was set up in a barn. Former marine sergeant Marvin Styles was in the middle of his exercise routine. "When you take a break, come find me!" he yelled over at Styles, receiving a grunt in return. Then he went to find J. C. Christman, the former TOPGUN instructor assigned to the group. He heard one of the ATVs fire up and went scurrying over to stop him. "J. C., hold up."

Christman turned and looked at him and then shut the machine down. "Yeah, what's up, Starr?"

"The Man just called and wants us to take a look at something weird in Alaska, some kind of fish kill."

"Fish kill? How would that involve us?"

"Don't know that it does. He just wants us to take a look at it."

"Hell, Starr, about all I know of fish is all you can eat on a Friday night somewhere."

"J. C., just go get Phillips. If the president asks where to go eat, I'll defer to you, okay?"

Christman just grinned and said, "On my way. Does she know I'm coming?"

"Not yet. She will." Right then, Starr spotted Styles coming out of the barn and walked over to meet him.

"What's up?" Styles asked.

"Guess there's some kind of fish kill up in Alaska. President wants us to take a look at it."

"Fish? What the hell we got to do with fish?"

"Christ, I just went through that with Christman."

"So what'd you tell him?"

"Same thing I just told you. He's going after Phillips," he said, referring to the computer guru of the group. "I gotta go call her."

"You do that. I'm going back to the gym."

Starr turned and walked back to the house to make the call.

Back inside the main house of the property known as the Ranch, Starr grabbed the secure landline and hit the button for Phillips's cell. She didn't have a landline. She answered on the second ring.

"Yeah, Starr."

"J. C. is on his way to pick you up."

"This about the fish kill they just picked up on in Alaska?"

Starr was stunned. "How the hell do you know that?"

"I like to keep up on what's going on."

Starr just shook his head. "Well, you're right. The president wants us to take a look at it. He wants an outside opinion."

"From what I've learned, it happened overnight, and looks like it's a total wipeout of everything living in that lake."

"And you know that how?"

"I've seen the photographs, how else?"

Again, Starr just shook his head. "Of course you have. Don't know why I asked."

"Actually, I don't either."

"J. C. should be up there in about two hours, give or take."

"I'll be waiting. Should I bring anything?"

Starr couldn't help himself. "Just your usual bright and cheerful personality."

Click.

❈ ❈ ❈

NSA Director Elliot Ragar had asserted himself right from the beginning that *he* was the man in charge. After assembling the entire research team with all personnel as directed by the president, they had boarded the NSA jet and flown to Alaska. They had flown directly to the airport in Bethel where three FBI helicopters were waiting. Aerial reconnaissance photographs had shown a small clearing approximately six miles from the small lake, their destination point.

The Centers for Disease Control and Prevention had sent four specialists along with full hazardous material gear, including suits, specialty instruments, and a portable lab. The idea of flying over the lake had been discussed, but not knowing what lay ahead of them, that idea was tabled.

"I really think it best that the four of us hike in to inspect the lake first. Not much sense in having the whole team die because we're in a rush. I understand it's imperative that we find out what's going on, but we *have* to maintain certain standards here, Director Ragar," Lawrence Larkin stated emphatically. He was the researcher in charge of the CDC team.

Ragar didn't like it, but he couldn't find a plausible argument against him. "All right, but I want you in constant touch with me personally. As soon as you think it's safe, I want to see this for myself. I have to report to the president."

"Understood, sir." The CDC team assembled their gear, donned their hazmat suits, and then started toward the lake. It was crystal clear, just after nine in the morning. Burdened down as they were, it was estimated it would take them at least six hours to reach the target, possibly longer. This chafed at Ragar worse than a bad case of jock itch. Patience had never been his strongest virtue, something he'd been called down on several times during his career. He went back inside the copter, opened a briefcase, and grabbed a secure satellite phone.

"Yes, Elliott. What do you have for me?" answered President Williams.

"Not much of anything yet, sir; this is more of an update. The CDC team left ten minutes ago to check out the lake. They're going to let me know the second they can determine anything. It was agreed that no undue chances should be taken until we have some idea what we're dealing with."

"That sounds wise, Elliott. How long before they reach it?"

"At least six hours, sir. We set down in the chopper as close as we could, about six miles out. They're suited up, bringing a lot of equipment with them, so it'll be slow going."

"Try not to chew the insides of your mouth out, Elliott. I know how impatient you can be. Don't take any unnecessary risks. Appreciate the update, and keep me posted." He hung up.

Elliott Ragar decided to try to utilize the time beneficially. He got on his computer and Googled *Fish Kills*. He decided to learn as much about them as possible while the CDC crew made their way in.

Charles Rockford, director of Homeland Security, had decided to make the trip himself. In his mind, he didn't want to take the chance of being upstaged by Elliott Ragar. He knocked on the chopper's door.

"Come in."

Rockford entered. "Elliott, any suggestions on what we might do while we're waiting?"

"I'm on the web trying to find out everything I can about fish kills."

"Care for a hand? I'm going to go nuts if I don't find something constructive to do."

Ragar was a bit surprised. Charles Rockford had not been the easiest man to get along with. *Might as well take advantage of free help.* "Sure, Charles. Help yourself to that desk and type in *moron* when it asks for the pass code."

"Moron?"

Elliott Ragar grinned. "Yeah, who'd ever think of it?"

Rockford laughed. "I can't argue with that."

Soon both men were deeply engaged in their search. Three hours went by before either man spoke. Ragar straightened up, stood, and stretched.

This caught Rockford's attention. "Getting anywhere, Elliott?"

"Yeah, I'm getting more puzzled. I can't come up with anything even close to what we apparently have here."

"Same for me."

❊   ❊   ❊

Dressed in their full hazmat suits, the four CDC researchers found making their way through the Alaskan forest difficult. Had the woods been thicker at the base of the trees, it would have been nearly impossible, at least not without damaging their suits. The temperature was cool enough that excessive body heat was not a problem. Slower than expected, the group made its way toward the lake. Twenty yards from the shoreline, the trees began to thin out, and glimpses of what was once a lake became visible. Within two minutes, all four were staring at a spectacle none really expected to see. They were looking at a solid mound of dead fish. Flies were already everywhere. Even birds had accumulated, beginning to feast on the buffet.

"Shit, Larry, do you believe this?" exclaimed Joey Tanelli, who was Lawrence Larkin's right-hand man. They had been working together for almost fifteen years.

"Not really. I've seen some major aquatic catastrophes before, but nothing like this. Get the portable satellite feed up and running. There are people who need to see this."

"It'll be up in five."

"Tracy, start collecting water samples—also half a dozen fish and some of those dead birds. Be *sure* you follow protocol to the letter. Alan, do a preliminary on the water. We'll have to do the fish back at the lab."

Larkin got NSA director Elliott Ragar on the phone. "Director, Larkin here. We've arrived at the site. It's like nothing I've seen before."

"Can you spot anything unusual from just looking at them?" asked Ragar.

"Their eyes are black—other than that, no."

"Black eyes?"

"Yes, sir."

"What does that mean?"

"Probably internal bleeding. We're going to wrap this up and start our way back before it gets too dark to travel. We'll find a place to hole up for the night and get back in the morning. We've got our samples on dry ice, so they'll be fine."

"Don't get eaten by a bear."

"Not to worry. Tanelli has that big Desert Eagle .50 with him. Damned gun could stop a bus."

"Understood. Check in every four hours."

"Yes, sir. We'll be back in the morning," he answered, ending the conversation.

"Sir!" Alan yelled over at him.

"Yeah, you find anything?"

"No, sir. Not a thing. Except for the biological waste from the rotting fish, far as I can tell, this water is fit to drink."

"*What?*"

"It's clean. Even the oxygen level is where it should be. Granted, there are other tests that need to be run to be absolutely certain, but from what I can tell, it's fine."

"The plot thickens," replied Larkin, who was known for his clichés. "Joey, you got that feed up and running?"

"Crystal clear, Larry. Beaming back video as we speak. I was just getting ready to launch our little drone for a fly around."

"Good. Concentrate on the shoreline and out near the middle. Don't take real long; I want to get away from this lake before dark."

"Fifteen minutes and I'll be done."

"Tracy, how are you doing with those samples?"

"Just about finished, sir," she replied. Tracy Bronn was the new member to the team. She'd graduated top of her class at the University of Hawaii and had been a great addition to Larkin's group.

While the other members were completing their assigned tasks, Larkin shot over a hundred photographs on his digital camera.

Finally, the group was packed up and ready to return. Larkin addressed his team. "Okay, everybody, nice and slow. It's almost dark, and we don't need any tears in anyone's suit to ruin the day. Joey, you get some good video for everyone?"

"Oh yeah. I already sent it back to Director Ragar."

4.

Rijah Ellhad had disembarked the plane and walked toward the taxi stand. Before leaving the aircraft, he had donned a disguise. He was now wearing a surfer-style blond-haired wig complete with beard. His dark skin would merely be thought of as a good suntan. He carried with him an old-fashioned army duffel bag. Complementing his appearance, it contained his gear, including his rifle. He hailed a taxi to bring him to a Holiday Inn on the outskirts of Portland, Oregon, a previously chosen meeting place. Room 333. He knocked twice and stepped back. The door opened. He entered, nodding at the swarthy-looking individual who had let him in. The nod was returned. He walked farther into the suite. Sitting around a table were two other men. Both were Iraqi nationals. One was another former member of the Republican Guard; the other had been a senior adviser to Saddam Hussein. All three were part of the group that had abandoned Hussein at the end. The swarthy man had been a member of Saddam's secret police. Assad Bassir, whose specialty was interrogation—or torture—had been recruited.

Jamil Abdul-Nasir rose to greet Ellhad. "You have done well, my brother. Our sources tell us the biological agent surpassed their expectations. No living creature in that lake survived. The speed with which death occurred was not to be believed. Allah has rewarded us for our patience and dedication."

Imad al-Bin agreed. "Yes, good fortune is to be ours. We will avenge Saddam's death at the hands of these infidels."

Rijah Ellhad asked, "When will we have access to the entire shipment?"

"Soon, Rijah, very soon. We needed to verify that it would work as claimed. Now that we have done that, money will be paid, and we should have our weapon within two weeks."

"Have we decided on the target yet?" Ellhad asked.

"No, that will have to be a full-group discussion. That will happen two nights from now at Ryyaki Ali's home." Ali was the acknowledged leader of this particular terrorist cell. They operated independently from anyone else. They had money, worldwide contacts, and a deep, seething hatred for America. They were determined to kill as many as possible. If they lost their own lives in doing so, there would be only honor and glory.

"Inform me of the time," stated Ellhad flatly. He turned and left.

❈   ❈   ❈

The president's "sword" sat along a table at the Ranch: USMC captain Richard Starr, retired; Sergeant Marvin Styles, USMC Force Recon, retired; Captain James, J. C., Christman, United States Air Force, active; and Darlene Phillips, recently of the CIA. They were located in what was considered their war room. It was where some of the ultrasophisticated computer equipment that Phillips had brought in and installed herself was located. There were eight new LED sixty-inch flat screens mounted along one wall. What Phillips could produce on the large monitors would make a Hollywood special-effects expert jealous. She had earned the respect of the others with her undeniable skills. Myra Banks, head of the CIA's cyber unit, almost had cardiac arrest when President Williams stole Phillips from her group to join the Department of the Presidential Office. Phillips's name was the only one of the four associated with the new agency.

Phillips's fingers started flying over multiple keyboards. After about twenty seconds, she sat back. Images of total devastation filled six of the screens from varying angles and distance.

"Holy shit!" exclaimed J. C.

"You ain't kiddin'," added Styles.

"Phillips, how close is this to real time?" asked Starr.

"We have the same photos that all other agencies have, although they don't know it. Guys, we've got a big problem here. These photos were taken by a drone launched by the CDC. On the far-right screen, you will notice a sequence of stills taken by a Lawrence Larkin, lead on the four-man CDC team that was sent in. Now watch this." Once again, she ran her fingers across one of the keyboards. The two screens on the far left momentarily went blank, and then pictures returned. "Far left shows the lake as it was late afternoon on the day before the kill was discovered. Next to it shows the lake at one hour past dawn the following morning. This entire event happened overnight. I've done some research, and I've found nothing in nature that has even come close to comparing with this. There is *no doubt* in my mind this was caused by man."

An eerie silence filled the room with only the humming of Phillips's computers heard.

Styles asked, "Is this going where I think you're about to take it?"

"You bet it is. Now, look at *this*," she said with her fingers back over the keyboard. Then she started to control what appeared to be a video game joystick. Slowly, the image on the left screen began to pan left and up. Then it stopped. Phillips began to slowly zoom in for a closer look. "I'll have to send this to the president. I don't think his people have this."

"Have what?" asked Starr.

"This. Look at the far left. Concentrate. You see that yellow spot?"

"Yeah," the three men answered in unison.

"Keep watching, guys." Slowly, the yellow spot grew, just slightly, but enough to be recognized as a figure wearing yellow.

"Is that someone wearing a hazmat suit?" asked Styles emphatically.

"Gold star for you, Styles. It sure is!"

Starr continued, "Why did you say that the president's people don't have this?"

"'Cause they don't have this program. I designed it, only one in the world. A satellite sends a signal. The signal contains the image. What you normally don't see clearly is the static that surrounds that image. I created a program that can clean up the static. We're the only people on the planet who have this information."

J. C. Christman whistled softly between his teeth. "Jeez, Phillips, that's some damned unreal work you've done here."

"And you boys all thought I was just another pretty face." This brought a round of chuckles from the table.

Styles spoke first. "No, Darlene, you showed us that quite some time ago." He'd used her first name, an unusual occurrence in itself.

"So, for the other two who are not as sharp as Styles here, we have caught someone putting something in that lake, and I'd guess he's testing a bioweapon."

Starr asked, "Where exactly is this lake?"

"In a very remote part of Alaska, which means it's *really* remote. Only way in or out would be by chopper. I've already got a program running searching the area for any sign of one for two days previous and two days afterward."

"Why only two days?" asked Starr.

"Couple of reasons. Two days seems reasonable to me, plus I'd have to hack into the archives to go any further. Not a big problem, but I've got a feeling we're working in a four-day window. I'll know soon enough."

Starr stood up. "Guess I'd better call the Man. Let him know what you've found."

"I've got a better idea," Phillips said. "Let's show him. I've downloaded this info on an encrypted flash drive. When you see him, call me on a secure line, and I'll give you the code. I can't give it to you now because I designed the code to be a rover. I'll have to run a sequence program, given the time and date, to be able to tell you what it will be at a certain time. No other way to open it. This material is too sensitive to be handled any other way."

"Smart," said Styles.

"I'll go make the call," asserted Starr.

5.

"Yes, Richard," President Williams answered.

"Sir, I have vital information for you regarding the situation in Alaska."

"We've been studying satellite photography ourselves. It is definitely concerning, to say the least."

"Yes, sir. What I have to show you will concern you more."

"What do you have, Richard?"

"Something I need to show you, sir, not just tell you. Phillips found something in the satellite feed."

"Richard, I'm sure we've seen it ourselves."

"Not this. Trust me. I need to see you immediately. I'm bringing an encrypted flash drive with me. You *really* need to see this, sir. ASAP."

The line was silent for a moment. "All right. Meet me at Camp David at 7:00 p.m. I'll have the security transponder numbers sent over. I trust Christman can get you there in time."

"Not a problem, sir."

"See you then." The president hung up.

Starr walked back into their war room. "J. C., I need to be at Camp David by seven. Can we make it in the chopper?"

"Easy. We'll leave at four thirty this afternoon. That'll give us plenty of time."

"Phillips, in your recon of fish kills, you stated you'd never seen anything like this one, right?" asked Starr.

"Affirmative."

"Phillips, you're beginning to talk like a marine," deadpanned Styles.

"No, I'm not; I didn't swear." They grinned at each other.

Starr rolled his eyes. "May I continue?"

"Please do," cracked Christman.

"Thank you. Now, the point I was attempting to make was to ask Phillips to search around for any other kind of unnatural phenomena, anywhere, that might have resulted in some type of devastation. Look for, I don't know, plant life, anything that is way out of bounds. Think outside the box. Have Sunshine Boy help you, if he can."

"Sure," Phillips agreed. "He can make us dinner."

"Hope you like boiled hot dogs," Styles muttered.

Five men converged on Ryyaki Ali's home. The door was opened as they approached. Two Middle Eastern men, dressed entirely in black with AK-47 assault rifles held at the ready, stood alongside the entrance as the men entered.

A large man in his early fifties greeted them. "Welcome, my brothers. Please follow me." He led them down a stairway and along a hall. At the end was a large metal door. Ryyaki Ali punched in a seven-digit security number on an electronic keypad, and the door slid open silently. "Come in, sit at my table." The room was impressive. It had two large flat-screen monitors along a full-length desk that housed multiple desktop computers. The table was made of solid rosewood, with matching chairs. A pitcher of water and a glass were arranged at each seating place. Everyone took a seat.

"We have complete security here. We may speak our minds without fear," added Ali.

Rijah Ellhad spoke first. "I would be comfortable not stating names aloud. I mean no disrespect, but that has always been our way. I see no reason to change."

Ryyaki Ali smiled. "As you wish. We are here to discuss the beginning of our revenge on these infidel Americans. We shall possess the means within two weeks. I have an idea I want to discuss with the group, as it is our decision to make together." Slight murmuring of agreement reached him. He continued, "My vision is to have multiple targets. The agent works so well that I feel it would be wasteful to use it all on one populace unless a particular venue comes to light. I've researched and believe we have enough to feed four major public water supplies. If you agree, we need to make choices."

Ellhad inquired, "Do you mean all at once or separate?"

"Separate. I believe that manner would instill the most fear in these infidels."

Imad al-Bin asked, "Which ones do you think best serve our purpose?"

"I'm not quite prepared to answer that tonight. I have an assistant working on that assignment as we speak. I will know by tomorrow. I seek the highest possible damage. The most populated areas will increase our revenge. That can never be too great." Murmuring of agreement again reached Ali's ears.

Rijah Ellhad spoke. "I like your plan. I would think as widespread as possible would also be a good thing. Let the Americans realize that no place is safe, that we can strike them anywhere. I will take you at your word that we can speak names freely in this room, but only here."

"My thoughts exactly," Ali replied. "Then it appears this will be a short meeting."

"It appears," Ali agreed.

T-Minus 64 Hours

Starr and Christman were met by an eight-man security team after landing at Camp David. Christman was directed toward the dining room while Starr was led to a small conference room. "Have a seat, sir." Starr sat. Two minutes later, a door opened. President Robert Williams entered the room. Starr immediately stood.

"Richard, it's just us. Sit back down."

"Yes, sir."

"What's so important you had to show me personally?" asked the president.

"Question, Mr. President. Any chance you have some large screens hooked to a computer somewhere? For this, bigger is better."

"Yes, and Richard, when it's only the two of us, call me Bob. Follow me." He led Starr out the door he'd come in and down a hall. Four doors to the left, they entered a larger room. Two men inside immediately stood. "Guys, I need the room." Both left.

"Bob, I need a secure line."

"The blue phone." The president pointed toward the table.

Christman picked it up and dialed Phillips. He put the phone on speaker.

"You near a computer?" she asked.

"Yes."

"Send me an e-mail."

"What about?"

"I don't care. Just send me an e-mail so I can reply to it."

"Okay." He sent the request. Within two minutes, he got a reply from Phillips.

"Okay, Starr. Now, plug the flash drive you've got into the computer. In my e-mail, there's an attachment. Open it up."

"Done," replied Starr.

"There should be a window that popped up with multiple choices; click on flash drive."

"It doesn't say flash drive. Closest thing is jump drive."

"Christ, Starr, I'd swear I was talking to Styles. They're the same fucking thing."

"Uh, Phillips, the president is three feet away."

"Oh. Uh, hello, Mr. President. Sorry about that."

"No need to worry, Ms. Phillips. I can understand the difficulty in working with the two of them." He chuckled.

"You have no idea, Mr. President."

Starr interrupted, "Can we get back to business?"

"Why certainly, *Captain* Starr," Phillips replied with more than a hint of sarcasm in her voice.

"You think *she* has it tough?" Starr retorted to the president.

"Did you click on the flash drive yet?" Phillips asked.

"Done," replied Starr.

"Okay. This will take about twenty seconds. Then the program will open. Just use your mouse normally. At the beginning, a window will pop up asking if you want a split screen. If you're on a large monitor, click Yes. Right click once to pause, twice to continue. Call me back when you get lost."

"Hold on a second. I thought you said that you'd have to give me the code over the phone."

"Originally, yes. I changed the program."

"Why?" Starr asked.

"To see if I could. I wanted to run a program that recognized a code I built into the flash drive itself. When you opened the attachment, it recognized the flash drive code and sequenced itself. Plus, it made it a little easier for you, and I also thought the split screen would be a help."

"Yeah, uh, okay. Thanks."

As soon as Starr hung up, President Williams burst out laughing. "Boy, does she fit in."

"Yeah, she does." Starr grinned. "That girl impresses the shit outta me. I don't know how you found her, but you couldn't have done any better."

Starr's attention went back to the screen, and he followed Phillips's instruction for the split screen. For the next half hour, Starr gave the president a narration of what he was watching.

"You say that speck of yellow is a man?"

"Man, woman, one or the other. It's definitely someone in a hazmat suit. On Phillips's gear back at the Ranch, it's a little clearer. You can just make out that something was tossed in the lake. Next morning, everything is dead. No doubt it's a bioweapon."

"Well, you're certainly right, as we do *not* have this info. Richard, I need to keep this."

"How will you explain how you got it?"

"That's the nice thing about being president. I don't have to."

"Well, as they say, rank has its privilege."

"Yes, it does, Richard. Yes, it does."

6.

A little after eleven o'clock at night, the CDC team arrived back at the landing zone. The portable lighting utilized was impressive. Two other researchers from the Centers for Disease Control and Prevention met them at the edge of the clearing and spent twenty minutes running tests before they were cleared. Finally, the original team was allowed to get out of their suits. All the samples were declared sufficiently contained. The six then approached the helicopter. Ragar and Rockford immediately brought Larkin into Ragar's helicopter, in which he'd set up a small office.

Ragar started, "Was it as bad as it looked? For time's sake, I've decided not to go myself."

"Worse. The pictures don't do it justice. Nothing in that lake survived. I've never seen or heard of anything like it. Makes the worst red tide kill I've seen look like a goldfish floating in a bowl."

"Could you tell anything at all?"

"No. Like I said before, water tested fine—didn't pick up any sign of a biohazard. Right now, I don't have a clue. Only oddity I saw was that the eyes of the fish were black. We won't know for certain until we're back at the lab, but my guess is coagulated blood. I don't know what killed those fish, but whatever it was, it's as strong as anything I've ever heard of. It's the speed that it worked in that's so damned scary. We have to get back. We've got a lot of work ahead of us."

Rockford asked, "You think it was a bioweapon being tested?"

"I can't say yet, but my guess would be yes. The only thing I can even think of that could have been a natural cause would have been gases coming up from the lake bottom due to volcanic activity. There are areas right now, they call them killer lakes, but its life *above* the water that seems to be affected, not in it. One other thing I found odd. Today there were birds feasting on the remains. Whatever originally killed the fish is no longer active. I seriously doubt our samples are any danger; we're just taking standard precautions. This whole incident is way beyond anything I've ever heard of."

There was a knock on the door. "Yes," answered Ragar.

"Wheels up in three minutes, sir."

T-Minus 52 Hours

Phillips surprised everyone by cooking breakfast at the Ranch the next morning—scrambled eggs with pepper jack cheese, homemade biscuits, thick slices of ham, orange juice, and a special Green Mountain Coffee she'd brought with her.

"To what do we owe this?" asked Starr.

"You can thank Styles," she answered.

"How's that?" Christman queried.

"Easy. He made dinner last night. I don't think I could take two meals in a row from him," Phillips retorted. A moment of silence was quickly followed by genuine laughter. "Speaking of, just where is Mr. Sunshine? I haven't heard a peep from him, and I got up early."

"Your early and my early are about three hours apart," a voice said coming in from the side of the house. Everyone looked over as Styles walked into the room. "And forgive me for pointing this out, but just *who* had two very large bowls of beef stew last night?"

"Desperate times call for desperate measures," Phillips deadpanned right back.

"Any more desperate and you probably would've swallowed the bowl," Styles gave it right back. "Breakfast does smell good, though."

Everyone grabbed plates and silverware and then served themselves buffet-style. Phillips had cooked a generous amount of everything, so no one was bashful. "Eat up, guys. Don't want it on the pancakes in the morning," Phillips cracked.

"Not gonna have to ask me twice," said Starr.

"Me either," chimed in Christman.

"Guess I'd better eat too. Don't want to hurt little Miss Frail's feelings here," Styles joked as a biscuit came flying in his direction. He easily caught it and took a bite. "Damn, Phillips. These are good. Maybe I'd better refer to you as Duncan Phillips," he said, bringing laughter from everyone.

"Yeah, that's me, all right. Just call me Crocker." She already had the coffee urn set up in the middle of the dining room table, and everyone piled in. The food was so good there was little talking. "There are more biscuits in the oven, guys. Anybody like some?"

"Hell yes. Bring 'em in!" J. C. hollered. Within twenty minutes, breakfast was over. All were enjoying the coffee.

"So how did the meeting go with the president?" asked Styles.

"Good, I guess. Blew him out of his socks when I showed him the video Phillips downloaded. He was *not* expecting that. He agreed with our assessment. As of now, we are in the mode."

"What can we do that everybody else can't?" asked J. C.

"Probably just about everything, at least quicker, when you get right down to it," replied Phillips. "I'm going to run a search on all aircraft that were in that area before and after. I'll take it out, say, seventy-two hours either side to be safe."

"How can you do that?" Starr asked.

"It'd take too long to explain it to you, Starr. All you need to know is I can. By lunch, I'll have the transponder numbers of every aircraft that's been in that area over that time. If we find anything suspicious, we can narrow down those particular aircraft, including departure and arrival points. That's a start."

"Won't other agencies do that also?" Starr asked again.

"Yeah, but they'll be way behind us by that time. They've got too much cross-referencing to do. I don't have to stay within their boundaries. I've also got another program running back across all the video we've already downloaded. I'm trying to come up with an infrared scan during the evening hours."

"Why? What are you looking for?"

"Anything. I won't know unless I look."

Starr continued, "Just how can you run an infrared scan on an existing video that was not shot using infrared technology?"

"To be honest, I'm not certain I can. I took the image of what we are sure is a person. I used that as a base for creating an artificial thermal image. I then wrote a program using everything else in the video, creating a colder image. It's hard to explain. The water is cold; so are the fish. Birds are warm-blooded, so I imaged them warm. I assigned a code for everything I could find in the video. If anything shows up in the video that was shot during the night, hopefully, the different coding will kick in and give me an image. I don't know if it'll work or not; never tried this before. Basically, I'm making something up from something I made up, if that makes any sense. That's how we came up with computers in the first place. Nobody knew anything until they tried. Figure I don't have anything to lose."

"Sounds like a solid idea, Phillips," Styles finally said. "If I were going in, I'd do a night jump. With a GPS fix, one could nail it spot-on. Even though it's in a remote area, it still lessens the chance of being spotted, especially considering what we think he's doing."

"I'm thinking the same thing," Phillips agreed. "I should have some answers by lunch or shortly after. Somebody else can clean up." She got up and left to return to her computers.

"Come on, guys. We can police this quick." All three men started grabbing the breakfast remains. "Can't have that one little biscuit sitting there all lonely," J. C. said as he stuffed it into his mouth.

"Thoughtful of you, J. C.," cracked Starr.

President Robert Williams had all the heads of his major agencies assembled. It was six in the morning. He'd removed his suit jacket. His necktie had been loosened, and his shirtsleeves were rolled up. It was a sign of the times as much the seriousness of the situation. Eight people were in attendance: the president, his new chief of staff, Laura Green, and the six directors.

"Gentlemen, I'm sure you all know Laura Green, my new chief of staff. I'm going to get straight to the point. There is now no doubt that we are facing a terrorist threat. This time, it involves a biological weapon, one that appears unfamiliar. I call your attention to the big screen. Watch carefully." A video began to play, and suddenly the image froze. "I want you to pay close attention to that yellow spot in the lower left-hand corner. Watch carefully," the president directed. Every eye was glued to the screen. The image grew larger until it could be distinguished as a person in a hazmat suit—small, to be sure, but no mistake. "Now watch," the president continued. The image seen appeared to be throwing something into the lake. The video rewound and played again. No one said anything. The screen went blank.

President Williams sat down. "What we just saw was exactly what it looked like. Someone dressed in a hazmat suit threw something into that lake. Twelve hours later, it was a body of dead water. Nothing survived."

Bernard Backersley, director of the CIA, was visually stunned. "Sir, where in the hell did you get *that* video?"

"That is not important, Bernard. What is important is that we have it."

Backersley looked around the table. "Has anyone else seen this?" Backersley was not used to being upstaged. All he received was a shaking of heads.

He turned his attention back to the president. "Sir, with all due respect, how do we know this video is factual?"

President Williams was in no mood to spar with Backersley. "Bernard, I realize that you are unaccustomed to information that you are unaware of; however, this is as factual as it gets. We need to focus on what the hell we're going to do about it."

"Well, it would certainly appear that if it was tested in water, then water would be the target."

"Good guess," Matt Sanderson of the FBI retorted sarcastically.

"*Enough!*" President Williams yelled. "This is *not* about who's the big dick here. Either get along or get out. I won't say it again." The room was silent. "I want everyone back here at two tomorrow afternoon to give your opinion on possible targets. If any of you want to work together, that's fine. I don't care. Just bring me ideas." He got up and stormed out of the room.

❋　❋　❋

Phillips and Christman had their own cabins that had been constructed at the Ranch. This was to allow them private quarters when present. Each was designed in a rustic country motif, were comfortable, and reasonably spacious. The open floor plan attributed greatly to the feel. A large brick double-sided gas fireplace in the center completed the effect.

Phillips had taken a smaller bedroom in the main house that was not being used and turned it into her personal computer room. She had taken a Sharpie and written on the exterior of the entrance door "Keep the Fuck Out," using this area when working alone rather than the war room.

"Bossy bitch," Starr had chuckled when he'd seen it. "Just another reason I'm not married."

"Starr, you couldn't con a Russian mail-order bride into marrying you," Phillips had shot right back.

"She's got you there," Styles threw in.

Close to lunch, Phillips walked out into the main living quarters. Starr was looking over some papers while Styles and Christman were nowhere to be seen.

"Where are the other two?" Phillips asked.

"Out in the gym. J. C. asked Styles to show him some basic fighting moves."

"Can you bring them in? I've got some serious shit to show you guys."

"Sure." He got up and walked out toward the barn that contained the gym. Walking in, he saw Styles helping Christman up off the mat. "Hey, Phillips has found some stuff she wants to go over."

"Fine by me," said J. C. "Styles is about to put me in a grave."

"You're doing fine, J. C. You gotta crawl before you walk," Styles replied.

"I'll be lucky if I *can* walk."

The three headed back toward the house with Christman limping slightly.

As they went inside, they heard Phillips yell, "Anybody want anything to drink?"

"Water," they answered in unison.

The three men followed Phillips back to her computer lair. "Have a seat," she said. She had the room set up very simply. There were three viewing chairs aimed at a row of four large flat-screen monitors. Two walls contained a continuous L-shaped desk with keyboards, smaller LED monitors, and other assorted equipment that none of the men would admit to not having a clue about.

"Okay, guys, here we go. The far-left flat screen appears black. It is. It's night. Now this is going to be real time."

Suddenly, a medium-size orange-red object appeared and crossed the screen. "That was an aircraft—helicopter, to be exact. That was at eight thirty the night before the person in the suit was seen." The blip disappeared, leaving a very small spot in its place. "That is our guy, who has jumped out of the helicopter. Styles, you were right." They watched in silence as the orange object seemed to just stay in one spot. Then slowly, it turned to a northeast direction. After a few minutes, the spot settled in one spot again. "He's down, right in the same clearing where the president's team landed."

The spot moved slowly a short distance and then stopped again. Suddenly, another small spot flared up. "My guess it's a campfire,"

Phillips offered. They watched for a bit until Phillips said, "I'm going to jump ahead a little bit."

The second spot diminished completely, and the original spot dimmed, but not entirely.

"He's settled in for the night," observed Styles.

"I agree," replied Phillips. "I'm going to jump ahead again. This next scene will be the following evening, after we've seen him throw something in the lake. I've highlighted the shoreline in gray for reference."

When the video started, roughly one-sixth of the lake had started to turn orange. It was brightest at the shore, while the color lessened as it got farther from lake's edge. "I'm going to speed this up about eighteen times," Phillips stated. For the next twenty minutes, the group watched as slowly the entire lake turned orange.

Christman asked the obvious. "Phillips, I know the orange represents heat, but what is that heat representing?"

"I'm guessing a couple of things. That toxic weapon has spread, killing everything in that lake, which is generating heat—the agent itself, the fish dying, maybe the starting of decomposition. Probably the act of killing the fish is causing heat. Either way, I figure this entire action took somewhere around seven hours to complete, give or take."

"Seven hours?" exclaimed Starr.

"Yes, maybe less. The really scary part is how small an amount must've been used to cause this," Phillips continued. "I was able to track that copter. It landed just outside of Bethel, Alaska."

"We've got a real fucking problem," Starr swore. "I've gotta call the Man." He got up and left.

Styles straightened up in his seat. "We have us a starting point."

7.

Ryyaki Ali was standing in a dimly lit warehouse on the edge of the industrial park just outside Portland's main shipping district. The early September weather was damp and chilly. He snugged his jacket closer to his neck, glad he'd worn a hat. He was meeting with a man whose nationality was unknown. He simply went by Smith. He was Caucasian, mid-forties, and everything about him radiated cold: his look, his appearance, his manner, everything. He had hair so blond at first glance it could have been mistaken for white. Ice-blue eyes combined with blond eyebrows and a skin tone suggested he was Scandinavian. He was fluent in several languages. He was undoubtedly one of the world's leading biochemists. He had gone off the grid ten years earlier. He'd spent that time developing a new synthetic toxin. Through a series of representatives, he had been introduced to Ryyaki Ali. Smith was in the act of peddling his wares.

"Your agent worked as you stated!" exclaimed Ali.

"Of course it worked."

"I would like to finalize our negotiations," Ali said.

"So would I," agreed Smith.

"I need to know the final amount of money you are requesting," Ali replied.

"That depends on how you want the agent to work. As I previously stated, I can modify the time element on how fast the agent reacts to water. The sample you received reacted in one hour. I can modify that up to fourteen days. The longer the delay, the more expensive it is. The time that the agent is active remains the same. In ten hours, it is virtually gone."

"Can that be modified, as well?"

"No. Once the activation process begins, it cannot be altered."

"I would like the agent to activate quickly."

The blond-haired man remained silent, thinking. "In that case, for the amount you requested, the cost would be one hundred million dollars."

"That is considerably more than I was expecting," scoffed Ali.

"It is what it is. No one is forcing you to purchase my product. You are welcome to look elsewhere. You will not find its equal."

"I will pay fifty million," Ryyaki Ali said.

"Then you will pay nothing, and this meeting is over." Smith stood to leave.

Ryyaki Ali threatened, "What makes you think you may just walk out of here?"

Ryyaki Ali had four of his guards with him, all with handguns drawn.

Smith turned and stared at him with a look that would freeze hell. "And what makes you think that the next drink of water you have will not kill you? Do you think I am so foolish as to not take my own precautions? You have insulted me. The price is now two hundred million dollars. You have thirty seconds to decide," Smith declared.

Ryyaki Ali was raging inside. He was sure he would be able to negotiate the price down, but his plan had backfired badly. He was also sure he could not take a chance that this man had not tampered with his own water supply. At that moment, he didn't trust this man that if he simply refused the product that he would just let it go. He was between a rock and a hard place, and he knew it. And this man Smith knew it. Ali also realized further attempt to negotiate a price reduction would be fruitless.

"Agreed, per my instructions on the timetable," Ali stated, not hiding his fury.

"Agreed. I will be in touch for the financial transaction and instructions on how the product will be delivered to you. You will wire half the money and you will receive the product, and then you will wire the remainder. Agreed?"

"Agreed."

The blond-haired man walked over to Ali and offered to shake his hand. Ali hesitated and then accepted the invitation.

"One other very important item," Smith added. "If you try to skip the second payment, you know what will happen."

"I will abide by our agreement. I have no wish to make an enemy of you. America is my enemy."

"Then I foresee no problems. I will be in touch with the delivery arrangements." With that, he turned and walked out of the dank warehouse.

Rijah Ellhad called Ryyaki Ali. He had heard the entire conversation by cell phone held by one of the guards. "I have people in place to follow him. Should we?"

"No. This is a very dangerous man. We will not give him any reason to suspect anything out of the ordinary. We will receive the weapon and then decide just how to proceed."

"He is asking for a very large sum of money."

"Yes, but for the pain we can cause the Americans, to me, it is worth it. I also don't want the concern of him attacking us. He fights by methods we are unfamiliar with. I believe that it would be in our best interest to just pay the amount and proceed. I was not prepared to spend that amount of money, but I believe it is the right path to follow. We may want to do business with him again in the future should our actions succeed."

"As you wish," Ellhad replied.

8.

Bernard Backersley was back in his office at CIA headquarters. It was surprisingly modest. Only his desk would draw any admiration, an early twentieth-century piece constructed from mahogany with a fine hand-rubbed oil finish that he'd imported from England. At the moment, he was sitting behind it bristling with annoyance. He was incensed that the president had shown him a video that he knew nothing about. Furthering his ire was the president not revealing how he had obtained the footage. Backersley was used to being the one holding the cards. He picked up his phone and summoned the chief of his cyber unit to his office.

Ten minutes later, agent in charge Myra Banks knocked and entered.

"Take a seat, Myra."

"Yes, sir."

"You don't have to 'sir' me when it's the two of us." Backersley had known Myra Banks for ten years, and they enjoyed a "friends with benefits" relationship, though very few people knew.

"What's eating you, Bernie?"

"I just came from a meeting with the president and the other directors. He had access to an extremely sensitive video that I knew nothing about. I couldn't get him to say how he'd obtained it."

"And you're mad because he had something before you."

"Damn it, Myra, it's my job to have everything before everybody. I can't figure out where in the hell it came from."

"Was it concerning the fish kill?" she asked.

"Yes. It was an infrared image that showed an individual tossing something into that lake. I wasn't aware that particular technology was far enough along to be utilized from a satellite and able to show that type of detail."

"Infrared has come a long way, but to pick up one individual's heat signal with that detail does surprise me, at least from the satellites that I think would have been utilized."

"Well, the president just showed it to me."

"I don't believe we have that capability, at least not yet. I could be wrong. I don't know of anyone else who might have it."

"Any guesses?"

The slender brunette sat quiet for a minute, curling her long hair around her right index finger, thinking. "I can only surmise that it could be done in one of two ways. Either somebody hit upon a new and much stronger technology, which I'm sure we would have heard about, or someone was able to write some type of program utilizing existing technology that created a much larger expansion into the revelation of minute detail. Given the choices, I'd bet on the second."

"Okay, who could do that?" Backersley asked, his ruddy complexion even redder than usual.

"Currently, no one who works for us. One woman comes to mind—Darlene Phillips."

"Isn't she the one that the president stole from us for that new DOP agency he created?"

"Yes. I worked with her for almost four years, and she's without doubt the best computer geek I've ever seen. She has a knack that can't be taught; it's just the way she's wired. Her ability to think outside the box only magnifies her capability. I'd say if anybody could create that type of program, it would be Darlene. That she's part of DOP would explain how the president obtained the video."

"How can we find out for sure? We need to know if it's us or someone else."

Myra Banks groaned inwardly. *For such an intelligent man, sometimes you ask the stupidest questions.* "It certainly seems to me it would have to be us; otherwise, how did the president obtain it? Bernie, I think you should come right out and ask. Use the pretext of national security. You should at least get your answer."

"I'm not sure I want Williams knowing what I know."

Both sat quiet in Backersley's office for almost five minutes, Backersley deep in thought. Finally, he looked up. "I'm starting to wonder if there isn't more to this DOP Williams created than just gathering intel."

"What do you mean?" queried Banks.

"Starting with the hit on those terrorist suspects back in Indianapolis, it appears that someone, or some group, has been a step ahead of everyone in certain matters. If Williams did have such a group operating at his disposal, this DOP group would be perfectly capable of giving him all the info he would need to dispense the information that all the other agencies have acquired. He's ordered that the DOP be kept in the loop on all terrorist activities in real time, so he's always up to date. That places him in the perfect position. Don't you see?"

"Yes, it would," she agreed, straightening up in her chair. "Christ, Bernie, if he got caught at that, it would make Nixon's Watergate scandal look like a walk in the park. Do you really think he's ordering assassinations?"

"We do it all the time."

"Yeah, but we're CIA. He's the president."

"One thing I'm sure about President Williams. I don't think there's anything that man wouldn't do if he thought it would keep this country safer. I remember when the bomb was discovered at Madison Square Garden. He was close to going over the edge. He wanted to bomb the entire Middle East."

"Let me ask you this, Bernie. Say if he was doing this, do you think it's a bad thing?"

"I think it should be our job."

"Well, it does seem like we're always getting called up to the Hill answering some damned congressional committee's questions.

Maybe he just thought it would be easier—go behind their backs, so to speak."

"If that's so, I want to know about it."

"Of course you do."

❈　❈　❈

Phillips came walking out of her computer room. The three men were sitting around the table where they'd eaten breakfast.

"Have you guys even moved?" she asked.

"Don't worry about us; have you come up with anything?" Starr retorted.

"Well, my only concern was whether I'd have to dust the three of you."

Styles burst out laughing. "Good one, Phillips. Actually, we just got back in from our weapons room, where I was familiarizing these two with some of my favorites. I want to start all of you on target practice. I know that you two guys can already shoot; I just want to knock any rust off your shooting skills. Have you done much shooting?" he said as he looked at Phillips.

"A bit, but I like that idea," Phillips agreed. "Most of my experience is with handguns. I have shot a shotgun a few times with my brothers. I'd like to practice with an AR-15 and get the feel of it."

Styles nodded in agreement. He continued, "We know that Phillips is proficient in Tae Kwon Do. Starr, you can handle yourself reasonably well. J. C., how about you?"

"I haven't had the extensive training you guys have had, but I suppose I'm okay. I wouldn't mind spending some time learning a few techniques from you, though, long as you don't break me in half."

"I won't."

Phillips interrupted, "Okay, to the point. As we know, the helicopter that picked up our suspect landed at a small airport outside of Bethel. Within minutes, a plane—a floatplane, to be exact—took off and landed outside Portland, Oregon. I've traced the registration numbers and identified the owners. The floatplane belongs to Northern Hunting Expeditions. They appear to be a legitimate business. I would not rule out that they would perform other services on the side; however, we don't know for certain if the floatplane is involved. I just thought it worthwhile to look into."

"I think we should follow up on it," said Starr.

"When do we leave?" asked Christman.

"One hour," answered Starr. "We know what to take."

Phillips interrupted. "Should I go or stay here?"

"Can you bring what you need to keep doing whatever the hell it is you do?" Starr questioned.

"Should be able to. I can download a couple of programs I need onto flash drives, and I'll make sure I have any uplinks I might need connected."

"Uh, yeah, do that. Remember, I know computer basics, but that's about it. I use a flip phone 'cause all I need a phone for are calls, texts, and to see what time it is. I don't even know how to turn on a smartphone."

"Well, I'll spend some time with you three and educate you just a bit," replied Phillips.

"Okay, guys," Christman announced. "Wheels up in one hour."

"One more thing, guys. I picked up some chatter referring to the Chemist regarding a potential attack here. I'll have to start researching him as time permits."

"Yeah, but first things first," stated Styles.

Bernard Backersley called Myra Banks back into his office.

"Myra, I want to know what this DPO group the president is running is up to. I want you to find out all you can about them. I want to know every member of that department and what they do."

"What if President Williams finds out what you're doing?" she questioned.

"It's your job to be damned sure he doesn't."

"Bernie, I have to be honest here. I'm not really comfortable nosing around in the affairs of the president, especially since he's got Phillips on that team."

"What do you mean—about Phillips, that is?"

"That woman makes me nervous. My gut is telling me that if I go poking around, somehow she's going to find out."

"Myra, your unit goes in and out of agencies around the world. Are you telling me you are afraid to nose around this DPO unit?"

"Not scared, Bernie, wise. Darlene Phillips can do more with computers than my entire staff. I'm not so egotistical to not recognize that. If we're discovered, it'll be our asses."

"Then probe gently. Maybe avoid Phillips entirely. See what you can find out. I want to know what is what with them. Don't do anything that makes you seriously uncomfortable."

"Bernie, this task is making me uncomfortable. May I ask you a straight question?"

Backersley gave her a look of slight annoyance. "Of course."

"Why in the hell do you want to take a chance on stirring up a hornets' nest? With all the shit going on in the world, it just seems that from a logical perspective, this is something we don't need to get caught up in."

Backersley leaned back in his overstuffed chair. He was quiet for a few seconds before answering, "I feel strongly that in order for me to do the best job possible, I need to know everything possible. Believe it or not, this is not about me being jealous or petty. If this group is doing more than believed, I'm not going to immediately condemn it. I just need to know the scorecard. I don't want to waste time trying to find out information about something if the answer is right in front of me. I don't know if that makes sense to you, but it does to me. This is how I operate. I need to know."

Agent Banks stood up. "I'll find out what I can," she said, and she walked out the door.

The main laboratory at the CDC facility, located in Atlanta, Georgia, was a dimmed hum of activity. Lawrence Larkin sighed in frustration as he reviewed yet another round of tests that revealed absolutely nothing. He tried stifling a yawn and looked away from his computer screen.

"You look exhausted."

Larkin swiveled around in his chair to face his boss, Director Michael Lang. Assistant Director Olivia Watson stood beside him.

"I've never seen anything like this. I've studied these samples inside out and upside down, and I can't find any solid evidence of what killed these fish. At best, I have an educated guess," offered Larkin.

Director Lang was a man of little patience. "And what might that be?"

"Okay, but remember, you asked for it. I've found, uh, for lack of a better word, residue in the coagulated blood taken from the samples. I have no idea what it is. Based on that, I think that someone has developed a synthetic bioagent that is activated by water. It does its thing, and after x amount of time, it disintegrates. From what I can surmise, it happens with extraordinary speed. Actually, unbelievable speed. I've studied the video, and this entire lake died overnight leaving no real evidence behind. Whatever this agent is, it causes the blood to congeal into a jelled condition, killing the host. Additionally, once this agent is activated, by the evidence we've learned from that lake, there doesn't seem to be a way to stop it; nor is there any reason to believe that there is any limit on how large an area it could kill. Conceivably, it could take out an entire ocean, if not every body of water on the planet. In my opinion, this just might be the most dangerous bioweapon we've ever encountered, and I also believe that most everything in the water, at least any species with blood, would be affected."

"*What?*" exclaimed Director Lang.

"You heard me. I can't come up with anything else."

Lang declared, "I've got to get this information to the president."

"Already done, sir. I had to wait almost three hours to get to you, so under the president's standing order, I've already informed the DPO."

"*You what?*" exploded Lang. "That's *my* job."

"Yes, sir, it is. However, as you were unavailable, and this is a national emergency, I felt the president should be informed immediately. I didn't mean to go over your head. I was only doing what I felt was my job."

"Of course, Larkin. You acted appropriately."

"Thank you, sir. Again, no disrespect intended."

With great effort to remain civil, Director Lang responded, "None taken."

9.

T-Minus 50 Hours

After Starr and company had transferred from their home-based helicopter to the group's jet, Starr came walking back from the cockpit after spending over an hour with Christman in what had amounted to a flying lesson. After the autopilot had been turned off, Starr had flown the plane, getting a feel for it. He noticed that Phillips had a cross look about her.

"Anything wrong?" he asked.

"Don't know yet," she replied, stopping what she was doing to address him. She stretched and sighed. "I've got programs in place pretty much all over cyberspace. You'd never believe it. One program I've installed notifies me if anyone does a search on any of the four of us. This program will also tell me where the search is originating from. Well, someone is doing a search on me."

Styles, who had been busy doing push-ups, stopped and joined them at the table. "What'd you say? Somebody is doing a search on you? Why?"

"Good question. Currently, it seems rather generic, but it's the location of the searcher that has me a bit uneasy."

"Where?" quizzed Starr.

"Langley."

"The CIA?" questioned Styles.

"Yes, and it's coming from the head of their cyber division herself, Myra Banks."

Starr looked at her and stated, "You know, there was a time I'd have asked you how you know that."

"You're learning, Starr."

"Can you tell what she's trying to find out?"

"So far, pretty much what my assignments have been since I transferred over to the DPO. I worked under her for three, maybe four years. She's pretty good. I don't like the idea that the CIA is investigating me. I have a bad feeling that *me* will ultimately mean *us*."

Styles spoke up. "Why would the CIA want to know what you, or we, are up to?"

"Bernard Backersley currently runs the CIA. He is off-the-charts smart and has an ego that would stretch across the Pacific. He does *not* like to not know about everything."

"What do you mean?" Starr questioned.

"You have to figure that he was shown the video I came up with. He won't like the idea that he didn't know about it, particularly where it came from."

Starr broke in. "The president specifically told me, when I asked about how he was going to explain how he got that, that he didn't have to. Rank has its privilege."

"True," Phillips answered. "But that won't stop Backersley from having a shit fit."

"So what do we do?" Styles posed.

"We don't do anything. I will keep a close eye as to where she goes with this and what she finds out. If it gets serious, we might have to address it in some manner."

"What do you mean by that?" Starr asked.

Phillips looked straight at him. "Make no mistake, Backersley could become a real pain in our asses. Maybe even an outright problem. He's an egomaniac who thinks he's above everyone else. Maybe nothing at all will come of any of this. However, we need to be vigilant."

"I agree with you," Styles broke in. "We don't need any bad surprises from the damn CIA."

"Trust me. I'll know what they're up to when *they* know what they're up to."

"Okay, I have to ask. How will you do that?" Starr inquired.

"Short version is that back when I was with the CIA, I installed what I call a 'mirror' program into their mainframe. What I mean is when someone uses a computer, there's a one picosecond delay that even the best firewalls can't pick up. During that delay, the mainframe splits the signal into two paths; one goes back to the originating computer accessing it, and the second signal goes to my installed program. Every single operation done by computer at Langley is backed up in real time to my program. I've downloaded every single word written at any computer there for almost three years now. Most are just filed away, unless certain ones I've earmarked are used."

Starr were stunned. The look on Styles's face suggested he was too. "You mean you hacked the whole fucking CIA?" gasped Starr.

"Well, yeah."

Styles asked, "Exactly what is a picosecond?"

"It's one-trillionth of one second."

He just looked at her dumbfounded. "One-trillionth? How far down does time go?"

"Currently down to one Planck time unit, which is the time required, at the speed of light, to travel one Planck length. Basically, it's the briefest physically meaningful span of time. Please don't ask me to explain any further; it gets very complicated."

Starr just shook his head. Finally, he said, "Is there any place you haven't hacked into?"

"Of course. I only infiltrate the important ones. I hacked the CIA because I thought we had a mole. Turns out I was wrong, but I didn't see any sense in removing the program. Never knew when it might have come in handy. Now we do."

"Aren't you the least bit concerned someone might find it?" asked Styles.

"Not really. If someone did come across it, the instant they tried to access it, it would self-terminate, leaving no trace."

"How did you learn this shit?" Starr asked, still stunned.

"I honestly can't tell you. It just came naturally. Some people can sing. I know computers. I learned how to type at eight, and the rest is history."

Styles looked at her and remarked, "I'm damned glad you're on our side."

"Yes, you are."

Starr got up and returned to the cockpit and rejoined Christman, leaving Phillips alone with Styles.

Phillips looked at Styles and said, "Okay, your turn."

"Huh?"

"I just relayed how I got to be where I am. What about you?"

Silence. Phillips was concerned she had touched a nerve.

"Guess it would be rude not to tell you some things. Short version is my mother died when I was quite young—before school, to be exact. Affected my father and me tremendously. I had always been somewhat of a loner, I guess, and that just drove me further away. I took to the woods. I liked being there, learned to track and later became adept enough to observe. By the time I was seven, I could tell you what animals had been through any part of the woods and how long ago. My dad got worried, so one Saturday morning, think I was about eight, he asked me to take a ride. We wound up at a karate dojo. Hell, I didn't know what karate was. He'd obviously been there previously; it was like they were expecting us. Next thing I know, I'm going there three afternoons a week and on Saturday mornings. The instructor said I had a natural aptitude for it. It also gave me a way to work out my anger issues about my mother. It didn't keep me out of the woods—that was my first love—but martial arts became a close second. Before the year was out, I was going five days a week plus Saturdays. Within two years, I was more than equal to boys who were five years older than I was and twice my size. At that point, my sensei took me aside and informed me that he wanted me to start training with his father. I'd seen him come around a few times but knew nothing about him. He spoke little English. He also held high-degree black belts in five different styles. He was tough. Next five years of my life, I always had bruises. I learned not just the different approaches and philosophies but how to easily blend them. Ultimately, I guess I just kind of conjoined them. Now the challenge is to keep my body in the proper condition to be able to do what I know."

"I never see you practicing any techniques, though," inserted Phillips.

"I don't have to. It's all totally ingrained in me. I've been doing this for over thirty years; you don't forget. You just have to be physically able to do what your mind doesn't forget."

"Well, I've never seen—hell, even heard of—anyone who works out like you."

"Doubtful if many do. It's just who I am, what I am."

"Do you have any regrets?"

"I'm not sure I fully understand what regret really means. Everything happens for a purpose. It's all part of a bigger picture. For whatever reason, I was, hell, I don't know, chosen for this life. I accept that."

Phillips looked at him intensely. "You've never spoken of this before, have you?"

"No."

"Why now?"

"You shared with us; only fair to return the trust. I've also come to terms that what has been my life for the last twenty years is over. I'm turning the page and moving on. I also realize that I'm not alone in this quest of ours. I have to learn to be more open, to accept the fact that I'm part of a team. This is uncharted territory for me. It hasn't been easy. From what I've seen and have begun to understand, make no mistake, I wouldn't have it any other way."

Phillips allowed herself a small smile. "That almost sounds like a compliment."

"It's fact. It is what it is."

"Still …"

Styles pretended to glare at her. "Don't push it." Changing the subject, he asked, "What do you really think of this CIA intrusion?"

"I think it's Backersley's ego. He doesn't like the idea that possibly someone else has a hit team. He wants to be the quarterback of that."

"Yeah, I've noticed a few of the CIA boys from time to time."

"How's that?" Phillips asked.

"I've run across them on and off. I can spot them blindfolded."

"Did they spot you?"

Styles laughed. "Not a chance in hell. A couple of them are actually quite good, but I can spot them just from the way they walk, the way they move. If we were observing one right now, watching him follow a target, I could tell you exactly what he was going to do before he ever did it. I gained that instinct from those years in the woods observing animals and their behavior. We're not that much different. I've learned you can't really teach instinct. It's something you either have or, with enough time, are lucky enough to partially acquire. You're not going to learn it from some instructor or in a classroom. Patience is the ultimate key."

"I found out that there's some top-secret location that the CIA utilizes to teach their best candidates. I know the CIA performs assassinations all over the world—inside our own borders, as well—even though that's completely against their mandate," Phillips offered.

"Yeah, I had to stop one once. The target had innocent company, and the agent was going to take them both. I couldn't allow that."

Phillips looked at him with slight admiration. "No, you couldn't."

Christman announced that they would be landing in Portland, Oregon. in half an hour. Starr, Styles, and Phillips gathered around the conference table. She announced she'd already made room reservations at a Holiday Inn located next to the airport.

Starr asked, "So how should we approach this, what'd you call it? Something Hunting Adventures?"

Phillips, with a look of disdain, corrected him. "Northern Hunting Expeditions. How many years did it take for you to get through high school?"

"No need for sarcasm. I'm just throwing out the obvious for ideas."

"Here's a novel approach," retorted Phillips. "Why don't we go in to inquire about a hunting trip? I mean, that *is* what they do."

Styles burst out laughing with Phillips joining him, leaving Starr looking exasperated. "I'm so happy to provide you both with humor," Starr deadpanned.

"Sorry, Starr, but that was funny," cracked Styles. "So who goes in?"

Phillips interjected, "How about Christman and me? He can do the talking and let me look around the place to see what they might have for electronic gear."

"Sounds like a plan," agreed Starr. "Marv?"

"Okay by me. J. C. knows what to say. Somehow see if you can work it around where the lake kill was without being too obvious."

"No shit," Phillips shot back dryly.

"This is about the easiest plan we've come up with yet," Starr said.

"What are you two going to do?" asked Phillips.

Starr and Styles looked at each other with Styles answering, "I think we'll nose around and see if we can figure out where the chopper came from. Figures that they probably work together since the floatplane damned sure couldn't land on a lake full of dead fish. Plus that keeps the copter out of your recon. Don't need to tip anybody off about anything."

"That makes sense," Phillips stated, nodding.

"Okay, that's it, then," Starr declared.

10.

T-Minus 49 Hours

Christman and Phillips walked through the entry door of Northern Hunting Expeditions. The front showroom was impressive. Photos of celebrities shown on hunting trips were hung on the walls for display. Several large animals that had spent considerable time at a taxidermist were featured, including a large brown bear, a grizzly bear, an elk, and a moose that just barely fit under the ten-foot-high ceiling. A middle-aged man dressed in casual business attire walked up to greet them.

"Welcome to Northern Hunting. My name is Tracy Howard. How might I help you?"

Phillips spoke first. "I'm giving my brother a hunting trip for his birthday. He has always wanted to hunt in Alaska, so that's where we are interested in going."

"Well, why don't we go back to my office and let's see what I might be able to come up with?" suggested Howard. "We offer customized expeditions to try to match as closely as possible what our client expects. We have an excellent reputation, particularly with many celebrity clients."

"That is good to hear," admitted Christman. "I'm anxious to see what you have to offer."

"Well, let's get started."

❖ ❖ ❖

With Phillips and Christman busy with Northern Hunting Expeditions, Starr and Styles had made their way close to a dock where three floatplanes were tied, not far from Northern Hunting Expeditions. They had discussed a basic approach. They saw a small office building with a sign above it proclaiming they had arrived at Seaport Flights. They walked inside and found a young man sitting at a desk.

"Be right with you gentlemen."

"Take your time," answered Starr.

Thirty seconds later, the man got up and walked up to them. "What's up?"

Starr replied, "Got a couple of questions. If we wanted to take a trip up to Alaska to do some fishing, you the guys we see?"

"Pretty much, although there are some spots we can't land in. We work close with a chopper company who can get you where we can't."

"What do you mean?"

"Well, some spots in Alaska are environmentally protected, and we can't land a plane on the lakes. In a case like that, some fishermen who are really particular where they go will charter a copter to take them close, and they hike in. We would take you as far as Bethel and chopper you in from there."

"No offense meant," continued Starr, "but say we wanted to drive. We've both always wanted to see Alaska or maybe just drive one way. Is there any chance you could set us up with that helicopter company?"

"No problem. We have some folks who do just that. You'd want to hook up with Inland Helicopter. We use them exclusively. In fact, I can give you a coupon that will save you 10 percent off the usual price."

Styles broke in, stating, "That would be great."

"Okay, then. My name is Jerry. Let me get that coupon and some brochures for you to take. My number is on the business card. Any way I can help, just give a shout."

"Thanks. We'll do that," answered Starr. He headed for the door with Styles. Before stepping through, Styles turned and asked, "Okay if we check out the plane? See how much gear we can take?"

"Sure, go ahead and check out the interior. We've got a mechanic down there performing some routine maintenance. I'll text him and let him know you're coming," said Jerry.

"Thanks," said Styles.

Walking out through the parking lot toward the dock, Starr queried, "Why do you want to see the planes?"

"Why not? You never know where you might learn something."

"I can't argue with that. He seemed legitimate enough."

"Remember, looks can be deceiving. Never take anything at face value."

"Sheesh, Marv, you're starting to sound like a philosopher."

"Yeah, that's me, all right. Hard to forget what you've learned the hard way, Starr."

"Again, can't argue with that."

Together they walked down to the first of three planes. Starr could tell they were older but maintained very well. "Look at those big radial engines. Those babies are torque monsters, just what you need to get off the water in a relatively short space. I'll bet they're loud as hell."

Styles had spotted the mechanic working on the second plane. The man was paying them no attention. Styles opened the entry door and hopped aboard. Starr followed. "There's quite a bit of room in here. Definitely enough to bring a lot of gear," Styles observed.

"More than I would have thought," Starr agreed.

Less than a minute later, they were both standing back on the dock. Styles walked toward the second plane but stopped at the big propeller in front of the one they had just been on. He looked as though he were studying the big rotary engine but in fact was checking out the mechanic. After about twenty seconds, he walked back toward Starr and motioned him back toward the parking lot and their rented Yukon.

"That mechanic is an Iraqi," Styles noted.

"How in the hell can you tell that from over a hundred feet away?" asked Starr.

"Easy. Remember where I've been the last fourteen years. I can tell the difference between an Iraqi, a Saudi Arabian, a Pakistani, or an Afghan. He's definitely Iraqi. He certainly did not want to be noticed. Most would have said something to us. He tried to hide behind his work. His mistake was working on the same spark plug. He was watching us."

They climbed into the Yukon, Starr driving, and pulled away.

"Marv, you sure picked up on shit that got by me."

"It's because of what I've done is why I picked up on it. If he'd been working on that first plane, you can bet your ass he wouldn't have been there by the time we got there. As it was, he didn't have time to leave. That I'm sure of."

"You can sure read people, I'll give you that."

"Only reason I'm still alive."

Phillips and Christman were leaving Northern Hunting Expeditions with several brochures on different hunting packages featuring expeditions all over North America.

"So what do you think of that group?" asked Christman.

"Hard to tell. We only really spoke to that Howard guy. He seemed legit. I didn't notice anything other than your run-of-the-mill computer system. Then again, that place may only be a front for whatever. I'm going to dig into that company big-time. Let's get back to the hotel."

Right then, Phillips's cell phone rang.

"Hey, Starr. We're just leaving, heading back to the hotel." She hung up.

"What's up with him?" Christman wanted to know.

"We're meeting up back at the hotel. He didn't say anything else."

"Guess we'll find out then."

President Robert Williams paced back and forth in the Oval Office. He felt very frustrated about the time it was taking to gather confirmed intel on the Alaskan fish kill. He grabbed the phone and spoke with his new chief of staff, Laura Green. "Laura, get Michael Lang on the phone."

"Right away, sir."

Ten minutes passed before the president's phone rang. "Michael, what have you found out?"

"Nothing positive yet, Mr. President. I have my best people on it, and we're working three different theories, but I cannot confirm any single one as of yet."

"Do you have any idea of when you might?" demanded the president.

"With certainty, no. My best guess would be within the next twenty-four hours, perhaps a bit sooner. Sir, we are running every test we have available to us, but we cannot afford to guess."

"No, you can't. I need you to do whatever it is you can, but you have to be certain of any results; that I agree with. Keep me posted."

"Absolutely," Lang was able to interject before the president hung up.

The president's secretary, Alice Pritchard, called him. "Sir, remember you have that ceremony in Baltimore tomorrow."

"What ceremony, Alice?"

"Honoring the governor. He's celebrating forty years in public service."

"Oh yeah. You're right. I forgot. I suppose it's formal?"

"Of course. Don't worry, I've got your nice tux all set. Plus you have your entire staff to help dress you."

"No need for sarcasm, Alice."

"Sir, whatever do you mean?" Alice asked innocently.

Director Lang then called Olivia Watson, his assistant director. "Tell me you have found something."

"Getting close, sir. Larkin appears to be correct; it seems as though this agent is synthetic. Someone created it. We still don't know how it seems to disappear. Larkin is now working on the theory that it somehow turns on itself. I tend to agree with this. There just doesn't seem to be any other plausible explanation. Whoever thought this up is a diabolical genius. Nothing in nature does this. It's an entirely new concept. Once this process starts, there doesn't seem to be any way to stop it. It just dies its own death in an unnaturally short amount of time."

Director Lang was short with his assistant. "I want a detailed written report on what we've found so far on my desk in thirty minutes," he said, slamming the phone down. He then called the White House and spoke with Laura Green. "Please tell the president I will have a report for him within the hour."

"Will do." The conversation ended without pleasantries.

Lawrence Larkin looked up as Joey Tanelli entered his office carrying two cups of coffee and sporting an angry look on his face

"I'll be damned if I can figure out just how this bug disappears. I can't positively ID this residue we've found in the blood. I've been working bioagents for over twenty years, and I've never seen anything like this," Larkin said, exasperated, taking the coffee.

Tanelli agreed. "It's beyond me. With everything we've done, we still don't know shit about how this works. Worse, we have no clue how to stop it." He sat down in the brown leather chair opposite Larkin's desk, placing his coffee cup on a cork coaster.

"I'm thinking the only way to stop this is simply not let it get started. It acts so fast, by the time any countermeasures could be taken, it's going to be too late, anyway. I'm inclined to believe the only way to beat this is to find whoever is responsible and remove the threat entirely," Larkin declared. "I doubt Lang is going to like this."

"Are you kidding? He's still pissed that you called the DPO, never mind his ass couldn't be found. I've worked under five directors, and this guy is a clown," fumed Tanelli. "The only thing he's really interested in is his power and keeping his ego intact. I was really hoping that with the change in the administration we'd get a new director. I still do."

"Good luck with that one."

11.

Myra Banks walked into Bernard Backersley's office. Backersley, on the phone, pointed for her to sit. She sat patiently for the two minutes it took him to finish his call.

Hanging up, he asked, "So what have you found out about Darlene Phillips?"

"What I suspected, primarily. She analyzes all the data that is fed to the DPO. She now has her mail delivered to a post office box. She started that ten days after she left us."

"Why do you suppose she did that?" Backersley inquired.

"It could be for any number of reasons. One might be that perhaps she travels. That is an educated guess."

"Traveling for what?"

"I'd say the DPO. I'm beginning to think there is more to this new agency than what appears. I will say again, this is making me extremely uncomfortable. I can't think of anyone I would rather not screw around with. I don't think you understand this woman's capability with computers. As smart as you are with everything, with computers, this woman is infinitely smarter."

"What is it about her that makes you so nervous?"

Myra Banks couldn't help but roll her eyes. "Haven't you been listening to me? I'm telling you flat out, this woman is dangerous. I have no doubt whatsoever that this lady can do things with a computer that I can't even dream of, and I'm damned good. I think we are playing with fire here. I'd rather spy on the president himself. I'm only offering you what I believe to be reality. What you choose to do with that information is up to you. I'll do whatever you ask, but I am warning you, we are on very thin ice with her."

Backersley was quiet for a moment before he straightened up in his chair. "Myra, I can't see how anyone could be that far above you in computer skills. That's why you're where you are. I want to know as much about this Phillips as you can find out, specifically what she does with the DPO. Be careful, but do it."

Banks got up to leave. As she headed for the door, she retorted, "Maybe they'll give us adjoining cells."

"What's that supposed to mean?" Backersley snapped.

"It means that this is going to end up biting us in the ass. Just you wait—I'll remind you of this conversation," she said, storming out.

❈   ❈   ❈

Backersley waited a few moments and then picked up a secure phone. After dialing a number, a computer-generated voice answered, "Yes?"

"I want you to do a search for me. Darlene Phillips. She worked for us up until a while back when President Williams snatched her from me to work for his new Department of the Presidential Office. Find out what you can. Be careful—she's supposed to be some real wizard with computers."

"I don't expect any problems," the voice replied.

"Good. Get back to me ASAP. I've got my girl on it, but she's scared of this woman. I want you to work on it also."

"My usual fee, of course?"

"If you get me the info I want, I'll double it."

"Consider it done." The call ended.

Backersley then placed a call to the president. The president's secretary informed Backersley that the president was in a meeting and would call him back shortly. Backersley hung up angry. He did *not* like being called back. He considered himself the president's most important asset and always assumed that his calls should be taken immediately. What he did not know was that President Williams was pacing in the Oval Office and simply didn't want to take his call. He knew that Backersley would not have any information that he did not already know and wasn't in the mood to listen to his complaints.

❋　❋　❋

Starr boarded the elevator, pushed the button, and headed for Phillips's room. She had scheduled a meeting for 6:00 p.m., and he had ten minutes to spare. He wondered if she had come up with anything. He had an uneasy feeling in his stomach, and that was bothering him.

One at a time, Starr, Styles, and Christman discreetly arrived. They found her with three laptops open on the coffee table in her room. "Grab a seat, guys. Be with you in a minute," she said with a surprising look in her eyes. "There's bottled water in the fridge."

Styles walked over and grabbed four and handed them out. The room featured a dining-room-style table with four chairs, and each grabbed one. Phillips joined them in about three minutes.

"Okay," Starr observed, "what's with the smirk?"

"Oh, just something I was expecting," she said with an unusual grin.

"Want to let us in?" asked Christman.

"Well, Myra Banks has been doing a search on me. In fact, she's doing one as we speak. She's starting to probe deeper, and she is specifically targeting the DPO." She paused as she took a drink of water and then continued, "I also got an e-mail notification from one of my special alerts. Remember I told you about some, uh, programs I installed in the CIA's mainframe when I was tasked with trying to find a mole? There is one other thing I didn't mention." She took another drink of water.

Starr, wanting to discuss what they had found at Northern Hunting Expeditions, was anxious for her to get to the point. "So get to it already."

"Patience, Starr, patience. It seems that Backersley has someone else also doing a search on me, probably trying to either verify what Banks can find or, as he probably hopes, find out more," she answered.

"And you know this how?" Starr asked.

"Obviously, one of my programs," Phillips answered, grinning.

"Can you find out who he's got doing the second search?" Christman asked.

"J. C., *please* ... I set this program up three years ago, and this is the fifth time that Backersley has gone to this individual for help."

Styles had been sitting quietly at the table, listening intently. Then he started to chuckle.

Starr, getting more impatient, snapped, "And what in the hell is so funny?"

Styles, ignoring Starr, looked at Phillips and nodded. "Good one, Darlene." Turning to Starr, he said, "Don't you see? Backersley has Darlene Phillips looking for Darlene Phillips."

Phillips looked at Styles and said, "You know, there just may be hope for you yet. That is exactly what he is doing."

Now, Starr was suddenly interested. "How are you doing that? I mean, what's going on?"

"I set up a fictitious character. I don't need to go into all the details, but he was introduced to this person by Mossad, although Mossad has no idea they did this. Every once in a while, Backersley has used this person for various tasks. I've fed him information, usually backing up what someone else has found out. He uses this asset mostly for confirmation purposes. Now before you even ask, I have *never* given him any info that was not available from other resources. If I had, it could have been construed as treason. That was a line I was extremely careful not to approach, much less cross."

Styles continued, "I assume there is financial compensation involved?"

"Absolutely. Quite handsome, actually. All the monies are placed in a secret CIA account. The CIA has so many unknown accounts I can assure you that no one knows how many and exactly where they are. I seriously doubt Backersley knows more than, oh, maybe 75 percent of them. I don't even know how many there are.

It'd take one hell of a long time to try to find them all, and I've got better things to do."

"So what are you going to tell Backersley?" Starr wanted to know.

"That depends on what Banks comes up with. I'll confirm what she finds, maybe throw a small, innocent bone into the mix, and call it a day."

The table was quiet for a moment, and then all of them were chuckling aloud.

"I've got to hand it to you, Phillips. Every time I think I might have you almost figured out, you pull one hell of a surprise out of your hat. That's something else," Christman added.

Starr interjected, "So what did you two find out at the hunting place?"

Christman looked at Phillips and nodded, so she took the lead.

"From all appearances, it seems legit. They've got a hell of a celebrity client list, just your basic office computer gear, and no one there that we saw seemed suspicious to me. Of course, it could all be just a front. I'm going to dig deeper and see if I can find anything. I'll check their computers and see if they are aligned with any others. I'll go through e-mails, correspondence, and the usual stuff. What about you guys?"

Starr answered, "We got the name of the chopper company they deal with up in Alaska, and Marv spotted an Iraqi working on one of their three floatplanes. Guess he was watching us pretty closely."

"What do you think?" Christman asked Styles.

"Don't ignore the obvious. We're looking into a terrorist activity, and we have an Iraqi in the mix. There's a connection somewhere, or it's one hell of a coincidence."

"If that's your conclusion, it's good enough for me," Phillips threw in. "I've learned not to question your intuition. What's their name? I'll dig into them."

"Inland Helicopter. Location is Bethel, Alaska."

Phillips was headed back to her computers before he finished the sentence.

Starr asked Christman, "So what kind of place was this Northern Hunting Expeditions?"

"Pretty nice. Had a lot of stuffed trophy animals on display. Don't think PETA would approve. Lots of photos of celebrities. Like Phillips said, it appeared legit."

"Looks like Bethel is our next visit," Styles said. "Might be a good idea not to land the jet there; we'll fly in close and drive. The plane might attract undue attention. Have a feeling it's a small town. We don't want to stick out."

"Good idea," agreed Christman.

Starr asked, "Anybody besides me hungry?"

"Yes, but no damned pizza," answered Christman.

Within minutes, four cheeseburger plates were on their way up to room 422.

After finishing a quick dinner, with Christman looking at a map, he suggested, "I have an idea. Why not fly the jet to Nome and rent a plane to go to Bethel? That way we won't be drawing nearly as much attention. Remember, this is small-town Alaska, and our jet will draw attention that we don't need."

Styles nodded, "Good one, J. C. That works for me. Be sure to rent something that we can haul some gear with. I'll go for a Cessna Stationair or Caravan. Either one will work fine. Those are common as mosquitoes up there, so we'll blend in. Hey, Phillips, you got a laptop to spare?"

"Sure. Use the one on the far end."

"Thanks."

Phillips came back to the table. She had eaten her dinner without ever taking her eyes off her computer screens.

"Myra Banks is definitely investigating the DPO. She's doing it under the guise of relations between the CIA and us overseas. She's fishing everywhere she can throw a line."

"Has she found out anything damaging yet?" Starr asked

"No, not really. She's confirmed J. C.'s identity, but you and Styles are under the radar. She got J. C.'s by a copy of his transfer orders. When there's time, I'm going to find out how that leaked. For now, she has little more than the official reports. Backersley must be on her ass pretty hard; she's gotten more brazen in her search. She has to know that I'll be onto her at some point. It appears as though she doesn't care. This has to be Backersley. She hasn't got the balls to do that on her own."

Styles allowed himself a small smile. Phillips was definitely one of the boys. A real feeling of satisfaction came over him as he realized just how well this team had jelled, especially after the rough start.

"You going to do anything or just let her fish?" he inquired.

"Let her fish. She's good, but not good enough. She'll never break through any of my programs, which are the only way she could ever connect any dots. Other than one of us getting caught and spilling our guts. And that won't happen."

"No, it won't," Starr said emphatically.

"Are we ready to head up to Alaska?" Styles asked impatiently.

"I suppose so," Starr replied. "J. C., how long will it take to get up there?"

"Flight time, maybe an hour—that is, if we don't want to draw attention," he answered while on hold on his cell phone. "That will do fine," the three heard him say. "We're all set on the Cessna out of Nome."

Styles looked at his watch. "Okay, let's go. We should be there a little after dark if we leave now. We won't bother to check out. Just leave the key cards on the table. Everybody okay with that?"

The other three nodded.

Phillips interrupted. "I've got something here. One of my programs intercepted some chatter on an underground website, and it's saying that an attack will take place here on Labor Day."

Styles swore under his breath. "Well, we don't have much time. Let's *move!*"

12.

Ryyaki Ali was holding a meeting with Jamil Abdul-Nasir, Rijah Ellhad, and Imad al-Bin. "I have given much thought to where we should strike. I would like your opinions on each. I have contemplated a public water supply; however, the timetable of the agent may not work to our advantage. I have considered a holiday spot involving water. This American holiday they refer to as Labor Day seems to bring these infidels out in celebration. There are many locations they flock to. One is Lake Mead in Nevada. Thousands of people will go out in their decadent lack of clothing on their boats. It also is the water supply for the center of these Western degenerate infidels, Las Vegas. We may also be able to infiltrate that source. Regardless, thousands will die along with everything in that lake. I believe it would make a very strong statement of our hatred for these depraved people. I will now listen."

The three men were silent. They knew better than to oppose any idea he suggested. Agreement was mandatory. All three nodded. No words were spoken.

"No one has anything to say?" Ali asked, feigning surprise.

Rijah Ellhad spoke. "It sounds like a good plan. I would suppose that you have worked out the timetable, the method of delivery, and the rest of the operational plans."

"I have. Now listen closely."

❈　❈　❈

Bernard Backersley had decided to go ahead and investigate this new suspected terrorist activity on his own, despite the CIA's edict of only working outside the borders of the United States. *Not like it hasn't been done before.* If he found something out that he felt needed sharing, well, then he'd cross that bridge. If he got called on the carpet from the president, he would claim he was only performing investigative research in an attempt to be helpful. He knew the president wouldn't buy it, but as long as he didn't initiate any physical action, he felt he'd be safe.

Ever since he'd had questions about the Department of the Presidential Office, he had changed his routine slightly. For this particular action, he'd begun using simple burn phones for communication rather than the official CIA phone lines. He'd already made several calls on one, so he decided to ditch that one. He grabbed a second unit and dialed a number. Everything discussed now with regard to what they were doing was outside normal channels. He didn't want anyone, including his own agency, to know what he was doing. Only the team operating under his direct control was aware. He was calling that team leader now.

❈　❈　❈

Styles came out the stairwell door in the lobby and immediately stopped. He never used the elevators, always the stairs. One pair of eyes had noticed his entrance. Styles nonchalantly walked over to the large breakfast area and poured himself a cup of coffee. He tried to act as an employee of the hotel. He grabbed a table near the entrance, where he could observe the entire lobby. The hair on his neck was immediately standing on end. He grabbed his cell and texted Starr, "Hold up." What had caught his attention instantly was the sight of four men in suits. Two were at the check-in desk while two were stationed near the elevators. The man who had noticed him was not paying an unusual amount of attention to Styles, though he did look over on a regular basis. *Trying to decide if I'm anyone worth watching,* he thought. Styles studied every aspect of the men, their dress, their attitude, the way they walked, the way the two at the service desk talked.

His cell buzzed slightly. Starr had replied, "?"

Styles texted back, "CIA. Coming back up." He finished his coffee and went back up the stairs. He entered the room, with the three looking at him with concern.

Starr spoke. "You say the CIA is downstairs?"

"No doubt."

"What are they doing here?"

"I think I can answer that," Phillips interjected. "Look, the CIA isn't completely stupid. My guess is they connected Northern Hunting Expeditions, had the place under surveillance, and followed J. C. and me back here."

Starr said, with a hint of sarcasm, "And you were followed?"

"It's a strong possibility," Phillips stated.

Styles interceded. "To be fair, they wouldn't have had a reason to think they might have been. This is not on them."

Starr continued, "Well, how did they get out here so fast? I mean, we just got here."

Phillips answered, "Starr, the CIA was already here. Even our jet can't go as fast as a phone call."

"How did they know to follow us?" Starr asked.

Phillips spoke again. "Another guess, but I'd say facial recognition on J. C. or me. We know the CIA is doing a search on me; it only stands to reason. Styles is the only one of us who is pretty much safe from facial recognition. The rest of us have photos on file somewhere. Even I can't delete all of them, though I'm trying."

"So what do we do?" J. C. asked.

Styles declared, "We get out of here. Phillips, can you delete all photos of us from the hotel's security systems? For the next fifteen minutes would also be good."

"Yes. It will take me about five minutes, maybe less."

"Do it," Styles directed. "We're going to leave the Yukon that J. C. and Phillips were driving here. We'll all go back in ours. Starr, you and J. C. get all our gear together on one of those hotel carts. Starr, find a hotel jacket, put it on, and then take everything to the Yukon and stow it. J. C., you and Phillips get ready to move the second she's finished. Take the stairs; there's two agents watching the elevators. Open the door, find me, and when I nod, you guys move to the Yukon. Don't stop, no matter what!"

Starr looked at Styles. "What are you going to do?"

"Make sure we get out of here without the CIA up our ass."

"Three minutes and I'm finished," Phillips informed them.

"Good. Starr, go find your jacket and get the gear to the Yukon. J. C., you and Phillips go down the stairs in six minutes. Wait for my signal." Then Styles was out the door and headed for the stairs. Silent as a ghost, he opened the door and stepped out into the concrete landing.

❈   ❈   ❈

Director Lang called the president. He waited only twenty seconds before the president picked up.

"Yes, Michael. What have you found out?" President Williams demanded.

"As we suspected, it's synthetic. Man-made. Somehow water seems to activate this agent. It coagulates the blood, rendering it useless. Death is probably rather quick. The shelf life on this new toxin appears to be short, but the effect is devastating. Any living organism that has blood in its system is susceptible. Nothing can survive its onslaught. The ramifications are unimaginable. Presently, once this agent has started, it's unknown if it can be stopped, so the key is prevention." Lang held his breath, waiting for the president to explode.

"Nice job on the report, Michael. Short and to the point, just how I like them. So where do you go from here?"

"We continue to study it, sir. Honestly, though, I don't know just how much more we can find out. We really need a live sample, and that won't be easy to procure."

"No, Michael, it won't. Keep me posted." The conversation ended.

The president thought for a moment, and then grabbing a secure phone, he called Starr.

"Sir?"

"Richard, I just wanted to bring you up to speed on the latest from the CDC."

"Ah, sir, would it be permissible to call you back? We're in a bit of a bind at the moment."

"What's the problem?"

"CIA."

"How in the hell is the CIA giving you a problem?" President Williams exploded.

"Mr. President, it would *really* be helpful if I could get back with you," Starr implored.

"All right, Richard, but don't take long. Backersley is already getting on my nerves. I want to know what he's up to."

"ASAP, sir. Thank you." Starr hung up quickly.

The president immediately called Coverley Merritt. Upon answering, the president inquired with fervor, "Has the CIA been keeping you in the loop?"

"Difficult to say, Mr. President. We get pieces of information from them but, curiously, nothing about this latest toxic threat. That seems rather odd. Far as I'm concerned, there's no way Backersley is keeping his nose out of this. Yet we've heard nothing."

"I'm not surprised, and I tend to agree. I'll handle Backersley. Keep me informed every step of the way. How are the others doing?" he asked, referring to the directors of the other agencies.

"Fine as far as I can tell. I suspect they keep a little to themselves, but nothing that concerns me, at least not at the moment. If that moment comes, I'll be on the horn to you immediately."

"Good to hear," the president replied, ending the call.

The elderly gentleman, who appeared to be in his late sixties, was disembarking at Baltimore-Washington International Airport. He had spoken very little during the flight that originated in Miami,

Florida. He had one of those grandfatherly smiles, one that would instantly make anyone feel comfortable. His eyes twinkled with innocence. The flight attendants immediately took a strong liking to him, giving him special attention. They brought him a blanket without being asked, along with a bottle of water, free of charge, which was unusual considering the state of the airline industry. A mere "Thank you," along with a nod of his head, was all that he offered in return. A young female attendant had assisted him to the restroom once during the flight. He walked with a pronounced limp, using a cane to compensate. As he reached the exit door of the plane, two of the flight attendants made a concerted effort to say good-bye and for him to be careful. The gentleman paused, and one at a time, he grasped their hands softly and said, "Bless you." Then he slowly walked away. He had brought no luggage, so he made his way to the shuttle that would carry him to the main terminal. Upon arriving, he made his way outside to the taxi stand. He easily hailed a taxi.

"Please take me to the Quality Suites motel near Halethorpe," he instructed pleasantly.

"Yes, sir. Do you have any luggage?" the taxi driver asked.

"No, young man, I'm much too old to bother with luggage. My son is meeting me, and he will have clothing for me."

"What brings you to Baltimore?" the driver asked.

"My grandson is getting married," he lied.

"Well, we are certainly having beautiful weather for a wedding."

"Yes. The weather is beautiful for anything. Anything at all."

Styles had just silently closed the door behind him, standing on the concrete landing on the fifth floor, when he heard the lobby door, five floors down, open and then close. Then a voice that said, "I'm in position," filtered up. *Jeez, where do they get these guys?* He was dressed in what had become his usual attire. Stretch blue jeans for ease of movement, dark T-shirt (this one black), with black sneakers. Silently, he made his way down the stairs, taking care to pay attention to any shadows the stairway lighting might create. Reaching the fourth floor, Styles was appreciative that the lighting threw the shadows back toward the railing and the rear of the stairwell, meaning behind his back.

Cautiously, he made his way down to the second floor. He was now two short flights of stairs, plus the center landing, above the fellow below him. He recognized him as the second man he'd seen at the registration desk. He knelt down to the floor and sneaked a glance over the edge of the concrete. The agent was looking through the crack of the door to the lobby, as he had not closed it securely. He was paying no attention to the stairway. Styles almost felt sorry for him. Worse, he had his back to the stairway. Styles watched him for two minutes. Not once did the agent move, continuing to watch the lobby. Styles straightened up and started down the second-to-last flight of stairs toward his quarry. At the landing, he paused, double-checked any shadows, and proceeded. Two steps above him and four feet away, he pounced. He simultaneously cupped his hand over the man's mouth and punched him hard in his right kidney and then immediately put him in a rear choke hold.

"Relax; I'm only going to put you to sleep. Don't fight it," Styles whispered.

In ten seconds, the man was out. Styles kept the hold for another five seconds and then lowered him to the floor. He reached down and pulled the man's communication earpiece from him. He inserted it into his own ear, making sure he turned off the microphone. *Might as well hear what they have to say.* He opened the door and checked the lobby. The two agents were still at the elevators. He looked around but didn't see the fourth. He texted Phillips, "Cameras down?"

"Yes."

He texted her again. "Move in two."

Slowly, he emerged from the stairwell so as not to draw attention. He moved over toward the main entrance as though he were entering from the street. He noticed a bit of a commotion over at the service desk. A door opened from behind the counter, and the fourth agent exited, followed by who Styles guessed was probably a manager.

Styles knew they would all be armed. He had his silenced Beretta in the small of his back but did not plan on drawing it. He judged the distance between the elevators and the service desk to be about thirty feet. He knew he could travel that and be over the counter in about two seconds. He judged the agent behind the counter to be early forties and probably the agent in charge at this scene. There was a large decorative pillar halfway between the elevators and the counter. Checking the angle, he knew it was partially concealing the area immediately in front of the elevators. That would give him an extra couple of seconds before anyone realized what was happening. *Nothing beats the element of surprise.* Walking casually toward the elevators, he noticed that none of the men were communicating.

Right then, the elevator chime rang, announcing its arrival. When the door opened, both agents riveted their attention to it. Out came a rolling luggage cart. A familiar figure dressed in a lavish hotel jacket with matching hat appeared. Styles had to suppress a smile as he strode quickly toward the elevator.

"Hold that for me, please?" he half shouted. One of the agents took three steps toward it and held the door. *These guys really need serious training.* He glanced toward the stairwell door and nodded. Then all his attention was devoted toward the two agents. As he walked past the first agent, Styles's fist shot out and caught the agent square in the side of his neck. Without stopping, he caught the agent and threw him into the second agent, knocking them both into the open elevator. Styles sprang after him. The second was fumbling, trying to get out from under the first agent, when Styles struck him with a vicious palm strike to his solar plexus. The air wheezed from his lungs. Though not knocked out, the man was sent to his back, helpless, gasping for breath. Whirling, Styles hit the button for the top floor and exited the elevator, heading for the registration counter. *Guy doesn't have a clue.* He glimpsed over to see Phillips and Christman going through the front door.

Styles was three feet from the granite countertop when the fourth agent realized he couldn't see the two that had been stationed in front of the elevators. He moved slightly to his own right for a better view of the elevators. As he started to become aware, Styles sprang onto the counter, landing on both his hands, pivoted, and kicked the agent square in the forehead, sending him sprawling back against a wall. Styles, immediately over the man, realized he was unconscious. Without a word, and avoiding looking at the two employees, he was back across the counter and headed out the door. He crossed the wide sidewalk, turned to his right, and began walking alongside the road. Walking less than one hundred feet, the Yukon that Starr and he had been driving pulled alongside, and he jumped in.

"What happened inside?" questioned Starr.

"Not much. Those guys were definitely not field agents."

Christman queried, "You didn't have to—"

"No, just knocked them out. Well, three of them. One I just knocked the breath out of and sent him and his partner for a ride up in the elevator."

"Aren't you worried about the witnesses?" Phillips asked.

"No. Eyewitnesses are the worst. You can have five people who will give five different descriptions. Unless someone has been trained by the military or law enforcement, generally people make lousy witnesses. That's why I needed you to remove us from the security tapes."

Phillips confirmed, "Taken care of. I deleted the last ten hours, so they have no image of us anywhere. Like I said, soon as I have time, I've got to do a better job of trying to get the three of us out of any system anywhere. I feel like it's my fault that they even knew about us."

Styles answered firmly. "Not true. Any of us can be found if someone looks hard enough, and apparently the CIA is. If this Backersley wasn't sticking his nose up our asses, it wouldn't have happened. End of conversation."

"Airport?" inquired Starr.

"Yes," Styles said. "I don't think there's anything here that Phillips can't find faster. Let's get to Alaska."

Reaching into a bag, Starr produced a cell phone. "J. C., be sure you don't speed. We don't need to be stopped for anything."

13.

The elderly man who had checked into the Quality Suites immediately went into the bathroom. In less than ten minutes, he had removed the disguise that had taken over four hours to apply, including the liquid latex that had dried into a remarkable mask. He then stepped into a steaming-hot shower. What emerged was a man of obvious Middle Eastern descent. Toweling off, he retrieved a cell phone and dialed the only number programmed into it. A voice answered a simple "Yes."

"I have arrived."

"Good. The van will be parked in the motel's parking lot within the hour. The key will be inside the driver's front tire on the ground. Everything you need will be inside. May Allah guide you in your mission."

"Allahu Akbar."

Sirhan al-Razar had come into America under a student visa. He had attended New York University and graduated with a perfect 4.0 grade point average. The day after graduation, he went underground. He had volunteered for this mission. It was generally acknowledged he would martyr himself, but he had no plans on dying. He was doing this for the money. He had been promised US $5 million should he survive. With an IQ of 160, he firmly believed he was smart enough to carry out his plan. He spotted several menus on the bureau the television was placed upon for restaurants that specialized in room delivery. He ordered a chicken dinner from KFC and waited for his food.

He had just finished eating when he heard vehicles pull into the parking lot. Looking out the window, he saw a dark van park. The driver got out and bent down as though he were tying his shoe. He then walked over and got into a dark sedan that promptly drove away. As anxious as he was to see the contents, he had decided to wait until it was late in the evening. He did not want anyone to notice that he was no longer an elderly gentleman.

He turned on the television in time to catch the local evening news. All of Baltimore was abuzz with the impending arrival of the president of the United States to honor the governor of Maryland. *With any luck ...*

The flight up to Nome, Alaska, was routine. Starr spent the trip in the copilot seat beside Christman and continued to learn more about flying the jet. Phillips was on her computers and spoke little. It was obvious she still felt responsible for the group being discovered. Styles spent the trip exercising. Christman had made arrangements for a private hangar, and Phillips had secured rooms at a Ramada Inn just opposite the airport. Once again, she booked four rooms to continue a random choice. When the plane was stowed in the hangar, three Ford Explorers were dropped off, the keys left in the ignition.

"Those for us?" inquired Christman.

"Yes," replied Phillips.

"Why three?"

"I want to stop doing patterns. Just trying to be cautious," she responded.

"Good idea, Phillips," agreed Styles.

By the time the four had checked into their rooms, it was past time for dinner. Phillips had said she preferred to have room service, as she had work to do. The three men decided to go to the in-house restaurant. They had requested a large table. After having their orders taken, with all deciding on cold beer, Christman brought up Phillips.

"I think she's blaming herself for us getting made."

"Wasn't her fault," said Styles again.

"We know that, but she's having a hard time buying off on it," injected Starr.

"Yeah, that's her. Best thing we can do is just leave her alone. She's not real big on cheering up," offered Styles.

"One thing for sure, I'm not sure what she's working on right now, but I'll bet she's kicking its ass, whatever it is," stated Christman emphatically.

"No doubt," agreed Starr. "So what's the schedule for tomorrow?"

"I want to check out that helicopter service in person. If she hasn't already done so, which would surprise the hell out of me, we'll have Phillips do a search on them," said Styles. "Might not be a bad idea to try to keep her busy with her computers. That's the one thing that might get her back on her game."

Both Starr and Christman nodded in agreement.

❈ ❈ ❈

After the three had enjoyed their steak dinners, they retired to their rooms. Though it was a little after ten in the evening, Styles called Phillips. "Hey, mind if I pay you a quick visit?"

"No, I'm just doing my thing. I'm in 416."

"I remember. Be right there."

Arriving two minutes later, he knocked softly on the door. It opened, and she invited him in.

"What's this about?" she asked.

"No big deal. I just want to make something clear. Darlene, you are unbelievable at what you do. This team would not have accomplished what it has without you. Not even close. We all have our roles, we all do them well, but not one of us can do everything. I know you are kicking yourself about being made. It wasn't anything other than a bad coincidence. It happens. Don't get me wrong; this isn't some damned pep talk. I know better than that. I just want to be sure you stay focused. I've said before, you don't have one fucking thing to prove to anybody. Catch the drift?"

Phillips was quiet for a few moments before she spoke, choosing her words carefully. "Normally, Styles, I'd probably get pissed at you for saying that, but I know it's not any kind of a 'feel better' speech or whatever. It's about looking out for the team, not about me. I get it. I also respect you for coming out and saying so. No problem on my end. I've found out some good info that we'll go over in the morning. I'm putting it all together now. I'm good, so how about letting me get back to work?"

"You got it. Good night." He stopped as he was leaving because Phillips spoke up.

"Thank you. Your confidence in me means more than you can imagine. I know that is something that, especially with you, has to be earned. I'm not afraid to tell you that does make me feel good and, most importantly, that I've earned my right to be here."

Styles walked up to her, placed his hand on her shoulder, and said firmly, "*That* you have done." With a simple nod, he turned and walked out. Heading back to his own room, he walked slower than usual, his mind going off in several directions at once. Back in his room, Styles was a little miffed he'd eaten so late. He did not like working out after just eating, so he did the next best thing. He cleaned his .40-caliber Beretta.

Sirhan al-Razar was so excited he could not sleep. The previous evening, when it was very late and activity had virtually ceased around the Quality Suites motel, he had sneaked out to the van, retrieved the key, and entered. He was pleased that the interior lights had been shut off. A crate was in the back. It was marked "Fragile—Handle with Extreme Care—Antique Glass." There was a DeWalt cordless driver in its black plastic carrying case behind the driver's seat. He grabbed the screw gun, which already had a star bit in place, and proceeded to unscrew the top and remove it. He was working by the light of his cell phone along with the lighting of the parking area. Inside were three smaller crates that had padlocks installed. He removed a key ring from his pocket and proceeded to unlock the top crate. He carefully removed the lid. He stared at what was inside, a Russian SA-18 third-generation infrared shoulder-fire missile. This was a highly sought system. Its passive guidance system emitted no signals, which made countermeasures difficult. It also had the ability to recognize and reject flares. It was great for bringing down airplanes up to ten thousand feet. It was perfect for bringing down a helicopter. He had memorized the firing sequence for this unit. He stared at it for over thirty seconds before replacing the padlock and screwing the crate top back into place. Then he very carefully scanned the entire area before slipping out of the van and coming face-to-face with a young man who was obviously quite drunk.

"Hey, man. You got a few bucks you could loan me?" he asked.

Sirhan al-Razar was instantly guarded. He knew what he had to do. "Yes, I could give you twenty dollars if that would help."

A smile came across the young man's face. "That would be great."

"It is in my front pocket. Let me get it for you." He reached out with a bill that was concealing a switchblade knife. As he was handing the twenty over, he thumbed the button upward, releasing the blade. As the drunk reached to take the bill, al-Razar dropped the bill and sank the blade up to the hilt just below the breastbone, upward into the man's heart. The man slumped to the ground, twitching twice, and died. Al-Razar looked around, checked all the windows of the motel, and was satisfied no one had seen him. He quickly dragged the body to the end of the motel to a large commercial Dumpster. Opening the half lid as quietly as possible, it appeared the Dumpster was about three-quarters full. He hoisted the body up and into it. He then reached around and covered the body with large black plastic garbage bags. He then lowered the lid back into place and retreated back to his room. He sat in a chair, staring at a noiseless television. He was literally quivering with nervous excitement.

14.

T-Minus 48 Hours

The next morning, President Williams convened a meeting with his top directors. All the major agencies were represented.

The president spoke. "I wanted to have a discussion with all of you about this latest terrorist threat before I leave for Maryland later today. First, I'd like Director Lang to read you in on what he has been able to ascertain about this danger. Michael ..."

Director Lang, of the CDC, rose and gave a recap of everything that was known about the threat.

The director of the National Security Agency, Elliott Ragar, asked, "What exactly do you mean by 'works with blinding speed'? Are you referring to how fast it kills?"

"I apologize, no. I mean how fast it can contaminate a body of water. I'm sure you have all seen the video. The only thing that appears to stop it is when it runs out of water. Otherwise, all indications are it will just keep multiplying and spreading, killing everything in its path that has blood in its system. It *is* possible that once this toxin has run its shelf life, it may just die out on its own; however, that is only an educated guess at best."

"Explain that exactly," directed the president.

"Conceivably, you're standing on a dock in Key West and you initiate this synthetic toxin. If it works in salt water, and we have no idea if it does as in fresh, within days all the world's oceans would be contaminated with every living creature in them dead. *That*, gentlemen, is how fast it can spread—and kill—and as of this moment, we don't have a single idea on how to stop it," described Lang. "If, however," he continued, "it were to die out on its own, there is no way of knowing exactly how far it might reach before it expired. Either way would be devastating."

"Mr. President, out of curiosity, why is the vice president not here?" inquired John Clayton, the chairman of the Joint Chiefs of Staff.

"He's on his way back from Japan as we speak. He has been brought up to speed." It was not a classified secret that the president did not care for Vice President Herbert Lamar.

Matt Sanderson, director of the FBI, asked harshly, "Do we know if we have a definite threat or target for this damned thing?"

"No, Matt, we don't. However, it doesn't take a triple-digit IQ to figure out that has to be its purpose," the president responded with more than a hint of sarcasm. "Bernard," he continued, referring to the director of the CIA, "has anything turned up in your world?"

"No, sir, not yet. I'm pressing every button I have trying to gain information, but so far to no avail. I will also say it's scaring the hell out of my fellow contacts. None of them have ever heard of anything quite like this."

"Gentlemen," the president continued, "we should be scared. Very scared. I believe that this is an attack on America; however, if this agent gets launched in the right manner, we cannot rule out that it could very well turn into a global event. We *need* to get a handle on this *now*! Leave no stone unturned, tap every resource, make up some, I don't care. But get me answers, *fast*!"

"Yes, sir," they replied in unison.

"Mr. President, how long do you plan on being in Maryland?" Coverley Merritt, director of the president's Department of the Presidential Office, inquired.

"As short a time as possible. If the governor wasn't such a huge supporter, I'd cancel, but Laura Green is being a pain in my ass," he said, referring to his chief of staff. This remark eased the tension in the room, but only slightly. "I will not be staying overnight. If anyone has any news, call me direct. Understood?"

The president stood and paused, looking down at the black walnut conference table so highly polished he could see the grim reflection of his own face in the surface. He then looked each director squarely in the eyes.

"Gentlemen, we absolutely *must* find the source of this contaminant. No compromises. No failures. Do whatever you must, but find this supply and supplier. Do your jobs!" He turned and walked through a door, determination in his step.

Styles was up at five in the morning, dressed for a run. He went down the stairs from his third-floor room two at a time. He walked briskly through the lobby, noting one employee at the registration desk and a second beginning to set up the complimentary breakfast. He nodded at the woman making coffee and headed out the door. He turned right and started into a brisk jog. His intention was to encircle the airport. The sky was getting brighter and promised to be a clear day. Not wanting to deal with cars and traffic, he entered the airport grounds through an open gate and decided to just follow the ten-foot-high chain-link fence around the airport. Easy enough, or at least it should have been.

He was approximately one-third of the way around, running on a paved access road for the airport, when he heard a vehicle coming up behind him. He moved over to his right, giving the vehicle ample room to pass. It didn't. He heard it slow up as it approached him and then matched his speed for perhaps fifty yards. Then blue lights came on with a blip of a siren. Styles slowed and stopped. A copper-colored Chevrolet Blazer, its white doors emblazoned with "Airport Security," pulled alongside with two guards inside. The one on the passenger side yelled for him to hold.

Great! He remained still.

"What are you doing out here?" demanded the officer in the passenger seat.

"Running," was Styles's reply.

"Why out here?"

"Didn't want to bother with traffic. Running around the airport seemed like a good idea."

"You know you are trespassing, don't you?" the guard responded testily.

"No, I don't. I haven't seen a single sign. If I had, I wouldn't be here."

Both the guards exited the vehicle. The one who had been talking was obviously the senior officer of the two. He appeared to be in his midthirties, exhibited an athletic build, and displayed an openly aggressive attitude. The second, the one who had been driving, looked to be ten years younger. Both were armed with Tasers and guns.

Glocks. Probably nine millimeter, Styles thought.

"I'm going to need to see some ID," the older one stated flatly.

"Sorry. Left it in my room over at the Ramada. I didn't realize you now need an ID to run." Styles casually took a step closer to the pair.

"You need to do anything I say," ordered the security guard belligerently.

"There is no trouble here. You can clearly see I'm not carrying anything. Hell, I've got on a T-shirt, gym shorts, ankle socks, and shoes. What do you think I'm going to do with that?"

"I think you're going to turn around while I cuff you. We'll take you back to headquarters and run a make on you to be safe."

Styles took another step closer, holding his hands out to his side as in an attempt to plead his case. "I don't think so. It would be better for you two boys to continue your rounds, or if you want, you can follow me. I'm not doing anything wrong, and I don't feel like being the subject of your morning conversation. A word of advice. Don't go for the Tasers or Glocks. It won't end well."

"On the ground," commanded the guard, reaching for his Taser.

Styles took a quick step toward him and executed a perfect front jump kick, catching the man squarely under his chin, snapping his head and shoulders back and then falling into a heap onto the pavement. Without stopping, Styles turned to the second man.

"Hey, I'm not part of this," he said with his arms straight out from his side. "Ed's an asshole. He hassles everybody. Thinks he's some king shit karate expert, but it looks like he's got quite a way to go. I've got no problem with you."

Styles stopped short. "So what are you going to tell your boss?"

"That he fucked with the wrong guy. Look, I leave in two weeks for the marines. They can fire my ass this morning, and I don't care. Day after tomorrow is my last day, anyway."

"Marines, huh? I just got out a while back, retired."

"Yeah, you look retired."

"Okay. We'll call it square. You'd better get your buddy to the ER. I know I broke his jaw," Styles directed.

"He's not my buddy. I can't stand him. I'd say he's lucky to have his head. I never saw anyone kick like that. Thanks for not taking my head off."

"Like I told him, I wasn't looking for trouble."

"No, you weren't. That's just what I'm going to write up. You got my word on that."

Styles stepped up and extended his hand. "Word from an ingoing marine is good enough for me. Good luck to you." Styles shook his hand.

"I'll put it on the radio that you're running the fence. You won't have any more problems. Hell, Ed's the only asshole we've got working with us."

"Appreciate that. Like I said, good luck." Then Styles was off and running.

Styles, freshly showered, met with Starr, Christman, and Phillips in Phillips's hotel room. Starr had gone down to the in-house restaurant and brought up breakfast sandwiches and coffee for everyone.

Phillips was visibly tired. She'd been up most of the night researching.

"Okay, guys, this is what I've got. Inland Helicopter. They are definitely suspect. I traced two bank accounts to the Cayman Islands and had to go through a dozen shell companies to get to the owners. Saudi. Any questions? Good," she said, not giving anyone time to ask one. She tossed a stack of papers onto the table. "Here's what I found out. Go over it when you've got the time. If Northern Hunting Expeditions is involved, it has to be minor. My feeling is they are not. I could be wrong. Chopper guys are definitely involved. Cross-referencing cell phone calls, I came up with one name. Not sure exactly where he fits in, but he's in there somewhere. Ryyaki Ali. Billionaire Saudi. Has four mansions in this country alone, a total of nine worldwide. One is a retreat outside Portland, Oregon, on about thirty-five acres. He enjoys a luxurious lifestyle. I have three other cell numbers, but I can't match to any names yet. I'll keep digging." Again she stopped for coffee.

Styles spoke up. "J. C., you go check on the plane, be sure it's fueled; whatever. Starr and I are going to pay Inland Choppers a visit. Phillips, get some sleep; you've earned it."

15.

Ryyaki Ali had returned to the warehouse to meet the man known only as Smith. Ali had six guards with him, all armed with AK-47s and Glock nine-millimeter handguns. As agreed, he had his banking information ready to present as additional proof that his payment had been made. He wanted no disagreement with this man.

Ali had waited ten minutes when a white Chevrolet Suburban appeared and parked. Smith got out, surrounded by three stern-faced bodyguards. No weapons were visible, but Ali had no doubt they were in possession of such.

"My bank has notified me that the transfer went as agreed," Smith stated.

"Yes. I brought records of my own in case you had any questions," Ali replied.

"No, all is well. I expect you to wire the final payment within ten days if you find that satisfactory."

"That is acceptable."

Smith turned and nodded at the Suburban. A rear door opened, and a fifth man got out, holding a wooden crate.

With no words spoken, he walked straight to Ryyaki Ali and placed the crate at his feet. He returned to the Suburban and climbed back inside, shutting the door.

Smith then approached Ali and handed him an envelope. "Inside are a few notes I made, along with a business card with only a phone number, and a cell phone. If you have further use of my services, call the number from that cell phone. I believe this concludes our present business."

"Yes."

The two men gave curt nods and parted ways.

Upon returning to Ali's immense home, one that most would refer to as a mansion, the group retreated to the downstairs secure room, one that had been specifically built to block any manner in which the room could be spied upon. It consisted of a long mahogany table that could seat twelve, with matching chairs. Along the side of one wall was a full-length desk, upon which sat three different computers. At the far end of the room, there was a walk-in safe, shelving installed upon three walls. Cash, arms, along with jewels and stolen art were stored. Only Ali could access this, as it was protected by an electronic keypad that also required his thumbprint.

"Stay here," he directed the four men who accompanied him as he walked to the safe. After punching in the code and pressing his thumb against the scanner, the large, heavy door swung open noiselessly. "Bring me that crate."

None of the other four men moved.

With obvious annoyance, he walked back to the table where he had placed the crate containing the toxin. "What are you afraid of? It is harmless until the agent is placed in water. Do you see any water here?" He impatiently grabbed the crate and took it into the safe, where he placed it upon one of the shelves. Without saying a word, he exited and closed the door.

The four men did not look entirely convinced, particularly Rijah Ellhad, who had personally seen the consequences of what that crate contained.

"Come, sit at the table," ordered Ali.

"How will we get there?" asked Rijah Ellhad.

"The most direct route from here. We travel Interstate 84 to

Interstate 15, take State Highway 169, and access the lake through what is called the Overton area. There will be heavy traffic, so thorough examination of vehicles will be limited."

"Will you be joining us?"

Ryyaki Ali gave him a look of annoyance. "No. I have other business to complete. You will be traveling with a woman who supports the cause. A couple will draw the least attention. All should go well."

"Forgive me for asking, but would it not be better to have others along to protect this package?"

Ali looked annoyed. "I have given this much thought, and as I just said, I believe a couple will draw the least attention. Rijah, if I thought you were not up to the task, I would not send you. Do you have any doubts about your ability to complete this task?" Ali asked in a semi-threatening manner.

"No. When do I leave?"

"You will leave in two days, on this cursed holiday these infidels celebrate. You will release the agent Monday afternoon upon your arrival. After that, kill the woman. We will leave no witnesses."

"Allahu Akbar."

Nazir al-Hadid called a burn phone number.

"Yes?" came a voice.

"I want to know that you are ready. I will leave for the fishing vessel in two hours. You are to meet me there in three hours. I have our escape means in place. Be sure you have eaten. We will have a six-hour journey after we complete the mission. Be sure to drive very carefully. Do you have any questions?"

"No, I am ready," answered Sirhan al-Razar.

"Then we proceed."

Styles and Starr had arrived at Inland Helicopter.

"How do you want to work this?" asked Starr.

"Straightforward, follow my lead, but your priority is watching my back for any shooters. Let's go," he said.

They walked in the Quonset hut–style building, a long, half-round structure made of corrugated steel. While the outside had been freshly painted silver, the inside was several different colors, including rust.

"What can I get you boys?" asked a gruff, scruffy-looking man. He definitely looked the part of an Alaskan; red plaid shirt, blue jean coveralls, boots. He was standing behind a four-foot-tall service counter.

"Who's top dog here?" Styles inquired.

"Well, I'm a co-owner, and since I'm the only one here, guess that'd be me."

"A few days ago, you picked up a man at a remote lake about two hundred miles from here and took him to hook up with a floatplane from Northern Hunting Expeditions. I want to know who that man was."

Starr had taken up a position just inside the doorway and five feet off to the side. His hand was inside his jacket on the butt of his nine-millimeter Glock, a pistol that Styles didn't particularly care for but Starr swore by.

"I wouldn't have any way of knowing just who you was talking about. We run three choppers, and it could have been any one of the three."

Styles's voice took on a razor-sharp edge. "I don't have the time or patience to ask you again. Who is the guy you ferried from that lake to the floatplane?"

"I don't give a fuck about your time or patience. Get the hell out."

Styles instructed Starr, "Check the building for any security cameras and the recorder or computer. Grab all of it." He looked back at the large man standing across the counter with an angry look on his face. Standing at least three inches over Styles and outweighing him by at least sixty pounds, he was badly underestimating Styles.

"All right, you want it hard, you got it hard," he snarled. When he came from behind the counter, he had a large hunting knife in his hand.

Styles backed away from the counter and stood still, letting the man approach him. He moved at Styles straight on, his right hand wielding the knife shot straight out at Styles's midsection. Styles turned to his left slightly, grabbed the man's wrist with his left hand, turned it over to the point of breaking, and then placed his right hand at the man's locked elbow, and using leverage caused by the wrist lock, he forced the man to one knee. "Drop the knife, or I shatter your elbow."

"Fuck you," the man growled.

Styles dug his left thumb into the nerve mass of the man's held wrist, which instantly caused it to spasm. The knife fell to the floor.

"Last chance."

The man tried to get up despite the pain. Styles drew his fist back six inches and drove it through the side of the man's locked elbow, ninety degrees of the opposite direction in which elbows are designed to pivot. The snapping of the joint could be heard across the building. The scream might have been heard across town. Styles grabbed the man by his throat and slammed him up against the cabinet that held the service desk. The man never saw where Styles's own knife came from. It just materialized right in front of his eyes, which appeared ready to bulge out of his head.

"I'm going to ask you again; if you don't tell me, I'll cut off an ear and then the other; I will carve you up like a Halloween pumpkin. *Now who was this man?*"

"I don't know his name; he was some kind of raghead. Sammy set up the deal."

"Who's Sammy?"

"My partner. He's on a flight right now," he choked out.

"Call him. Get me the man's name."

"I can't. No service up there."

"Use the radio."

"It probably won't work. He's three hundred miles out."

"Try," ordered Styles.

"I don't think I can walk."

"If your ass isn't on that radio in ten seconds I'm going to shatter your knee. Then you won't ever walk right again."

With a legitimate painful effort, the man struggled to move his feet. He was cradling his right arm, which was bent at a very unnatural angle. Styles grabbed the suspenders of his coveralls and helped him walk and then perched him on a stool in front of the radio.

"I'm familiar with aviation lingo, so don't say something stupid."

"6140 Charlie, this is base. Come back," the man said into the microphone. "Sammy, come back; it's an emergency." No response. "Sammy, come back. Emergency."

A voice emitted weakly from the speaker. "Yeah, I barely hear you, what's the problem?"

"There's a guy here needs the name of that raghead guy we flew in a few days ago and dropped off at Northern's floatplane. What's his name?"

"What business is it of his?" was the answer.

"Just give me the fucking name, or he's gonna slit my throat. Quit fucking around and give me the name."

"Who is this guy?"

Styles took the mike. "Give me the name, or when you get back, your friend's head will be sitting on the counter, minus his body. You've got five seconds."

"I don't have a name, just a credit card number. You can find it. It's filed under Northern Hunting. It'd be the last one run. Who the fuck are you?"

"Someone you don't want to cross. If this doesn't check out, you're both dead."

Starr came back from the office with the manila folder marked "Northern Hunting." "Got a credit card slip dated six days ago, prepaid. Name is a corporation from Portland, Oregon. No security cameras. What about him?"

Styles looked at the man hard. "You or your partner ever breathe a word we were here, there's no place I won't find you. Now I need to put you to sleep for a while." He instantly put the man in a rear choke hold, and in ten seconds, he was out.

"I'm surprised you didn't kill him," said Starr.

"So am I."

"Where to now?" Starr asked.

"Back to the plane, I think. Looks like we're heading back to Portland. Call J. C., and tell him we're on our way. Get hold of Phillips; have her meet us there."

"On it." Thirty seconds later, Starr informed Styles, "Phillips is already on her way. Girl is a workhorse."

"Yeah, she is. We'll have her check out this credit card and go from there."

Phillips was there when Starr and Styles arrived. Starr gave her and J. C. a quick rundown on what had happened at Inland Helicopter. Phillips grabbed the credit card slip, boarded the plane, and was back at her computer station, fingers flashing over her keyboard.

They were forty-five minutes out of Bethel when Phillips called Starr and Styles back to her workstation.

Styles asked her, "You get any sleep?"

"Enough for now. Here's what I came up with. This credit card tracks through six different corporations but ends at some company named Petroleum Assets. They sell refinery equipment and employ interesting personnel. One is Nazir al-Hadid. He appears to be the brother, or maybe nephew, of one Ami al-Hadid, who I believe had the misfortune of meeting Styles. His is the only name of familiarity. One other interesting prospect is Rijah Ellhad. He has flown back and forth six times in two years. He's an ex-captain in Saddam's Republican Guard." She paused and looked up. "Funny. Seems to be a lot of connections within certain groups." She continued, "They both appear to frequent Portland, Oregon, but I haven't established who or exactly why. Something else I found were other purchases charged to the same card. For someone who I would think would want to stay hidden, somebody is either very careless or very stupid."

"What was the card used for?" Styles asked.

"Rental car taken out ten days ago on a monthly lease. Five prepaid cell phones. Camping gear. And this is interesting, a rubber diving suit with full-face hood, but no mask, fins, or anything else."

"Maybe he already has that," offered Starr.

"Maybe. I just think it's odd."

"Where did he purchase this stuff?" Starr wanted to know.

"A big camping and recreation store in Portland. He bought it yesterday. The wet suit, anyway. The camping stuff was purchased six days ago."

Styles spoke up. "That would explain the trip to Alaska. He knew what he needed. The wet suit has me wondering."

"Sounds like he's planning a swim," stated Phillips.

"Or maybe for protection from something other than water," replied Styles.

"You think that this guy might be behind all this?" Starr asked, surprised.

"Not behind it, but the deliveryman. If someone is going to use this new whatever-the-hell-it-is as a terrorist act, somebody has to do something to get it started. Doesn't that make sense? So maybe a wet suit is adequate protection for whatever reason, maybe up until a certain point. I'd guess before it is somehow activated. From what we saw from Phillips's video and other info, we've learned that water somehow does that."

"Wow, Styles, that is quite a deduction. You must be working puzzles or something," quipped Phillips.

"Just common sense."

"I'd say we start with that camping store," inserted Starr, "while Phillips continues her computer thing."

Phillips, slightly rolling her eyes, offered, "It is called research, Starr. You know, the gathering of information?"

"I know. I just like to get you going once in a while."

"You don't have to try very hard to accomplish that," Phillips retorted.

Styles allowed himself a small chuckle.

Christman came over the speakers. "Guys, we're about fifteen minutes out of Portland."

Phillips clicked on her computer screen, and a printer started whirling. "I'm printing this to keep it off the Internet. Here's the name and directions to that camping outlet," she said, handing it to Starr.

"Thanks. The two of us going?"

"Yeah. We'll have J. C. secure the plane, and Phillips can get us some rooms and vehicles. I like the idea of mixing it up a bit; that was solid thinking. Get us two rooms in two different hotels this time and maybe something besides all SUVs, but nothing too flashy. Do get one, though," added Styles.

"On it," said Phillips.

Starr went forward to fill Christman in on what was coming up.

Styles sat down opposite Phillips. "Darlene, when you were with the CIA, did you have much interaction with actual chemical warfare tactics?"

Phillips had noticed that when it was just the two of them talking, he referred to her by her first name more than usual. "Not tactics as I think you mean. I did general research, mostly on actual agents rather than deployment."

"Okay. How would you use this?"

"Put it in a large body of water, maybe a large lake. See how it works on a larger area. So far, they've only used it on a large pond, at least that we know of. I would contaminate a holiday gathering since Labor Day is just around the corner. If this thing kills everything, if there were people swimming and boating, they would die also. At least if they were in the water."

"I agree. All right, what lake would you choose?"

She sat and thought for a moment. "Lake Havasu in Arizona, Lake Mead in Nevada, Lake Winnipesaukee in New Hampshire, or maybe Lake Okeechobee in Florida, which would be an ecological disaster but not harm that many people. Terrorists want to target people more than anything, at least far as I know. I think there's a big lake in Kentucky, but I don't remember the name of it."

Styles said deliberately, "If these guys are out of Portland, then I'd say either Lake Mead or Havasu, mainly because of the tourists, and it also makes sense because those two would be the easiest to get to."

Phillips nodded.

"Check out what's going on at those two. See if something might be more attractive than the other."

"You got it."

Ten minutes before Starr and Styles were set to leave, Styles said, "Hold it. Change of plans. Phillips, you got anything that would resemble a business suit?"

"Yeah, why?"

"I'm thinking you go into this camping store. Use your official DPO identification and get access to their computers and security video. See if there's any way to come up with a photo of our guy. I'll go with you but just hang off to the side. Invoke national security if anybody gives you any shit."

"I like that," agreed Starr, who had returned. "She can jump on their equipment, maybe save some time."

"Won't that advertise our presence?" asked Phillips.

"It may. Right now, I'm more concerned about stopping this threat than what the CIA or anybody else knows. We have to deal with this shit one step at a time, and right now, the threat is the priority," declared Styles.

Phillips nodded. "You're right."

"You might even persuade whoever not to tout our presence," suggested Styles. "Let's see how it goes."

16.

T-Minus 40 Hours

President Williams was walking across the lawn toward the waiting helicopter. He was not happy having to go to Baltimore, but he realized that it was one of those courtesy calls that he was required to make from time to time. He was accompanied by Tommy DeLancy, his personal assistant.

"Did my speech get revised?" the president asked DeLancy.

"Yes, sir. The changes exactly as you requested, all set for the teleprompter."

"I'd just as soon have a root canal as do this," complained the president.

"Yes, sir."

"You can also stop saying 'Yes, sir' all the time."

"Yes, sir. Uh, sorry."

The president just shook his head slightly as he mounted the collapsible stairs to board the chopper, saluting his military guards along the way.

"We'll be there shortly, sir," informed the copilot.

The president merely nodded and took his seat.

Two figures were walking down the docks toward a fishing trawler. One was carrying two duffel bags while the other was wheeling three medium-size crates on a dolly. No words were spoken. The vessel was tied to a floating dock that rose and fell with the tide. The ramp down from the main dock was long enough that at low tide the incline was not particularly steep, unlike some areas in the northeast where you had to practically hang on to the handrails to transverse the walkways. Upon arriving, they loaded their gear and quickly stowed the crates out of sight. They set about appearing as though they were performing routine maintenance on the craft. The boat was tied up near Fell's Point, across from the Baltimore Museum of Industry, where the celebration honoring the governor was to take place.

Nazir al-Hadid had been here several times, but it was Sirhan al-Razar's first time aboard. Both set about their tasks. One carefully opened the three crates and readied their contents. The other laid out two sets of dive gear just inside the wheelhouse. More was waiting for them tied to underwater scooters, small torpedo-shaped vehicles with a propeller at the rear that turned via an electric motor. A set of handlebars that could have been taken from a motorcycle were mounted rearward. To control the craft's direction, you either pulled up or pushed down to change depth or pulled left or right to change direction. Both had been modified with extra batteries to provide enough electricity for the approximate twenty-mile underwater trip that faced them. Able to achieve a speed of four miles per hour, not counting the current, which could raise or lower their ground speed, a five-hour journey faced them. They had spare scuba tanks, which would provide seven hours of air. Waterproof GPS units had been mounted to the handlebars to ensure not getting lost on the way to rendezvous with the yacht that would be awaiting their arrival.

Sirhan al-Razar set up a tarp as though he were initiating repairs. In fact, it would be used to hide their departure over the side of the boat.

Finally, all was set, and the waiting started.

With everyone having checked into their rooms at two different hotels, a Holiday Inn Express and a Ramada Inn, Styles and Phillips were on their way to Outdoor Hunting and Recreation Outlet.

"Drop me off just before the parking lot; don't want any security cameras to catch me traveling with you," Styles directed Phillips. "Same when we leave."

"Got it."

Little conversation had taken place. Both knew what they were to do. Half a block away, they saw the large retail outlet. Phillips turned into a bakery parking lot, and Styles got out. Before he shut the door, he said, "Sound check."

"Loud and clear," remarked Phillips, dressed smartly in a black business suit.

"Same," confirmed Styles.

Phillips pulled back out onto the roadway and drove onward to the retail outlet.

Styles started walking and was just entering the parking lot as Phillips was entering the store. Immediately, too much noise was coming in over Styles's earpiece.

"Turn your volume down when you get the chance. Too much background noise," he said.

Within fifteen seconds, the unwanted distraction disappeared, and he listened as Phillips coughed to be sure he could hear her.

"That's good.

Phillips approached the customer service desk and asked to see the store manager.

"I'm the assistant manager. How may I help you?" a younger man, perhaps late twenties, answered.

Phillips, all business, asked, "Is your store manager available?"

"Yes, he is, but he's busy with a supplier at the moment."

Phillips flashed her official badge and identification. "Phillips, Department of the Presidential Office. Get your manger, *now*!"

The man looked at her badge and ID carefully and then said,

"Yes, ma'am." Two minutes later, he returned with a short, chubby man in his midforties with a ruddy complexion.

"I'm Ted Longley. I've never heard of the Department of the Presidential Office."

"I'm Darlene Phillips, and I've never heard of Outdoor Hunting and Recreation Outlet, so I guess that makes us even." She handed him a card with the presidential seal embossed on the front. "There's a number on the front, a direct line to the Department of Justice, even though we're not part of them. They will confirm my identity if you have any questions. This is a matter of national security, and I don't have a lot of time and even less patience. Either make the call or shut up and listen."

Longley studied the card and the badge and then returned them. "How can I help you?"

Phillips held up a manila envelope. "You had a customer in here six days ago who bought some merchandise. I have a copy of his credit card receipt. I assume you have security cameras installed?"

"Of course," Longley replied indignantly.

"Take me to your office where your computer and camera equipment are placed. I need to do a search to try to match a face with this card."

"I'm sorry, Ms. Phillips, but I'm afraid that would be against our store policy to allow that."

Phillips's eyes blazed. "In two minutes, I'm either going to be in that office or you're going to be in the back of a federal agent's car, handcuffed on suspicion of aiding terrorism. You could be in GTMO before sundown. Which do you prefer?"

Longley swallowed hard. "Follow me."

The flight from the White House to the Baltimore Museum of Industry was to take just under half an hour. President Williams was going over his speech with Tommy DeLancy.

"I think you've got it down, sir," commented DeLancy.

"Not that much to get down. I want to be in and out of there in under an hour. I don't care what is going on, at the fifty-minute mark, you are to interrupt and tell me I'm needed back at the White House. Got it?"

"Yes, sir."

They were both looking out the windows of the president's helicopter. Off to the right were two identical aircraft, disguising which one the president was aboard. With less humidity than normal, it was a crystal-clear day, and looking out over the horizon, it was as though you could see forever. Four F-16 fighter jets were hovering three thousand feet above the president's craft. The three helicopters droned onward.

The president had returned to studying his speech, leaving DeLancy staring out the window. Suddenly, the helicopter flying the outside of the formation burst into a fireball. Stunned, DeLancy tried to yell to the president. Just as the words began to leave his throat, for a nanosecond, he felt extreme heat. He never had time to hear anything.

President Williams had just begun to look up from the noise of the first explosion, and then everything went black.

17.

Vice President Herbert Lamar jolted from the sound of his chief of staff's panicked voice. "What?" Lamar asked. "What is it, Irving?"

Irving Vickers handed the vice president a cup of coffee with cream. "Take a couple of sips, sir, and wake up."

Vice President Lamar took the coffee, took a sip, and then said, "What the hell is it?"

Vickers sat down opposite the vice president. "Sir, I just got word that President Williams has been assassinated. His helicopter was blown up over Baltimore. All three helicopters were taken out."

"*What?*"

"President Williams has been killed. It happened about four minutes ago. You are now the acting president until you can be sworn in, which will be as soon as we land. We're forty-five minutes out." Right then, eight F-16s converged around the vice president's aircraft.

"It looks like they're worried about us."

"*How?*"

"Sir, I don't know the details yet. Sounds like some kind of rocket fired from the ground. All I know is that all three of the helicopters were hit. No chance of survivors. Everybody is scrambling. We've gone to DEFCON 3. Everybody will be at the White House by the time we arrive. You will be briefed then. After that, it will be your call, Mr. President."

"My God. Sweet Lord, what the hell is going on?" He downed the coffee even though it burned his tongue and throat. "Get me more coffee. I need to think."

"Yes, sir."

Minutes later, Irving Vickers returned to Vice President Herbert Lamar.

"Sir, we've been strongly advised to divert to an alternative destination to be safe."

"Where?"

"It's still being decided, sir, but probably Norfolk. We should know in the next fifteen minutes. We'll also pick up a military helicopter gunship escort when we get low and slow. Every available missile defense system has been deployed."

"Keep me apprised, Irving."

"Yes, sir."

❈   ❈   ❈

Styles's cell phone rang. It was Starr. Styles heard tersely, "Have you heard?"

"Heard what?"

"The president's dead, killed about twenty-five minutes ago. His helicopter and the two decoys were all taken out by shoulder-fired rockets. Looks like they came from a boat that was docked by the museum where the governor's celebration was taking place. I don't know many details, but I deciphered that. Vice President Lamar is to be sworn in as soon as he lands, since he's on his way back from Japan. I'm not sure where he's landing; that's being withheld for security."

Marvin Styles was not a man who found himself absolutely shocked by news. Yet there he was. He was eerily silent. Then, "What's your thought?"

"He would want us to continue what we're doing," Starr answered, his voice heavy.

"I agree. We'll finish here and meet back in your room at the Holiday Inn. Does J. C. know?"

"I don't know. It's starting to hit the media. If he'd heard, he'd have called."

"Sounds right. You call him. We'll be back ASAP." No good-byes were warranted. He turned to look at some jackets and said to Phillips, "Did you catch that?"

"Yes," she said, her voice choking.

"Finish what you need to," Styles directed.

Phillips had been busy downloading pertinent information onto a flash drive. She had been able to match not only a photograph, but a driver's license to the credit card receipt. As soon as that downloaded, she was out of the office like a shot. She practically ran over the chunky little store manager without so much as a look in his direction, her black eyes radiating pure wrath.

She climbed into the rental car, a silver Ford Crown Victoria, and burned half the rear tires off leaving the parking space. She glanced at oncoming traffic as she approached the area's exit and gunned it. She slid up to Styles, who was inside the car in a flash, which was good, as she was moving before the door was halfway closed. They didn't speak.

Phillips's body was exuding absolute rage. "I can't believe it," she finally said.

"I can. It's been the ultimate goal of the jihad for over ten years."

"Is there any way it might have been prevented?" she asked, fighting back tears.

"No. When you've dealt with these religious zealots like I have, nothing surprises you. They would literally fight to the last man to achieve their warped objectives. It's like a cancer. The only thing to do is cut it out, eradicate it—and *that*, Darlene, is exactly what we are going to do."

"How?"

"By doing what we do best, one step at a time, and not losing focus. I don't mean to sound cold here. Just try to understand this is how I've lived for twenty years."

Phillips only nodded.

Twenty-five minutes later, all four convened in Starr's room at the Holiday Inn. They sat at the dining table in the suite, silent.

Finally, Starr spoke. "J. C., you know the basics, right?"

"Yeah."

"Marv and I already talked about this, but I want your and Phillips's feedback. I firmly believe that the president would want us to continue on finding and stopping this new toxic threat. I have no doubt about that."

They both nodded in agreement.

"J. C., how long would it take for us to get back to the Ranch and then back here? There's a specific reason why I ask."

"Around seven hours, maybe a bit more, round trip for the plane. Then the chopper flight back to and from the Ranch, call that ninety minutes. Total flight time would be about eight and a half hours. Plus the time we spend at the Ranch. Why?"

"There's something there. That's all I want to say right now."

Styles glanced at Starr with a quizzical look. He said nothing.

Starr looked at Phillips. "You can do your research from the air, right?"

Phillips was quite shaken as she answered, "Yes, you know that, but would it be prudent for maybe one or two to stay here, continue with the investigation?"

"Normally, I'd say yes, but not this time. I want to get there and back as fast as possible. I believe it is that important."

Styles stood. "Normally, I'd grill you hard about this because it's not making logical sense. I also know you've got your reason, and that's good enough for me. Let's get the hell back."

Christman said, "Everybody meet at the plane."

Without even a glance, everybody went about their business.

18.

T-Minus 37 Hours

Nazir al-Hadid guided his underwater scooter straight and true on a predetermined course at a depth of thirty feet. He glanced slightly rearward and saw his cohort Sirhan al-Razar following approximately eight feet behind him. He smiled as he thought back three hours earlier to when they had shot down the two decoy helicopters and the real Marine One from the old fishing trawler. Less than a minute later, he and al-Razar had slid into the water, untied their scooters affixed with spare scuba tanks from the dock pilings, and were traveling to rendezvous with a large ocean-traversing yacht. A waterproof GPS enabled al-Hadid to follow the track. They were about halfway through their journey. The water was chilly, but the wet suit was keeping him warm.

Al-Hadid was pleased that the sunny day provided good visibility. He looked around at al-Razar, as he often did, just to check. He had just turned back when he heard, and saw, a good-size boat pass overhead. He thought nothing about it. He never saw the fishing line that followed behind, and below, the boat. Suddenly, he saw al Razar being dragged through the water, passing him by less than five feet away. He saw the look of terror on al-Razar's face as his face mask had been ripped off. He just got a glimpse of a bright flash, and he could have sworn he saw a small fish just below his shoulder blade. Then it dawned on him. Sirhan al-Razar had been caught by a large fishing hook, and was helplessly being pulled away. Within seconds, al-Hadid had lost sight of him. He looked back and saw the empty underwater scooter slowing and starting to turn in a tight circle.

"Fuck!" he screamed underwater. There was nothing he could do, so he continued his journey, shaking his head in complete disbelief.

Bob yelled out, "Guys, I think I've got something already, and it feels big!" A fishing addict all his life, he was definitely the happiest aboard the forty-seven-foot sport-fishing boat that three couples had chartered and whose five-day fishing adventure was just beginning. It was a trip three years in the planning, and the party had already started. A twenty-thousand-watt stereo system rocking with the band Y's Factor was managing to drown out the twin diesel engines powering the boat. With drinks in hand, everyone was enjoying themselves.

The Baltimore Police Department Marine Unit was responding to a "body recovered" call when the two officers noticed something in the water ahead of them. The officer piloting the boat slowed, circled around, and came up beside it as it was bobbing up and down in the waves, yet obviously moving under its own power.

"What the hell is that?" said Sergeant Tom Rollins.

Officer James Wood responded, "Looks like one of those underwater scooters. Come up alongside, and I'll try to get a line on it." After several attempts, he managed to secure a rope around the guard of the propeller. He started to bring it aboard. He found he couldn't overcome the propulsion of the little craft. "Give me a hand. This thing's strong."

Sergeant Rollins placed the boat's shifter controls in neutral and joined his partner. "Shit, you weren't kidding," Rollins said as they both strained to reel in the scooter.

Finally, they were able to haul the rear out of the water, and the propeller immediately picked up speed without the liquid resistance.

"What in the hell is that doing out here?" wondered Rollins.

"Maybe some diver lost it. I don't see any diving flags anywhere. We'd better check with the glasses," suggested Wood, turning off the electric motor.

For the next ten minutes, both police officers scanned the horizon for any sign of a scuba diver. No boats anchored, no dive flags, nothing. They gave up.

Rollins and Wood might have been the only two law enforcement personnel in the Baltimore area not involved with the explosion of the helicopters a couple of hours before. Both were incensed about having to respond to their current call.

"Well, let's go check on this damned body," said Rollins.

Twenty minutes later, they were tied up to a chartered sport-fishing boat.

Sergeant Rollins hopped aboard and asked a man in white pants and shirt, "You the captain?"

"Yes, sir. The body is at the rear fishing platform. We covered it with a blanket. We haven't touched it."

"Good. Thank you."

Both officers proceeded to the platform and saw a shape under a bright blue blanket. Sergeant Rollins removed it, and there lay a scuba diver with a large hook clean through the lower part of his shoulder.

"How'd he die?" asked Officer Wood.

"It's hard to say. Probably drowned, but could have been trauma. I think we solved the underwater scooter mystery, though," answered Sergeant Rollins.

Miraculously, the swim mask was still in place. "Do we dare take it off?' asked Wood.

"Yeah, go get us gloves and evidence bags. We'll just be careful. I want to get a look at his face."

Wood was back in ninety seconds with the items.

Gently, Sergeant Rollins removed the mask. Staring at them through sightless eyes was a man of obvious Middle Eastern descent. Rollins looked at the man for a few moments and then bolted for his own boat. He was instantly on his radio. "Harbor Patrol, this is Rollins, on that body recovery call. Get everybody out here now."

19.

Three hours after the assassination, now president Herbert Lamar was sitting alone in the Oval Office. *My God, what is happening? Lord knows I've always wanted to be president, but not like this. Dear God, please give me the strength and confidence and your help in guiding me through the coming days.*

He summoned his chief of staff, Irving Vickers.

"Sir?"

"Get hold of Laura Green. Have her assemble *everybody*. I want the entire cabinet and all the directors of the security and law enforcement agencies to meet me at the White House in ninety minutes. No excuses—everybody. We'll probably have to use the White House briefing room. I don't want any media anywhere." *What the hell do I say?*

Twenty seconds later, Irving Vickers was on the line to Laura Green, President Williams's chief of staff. "Laura, I don't know what to say." The two had known each other on the DC conveyer belt for almost ten years. It was Irving who had suggested Laura Green replace Andrew Ladd after he'd been exposed as a traitor.

"There's really nothing to say for the moment, Irving. I've been expecting your call."

"The president wants everybody available for a meeting in ninety minutes, probably in the briefing room." He proceeded to list who was required to be there. "He and I haven't talked about it yet, but my feeling is no major changes will be made immediately. I wanted to ask you to stay on as my co-chief. I would suggest that you keep most of your staff, at least those you deem indispensable. We will have to work very closely in the coming weeks. Laura, this is going to take an exceptional effort to get through all of this, and I believe we are the key."

"Irving, my staff and I will do everything humanly possible to help in every way we can. I agree with your assessment."

"Laura, I don't even want to have to bother with swapping offices and all that shit. The president will obviously move into his new position, but for the moment, I strongly believe we need to keep the disruption to a minimum, if that's even possible."

"Just keep me posted as to what you need."

"Will do, and thanks."

"You are welcome, Irving."

Vickers returned to the president. "Sir, I've spoken with Laura Green, and everything will be set. I told her that it was my thought that we wanted to keep interruption to a minimum. I took the liberty of asking her to stay on as my co-chief for the time being. We are all going to need help during this time."

"Of course, Irving. I respect Laura tremendously. I thought she was an excellent choice after that mess involving Ladd. Make sure she knows she has full authority to keep whatever staff she might want."

"I've taken care of that, sir."

President Lamar smiled. "That's what I like about you, Irving. You anticipate well. Prepare yourself for some long hours ahead; this is not going to be easy."

"I realize that, sir. I have a comfortable sofa in my office."

"Good. You'll be using it."

Six hours after the assassination of President Williams, Nazir al-Hadid surfaced ten feet away from a splendid 110-foot ocean-traversing yacht at anchor.

It was just after dark, and al-Hadid's GPS unit had worked perfectly. The yacht was not overly lit up, not in the manner one would usually expect.

Two men were awaiting a different type of craft, one that would arrive silently. They had been on station for perhaps forty-five minutes when something surfaced ten feet away. It made its way to the platform. The two men reached down and hauled the underwater scooter aboard and then the man piloting it.

Nazir al-Hadid removed his swim mask and threw it into the ocean. "I never want to wear one of those again," he snarled. His swim fins followed.

Asobe Sydar hugged him. "You have done it, Nazir. You have done it." Then he noticed Nazir was alone. "Where is Sirhan?"

The second man handed Nazir a bottled water, which he eagerly accepted. He held up a hand while he gulped the entire contents.

"You would not believe it. From what I saw, it appeared like he was grabbed by a large fishhook. He was just yanked from his scooter, and then he was out of sight. He was right there, and then he was gone. A medium-size boat had just passed overhead. I saw a flash under his shoulder, along with a fish against him, and then he vanished. It can be the only explanation."

The second man, known only as Zahaar, questioned, "Was he dead?"

Nazir al-Hadid was in a foul mood after the nearly six-hour underwater trek. "How the fuck do I know, you idiot? It all happened in two seconds. You think I can swim faster than a boat?"

"No, I do not. I am only concerned if he were to be caught alive."

Al-Hadid realized his concern was appropriate. "Zahaar, I do not know. It seems unlikely if someone was hooked like a fish at such speed, I think he would probably drown, but I do not know this for a fact."

Zahaar added, "We can only hope. If the Americans were to capture him, they have ways that would certainly make him talk. We will have to closely monitor their news media for any information. Should we not call Ryyaki Ali?"

"No. We will not cause alarm without reason. If we find out definitive information, only then will we inform him. Do we have to stay in these waters?"

"It will not be a problem. We cleared customs without any problems. The Americans have no reason to check us again."

Nazir al-Hadid was not convinced. "Zahaar, I have just killed the American president. You do not think they will be checking every boat in the area?"

"Let them check. They will find nothing. Now strip off your wet suit. We will sink everything right here. Then we will cruise back into the harbor and find a nice anchorage. The Americans would expect a boat to be leaving, not coming closer."

"I hope you are right," he said as he stripped out of his wet suit. Everything was gathered into a large nylon net, including the underwater scooter. It was weighted down with over a hundred pounds of lead and then pushed overboard. It immediately sank out of sight.

"Nazir, go take a hot shower, and then join me for a fine meal. You have earned it. Asobe, inform the chef we will be eating in one hour."

Left alone, Zahaar looked at the spot where the net had sunk. Less than an hour before, another preceded it containing the body and paper documents, including a passport, of a crew member that al-Hadid now replaced. All the new paperwork in the same name but featuring Nazir al-Hadid's photograph was in place. He was confident that the yacht would easily clear any scrutiny should such need arise.

❈   ❈   ❈

Captain Richard Starr was sitting up front in the cockpit of their supplied jet, always paying attention to better learn the operation of the aircraft.

Phillips was busy working three computers at once, and Styles spent the time staring out the window when he wasn't doing push-ups.

After takeoff, Christman had an unusual conversation with flight control. When finished, he explained to Starr.

"We have the option to change transponder numbers, which identifies us as a federal agency plane on an emergency mission involving national security. It lets us run faster without the FAA getting their panties in a wad. Whenever they see a plane going supersonic and it's not military, it won't be long before military fighters show up."

"How fast are you planning on taking us?"

"Nine hundred miles per hour, perhaps a bit faster. We have a tailwind, so our ground speed will be around a thousand. It'll cut our travel time by at least a third."

"Good thinking."

Christman got on the microphone to inform Styles and Phillips. "Hey, guys, we're going through the sound barrier in a minute, so prepare." Christman climbed to forty-five thousand feet and leveled off. "Here goes." He pushed the throttles forward. Six hundred, six twenty-five, six hundred fifty miles per hour, then ... *Boom* ... eight, eight fifty, nine hundred, nine hundred fifty miles per hour. The plane was performing flawlessly; the last time they had gone this fast was when they had to leave the Middle East being chased by fighter jets. Christman looked over at Starr and grinned. "She's smooth as silk. Those engineers did a hell of a job with these performance modifications. Last time, I didn't have time to enjoy it."

"Last time, we were fifty feet off the ground."

"Yeah, well there *was* that."

Starr looked below. He could clearly see the silver outline of a commercial jet perhaps ten thousand feet below, which they were overtaking quickly. "Man, J. C., we're really moving, that commercial liner below looks slow."

"If it wasn't for their radar, they'd never know we were here. They'll think we're military."

"They won't see us?"

"Probably not, but if they do, we'll just be a spot in the sky."

The DPO jet was just starting its descent into Knoxville when Phillips called Styles and Starr back to her workstation.

"I've got some updated info on the attack. Three shoulder-fired missiles were apparently fired from a fishing trawler tied up to a pier a couple of miles from the Baltimore Museum of Industry, where the president was headed for the celebration for Maryland's governor. It's believed two suspects got off the boat and escaped using scuba gear and underwater scooters. Get this: it looks like one of them was accidentally hooked by a fisherman who had a line out from a charter boat. A guy reeled in the body, called the cops, and the agencies at the scene put it together. It looks like they're on top of things for once."

Starr looked at her and said, "Hooked? Like on a fishhook?"

"Yeah. Got him in the shoulder," she replied, shaking her head. "They're working like mad to ID him, but so far, no luck."

"Who'd you have to hack to get this?" Starr asked.

"Surprisingly enough, no one; it came from DPO. Merritt said that for now, everything is staying status quo. Guess we'll see how long that lasts."

Styles spoke up. "How do we handle this new arrangement with him?"

"We don't. I'll take care of it. I have to consider whether to resign from DPO or not. It could serve us better if I remain. He thinks I work from home, anyway."

Styles merely nodded.

She continued, "There are three decent motels within ten miles of Ryyaki Ali's estate. How do you want to work this?"

Starr looked at Styles and then answered, "Two rooms in two of them. Get us four vehicles, SUVs."

"See if you can get me a Jeep. Dark green if possible," Styles interjected.

"On it soon as I've gone over this," Phillips responded.

"Here's what I've come up with. And right upfront I'm going to tell you a lot of this is no more than an educated guess. This Rijah Ellhad seems to be the key. Like I said before, Iraqi national, former Republican Guard, now not much more than a mercenary." She passed them three photographs each. "Here are some pretty good head shots; the third is from the camping store, so that's only a week and a half old."

Styles remarked, "He's got what we used to call 'dead' eyes, eyes of a stone-cold killer."

"Just what I thought," agreed Phillips. "The middle photograph is a falsified passport photo, name of Jason Daniels. Can't believe that didn't get flagged. The first is where we get lucky. There is a restaurant called Marroni's; apparently, he likes Italian food. This restaurant has been robbed five times in two years, so they put a high-end security system in. It's linked into Portland PD's database, which is how I got it. Every person who enters is on video; he's shown up there six times in the last two weeks. I can't figure out if he's careless or what. No one who does this shit should be keeping any kind of a regular routine."

Styles spoke up. "The Republican Guard was an arrogant bunch. They actually believed they were the best military outfit in the world. I'd bet the arrogance hasn't left."

Starr nodded.

"This restaurant is only about twelve miles from that estate I was telling you about. My money says that ties him in hard," stated Phillips with conviction.

"Not taking that bet," replied Starr. "So now what?"

"Two things," answered Styles. "First, we all start eating Italian food, two at a time. Second, we put our own camera at the entrance so we can observe when we're not there. I'm going to recon that estate. When he shows up, we follow and hopefully recover that toxin. Then I take them out."

Phillips was still amazed at just how easily Styles could say that. "How many do you think there might be?"

"It doesn't matter. Space in the county morgue isn't my problem."

Styles, Phillips, and Christman were seated around the large dining room table located in what was referred to as the great room in the Ranch. They had made excellent time on their rushed flight from Oregon. Neither Styles nor Phillips had spoken much during the trip, Phillips busy on her computers, Styles lost in thought.

Starr came walking in from his bedroom with a large sealed briefcase. After setting it on the table, he addressed the others. "The president gave me this right after Indianapolis. He was clear it was only to be opened if something happened that prevented him from carrying out his duties as president. I was to open it with you guys."

He cut the seal with his folding pocketknife and, with a sigh, opened it. On top lay a manila envelope addressed to all four. He unclasped the envelope and removed a couple of sheets of paper.

"This is addressed to all of us." He read the contents aloud.

Richard,

It is unfortunate that you are reading this because it means that I have been disabled. I have something to ask you and your group that is extremely hard, but something I believe is critical to the safety of our country. I urge you to strongly consider my request. In my mind, there is no doubt of the importance of the work you four perform in service to our country. It must continue. One cannot compete if one's opponent plays by a separate set of rules, even worse when no rules at all are observed. That is what we face with the Taliban, al-Qaeda, Hamas, ISIS, and the rest of the zealots that are trying to destroy our way of life.

With the demise of Andrew Ladd, no one but me knows of your existence. It has to stay that way. Vice President Lamar will not sanction your actions. He may keep the DPO in place, but your group will be dissolved. You cannot allow that to happen. The only way I see that you can maintain your status is to go underground. Christman and Phillips will have to sever their ties with the military and DPO. This should be easy for Christman, as he may retire at any time. Not so easy with Phillips; however, since you are a civilian, this should not be overly difficult. I believe that if you stay with DPO, your real position may be compromised, but I leave that decision to you.

You will also be required to determine your targets. You know what I expected; continue and, if necessary, expand. Remember, it is the security of our country that is the basis for your existence. You as a group will decide. You four are the only ones I would trust with this immeasurable responsibility. In this briefcase, you will find everything you will ever need to perform your duties. There are also signed presidential pardons for all of you. Bear in mind they would be worthless outside our boundaries. I know what I am asking of you. If I had any doubt that you were not up to the task, I would not ask. You have my utmost faith to take this fight to our enemies, to use whatever means you decide is necessary. I must remind you that no innocents are to be involved. That is my only condition. Trust no one in your quest. Do what must be done. Please, protect our great country. May God look over you.

Robert Williams, President of the United States

Starr looked up to see no one looking at him. The three were completely focused on what he had just read. He took a quick look at what else the briefcase contained. After a minute, he placed the contents back inside and then looked up to see the others now staring at him.

"What else is in there?" asked Christman.

"The pardons and banking information. The Man was serious about giving us what we need. Phillips will have to confirm this, but I'd say we have pretty much unlimited funds at our disposal." Starr, who had been standing, sat down. "Okay, feedback time."

No one said anything.

"Come on, somebody's gotta say something," Starr pleaded.

"We get our asses back to Oregon and start doing the president's business," Styles snapped.

20.

President Lamar was striding toward the briefing room and caught up with Coverley Merritt, who headed up the Department of the Presidential Office initiated by former President Williams.

"Merritt, bring me up to speed on exactly what your department does. As you know, I haven't spent a lot of time around here since President Williams took office."

"We receive real-time information from all the agencies on terrorism. That way we can keep the president … uh, sorry, sir— you informed at all times of everything that might be going on."

The president dismissed the breech with a wave of his hand. "Is that *all* you do?"

"Yes, sir. We are an information-gathering agency only. We don't advise. We only inform."

"All right, for the time being, carry on. Be in the briefing room immediately."

The directors of major agencies, cabinet secretaries, and advisers were waiting in the briefing room as summoned.

The murmuring stopped as President Lamar entered the White House briefing room. Everyone stood and turned their attention to him. He walked to the podium and looked out over the gathering of the most powerful men in the country.

"Everyone, please take a seat." He then took some notes from Irving Vickers. He perused them and then intently studied the group. "I know we are all extremely horrified at what has happened, but wasting time talking about it is not going to get anything accomplished. You people know your jobs. I don't know all of you, but I will. For the time being, I do not plan on making any changes. We have too much work before us to complicate anything. I will rely on you to do your very best in not only bringing those responsible for this horrendous act of war on our country to justice, but also with this new toxin. I am read in on this and will meet with the FBI, CIA, NSA, Homeland, and CDC in one hour in the Situation Room. Heads of military also. People, let's get to work."

❈   ❈   ❈

Rijah Ellhad found himself in a quandary. Unknown to Ryyaki Ali, he had been seeing the woman whom Ali had chosen to accompany him to Lake Mead. She worked in his household as a maid, which was how the two met. While pretenses had to be kept, being in America had loosened her restrictions on what would normally be perceived as immoral behavior. She loved sleeping with Rijah. Not once in his life had he ever remotely questioned an order, but to kill the woman that he had very strong feelings for was going to be difficult. He knew that when the moment came, he would not be able to look her in the eyes; therefore, he was going to have to perform the act without her knowing what was coming. He had thought of many ways and finally had settled on simply putting a .22-caliber pistol behind her ear and pulling the trigger. A manner in which she enjoyed cuddling next to him would make it a physically simple task; emotionally would be a different matter. He had no doubt that when the time came, he would be able to perform the unpleasant deed. He just didn't like it.

Ellhad stayed in a small cabin on the edge of Ryyaki Ali's property. There were eight cabins clustered in a semicircle in a large clearing next to the woods. This small compound was approximately a half mile from Ali's main house. Ellhad's cabin was on one end of the circular row. The woman whom Ellhad kept company with lived in a cabin two down from his. They had been sneaking back and forth for close to a year, when Ellhad was in town. Ali had no objection when Ellhad had asked permission to take her to dinner at an Italian eatery he particularly enjoyed, as long as a chaperone was present. Ali was deeply rooted to his radical Muslim beliefs. Ellhad had no such loyalties. *I will miss you, Sahleea.*

With Phillips constantly on her computers, the return trip to Oregon was quiet. Starr was up in the cockpit, as usual, and Styles was threatening to push out the bottom of the floor of the plane, as he was doing so many push-ups.

Ninety minutes later, with the aircraft secure in a hangar, Starr and Styles had checked into a Comfort Inn, while Phillips and Christman had checked into a nearby Holiday Inn. Three GMC Yukons, two dark blue and one black, had been picked up at the airport, but the Jeep would have to be delivered. It had been promised by within the hour.

All four had decided to meet in Starr's room, as his was on the ground floor and easily accessible from the parking area without arousing any curiosity. Christman and Phillips had ridden over together, with Styles and Starr each driving one of the blue Yukons. Phillips walked in carrying three laptops and a printer and then proceeded to open them on the table in the room. She immediately started staring at the three screens. "I'm bringing up a Google Earth map of Ali's estate. Styles, do you need me to print it out, or can you get what you need from the screen?"

"The screen will do." He walked over to the table while Phillips pushed one of her laptops over to him along with a wireless mouse. He took them from her and sat down to study the image. He immediately clicked the mouse to zoom out. After a few seconds, he looked up at Phillips and said, "This is really good, very detailed and clear."

"Yeah, Google Earth has come a long way. I didn't want to use any of our satellites in case Backersley is keeping an eye on them."

"This works fine."

Starr looked at Christman and said, "Why don't we go to Marroni's, catch an early dinner, and plant those cameras?"

"That sounds good to me. How far is it?"

"Only about two miles down the road from here," Phillips answered. "Ali's estate is about sixteen miles away."

"I've got the whole duffel of electronic gear," Christman stated.

"Good. Bring it in, and we'll decide what we need," directed Starr.

"Be right back."

"I'll bring back some takeout for you two," Starr said to Styles and Phillips.

Both just nodded.

"No pizza," stated Styles. "Make it lasagna or spaghetti, with lots of meatballs and garlic bread."

"Got it."

Styles continued looking at the screen, even though he'd acquired the information he needed. He was evaluating whether he should talk to the group. He had seen a discernible mood change in the three. Anger was present, most visible in Phillips. Christman seemed somewhat detached, almost confused, while in Starr, he could sense genuine sadness. While they had all lost their president, Starr had lost a lifetime friend. Styles himself felt loss. He had grown to respect the president. The man had balls and wasn't afraid to use them. He decided to speak.

"Hey, guys, I need to say something." The three looked over in surprise, but all came over to sit at the table. "We're all boiling right now. We've got a right to. But we've got a job to do, a job that the president expects us to do." He purposely said *expects*, rather than *expected*. "I know that all of us want to go after the bastards that killed him. We will. But we have to finish this first. It's what he would have demanded. This is Saturday; Monday is Labor Day. That will be the timetable for the attack of this agent. I'm sure of that. We have to find these bastards and stop it. Once that's done, Phillips will read us into what everybody else has found out about the assassination, and we'll take it from there. We'll step on a lot of toes, but we won't get caught. We *are* going to be the jihadists' worst nightmare. We will leave the special signature so they'll know when we have visited. It won't be pretty."

The three were looking at him intently.

Phillips asked, "Do you think that the four of us on our own can really make a difference?"

"No doubt, at least not in my mind. *He* put us together because he knew we would jell as a team. We have, and I admit I'm the most surprised. But we work. All of us play an equally important role. In this world, besides my father, I have three trusted friends, and I'm looking at them right now. You three are not just my partners in this, but you have become my family. Trusting someone is the hardest thing in the world for me, but the three of you have earned it, in spades. We *will* continue this fight, and we *will* make a difference, a hell of a difference. That is not a promise, it is an absolute vow."

Everyone was dead silent; then slowly, all three nodded.

Starr said, "Marv, that's the most I've ever heard you speak in my life."

"It was more than in my entire senior year of high school."

Phillips spoke up. "I've got more info. I picked up some chatter about an event that will take place in this country on Labor Day. Styles, that confirms your suspicions on the timing. I'm also now convinced that Backersley suspects that 'we' exist. He's got Myra Banks working overtime on investigating not just me but the DPO. She has researched the Indianapolis affair, and it appears she is nosing around our European affairs, and not to beat a dead horse here, but the forehead marks are not helping. It ties us to these acts, and there is no way I can hide that fact."

Styles swore under his breath. "Does she know who we are?"

"Not yet, but she is trying hard to put it together. Whether or not she can connect us to the DPO is a different story. What she may guess and what she can prove are two different things at this point. She has my face on facial recognition. As soon as we act, in the same place I've been seen, it's only a matter of time. I don't know what to do," she said, obviously frustrated.

"For now, we stick to whatever plan we come up with. We'll

deal with the CIA after this threat is eliminated," stated Styles emphatically.

"How will we do that?" she asked.

"I don't know yet, but we *will* deal with them—that I promise you."

She just nodded, not entirely convinced.

❁   ❁   ❁

Styles had just toweled off from a scalding-hot shower when he heard a knock on his door. Quickly slipping on a pair of black jeans, he opened the door. Starr walked in carrying a bag of takeout food.

"J. C. and I got the cameras planted. Got two covering the parking lot, one on the front door, and one at the cash register."

"Good. If our boy comes in, we should see him and what he's driving. Why don't you three go back there for dinner? I've got something I want to do tonight."

"J. C. and I'll go back, but I think Phillips is glued to her computers. She barely even looked up when I placed her food on the table. Are you going to recon that estate?" Starr said.

"Yeah. If I can, I'll place some cameras—might even try for some mikes. Need to get a layout of their security. See if Phillips can hack into some of the security equipment providers around here and come up with anything. Start with the expensive ones. I've got a feeling this guy will have spared no expense. Don't worry if I'm gone most of the night. There's a lot I want to see before I decide how, and when, to attack. I'll have my ear set in, so you can talk to me if necessary, but keep it to a minimum. If I can't talk, I'll just squelch."

"Gotcha. If this guy comes in, I'd think it'd be a good idea to follow him."

"Agreed. Make sure everybody drives. On the chance that he does show up, be sure you three are out of there before he is, and then set up a standard double. With the comms, it shouldn't be too hard."

"You see anything on the aerial view you find interesting?"

"Yes, a group of cabins at one end of the property. I'm sure that's for the staff and guards. The house itself is on the opposite end with a lot of woods between; a poor setup from a security standpoint."

"Dogs?"

"Didn't see any signs, but I'm taking a tranq gun just in case. Don't want to have to shoot a dog if I can help it."

Starr couldn't help but be amazed at someone who could so easily take a man's life but absolutely shuddered at the thought of having to kill a dog.

"Don't say a fucking word, Starr. You know how I feel about dogs."

"I wasn't going to. I don't disagree."

There was another knock on the door. Starr, closest, went and opened it, allowing Christman and Phillips to enter the room.

Styles asked, "Any more news on this toxic agent?"

"No. President Lamar just went through a long meeting with everybody about everything. Merritt said that the president seems to be handling it surprisingly well. He confirmed that he's not going to make any real changes anytime soon; doesn't want to cause any further disruptions."

"Smart."

"I'd say so."

Starr offered, "J. C. and I are going to that restaurant because Styles wants to go play in the woods."

21.

T-Minus 32 Hours

Anyone on a beach on the West Coast of the United States was able to witness a purely stunning sunset. With the sparse cirrus clouds high in the atmosphere, colors of pink and gold were almost neon. Crystal-clear air, which was highly unusual for this time of year, only enhanced the colors.

Marvin Styles noticed none of it.

He had left his motel heading south on Interstate 205 and then got off on State Highway 213. The property he was looking for was about five miles outside the small town of Mulino. He had been able to locate a fire road that was only about two miles from Ryyaki Ali's estate. He turned off and proceeded a half mile up the road and found a good spot to hide his Jeep. He pulled off and parked. Styles was dressed in full camo, and he now went about applying flat camo face paint. When he was through, standing still, he was all but impossible to discern from the woods surrounding him. He decided to leave his AR-15 assault rifle, complete with silencer, hidden behind a tree ten feet from the Jeep. He'd decided that for tonight, his suppressed .40-caliber Berretta would be sufficient.

The map of Ali's land and buildings was imprinted firmly in Styles's mind. He set out on his hike through the woods. It was an enjoyable difference after thousands of hours in the sand. He knew that he would come upon the enclave of cabins first. It took him less than half an hour before he came upon an eight-foot security chain-link fence. He studied it carefully. He walked alongside for possibly a hundred yards. He saw no sign of any type of detection devices. Still he decided not to climb the fence. Instead, he looked for a tree that had a nice limb that spanned over the top. He spotted one immediately and noticed that fifteen feet away, he had the exact same situation. *In and out.* In less than two minutes, he was standing silently on the far side. From here on in, he would be in silent mode. He started forward, wanting the darkness to fall faster. He had night-vision gear with him. He knew that the cabins would be two hundred yards off to his right. He began his advance. The woods were very quiet. The leaves were still on the trees, rather than on the ground, making it much easier to remain silent while walking. In the distance, he could hear a vehicle start and a door slam shut. He could tell by the noise of the exhaust it was probably a pickup truck with an automatic transmission. He kept going.

By now, darkness had fallen, and he could pick up lights scattered through the trees. He was able to discern where the woods ended and the area opened up. He slowed, stopped, and got down on one knee and just listened. Two different voices could be heard. He smelled cigarette smoke and the odor of food being cooked. He made a quick check of his gear. He always secured it so that it would not move at an inopportune time and make noise, possibly alerting his presence to anyone. Very cautiously, he kept moving. Arriving at the edge of the tree line, he found a tree with a nice V in the trunk and stood behind it. He could now clearly see the eight cabins. He was opposite the sixth building, counting from his left. All the cabins appeared alike—small rectangular structures, each with a nice, covered, full-length porch on the front. A paved driveway ran up to each. Styles realized the entire road system was paved. *That cost someone some bucks.* Two trucks, a full-size van, and a newer BMW were parked. He decided he wanted to check the back. He slowly made his way around the end unit. Security seemed unusually lax. *Probably a hell of a lot different up at the house.* Arriving at the rear, the tree line was only fifty feet from the buildings. It was interesting that the tree line followed the curve of the buildings. Or probably the buildings were built to follow the natural curve of the tree line.

In his camo and paint, Styles was virtually invisible. Only with light at his back producing a silhouette would he be seen. There was still no sign of any real security measures. *Weird.* He watched the cabins for a full half hour. Three were dark; five had lights on. He started with the end cabin on his left. Proceeding in that direction would keep him on track to the main house. Though the cabins had blinds on the windows, none had been pulled. The first two cabins, lit, showed men eating dinner. Two in the first cabin, three in the second. Styles moved on. Cabin number three was dark. Cabin number four was lit. Suddenly, Styles froze. Light spilling out of the window revealed a set of rungs leading to the roof. *Guard platform.* He studied the roof for ten minutes. He scanned the roofs of the entire complex with his night-vision goggles. No sign of anyone. He waited ten more minutes and then cautiously continued. Cabin number four had a woman sitting at the kitchen table reading a newspaper. *Dressed pretty nice to be reading a newspaper.* Cabin number five also had lights on. Styles eased his way over toward it. He froze.

Standing less than twenty feet from him was Rijah Ellhad, former captain in the Iraqi Republican Guard. He was standing in front of a mirror in his bedroom. He was brushing his hair. *Getting ready for a date with the girl next door.* Styles decided to wait, which wasn't long. Within five minutes, the light switched off. Next, the kitchen light extinguished. Then he heard a door open and shut. Twenty seconds later, a knocking was heard, and then voices, both male and female, and then the sound of a door closing. Seconds later, a vehicle door opened and closed. Styles thought hard. *Has to be the dark BMW.* Then another door opened and closed, and he heard the sound of a car starting. *Definitely the BMW.* He heard the car back out of the driveway and then proceed down the long drive that had to have led to, and past, the main house. Styles went to Ellhad's bedroom window. It wasn't even locked. Slowly, he raised it and climbed in. He put on his night-vision goggles and navigated the cabin with ease. He placed a self-stick listening device under the front edge of the kitchen countertop, next to a wall-mounted telephone. He placed another one in Ellhad's bedroom, behind the mirror that Ellhad had just been using. Styles quickly searched the cabin. The only item of real interest was four boxes of nine-millimeter ammunition, but no gun. He thought for a second and then went into the bathroom and retrieved his cell phone. He texted Starr, "Strong possibility Ellhad heading to restaurant with date. Armed. 9 mm. Don't be spotted. Driving new BMW." Replacing his cell phone, he headed back to the window through which he'd entered. Easily slipping back out, he left it as he'd found it. He made his way past the next two cabins, which were dark, coming upon the last building, which was lit. He checked to be sure there was no light behind him to cause a silhouette. Satisfied there was none, he carefully looked inside through the bottom left corner of the kitchen window. He saw four hard Middle Eastern men whom he clearly heard celebrating the death of the American president. It took all Styles's self-control not to shoot the men. *Later ...*

Having checked the cabins, it was on to the main house. Through his earpiece, he could hear a double squelch, the signal that a conversation was desired. He walked past the tree line into the woods.

"Yeah," he said quietly.

"Phillips found something. She thinks there's a strong possibility that Ryyaki Ali may have also been involved with the death of the president. A credit card that tracked back to him was used at that camping store and also at a gas station an hour outside Baltimore," Starr said.

Styles could feel every hair on his body stand on end. "Got it. This is recon only. Out." He paused to think about what he'd just been told. It was obvious this Ryyaki Ali not only had money and connections but one hell of a network. Breaking that would be as important as anything else. Suddenly he found himself thinking about how easy it was when he was just a sniper. At least at that particular moment it seemed easier. He started moving, following the paved road. After ten careful minutes, he started to see lights through the trees.

Another double squelch. Once again, he retreated back into the woods.

"Yeah."

"Phillips has security info on Ali's house. You name it, he has it. Apparently no dogs, though. But figure on everything else," Starr passed along.

"Got it." From here in, he would become a ghost. Throughout his career in the Middle East, Styles had become familiar with the manner in which security measures were employed. He suspected motion detectors, pressure plates, and even lasers. His night goggles would pick any laser beams up; it was the pressure plates that he would have to be careful with. He estimated he was two hundred yards from the house. He figured that the serious security would start about a hundred yards out. He carefully made his way until he was within fifty feet of what he considered no-man's-land. He got down on all fours. From here in, he would crab and crawl. He took out a dimly lit magnetic compass. Every sensor plate he'd seen was comprised of metal. If he approached one, the needle on the compass, being magnetic, would react. Simple but effective.

Ever so slowly, and silent as a cat, he proceeded. He was eighty yards out when the needle on the ever-so-lightly-glowing compass swung counterclockwise to Styles's left. He held it at a ninety-degree angle, and the needle pointed at a severe angle down. Styles estimated the device was possibly two feet to his left. He carefully moved sideways a foot and then continued. He saw the compass needle react as he crawled away. He made a mental note of its location. He came across two more sensor units before he came to the edge of the tree line. Surprisingly, there was no fence. He did see two guards with assault rifles slung from their necks on either side of the drive, one hundred feet from the semicircle that pulled up to and past the massive front doors. The entire area in front of the entrance was covered to protect guests from rain.

He took his binoculars and switched off the night-vision option. He glassed the house carefully. He caught sight of two more guards on platforms on the roof. He carefully flanked the two guards' positions, which brought him behind the one guard who could potentially see him. The second roof guard was now out of his line of sight. He wanted to get close to the house but didn't want to be discovered. That was imperative. He used his binoculars to carefully search for motion detectors and found four under the eaves. He easily spotted the searchlights that the detectors would trigger. He studied the exact positioning of the motion detectors.

Fuck. No matter how he approached, there was no area that wasn't overlapped. He knew that Ali would have the best, and he figured they would probably sense out at least seventy-five if not one hundred. They were only about fifty feet apart. No way to approach without setting them off. Keeping one eye on his compass, he circled the entire house, taking almost two hours to do so. Every fifty feet was a motion detector. He counted six satellite dishes installed on the roof. He also noticed two more guard platforms on the roof at the rear of the house that were currently unmanned. Frustrated, he decided to head back. He wanted to try to plant some listening devices on the windows but knew the odds of him being seen were too great to make the attempt. He had wanted to place video cameras, but to place them in a good spot, he faced the same problem. Grudgingly, he began his retreat. He made it back to the cabins without incident, carefully retracing his steps.

As an afterthought, he decided to bug the cabin he'd seen the girl in since she was still out. The window, as in the cabin next door, was open. Slipping inside, he placed a transmitter in the same locations as in Ellhad's cabin. Then it was out the window, replacing it as he'd found it, and back into the woods. Traveling at an angle, he made it back near the first pressure detector when he froze and strained to listen. He was picking up on an extremely faint noise in the distance. Had there been much wind, he'd never have heard it. Two seconds later, he knew exactly what it was, and it could potentially prove to be a bigger threat than the guards. He had to find a place to hide, and quick. Not an easy task at night in the woods. He had an idea. He took two hasty strides over to a large tree and scrambled up. Ten feet up was a large branch, easily twelve inches in diameter. He clasped his hands and arms and hung under it, keeping as much of the branch as possible between himself and the sky. The noise increased. To someone unfamiliar, it would be unlikely it would have been heard. Even if it was, no notice would be paid to it. To Styles, it was a serious threat. *Baby drone.* And he knew it would be shooting film, both night vision and infrared. It was his heat signature he did not want it to pick up. If it only detected his hands and wrists, it was likely they would be read as an animal in a tree. The baby drone made three passes around the property and then left the area. Styles climbed back down out of the tree and made his way back to his Jeep he'd left almost seven hours earlier.

Climbing back in, he got Starr on his cell phone. It was just past three o'clock, Sunday morning.

"Yeah," a sleepy voice answered.

"Wake up Phillips. Tell her the CIA is in the area."

"What?" Starr blurted out.

"A baby drone just made a couple of passes over Ali's house."

"How do you know it's the CIA?"

"Too quick to be anybody else. I wonder if the FAA is having a shit fit. There's something in the air, and they have no clue what it is, because you know the CIA sure as hell isn't letting anyone in on what they are doing. From what I know, there is still a big stink going on over regulation of drones. See if Phillips can find out how much they know and what they're up to. If they're in the same game, we need to know, and I'm guessing they're damned close."

"On it." After disconnecting from Styles and before he could punch in Phillips's number, Starr's own phone rang. Through the speaker, he heard Phillips's voice.

"We've got a problem."

22.

President Lamar was back in the Oval Office with his chief of staff. They had just come from a three-and-a-half-hour meeting in the briefing room. They were now read in on everything known about the assassination of President Robert Williams and the threat of the new synthetic toxin. The president was exhausted. He looked around and saw everything the way the former president had left it.

"Irving, I believe you'll find some scotch in that lower cabinet over there. Pour us a couple." Vickers hesitated. "Irving, I don't think he would have minded."

Irving came back with the drinks and handed one to his boss. He sat down in a chair opposite the desk. "I have to tell you, sir, I'm a bit uncomfortable in here at the moment."

"You'll get used to it. It's been the day from hell—worse if I could think what that might be."

"Yes, sir."

"So what is your take on everything?"

"Well, sir, I'd say the immediate problem is this biological problem. I certainly don't mean to be disrespectful, but what's done is done. We have to prioritize."

"I agree, Irving. I don't know about you, but I'm famished." The president got his personal secretary on the phone and instructed her to order a meal for them both and have it delivered to the Oval Office.

"If you don't mind, sir, I'm going to go grab a quick shower and a change of clothes back in my office."

"Go ahead; I've got some calls to make." Once again, he got his secretary on the line. "A. J., get Elliott Ragar on the line for me, please." Exactly two minutes later, his phone rang.

"Director Ragar is on the line, sir."

"Thanks, A. J." He punched a button and said, "Elliott, I want you to keep me apprised the moment anything turns up. No matter what the time. You will be my unofficial lead on this toxic agent issue. Sanderson will lead on the other."

"Yes, sir. I won't hang up my phone before calling you."

"Very good." After placing the phone back in the cradle, he turned and stared out the window at the Rose Garden, lit up beautifully. *This is not starting out fun ...*

❊　❊　❊

Myra Banks was walking down the hall to Bernard Backersley's office. Her high heels were clicking loudly on the highly polished maple hardwood floor. *Bernie, I wish to hell I could get through to you about investigating the DPO. This is not going to end well. I can feel it.* She actually shuddered a bit from the slight chill going down her spine.

She walked past his secretary, nodding, knocked on his door, and then entered. He was talking on the phone; he pointed at one of the leather chairs in front of his desk, so she sat. She put the red folder in her lap. He ended his phone conversation and turned toward her.

"Bernie, I've got some more info on Darlene Phillips." She paused.

"And?"

"Phillips appears to do the majority of her work at home. Curious, though, it appears she spends quite a bit of time away."

"Where?"

"I don't know. There's no record of her using the airports—or trains, for that matter. She certainly would not use a bus. Her vehicle is extremely low mileage, so she doesn't drive, and I can't find any information as far as rental vehicles go."

"Well, if she isn't home, and if she isn't traveling, does she have a boyfriend or someone she stays with?"

"I thought of that. There is no indication she has a boyfriend, or any friends at all, for that matter. I can't find any record of her being with anyone at any time or anywhere. She just comes and goes; I don't know how, where, or with whom."

"Myra, how can that be?"

"You still don't recognize this woman's abilities. I have no doubt this woman could travel to the moon and leave no trace. For the last time, you need to comprehend that this one woman can do more with a computer than my entire staff."

Backersley was quiet for a moment. "Do you think she knows what the CIA knows?"

"I think Darlene Phillips knows just about anything she wants to know. Against my better judgment, I have her apartment staked out. The next time she shows up, I'll have a tail on her 24-7. I've tried to ping her cell phone, but that was a dead end. It's always turned off. At least the number we have on record. I'm sure she has burn phones. At one point, she was issued a satellite phone, but the records show it was turned back in over a year ago. Whether she did or not, who the hell knows."

"You and your team did an incredible job in tracking down this Ryyaki Ali. I have three teams in place and have a drone flying reconnaissance over the estate you found. Within the hour, we should have an idea of how many guards are on that property."

"Shouldn't you be turning this intel over to the FBI or Homeland or even the NSA? What about President Lamar?"

"What about him? He thinks I'm out of the country. He called two meetings, and I skipped them both. I've got bigger problems to worry about than holding his hand. When we're done, we'll concentrate on the Williams event."

"*Event?* Bernie, the president was killed."

"Yes, and it's unfortunate. However, everything that happens is an event to me. That's how I have to look at it. That's how I attack and solve problems, by looking at them as such and not letting them get personal. I couldn't do my job otherwise. Myra, I'm not trying to be cold or insensitive here; it's just how I work. It's how my brain works."

"That's hard to understand at times."

"I know."

"One other thing about Darlene Phillips. She was caught by facial recognition out in Oregon, *before* we even knew anything about Oregon."

"What the hell was she doing there?"

"My guess is running down the same leads we're chasing, only she is out in front of us."

"How in the hell could she have known that?"

"You tell me, Bernie. However, that also gives credence to my thought that there *is* more to the DPO than what is said."

Backersley was quiet. After a few seconds, he looked Myra Banks square in her eyes and stated emphatically, "You find out just what is up with her and this damned DPO."

Ryyaki Ali was internally gloating. He had accomplished what no other jihadist had ever attempted. He had assassinated the president of the United States. While the other men in his company were jubilant, he maintained the strictest of composure. No one in his immediate company had any suspicions that he was responsible. These individuals were participating in phase two of Ali's attack on America: the releasing of his newly acquired biological warfare agent. He held up his hand in a signal for quiet.

"Let us praise Allah for this unseen intervention on our behalf. Give thanks, but prepare yourselves, for we are about to begin."

T-Minus 28 Hours

At six thirty in the morning, Phillips addressed the team. "We've got a situation. The CIA is here. Styles called it last night with the drone, and he was right. They have three separate teams here. Two of them are sequestered one floor down at the opposite end of you two," she said firmly, referencing Styles and Starr.

That brought a look of both surprise and concern from Starr; Styles showed no emotion.

One team of three is the intel group. They are over at a Quality Suites; it's six miles from here. The teams over at the Comfort Inn are the shooters. My guess is they are planning an assault on the compound. The exact time hasn't been determined yet, but they are on standby. The problem for both of us is we don't know where the hell that toxin is."

"Yes, we do," Styles interjected. "Ellhad is the bastard that's going to deliver it. I'm sure of that. I'm also sure that it will be done Labor Day. They want to make a statement, and that would be the best way. Just like Indianapolis."

"How?" asked Phillips.

"He's ex–Republican Guard. I doubt there's anyone harder or sicker or especially more arrogant in that group than he is, so he'll be the one. He will leave within the next eighteen to twenty-eight hours, depending on his destination. I want to take him out away from the compound."

"Why not try to take the compound?" Christman asked.

Starr answered, "We don't know where the agent is. There could be contingency plans in place for such an attack. Too many variables we can't control."

"Exactly," confirmed Styles.

"Okay, that makes sense," agreed Christman. "But how do we stop the CIA?"

"We can't. We just have to stay sharp," affirmed Phillips.

Christman persisted, "How the hell can the CIA even be involved in this? I can see if it was the FBI, but the CIA?"

Phillips answered, "The CIA will go in strictly black ops. When it's over, Lamar's administration will credit the FBI, which will piss off the CIA, but there isn't anything Backersley will be able to do about that. Those two don't play well. The FBI probably isn't too far behind, but they have to jump through more hoops, which will cause delay. The CIA doesn't bother with hoops; it gives them an edge in response time. Merritt should have the info, but knowing Backersley, he's not coming clean. He doesn't give a shit about public opinion, but he wants the new boss to know he's top dog. The infighting between agencies is intense."

She continued, "It looks like there are five shooters. I hacked the motel's video and was able to see them check in. Or make that I actually saw three. The other three stayed around the vehicles. I did get a glimpse of all of them in the parking area. Ten seconds later, the video went down. It's in the motel's system. I'm betting our friends had something to do with that."

"You think they've got any idea we're here?" Starr asked Phillips.

"They don't know who we are. I'm sure they've got the registration list at the motels, but our covers will hold. From here out, I think we'd better stay apart. You can bet your ass everybody will be watched."

"So Ellhad didn't show last night," Styles said.

"No," Starr answered. "Phillips checked the camera feeds, but facial recognition proved negative."

"I've got a search on for any credit card he might have used before, but none has shown up," Phillips added.

Styles looked at J. C. "Get us a chopper that we can have on standby. I've got video on the main house. You and I are going to take a drive. Take your ride and meet me at that McDonald's about two miles back. We'll meet there, and then I'm going to show you where I think you'll be picking me up in that copter, and then we'll go pick up my 'baby,' just in case, and a couple of other things I might need."

Phillips spoke up. "There's one more thing. I got a call from a neighbor; some guy was asking about me, said he had a package I had to sign for. Asked her when would be the best time to catch me home. She just said she had no idea."

"Let me guess," Starr said. "You haven't ordered anything."

"Correct. According to Merritt, for the moment, DPO stays intact, but there's no way to tell what the new guy is going to do." She was still having a hard time calling the new president by name. "I'm still going back and forth on whether to stay or not, *if* DPO stays."

"Why don't we let that be a group decision when the time comes? That okay by you, Phillips?" Starr asked.

"Yes. Actually, I was going to ask that. We are a group now, a team. I think that all decisions that affect the group should be made by the group. Everybody okay with that?"

Everyone nodded.

"All right. I'm going to get back on my computers; I've got a lot to do."

"J. C., meet me at that McD's in half an hour. Okay, let's hit it," Styles directed.

The first place Styles drove by was the Quality Suites, and he immediately spotted two vehicles that screamed *agency*: two black Chevrolet Suburbans. *How the fuck you supposed to be undercover driving those? Might as well be driving a damned billboard.* Then he made a pass on the opposite side of the road that ran in front of the Comfort Inn where he and Starr were staying. Two more suspicious vehicles, but these were those new Dodge high-top vans. He wanted to get a look inside them, but he would have to wait until dark. Plus he knew they'd be watched.

23.

Bernard Backersley tried hard not to glare at President Lamar, but he just couldn't help himself. He was fully aware that his boss could see the contempt on his face, and he didn't care as he sat across from him in the Oval Office. He acted like he'd already served a full term, while in reality, he didn't even have his own coffee cup on the desk.

Backersley was getting his ass chewed out and did not like it.

"Backersley, I don't know or care about whatever relationship you may have enjoyed with President Williams, but with me, when I call a meeting of all my directors, I expect you to be there, and should you find that inconvenient, feel free to submit your resignation."

"Sir, my apologies; however, I was in the middle of assigning teams to observe and intercept people we strongly feel may be directly involved with this new toxin. Coverley Merritt has been read in on what we are doing."

"Backersley, let me see if I understand this. You have decided to take action inside our borders where you know it is expressly illegal for you to do so. Why have you not brought in Matt Sanderson and Elliott Ragar and turned your intel over to them?"

"Sir, I felt time was of the essence. I assumed Merritt would bring Matt and Elliott up to speed. I was waiting on contact from them and prepared to turn the entire operation over," Backersley lied.

"The fact that you moved teams into place within our borders is illegal. This is the crap that starts Senate investigations, and none of us need that right now. I want you to personally meet with Sanderson and Ragar immediately. I have already had my secretary contact them. You are *not* to leave the building until after they have been fully briefed. If you have material that you need that might be back at Langley, I suggest you figure out how to get it here. Got it?"

"Not necessary, sir. I have everything up here," he said, pointing to his head.

"I hope so." The president paused and then said, "You are to toe the line. I would rather not have to make changes in the middle of all this, but if I can't count on you to do your job in the manner in which you are prescribed by law, I will replace you immediately. Do you have any questions?"

"No, sir. Again, I meant no disrespect. I only thought I was putting my time where it was most beneficial."

President Herbert Lamar didn't believe him for a minute. One of the few things that President Williams had spoken with him about was Backersley's constant ignoring of protocol. "Get in line, Bernie. We won't have this conversation again. I want you to concentrate your efforts on the assassination of President Williams. Anything you discover will immediately be reported to Coverley Merritt. Irving Vickers will escort you to the office where I believe Matt and Elliott are waiting." He waved Backersley out, who got up and left without saying another word.

Styles pulled up next to Christman in the rear of the McDonald's parking lot. Christman walked over and climbed in. Rather than starting the Jeep, Styles turned and asked, "J. C., I'm trying to figure out if these CIA guys are here because of us or if it's a coincidence. Let me ask you something. Is there any way our jet can be traced to us?"

He was quiet for a few moments before answering, "No, not directly. It's registered as a federal government aircraft, but it's considered a loaner. There's no easy way to say who might have it on any given trip." Then he added, "But say Phillips wanted to find out. I have no doubt that using her black magic on those computers of hers, she could. And if she could, we'd have to be really naive to think it were impossible for someone else not to be able to do it. She's already told us that this CIA bitch is nosing around. My guess is it's at least fifty-fifty she may have put it together. If she's done that, I'm betting there's also a good chance that they think there just might be a bit more to DPO than what is officially acknowledged."

"I was afraid you were going to say that. I'm kind of surprised Phillips didn't offer that possibility."

"That would be a guess on her part, and we know how much Phillips doesn't like to guess. I'd bet she's already looking into it, and when she has something definitive to offer, our phones will start ringing."

"What do you think about this? Say they did follow the plane here. What would you think would be the easiest way to get them off our backs for a bit?"

"That's easy—leave in the plane."

"J. C., I need you here. I've got a plan in the works, and you're indispensable. I know you've been teaching Starr how to fly it. Is he there now? Can he fly that plane solo?"

"Yeah, I think so. I wouldn't want him getting our asses out of that slam like before, but just take it somewhere and bring it back; yeah, he should be good to go."

Styles thought for a minute. "Where could he go—an easy flight, mind you—that would take him four or five hours out?"

"Albuquerque, New Mexico. That'd be simple enough. What do you want him to do when he gets there?"

"Take a nap, I don't care. I just want our plane gone from here for eight hours or so. I want them off our track. If he leaves, we'll have Phillips track him, and if nobody takes the bait, we can bring him back."

"Okay, you want me to call him?"

"Hell no." Styles grinned. "I want to give him the news. I owe him one."

❈ ❈ ❈

Rijah Ellhad was just finishing lunch with Ryyaki Ali. Only the two of them were in the room.

"Are you set to travel, Rijah?"

"Yes. I am picking up the rental camper shortly. Everything is set. I only need to pick up the package."

"You may pick it up when you begin your journey."

"How big is it?"

"Come," Ali said, standing and then walking toward a door Rijah had never entered.

He followed Ali silently. They walked down a hallway to an elevator. Getting on, they descended two floors. The doors opened into a spacious room where everything appeared to be stainless steel.

"This is one of my preparation rooms," Ali informed him. There were two men in white uniforms resembling what one might find in a restaurant kitchen.

"Who are they?" Ellhad asked.

"They are of no consequence to you."

Ali kept walking toward the far end of the room to a set of double doors. He punched in a password on the electronic keypad. The doors opened silently. Upon entering, one of the first things Ellhad noticed were large red panic buttons, two on each wall. He didn't ask their purpose. Ali led him to a table. On it sat a metal crate with a hinged top. It was the size of a small microwave. Next to it sat the wooden crate it had arrived in. Ali opened the top. Inside, set in a foam-like material, similar to what would be found inside a gun transport case, were four aluminum vials. They were sealed at the top by what appeared to be a strange-looking cork.

Ellhad was apprehensive even approaching the table.

"Come, Rijah. There is nothing to be afraid of. Look." Ali leaned over and picked up one of the vials. "See, nothing to be concerned about. Just don't break the seal." He held it up for Ellhad. "Take it."

Ellhad cautiously took it from Ali's hand. He was struggling to control his nerves. He had seen horrible things through the Iraqi wars with the Americans, he had performed horrific acts on people Saddam Hussein considered his enemies, but what he had seen on that small lake in Alaska had made him gasp in fear. To think what was responsible for that was in this container scared him like nothing before.

"That seal will dissolve on contact with water. It will take approximately two minutes, more than enough time for you to toss them into the lake and withdraw."

Ellhad handed the vial back. "Yes."

"Come pick this up when you are ready to leave."

Twenty minutes later, Ellhad was back at his cabin. He walked next door and knocked.

Sahleea Mahad answered and smiled at him. "Rijah, come in. You know you don't have to knock."

"Yes, I do, for appearances."

"If you insist." She closed the door and kissed him. "I miss you."

Ellhad grinned. "I only left you a few hours ago. How can you miss me already?"

Sahleea smiled. "I miss the things you do to me."

"Then I should do them some more."

Styles made a sudden U-turn and headed back toward the Holiday Inn.

J. C. asked, "What's up?"

"I want to see if Phillips and Starr are being watched."

"Okay. Good idea. What's the plan?"

"You stay with the Jeep."

"Gotcha."

Nine minutes later, the Holiday Inn appeared up on the right. Styles pulled into a Red Lobster restaurant and parked.

"You stay put. Call Starr and Phillips and tell them to stay put. I'll call them if I want them to do anything." He jumped out of the Jeep and began walking. He was dressed casually: blue jeans, black Reeboks, gray short-sleeve sweatshirt. To a casual observer, he was just a guy walking. To someone paying strict attention, they would be surprised at the rock-hard muscles in his arms. Not overly bulging like a bodybuilder, different, just skin stretched tightly around each individual muscle that was extremely definitive in form.

He approached the Holiday Inn and acted like someone who was a guest there just out for a walk. He stopped as though he were catching his breath and surveyed the entire grounds and saw nothing. He kept walking, ending up at the registration lobby. He walked in and grabbed some of those brochures advertising tourist destinations in the area. He walked back out acting like he was studying them. He took the stairs up to the second floor and walked its entire length. Nothing. He took the stairs up to the third and final floor. Nothing. He walked around to the back side and stopped just short of the railed walkway that led past all the rooms. This was obviously an older Holiday Inn. He looked very carefully over the pool area and spotted an observer. A woman was in a lounge chair by the pool with a book. Styles noticed something wrong. *Hard to read when you're not looking at the book.* He watched her for six minutes. Not once did she turn a page. What Styles didn't understand is why she was watching the wrong side of the motel. *Did I miss somebody?* He withdrew, and from the corner, he watched the parking lot. He checked each vehicle in the area. No one sitting in a car, no cars with dark-tinted windows. *The fucking registration clerk.* He had video to watch with.

He called Starr. "You still with Phillips?"

"More or less. She's next door on her computers."

"At least one of you is being watched. A female out by the pool and the registration clerk. Call Phillips. In exactly twelve minutes, I want you guys to bug out. Take everything. Try to wipe your prints. Don't get in your vehicles. Cross the street, go left, Red Lobster, get in the Jeep."

"What about the security video? Do you want Phillips to hack in and erase it?"

"No. I'll take care of it. I'll see you at the Jeep."

"Roger that."

Styles made his way back down toward the registration lobby. He walked back in, directly up to the desk.

"Yes, sir?" a well-built blond man in his early thirties asked. "How can I help you?"

"I have a question."

"Do my best to answer it."

"Who are you watching?"

"Excuse me?" he asked, his tone turning.

"Who are you watching? You're no damned clerk."

The smile disappeared. "Well, now I guess I'm watching you."

"Not for long."

The blond-haired man hopped over the service desk and approached Styles. "You're going to have to come with me."

Styles didn't reply. He merely turned slightly as the man approached him. Styles saw him move up on the balls of his feet. He saw the man's left knee bend ever so slightly. *Kick to the chest.* Then he sprang, foot striking out with fury to where Styles's chest had been an instant before. It caught only air, and in the split second that he withdrew his foot, Styles struck, a savage kick to the outside of the man's right knee, the leg holding his weight. The knee snapped sideways, sending the attacker to the ground. Styles was surprised he made little noise. The man reached behind his back, and Styles was on him. As the attacker's hand came out from behind his back holding a nine-millimeter Glock, Styles grabbed the man's right wrist with his right hand, twisted it hard in a counterclockwise direction, straightened the man's arm, and brought his left fist down through the side of the man's elbow, shattering that joint. The gun fell to the floor. Styles had driven the fight out of the man. Styles knelt down beside him and saw the hate pouring from his eyes. He'd been badly beaten and hated it, hated that more than the pain.

Styles asked him once more. "Nothing personal, but I've gotta know who you're watching. I won't ask you again."

"Fuck you," he said between clenched teeth.

Styles was caught in a dilemma. He remembered President Williams's directive: "No innocents will be hurt." He quickly searched the man and found his CIA identification. "You don't belong here. Sorry."

Grabbing the back of the man's head with his left hand and his lower jaw with his right hand, he violently snapped the man's neck. Styles picked him up, slung him over his shoulder, and carried him back into the office sitting him in the desk chair. He turned the chair to make it look as though the man was merely looking out the window. He saw the security equipment on a shelf mounted on the wall to the right of the desk. Styles walked over and pushed the button that ejected the DVD. He slipped it into his pocket. He noticed two flash drives plugged into the computer. He grabbed both of those. He was tempted to try to see if there was a backup on the computer, but he was worried about time. *Phillips can deal with that.* Before he left the office, he unplugged the entire system. Seeing some low-voltage wires running from a cabinet, he took his knife and cut them. Sure enough, a nice spark arced. *So much for the battery backup.* He was already on his cell phone calling J. C.

"As soon as Phillips gets there, have her run a check on that hotel's security system. I think I've got it, but see if she can get in to see if there's some kind of backup. I unplugged everything and cut the battery backup power, so I don't know if she can do that now or not, but it's a priority. I don't want any pictures of any of us in their system."

"Got it.

"I'll be there in three minutes."

"Waiting on you."

24.

President Herbert Lamar was meeting with his chief of staff, Irving Vickers, who was disagreeing with his boss about Bernard Backersley.

"Sir, we have two monumental issues at hand. I don't know if the two are directly related, but we can be sure that in one form or another it will track back to the jihadists. We are at war, sir, and I think we need to give the CIA some wiggle room on their mandate, as long as they can keep their operations behind a curtain."

An exasperated President Lamar responded, "Irving, I don't entirely disagree with you, but if we knowingly allow Backersley free rein, and it's discovered, they will crucify us up on the Hill."

"What is the worst of two evils, sir? Getting heat from some senators or saving this country? Because that is what it comes down to. We have a biological agent that by all accounts will be released shortly, with everyone agreeing the Labor Day weekend would be the prime time. Sir, that's in three days. We need to do everything in our power to stop this, and right now, the question of legality isn't at the top of our concerns."

President Lamar was silent, but in his mind, he knew Vickers was right. "Get Backersley, Sanderson, Ragar, Rockford, Clayton, and Merritt here immediately."

Vickers was out of the Oval Office like a shot.

Herbert Lamar was born and raised in the Bible Belt. He was a

God-fearing man, considered by most ultraconservative, and had been placed on the ticket for the Far Right's vote. He had not gotten along with his former president because of some fundamental differences in ideology. For the good of the party, they had kept those differences in check, at least from the public eye. Privately, they had downright disliked each other. Lamar now found himself in a position he never imagined. Confident in his ability, he strongly wished he was working with people of his own choosing. Right now, that was simply not possible. He had to play the hand he was dealt. He was coming to grips that he was going to have to make concessions, but that didn't mean he had to like it. *This is going to be a very long weekend. God, help me get through this.*

❖   ❖   ❖

Styles quickly climbed into the back of the four-door Jeep Wrangler. The Jeep, with Christman driving, was moving before the door had closed. Quickly, he relayed what had happened.

Starr, sitting next to him, asked, "What made you decide to kill him?"

"No choice. He's trained. He would have given an accurate description of me. I remember what the Man told us: no innocents. He was CIA, illegally operating within our own borders. That is expressly against the law. For what it's worth, I didn't like it." He leaned up to Phillips riding in the front passenger seat. "Here," he said, placing three items in her hand—a recordable DVD and what he thought were two flash drives. "I took these from the security recording unit."

She looked at them closely. "This is a wireless connector. That means that the recording unit was integrated with the computer, which means that all the images from the security cameras will be stored in its hard drive, as well. This might be to our advantage. J. C., find someplace to park, quick."

Christman pulled into a strip mall.

She turned back to Starr and handed him one of her laptops. "Open it. On the desktop, you'll see 'cabin.' Left click that. When it opens, you will see a split screen, each with a transcript. On the left is Ellhad's cabin; on the right is the woman's. Read through it, and see if there is anything mentioning when he might be leaving. I need to concentrate here."

No one spoke.

Styles and Christman watched in amazement at the speed of Phillips's fingers flying back and forth between two open laptops, one sat in her lap, the other precariously perched on the Jeep's center console. Christman cautiously reached over and held it steady.

"Thanks," said Phillips. Six minutes went by, and no one spoke a word. Unconsciously, everyone was even breathing quietly. "*There*," she said triumphantly.

"What did you do?" asked Styles.

Phillips wiped her brow, as she was actually sweating. "First I hacked their computer and confirmed that no one had seen any of the footage. Then I transplanted Styles's face with one of a known terrorist. Then I had to match the skin tone of Styles's hands to match his new face. Now when they go back through the video, they'll think it was a terrorist who killed that CIA agent."

"What?" exclaimed Starr, looking up from the laptop Phillips had given him.

"Don't make me explain it again. Just read."

"There she goes, getting all bossy again."

"Wouldn't have to if you did as you were told."

"Like I said," he remarked, bringing a chuckle from everyone.

"We need to talk," pronounced Styles. "J. C. and I think that the CIA somehow traced the plane to DPO, and that's why they were sitting on you two," he explained, referencing Starr and Phillips.

"You're half-right," interjected Phillips. "It's me. They caught my photograph leaving it. That was the next thing I was going to bring up. The CIA is here because they are right behind us on Ryyaki Ali's ass. Protocol would be for them to photograph or video anyone arriving on public and private aircraft. I'm sure I came up on facial recognition. I was probably followed from the airport. It was only a matter of time. The CIA does have some talent, and they are relentless, particularly Backersley. He won't play by the rules. He'll tell Lamar whatever he thinks he wants to hear. I'm sure at some point he'll have to play with the FBI and Homeland, but until his ass is against a wall, he'll act on his own."

Starr asked, "Do you think he's put it together about this team?"

Phillips was quiet and then replied, "He probably has suspicions. He's the CIA. It's what they do, so that will probably be his first guess."

"So what do we do?" continued Starr.

"If we want to continue this, we have no choice. We have to go dark. I mean completely dark. I know you guys know what that means."

The three men nodded.

Styles spoke up. "I think this is a conversation for a later time. We need to stick to business at hand."

❈　❈　❈

Styles turned and looked at Starr. "You're gonna love this. We need you to take a little trip."

"What do you mean?"

"Gotta figure the CIA has eyes on the plane. I have to have J. C. with me. Phillips needs to be on standby with her computers. So that leaves you."

"So what is it I need to do?"

"Fly the jet to Albuquerque."

"*What? By myself?*"

"You can do that. It's an easy flight," urged Christman.

"I don't have the license yet."

"Who gives a shit?" snapped Styles. "We need you to get the CIA's attention diverted, if only a little, and that's the best way."

"So what do I do when I get to Albuquerque?"

"Get out, rent a car, drive around, stop in a restaurant, go to the men's room, go back to the airport, and fly back here. We need you gone at least eight hours."

Starr looked at Christman. "You really think I'm ready for this?"

"If I didn't, I damn sure wouldn't tell you otherwise. You can do this, Starr."

"Okay. I'll give it a shot."

"*Fuck* you'll give it a shot. You'll do it and get your ass back here. By the time you get back, we're going to be ready to get the hell outta Dodge," barked Styles.

"Okay, okay, calm down. Christ, it just caught me by surprise, big-time."

"One more thing," said Styles.

Starr audibly groaned.

Styles continued, "We're leaving the vehicles that J. C. and Phillips drove at the motel. Cops will find them easy enough. The CIA damn sure took down all the plate numbers. I know they're rented under one of our dummy companies, but—*shit!*"

"What's wrong?" Phillips and J. C. asked together.

"Fingerprints!"

"Relax. We wore gloves," assured J. C.

"Both of you?"

Phillips nodded in agreement and added, "We purposely didn't wipe them down so they'll have fun running who knows how many sets of prints through their system."

"Good thinking, guys. Seriously, I didn't think of that."

"Well, somebody has to be the brains of the outfit," cracked J. C.

"Heaven help us," muttered Styles with just a hint of a grin in his expression. "We'll need to pick up two more vehicles."

"Get them at the airport, since we're going there, anyway," said Starr. "Phillips—"

"On it."

Looking back at Starr in the rearview mirror of the Jeep, Christman stated, "You're fine on fuel. Just remember that when you are in contact with the control towers, keep it short. We've spent enough time on the automatic pilot, so once you're up, just punch the On button. I'll set it up for you. Look, you're going to be fine. You're actually past due to solo that bird. If you have any questions, I'm a phone call away, but I know that you're good to go. You know how it flies; just remember what you've learned."

"Yeah."

"Phillips," said Styles.

"Yeah? I'm just finishing up with the cars."

"Good. Is there any way you can intercept communication between these teams and whoever is directing them?"

"Probably, but it'll take a while. I'll have to discern who Backersley is directing out here. He's hands-on everything over there. He designates, but no decisions are made that aren't his."

"What about the assistant director?"

"In name only. He's just one of many managers. Myra Banks is his most trusted adviser, besides being the head of his cyber department."

"Give me your take on Banks again."

"She's good. Strongest part of her game is organization. Weakest is she won't think outside the box."

"What would be your best guess on what Backersley is doing?"

"I don't like guessing, but here's what I think. Backersley's downfall is his ego. No question. He's going to be a dog on a steak with the three things that are forefront in his mind right now."

"And those three things are?"

"First, the toxin; second, the assassination of President Williams; and third, us, or at least the DPO. I strongly believe he is beginning to think there's more to the DPO than what he's been told. Backersley is extremely smart. His IQ is off the charts. It is difficult, next to impossible, to try to get anything past him."

"So right now he'd be concentrating on the agent?"

"He's giving all three equal time. Make no mistake about it. This man is a very strong adversary."

"Anything you can do to slow him down or even get him off track?"

"There's always something I can do," she replied with a gleam in her eyes.

Starr spoke up. "Looks like Rijah Ellhad is leaving tomorrow morning on a camping trip. He's talking to this woman—looks like her name is Sahleea. He's picking up a rental tow-behind RV today."

"That's it, then. He'll pick that up, go back, and get the rest of his gear along with that weapon. Starr, you need to get back straight away, as we'll need you in the morning. I'll be watching and let you know what he's driving. I need you to plant a tracker on his truck. I hope he has to stop and gas up, because that'll make it easier for you, but no matter, whatever you have to do, get a tracker on that truck. J. C. and I are going to swap vehicles for the time being. I want to go back past the Quality Suites, and the Jeep has been seen driving in the area. When we get to the airport, Starr and J. C. will go in and pick up the keys. That should keep Phillips away from the cameras. We'll meet you guys over at the hangar."

"Got it," answered Starr.

When Starr and Christman got out, Phillips jumped behind the steering wheel, as Styles relayed he would walk to the hangar. She pulled up, got out, and walked through the large retractable doors. The DPO jet was set to be pulled outside.

She had decided to retrieve a couple of blank flash drives and was fifteen feet inside the hangar, walking toward the jet, when a voice shot out from off to her right, in the shadows. Two men came walking toward her.

"Hold it right there, miss."

Phillips turned and looked at the two men, saying nothing.

"Are you Darlene Phillips?" asked the larger of the two.

She said nothing and was glad she'd left her purse and computer bags in the vehicle.

"Yeah, that's her," replied the first man's companion, looking at a photograph.

"You'll need to come with us."

Phillips flashed her DPO identification at them. "I'm with the DPO, on official government business, and I'm not going anywhere with you."

The second man put the photograph back in his pocket as both men advanced toward her.

A black Chevrolet Suburban came screeching to a stop ten feet outside of the large doors. It sat there idling.

"That ID goes nowhere with us. Now walk toward the Suburban or we'll carry you."

Very casually, Phillips slipped out of her shoes.

"Go open the rear door. I can handle her," ordered the larger man.

The second man immediately turned to follow directions.

In a flash, Phillips had tied her long black hair into a ponytail. She was dressed in her usual black jeans, with a long-sleeve, very dark gray T-shirt-style top. She had put away her ID and now stood facing the man at a slight angle.

"Not that it matters, but who are you? Do *you* have any official identification, or is this just some half-assed attempt to kidnap me?"

"Lady, you can make this easy, or you can make this hard; your choice."

"I choose hard."

He stopped eight feet in front of her to evaluate his opponent. He saw no fear in her eyes, just determination. Suddenly, he just rushed her, intending to grab her arms. He never really saw the back of her foot as it connected solidly with the side of his head, sending him sprawling.

Upon seeing this, the second man joined in. He advanced much more cautiously as the first man was picking himself off the ground.

Phillips had backed up close to the fuselage of the jet, eliminating any chance of either of the men getting behind her.

The two men flanked her and approached much more slowly.

"Why don't we just Tase her ass?" the smaller man asked.

"I owe her one," was the response.

Phillips balanced slightly on the balls of both feet. Both men lunged at once.

Phillips executed a perfect side kick to the solar plexus of the smaller man and delivered an elbow to the forehead of the larger man just as he was able to grab her around her left shoulder and under her right arm. He was dazed but still maintained the grip. She spun hard to her left, bringing her left hand up, over the man's arm, into a knuckle strike perfectly into his nose. The blood immediately started pouring as he yelled in rage.

She saw a third figure appear in the open doorway who was

instantly moving toward her. Suddenly, that man, whom she now recognized as Styles, was on the ground in convulsions. A woman was behind him holding the Taser that she had fired into his back.

Shit ...

The woman was walking toward her, reloading her Taser.

Phillips had no intention of being Tased; she'd had enough of that earlier.

The big man tried wiping the blood streaming down his face and approached her again, fury in his eyes.

The smaller man was just now getting his breath back, and he warily approached.

"You two morons just get the hell out of my way," the woman ordered.

Luckily for Phillips, the larger man's ego wouldn't allow that.

"You don't learn very well, do you?" Phillips egged him on.

The man's indignation had gotten the best of him. He approached Phillips again, this time receiving a kick under his jaw and two quick punches to his face. Phillips then pushed him toward the woman and ducked low. The man reared up like an enraged bear and caught two darts between his shoulder blades for his trouble. He instantly went to the concrete floor, writhing in pain. He had intercepted the Taser contacts intended for Phillips. The second man was now scrambling to intercept Phillips while the woman reloaded her Taser again.

Suddenly, Styles appeared beside the woman, a redhead in her early thirties, and kicked the Taser unit out of her hand so hard that it flew halfway across the hangar and skidded to a stop on the floor. Then he pushed her toward Phillips. "You take *her!*"

"Glad to."

Styles approached the second man like a coiled snake as he was scrambling to procure his own Taser. He was just clearing the unit's holster when Styles launched a vicious side kick and caught the man right on the bridge of his nose that drove him backward. Following him, he drove two brutal punches in the center of his forehead, knocking him unconscious. He turned just in time to see Phillips squaring off against the woman he'd just kicked the Taser from.

"Any chance this might be just the two of us?" asked "Red."

"Wouldn't have it any other way," declared Phillips.

The two women circled, eyeing each other up. Suddenly, the redhead threw a hard, fast kick to the side of Phillips's head, which Phillips barely blocked. It caught Phillips's attention. The woman in gray then launched a straightforward attack—three punches that caught only Phillips's arms that that she used to block with, a kick that missed, and an attempt at a flying knee.

Styles watched with concern.

The woman then tried a spinning back kick to Phillips's head that missed badly, providing the opening Phillips had been waiting for.

Ducking under the kick, Phillips pivoted and side kicked the woman square in her stomach, connecting hard. Her opponent groaned but recovered. Phillips feigned a punch to the forehead but closed with a knee to the woman's chest that connected with authority. The redhead had been hurt, but she kept her arms and guard up. Phillips executed a spinning back kick, but rather than go high, she went low, right at the woman's knee, which knocked her off her feet. Phillips backed up and motioned for her to get up and continue the fight.

Back on her feet, the woman advanced cautiously, too cautiously. Her guard was a little too far apart, allowing Phillips to connect with a perfect front-jump snap kick that rocked the woman hard. Phillips jumped in close and fired off three hard punches to her opponent's sternum, followed by two more to the bridge of her nose and her forehead. The redhead fell to the ground, the fight knocked out of her. She lay on the ground staring up at both of them, hatred pouring from her eyes.

Styles walked back to the man he'd knocked out and grabbed the Taser from him. He walked back to the woman, stood over her, and snarled, "Just want to make sure you know how this feels," and started to shoot her in the chest.

Phillips said, "Hold up." She walked over and took the Taser from Styles. "I don't want anyone to accuse you of being sexist."

"If she wants to dish it out, she needs to be able to take it," snapped Styles.

"True, but allow me."

Styles relented.

"Here, bitch," Phillips said as she fired the electrical darts directly into the woman's chest.

She started convulsing. After eight seconds, she stopped and was barely conscious.

"You okay?" he asked Phillips.

"No, I was just getting started."

Right then, Christman and Starr drove up, got out, and immediately came running over.

"What the hell happened here?" Starr growled.

"Three guesses," Phillips answered.

Styles was still so mad about getting Tased that he was pacing back and forth like a hungry lion. "*Damn*, that hurts."

"Yes, it does," Phillips retorted, giving him a sweet smile. "Remember that elevator?" She did not receive a reply, only a nod.

Christman went over and dug through the smaller man's pockets, producing CIA credentials. "Well, what do you know! CIA."

Styles was finally starting to calm down, just barely, and directed, "Phillips, get us one more car from Enterprise. One with a big trunk, and make sure it's a credit card we've never used before."

She just nodded, walked back to the Tahoe she'd driven over, sat in the backseat, and then made the reservation.

"J. C., drive me back over there, since you two were just in there. Starr, grab some wire ties, and tie these three up *good*. We'll be right back."

In eight minutes, two vehicles parked close to the door, one being a new Ford Taurus.

Styles got out of the Taurus and spoke. "Line these three up alongside each other on the floor. Put their CIA IDs on their chests and take some photos. Then hold the IDs up against a recognizable background; no doubt where the photo is being taken. Be sure the photos are time and date stamped. J. C., will you back that Taurus in here?"

"Sure."

After the photos were taken, Styles popped the trunk. He looked it over. "We can get two of them in here."

"What about air?" Phillips asked.

Styles walked around and came back with a lug wrench rather sharply wedged on one end. Gripping it tightly, he used it as a large punch, quickly producing four holes in the side of the vehicle. "There, that *should* let them breathe. We'll toss the woman onto the floor of the backseat."

Styles walked over to the three CIA agents trussed up on the ground. All three were conscious. He knelt down beside them.

"This should be pretty easy to understand. Normally, I'd just kill the three of you, but as we are basically on the same side, I'd rather not if it can be helped. So here's the deal. We've got your IDs, photographed both on you and against a recognizable backdrop. They are time and date stamped. What you tell your boss is your problem. If you say anything to describe us, then it becomes my problem. The first thing that will be done is those photographs will be leaked to the press; CIA operating illegally in this country. That will cause your director problems. Then I will come after all three of you, and I *will* finish this—permanently. You three will be tossed into that car. You have my word that we'll let the proper people know of your whereabouts within thirty-six hours, possibly sooner. You're not going to like that, but it beats being dead. You two guys go in the trunk; the woman goes on the floor in the backseat. I'm going to have to tie you so you can't kick. Sorry, but it has to be that way."

Styles got up and, grabbing the long wire ties, walked over to the Taurus. "Starr, you and J. C. bring those guys over here."

J. C. and Starr walked over to the smaller man, hoisted him up, dragged him to the trunk of the Taurus, picked him up, and tossed him inside. Styles rolled him over onto his stomach, bent his legs backward at the knees, and hog-tied his feet toward his hands. He then doubled up all the wire ties to ensure the man could not escape. He turned and said, "Next."

After J. C. and Starr brought the larger man over, he repeated the process. He then used duct tape to gag both men, cutting a slight slit between their lips to aid their ability to breathe, and then double-checked to be sure there would be no way they could pound on the vehicle; satisfied, he closed the trunk.

"Okay, bring that woman over here."

She wanted no part of going into that car and tried to resist. Phillips walked up to her and slapped her hard in the face. "Listen, I know what he said; I don't have a problem in killing you right here and now. So either get in the damn car alive, or get in dead. *Your choice.*"

She settled down somewhat, and Starr and Christman got her onto the floor in the backseat, on her stomach.

Styles proceeded to tie her in the same manner. Looking at Phillips, he said, "Follow me; I'm going to park this in the last row in that rental lot." Glancing at J. C., he directed, "You get him up and running, and then she will go back to his room. You stay with her until you hear from me." Looking at J.C., he said, "Let me have your car keys. Mine will be on top of the tailpipe. You ride back with her." Looking back at Starr, he said, "You'll have your ride when you get back. Everybody set? Let's go."

25.

T-Minus 26 Hours

CIA team leader Martin Larrow, known as Marty, was on the phone to Langley. Holding for Bernard Backersley, he was conversing quietly with Sandi Davis, the female agent stationed poolside.

"So you never saw anyone? Anything? How in the hell can that be? For Christ's sake, Sandi, he was killed right under your damn nose! Look at the fucking mess we have. Everybody but Santa's elves is nosing around. I have no idea how to explain this. Backersley is going to throw a shit fit." He held up a hand to stop her response as his cell phone rang.

"Yes, sir," he addressed Backersley. He gave Backersley a quick rundown on what had happened at the motel. Davis could hear Backersley over the cell phone, which was not on speaker, from five feet away. The look on Larrow's face was painful.

"No, sir, the second agent saw nothing. The video system was compromised, but we do have footage on the computer. No, sir, I have not seen it. The FBI is in charge. They got here about ten minutes ago. They chased everyone out, including me. I know one of the agents here, so as soon as I can, I'll speak to him. No, sir, I told them I was in the area visiting family. No one is aware of Davis's status." He paused listening to Backersley. "I will call you immediately, sir." He closed the phone.

165

"Sir, Claude had me watch the back. I had no view at all of the front or sides of the building. I didn't like my positioning, but he wasn't up to debating it," Davis told her boss.

Marty Larrow knew he couldn't doubt her on that fact. Claude Dole was a prick who really despised working field operations with female agents. He might have excelled during the fifties, but in the current world, despite his young age, he was a dinosaur.

"Go to the safe house and wait for me." He turned to see an old friend waving him over. FBI special agent Paul Hedges greeted him.

"Tough day. Marty, what was the CIA doing here?"

"Paul, I honestly don't know, and if I did, you know I couldn't comment on it. Like I said, I just happened to be in the area and got a call to stop in and lend a hand if I could."

Marty, we go way back, and we'll always be friends, but we both know you're feeding me a line. The CIA never just happens to be anywhere." He stepped around a corner, motioning for Larrow to follow. "I don't know what's going on, but here's what I do know. The security discs and backup were taken, but they didn't know about the backup in the computer. The footage shows a man of Middle Eastern ethnicity attacking your agent. I watched it three times, your man looked like he could handle himself, but he was no match for this guy."

"You say he was Middle Eastern?"

"Yeah, we're running him through facial recognition right now. If he's anywhere in the system, we'll find him."

"Any chance you got him in a vehicle?"

"No, he withdrew right through the front door and walked toward the street. That's the last we have of him."

"Where is the employee who was supposed to be on duty?"

"She was sent home by your man. He wouldn't allow her to call her manager. There was a second employee scheduled to come on duty within a half hour but was called to stay out. Marty, this is going to get messy. My boss is going nuts about the CIA being here."

"Trust me, he's not half as pissed as my boss. My next posting might damn well be the Arctic Circle."

"Between you and me, is there anything you can tell me?"

"Between you and me, Paul, I'll tell you this: it has something to do with a rumor of a possible terrorist action. Not necessarily here, but something was intercepted, and it was believed that a meeting might take place here. This was an observation-only mission, nothing more. The last thing we need is a CIA agent turning up dead, much less here."

Paul Hedges knew his friend was being up front with him. Their friendship went back to high school football. Hedges was an usher at his friend's wedding. "I'll call you later. Now get out of here before my boss gets hold of you."

Nodding, CIA agent Marty Larrow turned and left.

Walking back inside, Hedges heard, "Where the fuck is that CIA asshole?" *This is not going to be fun.*

"Was that the guy in the black suit?"

"No, Hedges, he was the guy in the Easter Bunny outfit."

"I believe I saw him leave, sir. I did not know that's who he was."

"Why were you outside?"

"A quick smoke, sir."

"Well, if you're not too busy feeding that disgusting habit, do you suppose you could bother yourself to try to help out?"

Hedges was struggling to stay professional. Agent in charge Dan Gare was a boisterous jerk. He had ten months until retirement, and it seemed like he was trying to make life as miserable as possible for everyone around him with the time he had left.

"What do you need, sir?"

"I need answers, preferably before they boot me to the curb." Gare was not taking retirement well. In reality, everyone who knew him thought it couldn't come soon enough.

"Our forensics team is on the way. They should be here in fifteen, maybe twenty minutes. I've been keeping everyone away like you instructed, sir. The local PD is having a fit."

"Like I give a shit. I don't want to see a single face I don't recognize. If I do, it'll be your ass where they'll find my boot."

"Understood, sir." Hedges walked out.

Bernard Backersley had no intention of mentioning the incident in Portland, Oregon, to President Lamar unless directly asked, and even then, Backersley would brush it off as a mere unfortunate circumstance. Backersley would press they had much more important items to address. In truth, he was seething over having had an agent killed, particularly because it happened inside American borders. Nothing caused him more grief than explaining any actions inside the country when they were discovered. Four times he had been summoned up to the Hill to explain such incidents. Four times he had left intact but presently had some very powerful senators as sworn enemies. He didn't care. He had a job to do, and if they could find someone better, that was their choice. As long as he was in charge, he would do things his way, and damn them if they didn't like it.

He had talked to his own AIC, Martin Larrow, and had a suspicion of what might have happened. At that moment, his phone rang.

"Yes, Martin."

"Sir, I spoke to that friend of mine. He saw the video footage personally. A man of Middle Eastern descent attacked and killed Agent Dole. There was no doubt on that point. They are running him through facial recognition as we speak, along, of course, with us. If his group should ID the man first, I'll know immediately."

"Are you trying to tell me that some religious fanatic knew we were running an operation at that particular motel? We were on station what, less than an hour?"

"Approximately forty-five minutes, sir."

"So they knew we were there inside of forty-five minutes? Martin, I did not know that, and I run this agency."

"Yes, sir. I can't explain it. When I have answers, you will have answers. I simply cannot tell you what I don't know. I am not foolish enough to guess."

Backersley sighed heavily. "All right, Martin. Keep me posted in real time."

Special Agent Larrow knew that meant 24-7. He called the leader of his response team and filled him in on what had happened. Agent Robert Randall listened and only replied one word: "Shit." Next he called the leader of his intelligence team, Special Agent Toni Latell, and informed her. She had already found out. Not surprising.

"Is that crotchety old bastard Gare AIC?"

"Yes." Larrow knew that Latell and Gare had a history, and not a good one. Latell had quit after working under Gare for only four months. She had made quite a stink when she left, strongly accusing him of inappropriate conduct. It was her computer skills that got her a probationary position at the CIA, which now was six years ago. She had quickly worked her way up the ranks and was now the cyber team leader for the West Coast surveillance unit, which of itself was somewhat of an oxymoron. Larrow found her to be professional and quite competent. She also didn't question the aspect of sometimes working within national boundaries. That was a plus.

"You want me to widen the scope of the assignment?"

"Do as you see fit."

"Yes, sir."

Larrow knew he could trust Latell to be discreet. She routinely found out items of particular interest by her own initiative.

US Marine captain Richard Starr, retired, sat by himself in the cockpit of one very expensive jet aircraft. He was sweating. While he had countless hours sitting beside his assigned pilot, J. C. Christman, learning the plane, this was his first time alone. *Calm down, Starr. You know how to do this.* He keyed the radio microphone and contacted the airport tower. He gave the plane's identification numbers and requested instructions for takeoff. As Christman instructed, he kept it short and sweet. Christman had filed the flight plan for him, written up a quick set of notes that he'd taped to the copilot's seat, and slapped him on the shoulder when he left. "Read you loud and clear," he replied.

The hangar crew had positioned the jet on the tarmac. He started the engines, went through his cockpit takeoff checklist, and then eased the throttles forward. He wiped his brow. Very deliberately, he followed his instructions, got in line behind a Delta commercial jet, and waited. The big Delta's engines roared, and it started down the runway. As it reached the halfway point, Starr heard his radio crackle with his instructions to proceed. He opened the throttles on the modified aircraft. With engines producing more than twice the thrust as the original the plane had been built with, it gained speed with authority. As he saw the big commercial craft in front of him ease into the air, he couldn't help but notice he'd already closed the distance behind it considerably. "This isn't a race," he heard over the radio with a hint of laughter. He gently began the rotation of his craft by pulling back on the wheel.

Suddenly, Starr felt the powerful bird smoothly leave the runway, and he was free of gravity. He was no longer nervous, feeling like a kid who had just mastered riding a bicycle. He could feel the grin on his face.

He was instructed to begin a long, winding turn to his right. He complied. He was now lined up for his flight straight to New Mexico. As he passed four thousand feet, he decided to open up the jet engines even more. Effortlessly climbing at four thousand feet per minute, he reached his thirty-five-thousand-foot flight plan altitude in less than ten minutes. He leveled off, cruising at six hundred miles per hour.

❈　❈　❈

Christman, after returning to the motel with Phillips, was concentrating on the laptop that Starr had previously been watching, which contained a real-time transcript of any conversation taking place in either cabin that Styles had previously bugged.

"Besides sounds I'd really rather not describe, Ellhad told his girlfriend that he had to leave for a bit and would return later."

Phillips acknowledged the information with a wave of her hand, her eyes transfixed on three laptop screens.

Suddenly, a sequenced knock on the door was heard. Christman got up and let Styles in.

"No reports of any plane crashes so far?" Styles asked, only half joking.

"No. Don't worry, he'll be fine. Soon as he gets up in the air, he'll be like a kid in a candy store. He can handle it."

Phillips spoke up. "Langley has been informed that our plane has departed. They've even got the flight plan. There will be an observation team waiting for him in New Mexico. Should we call him?"

"Why not?" Christman suggested. "We'll have him fuel the plane and then come back home. That ought to mess with their heads a bit."

Styles couldn't help but chuckle. He had noticed that even during tense times, the group had become so comfortable working with each other that there was an overall change in the emotional attitude of everyone, including himself.

"Not bad, J. C., not bad."

"What's going on over at that motel?"

Styles turned serious. "Place is crawling with everybody. I didn't see that much, but it looked like the locals were just observing from the parking lot."

"Ouch. That's gotta be pissing them off."

"No doubt about that. The FBI gets pretty damned bossy."

"I'm surprised you've had so many run-ins with them."

"Just a couple of times, mostly just watching. It's their method of operation. They look at the country as their personal sandbox, and they don't like to share. Hell, the only time I've been involved with them was in Iraq—some kind of murder that they thought had been the result of a bombing, so they were investigating; they were total jerks." Styles started chuckling.

"What's so funny?"

"About ten, maybe twelve years ago, I was watching three locals who had been zeroed for me to take out. They were gathering intel on some plan they were hatching. I think they were going to bomb the same place twice. The FBI had sent a team over there to help with forensics, and there was this one guy in charge that was just a total ass wipe. That night, there were about six of them over at a lounge on base. They stayed in civilian quarters there, although they had full access to this particular bar. Well, I happened to catch this jerk in the men's room. I guess I happened to comment about his, uh, lack of professionalism. He started chewing on me, so I stuffed his head in a toilet, one that someone had conveniently forgotten to flush, and no, it wasn't me."

Christman laughed out loud. "I'd have paid money to see that."

"He had it coming. Think his name was Gary or Gore or something like that."

26.

T-Minus 25 Hours

Styles decided he should go for a quick run. He hadn't exercised much over the last two days and was getting edgy. Christman had moved over and joined Styles, bunking with him. Phillips had moved into J. C.'s room, leaving Starr to join the two of them when he got back from New Mexico, having to take the couch. The decision had been made for Starr to return around ten that evening. Christman had shown Starr how to change the transponder numbers on the jet so that it wouldn't be immediately identified as the plane that had just previously arrived, the theory being that since it was probably being watched, the changing numbers might cause confusion.

"We'll at least see if the CIA is on their toes," commented Christman. "I think this misdirection was a good idea if it draws just a bit of attention away from us."

Phillips had sat down with the two of them to share what she'd found, causing Styles to hold up.

"I have no doubt that Ryyaki Ali is connected with President Williams. I don't have the proverbial smoking gun, but I've got spent shell casings. I think we need to have a conversation before you kill him," she said to Styles.

"We need to get a time line down. Day after tomorrow is Labor

Day. Ellhad is more than likely leaving at some point tomorrow afternoon. He's going to want to travel with people on the road, trying to blend in. I need to catch up to him by the time he reaches Lake Mead; earlier would be better. J. C., you're on standby with the chopper. I'm thinking of having Starr follow Ellhad just in case we have to switch gears. What's the most popular color car on the road?"

"Silver sedan? Maybe white?" offered Phillips.

"I'd go with silver," agreed Christman.

"Get Starr a full-size silver sedan to pick up when he gets back. Hell, might be cheaper to buy a damn car dealership," Styles grumbled.

"Consider it done," assured Phillips.

"How are you going to *talk* to Ali?" inquired Christman. "It's not like we're going to have all the time in the world."

"I might have to just get medieval on him," replied Styles.

"Up for a suggestion?" asked Phillips.

"Sure."

"Chemicals."

Styles thought about that. "Yeah, I remember your work on Andrew Ladd."

"That was just an example. I'm quite familiar with them, and they can work quickly."

Styles looked out the window. He wanted to get running, but knew this aspect needed to be established. Turning to Phillips, he asked quietly, "You ready?"

Neither Christman nor Phillips was used to hearing Styles using such a soft tone.

"Ready?" she asked.

"Yeah. It's time for you to become a field agent; you up for that? We don't have the time for you to teach me about drugs. I use a different approach, but for this, I think your way is best."

She stared him right in his eyes. "Yes."

Styles looked right back at her and grinned. "Of that, I had no doubt. One condition: we can't have you get hurt—or worse. I'll do the heavy work, but I'm sure you'll get a little dirty. Besides, since this will be a daylight raid on their compound, two shooters are better than one. I know you can shoot."

"What about me?" questioned Christman firmly.

"J. C., you're on chopper duty. Unless you can rent one with an M60 machine gun mounted, it's gonna be hard for you to fly and shoot."

"I'll buy that, but why don't I bring a little something with me so when I'm waiting on you, I can bring something to the party if I get the invite or if I have to crash it?"

Styles thought quickly. "All right, but you don't attend unless I invite you. Understand? No buts about it. Bring one of the suppressed ARs and a suppressed pistol. However, if someone crashes your party, feel free. Just use good judgment."

"Got it, loud and clear."

"Okay, Phillips, I want you to—"

"Taken care of," she interrupted. "I've been practicing on my own. I took a clue from what you like and pretty much copied it. I had an AR built, along with a Beretta. A .40. I've put about two thousand rounds through the AR and maybe three hundred with the pistol. I'm competent."

Styles face showed surprise. "You've got them with you?"

"Of course."

J. C., exclaimed, "What the hell? Where? I didn't see them."

"J. C., a girl has to have some secrets."

"My kind of girl."

"I will *not* disagree," voiced Styles.

"So when do we go in?" asked Phillips.

"I'm going later tonight to plant some more cameras. We'll go in tomorrow after Ellhad leaves. Do you have access to their camera feeds in the field?"

"Styles, *please.*"

"Sorry, I withdraw the question."

"You are forgiven."

"Thank you. I'm going to go for a run. When I get back, we'll get some dinner. That okay?"

"Fine," they said in unison.

Phillips left to go back to what originally had been J. C.'s room, wearing her hair up under a ball cap.

Christman went back to study the laptop that he'd been watching earlier for any signs of further conversation.

Styles changed clothes. Rather than his usual running attire, he changed into sweats, including a hooded top. He tied it in place and went out the door looking like a boxer in training. He stretched and then started out along the road. Twenty-five minutes later, he was within sight of the Holiday Inn. The motel was still closed to the public, although the action had died down. Styles ran through the parking area as though he'd done it a thousand times before.

"Hey, where do you think you're going?" shouted someone.

Styles turned and yelled back, "Just cutting through here like I always do!"

"Not tonight. Don't you see the crime tape? It doesn't say, 'Welcome.' Now turn around."

"What happened?"

"Read the fucking papers. Now move along."

"Sure, Officer; didn't mean any harm." Styles withdrew and headed back to the Comfort Inn.

Arriving back at the room, Christman was absent. Styles grabbed a quick shower and had just finished changing back into his familiar clothing of choice: jeans, sweatshirt, and athletic shoes. He was still sporting his three-day growth on his face—something Starr pointed out at every opportunity.

"What's up?" he greeted Christman.

"Been over with Phillips. I was wondering who the CIA was watching over at the Quality Suites since we're here, and they were at the Holiday Inn."

"Funny you should mention that, J. C. I was thinking the same thing running back here. I went by there just to check it out. Nothing new. Then I got thinking …"

"Well, Phillips says she knows why. She booked a room there under D. Phillips. Guess that got the CIA's attention. I think she was just screwing with them. I have a feeling she knew they were onto her, as far as DPO goes, anyway."

Styles lay down on the floor, hooked his feet under the bed, and started doing sit-ups. "You know, J. C., now with the president gone, we're going to have to make some hard decisions. It's not a problem for me, and I know how I can square it with my dad."

"How, if you don't mind my asking?"

"Not at all. I'm just going to lay the cards on the table about everything. Then I'm going to tell him he has to go dark too. That way we can still have a relationship, and no one will be able to find him to use him against me."

"How would they find that out—about you, I mean?"

"Don't know that anyone would, but plan for the worst. That's what's kept me alive all these years." He paused doing his sit-ups for a moment to look at J. C. "I've been through some really deep shit, and that's how I got through it: *always* plan for the worst."

The practiced sequential knock sounded from the door. J. C. opened it, and Phillips came walking in with four bags. "Beef stew and biscuits from Cracker Barrel. I thought we could use a change."

"Thanks, D," said Styles.

Phillips grinned as she spread the food around the table. "Everybody has two orders; they aren't real big. Don't worry, J. C. I got extra biscuits."

"I *was* concerned," he joked.

While they were eating, Styles asked Phillips, "So do you think the CIA was there specifically to watch you?"

"No, two birds with one stone. They're onto Ryyaki Ali, just like I said. So is the FBI. I guess J. C. told you about the room I booked. Funny how such a simple trick can fool those agencies. It just confirmed what I strongly suspected."

"How deep are you being investigated?" asked Christman.

"Myra Banks would love to know what I had for breakfast."

177

T-Minus 22 Hours

Styles's phone rang, and it was Starr. "I'm back. Anybody need anything?"

"No, we're set. Grab yourself some takeout if you're hungry and get back to the Comfort Inn. You're bunking with J. C. and me in my room. Phillips is in yours.

"Gotcha," he said and hung up.

"Flyboy back okay?" Christman asked.

"Yeah, he's on his way back here." He continued, "Phillips, you've been unusually quiet. Something on your mind?"

"A lot, actually. As much as I've been searching, I haven't been able to gather much new information, at least not as quickly as I expected. This issue with Myra Banks is starting to piss me off. If Backersley spent the time working what's important rather than what feeds his damned ego, he'd get more done."

Styles got up from the table and sat down across from her. As usual, she was sitting on a sofa with three laptops open in front of her.

"Talk to me."

She sighed. "Backersley is going to be a problem. He's got Banks running every search on me possible: phone records, credit cards, bank accounts, probably the library. She's even hacked the Interstate Highway System checking for my E-ZPass cards. She's the one who got my photo at the Portland airport, possibly that hunting store, and at the car rental center. They have cameras there, and I didn't see them. I'm *really* pissed I didn't pick up on that. I was sloppy, and sloppy could get us all killed."

"It could have been any one of us at that counter. Don't beat yourself up over it."

"But it wasn't; it was me, and I'm supposed to think about that shit. That's *my* job."

"No. Your main job is gathering intel. You were picked for a reason, because the president thought you were the best person for this job. He was right. That is the only thing you need to keep in your head. Like I've said, we all have a specific job within this team, though I'll be damned if I can figure out Starr's." That brought some much-needed laughter. "We all need to keep in mind that at any time, shit happens. How all of us remain focused determines how we deal with it," Styles continued. "Look, as we go forward, all our roles will continue to expand to a degree, but we all will always have our primary responsibility. Hell, Starr just flew our plane. You'll be in the field. J. C.'s helping on the computers. I'm even cooking. Darlene, *please*, let it go."

"You're right. I have been kicking myself, and it's been affecting my focus. I've set a trap for her. I know one more place she will eventually get to, and when she does, she'll know she bit off more than she can chew."

"Phillips, you're not going to blow up Langley or anything, are you?" Starr asked.

"Relax, no. But I am going to send Ms. Banks a very strong message, a very strong personal message. It should stop her from any more searching, but if it doesn't, well, she'll only have herself to blame for what will follow. Guys, I'd really like to leave it at that."

"That's fine by me. You okay with that?" Styles questioned.

"Okay with what?" Christman replied innocently.

"Thanks."

Styles asked, "J. C., get me those video bugs and a GPS transmitter. I'm going to place that in the clearing where I want you to land the copter if we need you. I was going to show you this afternoon, but that's all down the tubes. Make sure everybody has their comm sets on. Tomorrow is going to be a hell of a day, so get some rest. I won't be gone very long, a few hours at most. This is a get-in, get-out deal."

It was just after nine when Styles found himself back in the same place as the previous evening. He'd had no problem remembering where the security devices were hidden. He was just inside the tree line with the cabins to his right. He carefully made his way to a tree he'd spotted where the lights for the parking area would not cause a glare on the camera lens. He attached one of the video cameras, which featured both wide-angle and zoom capability. Looking hard at the rooftops, he saw guards positioned as previously. The one closest to him was paying more attention to the back of the cabins. *Odd.* The second guard was on the far end. He could see the glow of the cigarette he was smoking. Styles paused and carefully smelled the air. Despite the different fragrances that the woods offered, he could make out the odor of the tobacco. *They're upwind.* That was good not only for scent but noise, as well. Again he was dressed head to foot in full camo, including face paint on his face and hands. The BMW that he was certain Ellhad had left in the night before was parked in the third parking spot from his position. To its right sat a pickup truck and a four-wheel-drive dually pickup. *That will be the tow vehicle.* Only the cabin at the far end had lights on. He calculated his odds as very strong that he could make it to the truck to plant a transmitter on the large truck. He made his way along the tree line until he was at the most advantageous point of attack. He estimated he was eighty feet from the truck. One place, just about middistance, was going to be the most dangerous. It was the area that was bathed in the most light by the streetlamps. He got down and started to belly-crawl. He would advance a body length at a time and then pause and repeat the process. He went through the lighted area nonstop. A few seconds later, he found himself at the rear of the target. He crawled underneath and affixed the transmitter. This was a strong unit with a range of just over one hundred miles. *This will save Starr some hassle.*

Suddenly, a door opened, and Styles froze. The cabin up at the end with the lights on had an individual walking out of the door. He lit a cigarette and continued walking toward Styles, in front of the parked vehicles. A second man emerged and walked around the far end of the last cabin. *Fucking guard change.* The man on the roof to Styles's right moved off the platform and started down the ladder. The two engaged in a short conversation before the new arrival went back up the ladder. The second guard went into the cabin directly in front of Styles. Lights came on. *Shit.* Seconds later, the man who had been on the far end of the roof came walking toward Styles.

He entered the cabin just to Styles's left. Lights came on. Styles had no choice but to lie and wait under the truck. The front windows of both cabins did not have any curtains or blinds drawn, and light was pouring out. It was too risky for him to move. He waited. Within ten minutes, the lights in the cabin directly in front of him were turned off. *One down.* Unfortunately, the lights in the cabin to Styles's left remained on. Fifteen minutes went by, and nothing changed. Styles had not seen any movement from the cabin. He studied the area directly behind him. There was a large clump of bushes sixty feet away at his five o'clock. After waiting another five minutes, he decided to go for it. The ultimate destination was the main house to place surveillance cameras. Silent as a cat, he belly-crawled backward, five feet at a time. Still nothing changed. He kept going, finally reaching the shrubs. Now all he had was ten feet to the paved drive and the tree line ten feet past that, and he was on his way. *So far, so good.*

Undetected, he arrived at the main house. He secured the first camera, much more advanced than the ones he'd had the previous evening, capturing the front door, a second to capture the driveway out to the main road, and a third and a fourth to capture the front and sides of the house. Satisfied, he began the trip back to his Jeep. He was only fifteen feet back into the trees when the front door of the house opened. Styles saw a man he thought was Ryyaki Ali. The second man was unknown. They were speaking in Arabic. While not fluent, Styles had picked up enough to make most of the conversation out. The blood in his veins froze when he heard a word that translated to *assassination.*

He crawled back as close as he dared. The two men continued speaking quietly. He was not able to pick up much more of the conversation. One name was overheard: Nazir al-Hadid.

Six minutes later, the second man started walking toward the cabins, while the man Styles was sure to be Ryyaki Ali went back inside. Twenty seconds later, the lights in the stately mansion began to darken, and Styles was making his way behind the tree line, headed for his Jeep.

Less than two minutes later, the familiar odor of cigarette

smoke alerted Styles. Thankfully, there were many pine trees in these woods, which meant pine needles on the ground, making it easier to be quiet. He got a fix on the location from the wind direction and started scoping the area with his night goggles. It took him less than twenty seconds to locate the source. Another guard on a platform built into a tree. He was surprised. *How did I get through before and not see one of these?* Then he realized that he was at least two hundred feet to his right from where he'd come through before. After checking for the pressure plates, he'd become complacent, which was not like him. Mentally, he slapped himself on the back of his head. He studied the man carefully, coming to the conclusion that he was not wearing night-vision gear, at least not for the moment. He slowly eased off to his left, being careful to keep trees or shrubs between him and the man on the platform. In less than five minutes, he was comfortable he was out of any danger of the man spotting or hearing him. Then the lights came on.

Styles didn't know how, but he'd triggered something that caused lights that were secured to the very base of trees that illuminated upward, virtually lighting up the whole area. He heard men yelling. He was on the fringe of the area that was lit, so he did the unexpected: he retreated back toward the main house. With his silenced Beretta in hand, he walked as briskly as possible without sounding like a herd of deer. He zigzagged from large tree to large tree, constantly keeping aware of the direction voices were coming from. He was virtually surrounded. He could now make out voices coming up from the cabins. He weighed his options and decided on doing the unexpected. Rather than run away from them, he would advance directly at them. Shots rang out, but he heard no bullets whizzing through the trees near him. He continued his backward retreat. He froze and got down on the ground. Two guards were coming straight at him, not more than fifty feet away. He remained motionless. Suddenly, the area he was in lit up. The two guards had triggered what he now surmised was a battery-powered light system. If he stood up, he would be seen. *Shit!*

Frozen to the ground, the guards passed him by less than ten feet. As soon as they were thirty feet behind him, he stood up in a crouch and started to move. Suddenly, a searing pain shot through his right calf, followed by the loud crack of a gunshot. A guard on a tree platform had spotted him. Now he had no choice; he had to run. Continuing his zigzag pattern, he tried to keep trees between where he thought the gunshot had come from and himself. He had no intention of getting into a firefight at the moment. Escape was the only thing on his mind. Three more gunshots followed, and he heard the bullets crashing through the branches just above him. He kept going. His calf was burning like hell, but he wasn't having any difficulty in moving, so he guessed it was merely a flesh wound. On he went.

Styles was still making his way back to his Jeep when again he froze. Now that he was wearing his night-vision goggles as a precaution, the flare of a match lighting a cigarette up ahead in the trees was the equivalent of a strong flashlight being shown in his eyes. The bright mini-explosion calmed down, and he could see another guard perched approximately fifteen feet off the ground, his AK-47 held at the ready. This time he could determine it was a hunter's deer stand, an aluminum unit that could be easily transported and set up. *These guys were not here last night—has to be the toxin!* As before, he eased back and around this new threat. He skirted past on his highest mental alert. No doubt Ryyaki Ali had stationed security in the woods surrounding the property. The only question was how many? Silently, he continued his trek back to his Jeep. He did not run across any more sentries. The moon had come out from behind the clouds and was now shining quite brightly. Not quite full, it still lit the area up well enough that Styles comfortably discarded the night goggles. He reached the tree line and could see his Jeep less than a hundred feet to his left. Still cautious, he stayed just inside the woods until he was opposite his Jeep. He removed the small pack he was wearing that contained his gear. He walked up and opened the driver's door, intending on tossing the pack onto the passenger's seat. What he got was a gun barrel thrust in his face.

Styles put his hands out to his side and backed up two steps with the man dressed all in black following him, the gun barrel never wavering from his face. The two men didn't speak.

A second man came up from behind the Jeep. He appraised the man in front of him, dressed in full camo gear, including face paint, being held at gunpoint by his partner.

"Just who the fuck are you?"

Silence.

"I asked you a question."

Silence.

The second man nodded at the man holding the gun, who lashed out with his pistol and cracked Styles across the forehead. Styles flinched, but nothing more. Blood began running slowly down the right side of his face. Still he said nothing.

"Hard-ass, huh? Okay, I'll ask once more, and either you answer, or you lose a kneecap. Now who in the hell are you?"

Silence. Once again the second man nodded to the man holding the gun on Styles. The instant the gun started to move downward, Styles jerked to his right, reached out, and snatched the gun right out of the hand of the man holding it. He did not want the gun to go off. The gunshot would be as loud as a cannon in the still woods, and it was certain the guards in the woods would hear it. As the gun cleared the man's hand, Styles stepped up and punched the man viciously, directly in the throat, killing him. The second man had made a horrible mistake by not having a gun trained on Styles. As he was trying to draw his weapon, Styles delivered a hard palm strike to the man's chest, just below his heart, knocking all the breath out of him. Styles wanted him alive. The man fell to the ground gasping for air. Styles did a quick search and found some wire tie cuffs in his back pocket, and he secured the man's arms together by his hands behind his back. He quickly scanned the area and saw no sign of a vehicle. He went back to his Jeep, opened his small pack, and removed a roll of Gorilla tape. He ripped off an eight-inch piece, put the roll back, and walked back to his captive. He firmly placed the tape over the man's mouth, making it even harder for him to try to breathe.

"Relax. You'll live, for now."

He turned his attention to the dead man. Picking him up and slinging him over his shoulder, he walked into the woods opposite Eli's estate, about two hundred feet, and tossed him on the ground. As bright as the moon was, he had no difficulty in finding several branches and placed them over the body. If someone walked directly up on it, the corpse would be easy enough to see, but from twenty feet away, it would likely remain hidden.

Styles went back to his captive, who had now regained most of his breath. Styles could see the hatred in his eyes. Styles studied him. A man in his early thirties, excellent shape, and dressed in what would be considered a civilian black ops outfit, completely black. Styles picked him up and positioned him leaning against the driver's-side rear tire.

"Now I'm going to ask some questions, and you nod yes or no. Understand? If you refuse, it will not go well for you. I'll also tell you this. Cooperate and you live. That's straight. Otherwise, you join your friend. Now, are you CIA?" Searching the man had revealed no identification.

The man remained motionless, eyes spewing venom at Styles.

"I don't have time to waste. I think you're CIA. I can tell you we're on the same side. But I need to confirm. Last time, are you CIA?"

Still nothing.

Styles shook his head. "I gave you a chance. That's all I can do." Styles reached down and hoisted the man up onto his shoulder then started walking into the woods in the same direction he'd already gone. The man started squirming hard.

"Settle down; you're not going anywhere." He started making noises. Styles ignored him. After a short distance, Styles gently set him down. For a moment, his captive thought that just maybe he might live. Styles walked behind the man, grabbed a handful of his hair, yanked his head back and, with his knife, slit his throat from ear to ear. He wiped his knife on the back of the man's shirt. Blood was cascading down his shirt. He let the man fall forward. Once again, he tossed branches over the body and then turned and walked away without ever looking back.

Climbing into his Jeep, Styles began to slowly make his way back to the motel, while he was wiping the black camo paint off his face and hands. He started cruising parking lots of every business that was still open, mostly bars. He'd driven through four and still not found what he was searching for. He passed a couple of fast-food chains that were still open, but it would be too easy for him to be spotted in what he wanted to do. He kept looking. Finally, he found what he was looking for in the parking lot of a strip club: another green Jeep. He pulled into the far end and parked. Getting out, he paused for a moment at the back of his own ride. Then he headed straight for the second vehicle. Ninety seconds later, he returned to his own. Thirty seconds later, he was leaving the parking lot, with a different license plate on the rear. *Somebody's gonna have a real hard time soon!*

27.

T-Minus 21 Hours

Phillips gave the knock on J. C.'s door. Entering with a laptop in hand, she sat down at the table and opened it.

"This is going to be real time. Everything that comes through will go into a file. The feed should start in about two minutes."

"That was fast."

"When Backersley says jump, they don't question it."

Suddenly, the door burst open, and Styles walked in. "Anybody on guard here?"

"Well, you do have a key," offered Starr.

"How hard is it going to be for the CIA to get a key? Listen up. We've got a CIA hit team at the other end of the building, two floors up. They are hot on our ass. I had another run-in with them in the woods where I parked. They were waiting for me."

That got everyone's attention. "How the fuck?" Christman muttered, who woke up from the sofa when Phillips entered.

"My guess is they're watching Ali's place too. They spotted my Jeep and waited."

"What happened?" Starr asked suspiciously.

"Didn't end well."

"Jeez, Marv."

"I don't want to hear it, Starr. Besides having a gun stuck in my face, smacked with one, and getting shot, we've got a job to do, and until somebody proves me wrong, as far as I'm concerned, the CIA is basically made up of clusterfucks, not to mention they are operating illegally in this country." Looking at Phillips, he added, "Present company not included."

"*Shot?*" all three exclaimed.

"Yeah, think it's a flesh wound in my calf. Let me get my first-aid kit." He rummaged through one of his bags and returned to the table. "Sorry, Phillips, but I've got to take my jeans off."

"Let's see the wound," she replied.

Styles sat in his underwear and a T-shirt, and the others crowded around him. "Just what I thought: nothing but a good crease!" Styles exclaimed. "Starr, hand me that small yellow bag." Taking it, he tore open a corner and poured a tan powder all over the wound. "It's a coagulant; it'll stop the bleeding, though it's not too bad. Grab one of those large nonstick bandage pads and the tape."

"Here, let me," said Phillips. "I've done this before." Quickly, she dressed the wound. "There, that should work. We'll need to change it twice a day. It looked pretty clean."

"So what happened?" Starr demanded.

"They've increased security, added a battery-powered security light system in the damn woods. Place lit up like Vegas. Guard up in a tree stand got me. Worse part is they'll be on high alert." Then Styles recounted what had happened with the CIA agents.

Starr started to interject, but Styles interrupted him. "Starr, *quiet.* I've come across the CIA too many times, and you can count on them fucking something up in one way or another. That whole damned agency is egotistical, and we don't have time to be nice. We've got a synthetic toxin we need to stop before all fucking hell breaks loose, and I don't have any confidence in the CIA to deal with it. Besides, they're not even supposed to be here. *We've* got a job to do, and *we're* going to be the ones who do it. Got it? Things have changed, and everybody here had better get that through their heads. If we're going to do what President Williams has asked of us, then *we don't play nice.* I'm not saying we start killing at random, not at all. With the exception of my father, I don't trust anybody outside this room. I don't know if I ever will, but we have to all be on the exact same page, and that is we do anything to get the job done with respect to the one condition we work under. Either we throw ourselves totally into this, or we go home. Right here, right now, we make that decision, and it won't be brought up again. And no offense meant here, Starr, but you don't question what I do. We don't question Christman's flying skills, we don't question Phillips's ability on computers, and we don't question your usual common-sense voice of reason. You're right, Starr. I'm a killer, have been now for well over fifteen years. I don't particularly like it, I don't get off on it; it's a job I just happen to do well. It's a job that has to be done. If I can live with it, you have to be able to, as well. And you questioning me when I do is getting on my nerves. Here's the deal. I don't unless I have to. Tonight, I had to." There was no anger in Styles's voice, just respectful firmness.

"Marv, I apologize. I did not mean to question your actions, and I'm sorry if it appeared that I did, and I feel the same way about this group," Starr replied.

Phillips spoke. "I'm in this, all the way." Without even looking at him, she added, "And I know J. C. is, as well, and the both of you."

Starr walked up to Styles and looked him straight in the eyes. "I'm sorry. Of all the people I've ever known, in and out of the military, there is absolutely no one I respect more than you. It will never happen again."

"If anybody dares to say 'group hug,' I'll shoot them," Styles replied with just a hint of a grin. "What have you got on the laptop?" he inquired, joining Phillips at the table. The other two brought chairs around and sat, as well.

"The CIA drone. It's just starting the live feed. All the orange blotches we see will be people. At least the ones that are larger than a quarter inch. Pinpoints are small animals. A rectangular one will likely be a deer. Anything bigger than a half inch is not living but a heat-generating object. Okay, everybody count."

No one spoke for eight minutes, the time it took for the drone to make three passes over and around the entire estate.

"Ten," said Starr.

"I got twelve," piped up Christman.

"Styles?" quizzed Phillips.

"Ten people, three deer, four smaller animals, and something else that's generating heat."

"What were those two dim, yellowy objects at the beginning?" Christman inquired.

"Bodies," stated Styles flatly. "Looks like ten guards tonight, definitely upped them from last night. Means the agent is on the premises. The cameras and transmitters are all in place. J. C., I'm betting that Ellhad is going to rent another truck. There is a dually on the premises that I got a bug on, but it doesn't make sense to use their own vehicle. With a decent-size tow-behind camper, he'll want a three-quarter ton at minimum, if he's got half a brain."

"Why use the truck and camper?" asked Christman.

"It will allow him to blend in with all the other people traveling over the holiday weekend."

"I'll be on station to intercept and follow him by seven thirty. If he does get another truck, I'll get the bug on it. I've got a question, though," said Christman. "If we're sure that toxin is on his property, why not just go get it now?"

"Same deal. Too much chance if we go busting in there now that somehow they'll have some kind of contingency plan in place to get it out of there. If we go after Ellhad when he's by himself, then there's no backup," Styles explained.

"But isn't that taking a bit of a chance?" continued Christman.

"It's all a chance, J. C., every bit of it. This mission has two equal parts in my mind. Once that toxin has left Ali's estate, I go in and eliminate everyone. Part two is stopping the agent. There's one other thing. Tonight, I overheard a conversation between who I'm sure was Ali and an unknown, but I think it was Ellhad. I'm not fluent in Arabic, but I did hear the word *assassination* and the name Nazir al-Hadid. Far as I'm concerned, that definitely ties him to both events."

Christman whistled low under his breath, something everyone was accustomed to when breaking news was brought into the conversation. "No shit," he muttered.

"Phillips, could you tell if there was any CIA reaction to Starr's little journey?" Styles inquired.

"Oh yeah," she answered. "They had a team waiting for him at the airport. You were right, him going down there and just fueling up really got them wondering. I was laughing listening to them."

"Listening?"

"Oh yeah, I hacked into the cell towers. It was a breeze."

"One more thing," Styles said. "This group is a democracy. Decisions about who the group goes after, how we do it, and decisions that involve the group are just that: a group decision. The fact that we all have a specific role to play and at times we help each other as required and how we perform our specific roles is obviously up to us. I just wanted to clarify that. Okay, everybody get some sleep. We do a final analysis at six thirty sharp."

❋ ❋ ❋

At 6:28 a.m., Styles opened the door, and Phillips joined the three guys in the motel room they were bunked in. Starr was in possession of the GPS receiver tracking the vehicles Styles had targeted. It displayed the truck still parked at Ali's compound. Styles was leading the assembly.

"Phillips, you'll be with me. Dress in full camo, including face concealment. Bring your armament, including suppressors, and your interrogation kit. Starr, you're going to have to supplant J. C. on the surveillance of Ellhad, since he needs to be in the copter. Be sure to have a full complement of gear with you. I want you to take up the position I marked on the map. That's the only way away from Ali's property that Ellhad will take. We'll keep in touch via our comm units. J. C., I already planted the GPS transmitter in the small field you'll use as the landing zone. Phillips, we have to be careful in avoiding the CIA or FBI going in. We don't want to get into a firefight with them."

"Do you want me to go ahead and land or just circle around?"

"Circle. When you file your flight plan, mention that you're on a photography assignment. You'll only land if we call for an extract."

"How far do you want me to stay back?" asked Starr.

"No more than a mile. You need to be close enough so that if he swaps for a rental, you can be sure to see what he's in. That's when you'll have to get a transmitter on that truck. There's a strong possibility that he won't stop. In that case, don't under any circumstances lose track of him. The one shot you should have is when he goes to pick up that camper rental. I didn't see one on the property. Anybody got any questions?"

All three shook their heads.

"All right. Starr, you're in the silver sedan. Phillips, you and I are in the Yukon. J. C. takes the Jeep, but remember, it has a stolen tag on it. You'll be leaving it at the airport, so wherever you park, be sure to back in. Phillips, we leave in thirty. Let's go."

Twenty-eight minutes later, Styles and Phillips were the only two at the motel. They were walking toward the dark brown Yukon they would be driving. Styles had loaded his gear earlier. Phillips was carrying hers. Styles opened the back passenger door, and Phillips threw her equipment across the backseat. Styles looked around carefully; no one appeared to be paying any attention to them.

Styles got behind the wheel, and they headed out.

"Any words of advice?" asked Phillips.

"Keep a three-sixty awareness and a close eye on your compass once I give you the signal. Hold it as I showed you; it'll detect a pressure plate. Now listen to me. Darlene, this is not about prisoners. This is about killing terrorists. When you shoot someone, and you will, be sure they are down. If in doubt, put one in their head. This is important: how far out are you accurate with your AR?"

"Four hundred yards with the sniper scope."

"How about with your EOTech?"

"Deadly to seventy-five, accurate to a hundred. That's what's mounted now."

"Good enough for me. We're going to get in close and hole up.

After Ellhad leaves with the camper, we'll clear the cabins and then the main house. There will be at least two guards on the roof of each cabin on the end, possibly four. There are also sentries in deer stands in the woods. We take them as we come across them. We have to assume they have radios, but they probably won't use them on a regular check-in. When we start in, be sure you have your subsonic rounds loaded. Once we get ready to start the clear, we'll change over to green-tips," he continued, referencing the armor-piercing rounds. "Last thing: anybody in there is considered a hostile. Anybody. You okay with that?"

"I'm okay with all of it," she replied sternly.

28.

CIA Team Leader Marty Larrow was awakened by his cell phone ringing at four in the morning. Groping for it, he answered, "Larrow here."

He was informed that the two agents charged with keeping an eye on Ryyaki Ali's estate had not checked in and could not be raised by either cell phone or radio. The agents had been located by obtaining a fix via their cell phones. Both were dead. One had had his throat cut, while the other had severe bruising and swelling in the front of his throat, suggesting the man had suffered severe blunt force trauma. Some type of strike.

"Does it look as though Ali was responsible?"

"No way to know that at this time, sir," asserted Special Agent Ryan Back, who had discovered the bodies. "Latell informed us that they had missed two checks, and we could not contact them. She was able to locate one of the cell phones; we went to the location and made the discovery. The agent who suffered the knife wound, that would be something a Taliban fighter would do, but the blow to the throat, that's not their style. We should know more after the autopsies." The call ended, and Larrow threw his cell phone across his motel room.

He had to call Backersley. He was dreading it. Plus, he had no phone. He was set up in a room four down from Latell and her intelligence unit. He stormed down. He knocked hard, and the door opened immediately. One of Latell's assistants ushered him in.

"Sir, we've been expecting you."

"Set me up on a secure line with Backersley," he ordered. Forty-five seconds later, he was handed a satellite phone. "Please hold for Director Backersley," he was told.

Two minutes elapsed before Backersley picked up. "Backersley here."

"Sir, Larrow here." He proceeded to give his boss a rundown on current events.

"Agent Larrow, allow me to ask you a question. If your agents were watching Ali, would it not make reasonable sense to presume that Ali probably discovered them?"

Larrow was pissed. "Obviously, I have thought of that, sir, but they were not on Ali's property. They were under strict orders not to enter his compound for any reason. The manner in which they were killed raises some doubt."

"How were they killed?"

"One had his throat cut—that would be Ali's style—but the other one suffered a severe blow to his throat. That isn't."

"I would operate on the presumption that Ali was indeed involved; however, keep your mind open to other scenarios."

"Sir, these were two well-trained agents. It would have taken a highly skilled team to take them out."

"Larrow, you have lost three agents in less than a day. We are the ones who are supposed to take people out, not having people taken out. You continue to run logistics on the surveillance of Ryyaki Ali, but any intel on the three agents goes directly to Rob Randall. Understood?"

"Sir, with all due respect, Randall has a bad habit of shooting first, and he won't bother about collateral damage."

"*Three agents down, Larrow, three! Don't you dare lecture me about collateral damage! If you have a problem with that, get your ass back here!*" Backersley yelled loudly.

"Understood, sir," Larrow acknowledged reluctantly.

"Good."

Randall turned loose. What next?

"Ryyaki Ali could employ any number of teams that have skill. The man is wealthy beyond most people's comprehension. I want three-hour updates." Larrow's phone went dead.

Larrow turned to Toni Latell, who had entered the room. "Toni, when was their last check?"

"At eleven thirty, sir. They reported a dark green or black four-door Jeep Wrangler parked in an obscure location next to Ryyaki Ali's property. We have the plate number. We're running it now."

Larrow cringed inside. "And why did you wait until now?"

"Sir, we just discovered the problem fifteen minutes ago."

"Agent Latell, the problem started one second after they didn't check in."

"Yes, sir. If it were any other agents, I would have informed you immediately, but Jackson and Hutch have a history of not keeping to schedule. I just didn't see a problem at that moment. My fault."

"I am well aware of Jackson's peculiarities. I can't say I don't agree with your particular assessment. It gets worse. All intel with regard to the downed agents goes directly to Randall."

"Randall, sir? Are you sure about that?"

"Straight from the director, Latell. We don't have any choice."

"If you say so, sir. Better get the women and kids off the streets."

"No shit. I need a cell phone."

Latell went to a small case, retrieved one of the standard-issue phones, and handed it to him. "Broke another one, sir?"

Larrow just glared at her and returned to his room.

T-Minus 7 Hours

At seven thirty that Sunday morning, President Lamar, along with his chief of staff, was convening a breakfast meeting with the directors of his different security agencies. Absent was Coverley Merritt of the Department of the Presidential Office.

"Good morning, gentlemen. Please read me in where we stand."

Elliott Ragar and Bernard Backersley took turns in bringing the president up to speed on everything that had transpired since their last meeting.

"You mean to tell me you've lost three agents?" The president bristled.

"Yes, sir. I have turned that aspect of the operation over to the lead on our response team."

"What aspect of what operation? Backersley, what did you not understand about turning over all your information to Sanderson and Ragar and withdrawing? Hell, man, you are the CIA; it is completely illegal for you to be operating inside our borders." The president was visibly angry.

"Sir, I lost three of my agents before we had the chance to withdraw. With all due respect, I am *not* turning that aspect over to anybody. We take care of our own. We will operate with all due caution, but the CIA will continue to conduct the investigation into the deaths of three CIA agents. If you find that disagreeable, you may ask for my resignation." Backersley was not going to give ground on this point.

The president was quiet for a few moments. "All right, you continue that, and only that. If I find out that you have stepped outside those boundaries, you will be fired. If this blows up in my face, you will be fired. If my coffee gets cold, you will be fired. Is there anything about what I just said that you don't understand?"

"No, sir. Not at all."

Elliott Ragar, director of the NSA, spoke up. "Sir, I understand how Director Backersley feels. I would feel the same." There were a few looks of surprise on some of the faces in attendance.

Matt Sanderson, director of the FBI, asked a question. "Sir, I have noticed the absence of Merritt in the last meetings and was wondering why."

"I have decided that the DPO that President Williams initiated is unnecessary. Under my administration, heads of agencies are going to be more cooperative with each other and me, or they will be gone, thus eliminating the need. Merritt will be reassigned. He's a good man. I won't make it official until we have eliminated this biological threat. I don't want distractions."

"Yes, sir, and if I may say so, I believe it's a good call."

"You may not. Worry about your own agency; I'll worry about all of them."

❈   ❈   ❈

Toni Latell nearly jumped out of her chair when the door to the motel room that she and her assistant, Jay Sling, were using as a temporary HQ burst in. Latell spun around in her chair ready to chastise whoever couldn't even bother to knock but froze in place. Special Agent Robert Randall was walking toward her. He was the leader of one of the CIA's most respected, and definitely most feared, response teams. Randall was a man who instilled fear. At six feet and five inches tall, weighing 260 pounds, he made most men nervous. He kept his head shaved smooth except for a black mustache and goatee-style beard. Dark eyebrows and dark brown eyes completed the package. His left eye twitched occasionally, the everlasting effects of a concussion grenade. He was an avid weight lifter and looked it. The personality of a snapping turtle with a sore ass was the icing on the cake.

"You know this has pretty much been turned over to me, right?"

"I know that Agent Larrow is in charge of logistics and that any action taken shall be coordinated through you."

"Fuck Larrow. We should've gone into that facility already. We're wasting time."

"We don't know if Ali is in possession of the toxin yet. That is what we're waiting on."

"Why should that be a problem? We go in, take the place over, and wait. What's so damned hard about that?"

"Agent Randall," she replied, standing her ground. "That is a question that needs to be taken up with at least Agent Larrow or Langley. That is not my call."

"Langley told me I was in charge."

"Langley told me that you were both in charge of separate operations of this action. I can get whomever you might want to speak with if you need clarification."

"Latell, I don't work on clarification. Where is Larrow?"

"I'm sorry, but I'm not his personal secretary or babysitter. Why don't you try using your cell phone and call him?"

"Latell, don't think I won't shove a cell phone up your ass just because you're a female. All I want from you is information. Is that understood?"

"No, it's not. I take my orders from Larrow, who is my immediate superior. I pass on to you what he tells me to. You are not in my chain of command. I know that most people are scared shitless of you; I don't even blame them. But if you give me problems, ultimately you will answer to someone who is not scared of you, so go fuck yourself."

In response, Randall leaned over and grabbed her computer monitor and sent it flying across the room. "Next time you decide to give me shit, that'll be you." He stormed out of the room.

Jay Sling exclaimed, "Are you out of your mind? That psycho has killed more men than some army platoons!"

"He's an ass." But she couldn't stop her voice from shaking.

J. C. Christman was walking out of Air Rentals. He had chartered a helicopter for seventy-two hours, citing a high-paying photography assignment. The rental transaction went smoothly after Christman showed his pilot's license with multiple endorsements, including rotorcraft. He was assured that his Jeep would be secure, and he backed it into the concrete building that was located at the far end of Portland International Airport. The chopper was a newer model, could comfortably seat four besides himself, and had storage for the "photography" gear. He had told the owner that he had some errands to run and would be back for the copter in a couple of hours. In reality, he was going to pick up gear from the DPO jet.

Ninety minutes later, he returned and pulled the Jeep up tight to the chopper. He loaded the equipment he'd retrieved and stowed it securely. Lastly, he covered everything with a black tarp. He returned the Jeep to its original parking space and then walked back to the copter. After going through his preflight inspection, he climbed into the pilot's seat and started the blades whirling.

Starr was driving, seeking a good spot to pull in and wait. He spotted a strip mall on the right. Besides all the little chain stores one usually finds in such a place, there was a Burger King at the end. *Might as well get some food.* He pulled up to the drive-through and ordered five egg-and-cheese breakfast sandwiches on biscuits. These he could eat cold as well as hot, giving him something to nibble on during the day since he didn't know when he would be stopping again. He had brought along several bottles of water, so drinks were not a problem. After receiving his order, he found a parking spot one row back from the road, close to the exit, allowing him a quick exit when the time came. There was a row of neglected bushes planted next to the road, which would provide further cover even though he was not worried about being spotted. Ellhad would have no idea that he was even there, much less what he was driving. Now parked and in position and watching the GPS tracker, he had seen the vehicle he was monitoring move slightly. He zoomed in and was able to determine it had moved to the main house and parked. The road wasn't too busy, and Styles had provided him with a reasonable description of the pickup truck he would be tailing. Now he just had to wait.

Styles and Phillips had pulled into a Home Depot. Phillips had pulled up Google Earth and zoomed down on Ryyaki Ali's estate. With a few clicks, the image was amazing. You could easily see individuals on the property.

"Do a perimeter search. That is where we might see some friendlies."

"Gotcha."

Styles watched as Phillips performed her magic on her laptop. The connection between the two reminded him strongly of himself and his sniper rifle. Synergy.

"I've got a vehicle that's partially hidden just off the property. I don't see any individuals." She turned the screen so he could see for himself.

"Show me the position on an overlay of the entire property."

Phillips complied. "Is this what you want?"

"Yeah. Looks like they're about two hundred yards south of where I went in. That's too close. We're going to go in ninety degrees from them, here," he said, pointing toward the electronic map. "That allows a good distance between us, just about a mile."

"Won't they have the place surrounded?"

"No. They're just watching the outskirts. If they're that close, I'm surprised they got past the guards up in the tree stands. That's pretty smart."

"They might have run a recon with infrared over them like we did. Even though they can't do that from a satellite, they can certainly do that with a drone."

"Maybe." Styles started the Yukon and pulled into traffic, while Phillips fired up her laptop that received the video feeds from the cameras Styles planted.

"On second thought," Styles advised, "keep the subsonic rounds loaded. We might be better off keeping noise to a minimum with those agents so close."

"How's the leg?" she asked.

"Little sore; it's no concern."

29.

T-Minus 6 Hours

President Lamar had called Coverley Merritt into the Oval Office. "Have a seat, Coverley." Merritt sat down across the desk from the president. "I'm going to make some changes; some of them involve you. I'm not convinced that this DPO is really necessary. Under my administration, the heads of agencies are going to work together, or they'll be looking for new jobs. Therefore, I'm going to eliminate this. You're a good man, and I don't want to lose you—or worse, waste you—so I'm going to have you assist Elliott Ragar of the NSA. I want to get through this biological problem before I announce it; we don't need any distractions. I just wanted to give you a heads-up. I'd like you to keep this under wraps until I make it official. If you have some extraordinary people under you, I'd like you to make a list and submit it to me. Good people are hard to find. Be sure that loyalty weighs in any decisions you might suggest. For now, it will be business as normal; just be aware that change is coming. Do you have any questions?"

"No questions, sir. However, I'd like permission to speak freely."

"Go on." Just then, the president held his hand up to stop Merritt as a knock on the door came and coffee was delivered. The assistant set one cup in front of the president and the second one in front of Merritt. Once the president's assistant had left the room, closing the door behind him, Lamar motioned for Merritt to continue.

"I'm not making comparisons here, understand. Your predecessor found the different directors quite often did not play well together. This new department he created eliminated much of the friction. I applaud your expectations, but quite honestly, sir, I believe you will find that particular expectation much harder than one might think."

"This is not a frivolous decision, Coverley. However, for me, I believe it is the correct one."

"Whatever you say, sir, I serve at the pleasure of the president."

"Good. I believe you will enjoy your position at the NSA. I'll be in touch, and keep me up to date as you find necessary. Thank you, Coverley. I do appreciate your support."

"Yes, sir." Merritt left, nodding toward the president.

Elliott Ragar, Matt Sanderson, and Charles Rockford had decided to meet privately. They had arranged to convene at a restaurant a short distance outside Washington. They had requested a table in the far corner. While there were a few men also dressed in suits, most were in casual wear.

Ragar spoke. "As we all know, Backersley lost three agents yesterday and last night."

Both Rockford and Sanderson nodded.

"He is supposed to turn over anything he finds to us. Either of you received anything?"

"Not a thing," answered Rockford.

"I haven't heard from him," replied Sanderson. "His ego is going to toast him one of these days."

"We'll be lucky if it doesn't toast all of us," snapped Ragar.

Sanderson added, "My people tell me that he has an intelligence unit there, as well as a response team. It's believed that Robert Randall is leading the response team."

"Christ, isn't that the same SOB that caused all that shit in Italy two years ago?" questioned Ragar.

"Yeah. He's good at his job but can't see past his own ass. He doesn't care who gets caught in any crossfire. If he's out there, and Backersley turns him loose, there'll be hell to pay."

❈ ❈ ❈

Starr's attention picked up. The little dot representing Ellhad's truck was on the move.

"We've got movement on the truck," he stated over his comm set.

"Okay, Starr, he's all yours. Don't screw this up," asserted Styles.

"You do your job, sonny boy, and let me do mine."

"Keep us posted."

"Roger that."

Phillips interposed, "Confirmation on the truck's location."

"You got anything else going on?" queried Styles.

"All other cameras show quiet. Hold on. The truck is still moving."

"Starr, Phillips says the truck is moving."

"I can see that. I got a good idea. Don't call me; I'll call you."

"Don't get so touchy." Styles grinned as he spoke.

"Tell him that Ellhad is about ten minutes from him," offered Phillips.

"Phillips says he's about ten minutes out from you."

"How does Phillips know where I am? Never mind. I retract the question."

"You're finally learning," Phillips responded after donning her own comm set.

Styles called out, "J. C., you got your ears on?"

"Loud and clear. I just finished the preflight on the chopper. All the gear is loaded up. I did not touch your favorite toy."

"No reason to; I won't need it here, at least not at this location. We may grab it. I don't know yet."

"I'm going to take this bird over to a small uncontrolled airport that's only about twenty miles from you. That's a good staging place for me. I can be on-site in under ten minutes if need be. Just tell me when you want me airborne."

"Roger that, J. C."

"I've got the truck in sight. I'll check back in," interjected Starr.

"Roger that, Starr. Do not let him spot you."

"He won't."

Styles found a spot where he wanted to park the Yukon. It was in the middle of a large cluster of shrubs that also had a monster maple tree with branches hanging directly overhead. It was a good hiding spot from both the ground and the air.

"I'll be right back. Get your gear ready." He made a quick ten-minute sweep of the area and came back satisfied no one was nearby. He saw Phillips just tucking her ponytail up into a camo watch cap, pulling it down to the top of her ears and farther down the back of her neck.

Surveying her, he said, "Good job. Now let me paint you." He applied a combination of green and brown paint to her face, neck, ears, and hands. Finished, he stepped back and nodded. "You'll be invisible from twenty feet away in the woods." Next he applied the paint to himself. Finally, he grabbed his own gear. Phillips noticed he had three throwing knives. "One last thing," Styles said. "Hold out your fingers." Doing so, Styles applied Nu Skin to her fingertips, then his own. "This will eliminate fingerprints."

"Better than gloves."

"Oh yeah. Are you ready?"

"Absolutely."

"Okay, be sure you have your comm in place. Stay ten feet behind me and off to my right. When I stop, you stop. When I move, you move. Don't use the comm set unless I do. We'll use basic hand signals. Every minute we'll pause, and you use your smartphone for a camera view. We don't want to walk into anything. You good?"

"Yeah. Thanks for the shot at this."

Styles turned and stared at her hard. "If you weren't ready, you wouldn't be here."

She nodded.

❈   ❈   ❈

Phillips's heart was racing. She was ten feet to Styles's right when he motioned for her to stop and signaled her to look up and to her right. She got down on one knee and scanned hard. Then she saw what he'd seen: a guard in a tree platform. She saw Styles motion with a slashing gesture across his throat. She knew what that meant. She very carefully and quietly repositioned herself next to the base of a medium-size tree. She used a low branch to rest her AR-15 on. She quietly clicked the safety off. She turned on the EOTech scope. Looking through it, she placed the holographic red spot on the bridge of the guard's nose. She breathed in once, twice, and when the air was out of her lungs, she gently squeezed the trigger. To her ears, the action was loud, and she instantly was afraid she'd been heard. She saw the guard thrown backward out of the tree stand, never attempting to break his fall. He hit with a thud. She froze. Then she remembered to breathe again. She looked over at Styles. He nodded and then motioned for them to move on. He signaled one of three, meaning two more guards to go. Forward they moved. They came upon the two up in the trees, with Phillips removing one more, and Styles the second.

They were just behind the tree line observing the cabin on their end. He motioned for her to take out the guard on the roof closest to them while he zeroed in on the second at the other end of the small complex. She moved off slightly to the right for a better sight line. She took up her position, lowered her rifle, and nodded that she was ready. Styles motioned back, *In three.*

Both took aim, and three seconds later, two rifles spat out two barely audible rounds that penetrated one guard in the center of his forehead, while the second entered just in front of an ear. The action of the weapons reloading was the only noise actually heard. The two men crumpled silently.

Styles nodded approvingly at Phillips and directed her to start at the first cabin while he took the second. He had decided that each taking a cabin would reduce the time factor, with the added benefit of demonstrating to Phillips his faith in her. They advanced on the complex. Taking care, they reached the first two doors and simultaneously entered. Styles's was empty, but he heard a slight thud next door. Ten seconds later, he was back outside and watched Phillips exit. She nodded. Slowly they made their way to the next two cabins. There were men in each, one in Phillips's and two in Styles's. In three seconds, those men were down, and as before, a quick search of the bathroom and bedroom revealed the cabins were clear.

Back outside, they made their way to the fifth cabin. Several voices could be heard inside. Styles motioned that he would go in first, with Phillips right behind. They entered as virtually one and found four men sitting around the kitchen table playing cards. They looked up and with surprise on their faces were all shot in the middle of their heads. The remaining cabins were empty. Checking the back, they regrouped as they heard voices coming from the front. They were talking excitedly.

"Sounds like reinforcements," whispered Styles.

"Yeah. The loudest one is throwing a fit about not seeing the guards on the roof."

"Let's go."

They quickly made their way back around one end of the cabins and came face-to-face with two guards heading for the ladder that led to the roof. The two groups saw each other at the same instant. Styles was faster. From his hip, he shot both men in the chest. He heard Phillips shoot twice and saw both men's heads jerk hard.

They scurried to the front corner and looked around carefully. One man was close to the other end of the cabins, while the second man was just entering one.

"I'll take the far guy; you watch that door," Styles directed.

Styles took aim and shot the far guard right between the shoulder blades. He put two more rounds in him to be sure. He simultaneously heard a screen door open, and Phillips's AR spat twice, sending that guard bouncing off the doorjamb and falling back inside.

"Make sure he's dead," Styles instructed.

As Phillips headed for the cabin door, Styles took up position in front of a truck. No one else appeared.

Rejoining him, Phillips confirmed he was down.

"That clears this. We'll hit the roof and prop the guards in position. Then we secure the house. Remember, you hold up outside and keep watch. Don't come in until I signal you. If anyone should approach, warn me; I don't want a body lying outside if we can help it."

Phillips nodded. Ten minutes later after skirting the trees, they were at the main house. Phillips veered off, found a good spot, and set up to monitor everything. Once she was out of sight, Styles looked and saw two more guards outside of the house. Both had arms at the ready. Five feet behind the tree line, he took aim and center punched each man in the middle of his forehead. Quickly, he crossed the drive and dragged each man around to the side of the house, depositing the bodies behind shrubbery. Then he carefully approached the front door. He hugged the wall, hoping it would keep him out of sight from the security cameras. He got to the door undetected. He turned the knob and found it to be unlocked, which surprised him. He eased it opened and looked in. No one in sight, and no sounds could be heard. He opened it slightly farther, slipped inside, and silently closed it behind him. He immediately crouched down and surveyed the room. It was a massive entrance hallway decorated in lavish silk hanging from the ceilings and opulent Middle Eastern furnishings that continued into the massive living room.

Staying tight against the wall, he slowly made his way through the massive chamber. He could now vaguely hear what sounded like two voices coming through one of the several doorways that led from the rear of the room. He scanned for any cameras and saw none. He made his way toward the sounds. The door to the room that the conversation was being held was partially open, allowing Styles to observe it was a conference room. Two men were inside and appeared to be disagreeing about something. Styles listened for a few moments and discerned that it was about the decadent behavior of Westerners. Inwardly, he shook his head. He'd already decided that Ryyaki Ali was not one of them. He opened the door slightly with his silenced gun barrel and shot both men dead center in their chests, hoping that would keep them in their chairs. One did, but one fell. Styles quickly entered the conference room and hid behind the door. Thirty seconds passed, yet no one else approached.

Cautiously, he continued his search, closing the door behind him so the two bodies would not easily be seen by anyone just walking past. Three minutes later, he was convinced no one else was on the main floor. Quickly, he ascended the stairs and checked out the second floor, which consisted of bedrooms and bathrooms and two sitting rooms. All were empty. Just as quickly, he descended the stairs and searched the main floor again. No one. *This is odd.* Only one way left to go—down. He found the stairway leading below and started down. A shadow alerted him, and he ducked just as one of Ali's guards had attempted to jump him from behind. A knife blade had missed him by inches. Whirling, Styles saw the man in front of him was not wearing any shoes. *No wonder he was so damn quiet.* The man was looking at Styles with a maniacal grin. He tried two front thrusts with the blade at Styles's chest and neck. Styles blocked both attempts with his AR. The guard changed grips on his knife, and in the instant he brought his arm back to try a sweep thrust, Styles brought the butt of his rifle straight out and caught the man in the throat. He dropped the knife and immediately clutched his throat. Styles knew the man was done; he'd crushed the larynx, leaving the man powerless to breathe. Slowly, he slumped to the floor against the wall.

With rifle at the ready, Styles did two 360-degree sweeps. He was expecting men to come pouring out like ants, yet no one came. *Weird.*

He could faintly hear voices, so he crouched and continued downward. Reaching the bottom of the staircase, he followed the sounds, which led him to a large office. Three men were inside, one large man sitting behind a huge desk, and two others sitting on a sofa just to the right of the desk. Immediately, he knew who Ryyaki Ali was. He paused, listening. They were openly toasting the death of the American president. Styles could feel his blood beginning to boil. He opened the door and shot both men on the sofa directly in the center of their foreheads. He advanced on Ali with the barrel of his gun staring him in the eyes. No words were spoken. Styles walked around the desk while Ali turned to face him. There was no fear in Ali's eyes; if anything, there was contempt. Styles looked down at the three-hundred-pound man sitting in front of him and then hit him with the butt of his rifle in the forehead, stunning him but not seriously injuring him. He clicked his comm set to alert Phillips.

"Come inside; go through the main room and down the hall to the stairs. Go down. Meet me in the office."

"Affirmative."

T-Minus 5.5 Hours

Robert Randall, the CIA response team leader, stormed into the motel room his men were using as their staging area.

He looked around at his squad and said, "Gear up, boys. We're heading out. Bring the AK-47s."

Second in command Pete Locker asked, "We got the go-ahead?"

"Yeah, I just gave it to you."

He looked at the other two men and stated, "You heard the man. We leave in ten." Turning to Randall, he asked, "We hooking up with Jonesy?" He was referring to the man already on-site in the woods outside the suspected terrorist's property.

"He's waiting for us."

Six minutes later, the four men—each carrying an extra-large black duffel bag—climbed into a black Chevrolet Suburban. With Locker driving, Randall issued instructions.

"Jonesy has reconned the area and given me the layout. We're going to hit the cabins first and then the main house. No prisoners. I expect to find that bioagent at the house, but if it's not there, we beat where it is and how we find it out of whoever. We don't have time to waste here, so we go in fast and hard."

No one else said anything.

Half an hour later, they met up with Jonesy. "You boys ready for a walk in the woods?" he asked jokingly. He was the only one in the group who had what might be considered a sense of humor. It drove Randall nuts, but Jonesy was as good a recon man as he'd seen.

"Of course; that's why we brought a picnic," Randall snarled at him.

"Quite thoughtful. Okay, time to play follow the leader. We're going to circle around and come in on the far side. That's the safest way in."

"Is it the fastest?" Randall demanded.

"No, but it's the quietest and least guarded. It's only about fifteen minutes longer, and I've got the route well cleared. It's quiet, pine needles. Jeez, boss, calm down; you'll get to shoot somebody pretty quick."

"You don't get us there in time, it'll be you."

"We'll get there quicker if you stop bitching."

Randall took a step toward him, but Jonesy was already leading the way into the woods. Five figures, all dressed in black, disappeared into the trees.

30.

Starr had no problem picking up Rijah Ellhad, noticing as he pulled in behind him that he had an attractive woman accompanying him. Starr drifted back approximately half a mile, where he could still keep the vehicle in sight.

Ten minutes later, Ellhad pulled into an RV rental site. The woman stayed in the truck while Ellhad went inside the office.

Starr decided now was his chance. He pulled up his silver sedan over near another rental RV unit. He got out and looked it over. Then with a GPS transmitter in his hand, he walked toward the office. He approached the rear of Ellhad's rental unit from the driver's side. He easily planted the tracker up under the wheel well of the rented RV unit and then walked on toward the office. He opened the door, and seeing the staff member busy with Ellhad, he excused himself and said he would return.

Ten minutes later, Ellhad reemerged and returned to his truck. After a short discussion with his companion, Ellhad pulled his truck over next to a larger GMC dually truck, already hooked to a nice tow-behind RV. They got out, and Ellhad unlocked the dually. Returning to his truck, he started to transfer his gear from one truck to the other. Several suitcases, three large duffel bags, and a couple of boxes were taken directly into the RV. Finally, Starr, who had parked across the street, saw Ellhad lock his own truck, climb into the cab of the dually, and pull back out onto the road. Starr again fell in behind him. He knew that he would be harder to spot with Ellhad towing the large camper.

Ellhad turned to Sahleea and said, "We are on our way to Lake Mead. It was a surprise that Ryyaki Ali let us go alone."

"Yes, I am surprised, as well, but I'm not complaining."

She took Ellhad's hand and placed it on her leg, high under her skirt, giving him a playful smile. "Do you know what I am thinking?"

"Yes, but you must continue to think. We have to get to Lake Mead before dark."

Pouting, she said, "You always seem to be in a hurry."

He glanced over at her. "Not when I am with you."

"No, not then. That makes me happy. How long will it take for us to get there?"

"To where we are going, maybe ten hours," he lied.

"That is a long ride, Rijah."

"You will get a longer ride once we arrive."

"Promise?"

"Promise."

T-Minus 5 Hours

Phillips walked into the office of Ryyaki Ali to find him bound to a chair. She noticed a large red welt in the middle of his forehead. She paid little attention to the two bodies on the couch.

She approached Styles, who was sitting on the edge of Ali's desk.

"We ready to go?" he asked.

"Yeah. Let me plug this into his computer." She inserted a flash drive and portable hard drive. Without a word, she withdrew and opened a small leather case. Inside were four vials and a syringe.

Styles leaned down close to Ali and stared him right in his eyes. "I'm going to ask you some questions, and you're going to answer them. If this goes smoothly, you will only die. If it doesn't, I'll castrate your worthless ass, and you won't have any fun with your virgins. Understand?" Without waiting for a reply, he nodded at Phillips.

She took two of the vials from the case and put equal amounts of each into the syringe. Without a word, she raised the sleeve of Ali's long robe, found a vein, and inserted the needle. Within seconds, Ali's eyes began to glaze slightly. "Give him a few more seconds."

"Where is the bioagent you tested in Alaska?" Styles asked. He received only a mumble in return. Styles slapped his cheeks firmly. "Think. Where is that bioagent? Where are you going to release it?"

Once again, only a mumble emerged from Ali.

"Hold up a second," said Phillips. She retrieved the same two vials and added a smaller portion to the syringe. Then she pulled a third from the bag. "This is Adrenalin. It'll wake him up, whether he wants to or not." For the second time, she inserted the needle into Ali's vein. Ali's eyes immediately changed. The glazed look was gone and was replaced by a look of fearful confusion. "He should be more cooperative now."

"Where is the toxin? Where are you going to place it?"

Fighting, Ali answered, "Ell … Ellhad." He was fighting hard against the drugs.

Styles slapped him again. "*Where are you placing that bioagent? I won't ask you again.*" Styles allowed Ali to focus on the knife he was holding in front of his eyes.

As hard as he tried, Ali could not stop from answering. "Meeaad. La Meeed."

"Lake Mead!" Phillips exclaimed.

Styles continued, "Were you responsible for the killing of the president?"

Ali visibly squirmed, fighting even harder against the drugs.

Styles pressed harder. "*Did you kill the president?*"

"Al-Hadid. Nazir al-Hadid," Ali stammered.

"Is he Ami al-Hadid's brother?"

Ali only barely nodded.

Purely on instinct, Styles whirled the man around in his chair and furiously drove the blade of his knife into the left eye of Ryyaki Ali, twisting it upward. He did it forgetting Phillips was only five feet away. "Rot in hell, you son of a bitch!" Styles snarled at the man. He turned and saw Phillips looking at him. "Sorry you saw that."

"Why?" she answered. "I only wish I did it. The brother of the man *we* killed murdered our president."

Styles noticed she'd said *we*.

Phillips walked up to Styles and stated, "This is a war, isn't it?"

"Yes, it is." He clicked his comm set. "Target is Lake Mead; we don't know exactly where. Starr, you still got him?"

"Sure do."

"Do not lose him. He's definitely got the agent."

"Don't worry. He's not getting away."

Five figures, dressed in black, assembled just behind the tree line at the center of the small complex of cabins. They carefully observed their targets with binoculars for two minutes.

Locker whispered to the team leader, Randall, "I only see two guards on the roof," receiving a nod in return. Without being told, he screwed a retrofitted silencer on the end of his AK-47 and began making his way inside the tree line to a point where he had a clear shot at both guards. Two barely audible sounds were heard, and Randall saw both guards slump.

Within two minutes, his team converged on the cabins from each end. It took little time to ascertain all occupants were dead. The squad convened in the front of the small complex.

"Boss, everybody's dead," Locker informed Randall.

"I can fucking see that. So who the hell killed them? We're the only team here."

"Apparently not." Locker regretted the words as soon as they left his mouth. The look he received from Randall scared him. "Sorry."

"Let's get to the main house. Double-time at the tree line." Randall led his team at a fast pace toward the house, the rear man constantly keeping watch to the rear. All five were armed with Russian AK-47 full assault rifles, taken off the Taliban, which fired the distinctive 7.62×39-millimeter round. This was Randall's strategy whenever he operated within the boundaries of the United States. Any brass casings that might be found at a scene of a firefight would draw suspicion toward radical Islamists, he reasoned. They also carried Glock nine-millimeter semiautomatic pistols strapped to their sides, which were becoming widely accepted around the world.

Phillips was just about to step out the office door when she whistled for Styles.

"We've got company coming up from the cabins. My guess would be the CIA response team." She watched her electronic notebook that was receiving the security camera signals Styles had placed.

"How far out?"

"Two minutes, three at the most. I need ninety seconds for his computer to download on my portable hard drive. I need that flash drive left in place."

"I'll get it. Get to your observation point. Now."

Phillips took off at a run without even looking at him.

Styles whirled back to Ali's desk and waited for the red light to turn green. It seemed to take forever. The instant the color changed, the portable hard drive was his, and he was sprinting back from the lower level to the second floor and crawling out onto a balcony. He stayed low. He didn't want to have to fire on the CIA team if it could be avoided. He knew the basic CIA clearing technique would leave one man outside, figuring he would have two minutes, maybe three, before his own position would become precarious. The idea was to get away without being detected, which was not going to be easy. Depending on where the one agent set up outside, he was hoping to swing down and take the man out without killing him. After all, he'd already killed three, and though he had little use for them, he really wasn't trying to start a war with the CIA. The time the response team would take in clearing the remaining parts of the house should allow Phillips and him to get away. That was the plan, anyway. He clicked his comm set. "J. C., get your ass in the air to the extraction point. We've got company."

"On-site in twelve minutes."

"Roger."

Twenty-five seconds later, peering through a potted plant, Styles saw four figures approach. *They know what they're doing.* He saw that the first man was extremely large and immediately knew who it would be. Silently, the men approached the house, and he heard the front door open. He heard his comm set click, and then Phillips's voice came over quietly. "Minus one at the house."

Styles thought for a second. He clicked back at Phillips and said low, "Watch your six." *So much for that idea.* He was in a dilemma, and he knew it. Phillips came first. He clicked her again. "Climb a tree and stay rock steady, but be ready for anything." Receiving a double click in return meant she'd understood. Styles secured his AR-15 firmly against his back and got ready. This was not going to be fancy. Silently, he eased out and looked below. Sure enough, there was the agent four feet to his right. Styles eased over the top railing and lowered himself by grabbing the bottom rail, now hanging well over the edge of the massive porch, moving three feet to his left hand over hand, and then dropping the six feet to the ground, striking the agent at the base of his neck and rendering him unconscious. *So far, so good.* He rolled and quickly stood, unslinging his rifle in the process.

The noise of the front door opening sounded like a cannon shot in Styles's ears, and after dropping his AR, he was instantly moving toward it. Robert Randall walked through, coming face-to-face with Styles. His expression was of shock seeing his own agent on the ground and a man dressed in full camo moving in a blur toward him. Randall had shouldered his assault rifle, not expecting to find trouble in the yard, a mistake caused by arrogance.

"What the—" was all he managed to get out before what felt like a wrecking ball explode into his chest as Styles launched a vicious attack. Randall was kicked so hard that he bounced back off the wall next to the door and right back toward Styles. Most men would have collapsed under the assault, but Randall managed to stay on his feet. He was hurt, but not down. He immediately tried to circle Styles. His ego would not allow him to go for his weapons, a critical mistake. Randall took a step toward Styles and promptly received a brutal kick to the side of his knee. Styles, inwardly, couldn't help but be impressed. Randall threw a monster haymaker at Styles's head, which Styles narrowly avoided. A second punch by Randall, a body shot, was blocked by Styles, who then turned into his man and drove his elbow squarely into Randall's face, breaking his nose and the orbital bone in his left eye socket. This seemed to only enrage him more. He swung wildly at Styles's head, catching him in the shoulder enough to send Styles sideways two steps.

Strong.

Randall paused for a second to catch his breath, and that's when Styles moved to finish the fight. He started with another kick to the already injured knee and then instantly sprang into a front jump kick, catching Randall full under the jaw and causing him to bite his own tongue in half. Howling with rage, Randall still did not go down.

Fucking guy's a bull. Styles then drove two brutal punches into the man's broken nose, blinding him with his own tears. Finally, after a crushing punch to the bridge of the man's nose, he crumpled to the ground. Styles turned to dash across the road only to see a figure in black leveling an assault rifle at him. Just as he started to hurl himself to the ground in a desperate attempt to avoid the bullets he knew were about to spit at him, he saw the man's knee explode, bone shards and blood tearing out of his pants as the man fell to the ground screaming in agony. In three seconds, Styles, after grabbing his AR, was across the road and into the trees. Fifteen feet past the tree line, he could hear all hell breaking loose behind him. Six strides later, Phillips was at his side. He could see the grim look on her face. He only nodded at her as they both disappeared into the woods, bullets whistling about them.

President Lamar told Irving Vickers, "I want to split the responsibility of finding this toxin and the assassins into two groups. I'm convinced that everybody right now is trying to do too much. What are your thoughts?"

Vickers paused before answering, "I agree, but we need to have the right bunch on the right topic."

"I agree. Bring Laura Green in, and have her help you decide. She would have a better feel for whose strengths would better fit where than we probably do, and she wants to help."

"I would have suggested that myself, sir. I'll call her immediately."

As Vickers left the Oval Office, President Lamar was concerned. He couldn't help but feel that somehow the two issues at hand were connected, though no one had yet been able to connect any dots. He called A. J., his secretary. "Get me Coverley Merritt on the phone," he said. Two minutes later, his phone rang. "Merritt? Have you heard of any possible connection between the assassination of President Williams and this toxic agent?"

"Nothing solid, sir, but there are rumblings among some that there very well could be. Personally, I find it too coincidental."

"I feel likewise. Get with the directors, and be sure that they understand the importance that any correlation between the two must be found."

"I'm sure they already know that, sir, but I will remind them."

"Good."

President Lamar sat at his desk feeling a bit overwhelmed. He knew he had to make a televised address to the nation, but he wasn't sure exactly what to say. Everything he kept thinking sounded redundant. He also couldn't even hint at the bio issue. He called Irving Vickers.

"Get a speech prepared to address the nation on President Williams for me. I want to see a draft in four hours."

"Already been working on it, sir."

"Irving, what would I do without you?"

J. C. Christman was hurtling his rented helicopter to the designated landing spot as fast as it would go. He knew that thirty seconds could make the difference between a successful extraction of Styles and Phillips or a disaster. He keyed his comm. "One minute out."

"Roger that," came Styles's reply.

Fifty seconds later, the bird flared in for an emergency landing, with the skids just touching the ground, when the door flew open with Phillips and Styles bursting through.

"*Go!*" yelled Styles.

Christman had the copter back in the air before the shock absorbers in the landing gear had even rebounded. He was flying ten feet above the treetops with the throttle to the stop.

Phillips had made her way to the rear seat and was buckling in while Styles was strapping into the copilot's seat.

"Where to?" hollered Christman.

"Find Starr." Looking back at Phillips, Styles wasn't the least bit surprised to see she already had two laptops open.

She looked up at Styles. "Ali's security footage is uploading into this second laptop. It wasn't wired into his hard drive that we downloaded."

"How long will it take?"

"Depends on how much info we upload. I'm trying to get all I can. Could be ten minutes; could be an hour."

"Any chance that CIA team could screw that up?"

"No. They'll bring in an FBI tech forensics team, and that'll take a bit. Besides, if they try to remove that flash drive I stuck in, it will self-destruct and take out the computer's hard drive. When the upload is complete, it's all going to be history, anyway. We don't need the CIA getting in our way."

Styles nodded. "Where was the second computer for the security system? I didn't see it."

"On a shelf. You were busy interrogating Ali. I figured that's what it was, so I stuck an upload stick in it. Saved me the time of having to hack it."

"You mean that flash drive-looking thing?"

"Yeah."

Bernard Backersley was in his office glued to his large flat-screen monitor. He was watching events unfold in real time via a helmet cam of the raid on Ryyaki Ali's compound. Myra Banks, head of his cyber unit, was with him. They didn't speak once the assault began. When the suspected terrorists had been found dead, words were finally exchanged.

"What the hell is going on?" Backersley snapped to Banks and the agent wearing the helmet cam.

"We're not sure, sir. We're clearing the area."

"Looks like somebody beat us there," observed Banks, which drew a hard look from Backersley.

"Could Sanderson have sent in a team?" he asked, referencing the director of the FBI.

"Doubtful. I would have heard about it."

"You sure?"

"Absolutely. We've been monitoring all FBI communications," assured Myra Banks. "No mention of any tactical advance."

"Then who the hell killed those guys?"

"Bernie, I don't know any more than you."

Backersley hit his desk in frustration. "I don't like anybody interfering in something we've got our hands on."

Realizing his mood, she did not remind him of the fact that their action was completely illegal.

"Director," a voice was heard over the speaker. "We're coming up on the main house. So far, all hostiles found are down."

"Any idea of who's been there?"

"No, sir. I'll not be in vocal contact while we clear the house."

"Understood."

Not taking his eyes off the flat screen, Backersley asked, "Have you found out any more on Darlene Phillips?"

"No. We've confirmed she spends a lot of time away from home, as you already know, but I can't establish where. I've investigated the DPO inside out. I can dig so far, and then it's like hitting a wall."

Backersley turned and looked at her. "What do you mean?"

"Like I told you, by all appearances, it's strictly an intelligence-gathering operation, but as I've said before, I think there is more to it."

"What have you learned from Merritt?"

"Not a damned thing. Bernie, if there is another aspect of the DPO, I'm not sure that even he's aware of it. I've hacked his e-mail, his in-house communiqués, phone calls, and absolutely nothing comes up. I mean nothing."

"How could something be going on in his own agency and he not know of it?"

"You tell me. You're the king of working around the rules."

"And your point is?"

"There isn't one. President Williams set that up. It's possible, and quite highly probable, that if there is a tactical or operational aspect within the DPO, President Williams might have been running that himself. To me, that would make perfect sense."

Backersley nodded. "I see what you mean. Good catch."

Banks nodded at the screen, and they both began paying close attention as the main house of Ali's compound came into view.

31.

T-Minus 3 Hours

Starr was about half a mile behind Rijah Ellhad's rented RV. They were traveling toward Lake Mead at a leisurely pace. Starr's earpiece crackled.

"I've got our cargo, and we are headed your way," Christman informed him.

"Roger that. We're on I-84 eastbound and probably headed to State Route 93. That goes straight into Vegas and Lake Mead. We're only going about sixty-five, and traffic is pretty heavy."

Styles broke in, "You're tracking device working okay?"

"Affirmative."

"Good. We're going to find some place to rendezvous so Phillips can join you. It'll be easier to work her computers from your rig than this copter."

"Copy. Let me know where you want me to pull off."

"We'll get ahead of you and scout out some truck stop where we can land, and get back with you."

"Roger that. You guys get what you need?"

"We think so. Confirmed some suspicions and got more intel. Phillips will bring you up to speed. We should close on you within the hour."

"Let me know."

Starr had unwittingly crept closer to the rig he was following and had just begun to drop back when he saw the turn signal activate. Ellhad was leaving the interstate and pulling into a large fuel stop with several retail stores within. Ellhad bypassed the fuel pumps and headed straight to a large Hess retail store. He parked in the specified parking for large vehicles, and with the woman accompanying him, he walked inside.

Starr pulled over in front of a Wendy's. *Pit stop. Might as well go too.* He hit the can quickly, washed his hands, and then grabbed two burgers and a large water to go. He'd eaten all but one of his breakfast sandwiches out of boredom. He was back in his Yukon and had finished one sandwich when he saw Ellhad and the woman reappear. They were immediately under way again.

"Hell, I never realized how damned boring following somebody could be," Starr muttered to himself. "This is getting on my nerves."

"Stop your whining," Styles said over the headset, laughing.

"Screw you," Starr snapped back, forgetting that everyone could hear what he'd just said.

"Maybe we could all sing songs," Christman suggested, bringing more laughter.

"One more crack and I shut off the headset."

"Don't be so touchy," joined Phillips.

"I'm not touchy, I'm bored. We're driving sixty, maybe sixty-five, and it's taking forever to get anywhere."

"Enjoy it while you can," directed Styles. "The shit'll hit the fan soon enough."

"Guess you're right."

Christman interrupted, "I gotta call in the flight plan change."

While Christman was talking to flight control, Styles turned in his seat and asked Phillips, "You find anything?"

"Yeah. One of the guys on the CIA team is wearing a helmet cam and providing a live feed back to Langley, probably Backersley."

"Did they get us on camera?" Styles questioned with concern.

"No, I don't think so. I'm following four different programs at once here, but it appears that when we were engaged outside, the cameraman was in the house. Backersley found out about six minutes after we hit them. From the conversation I've heard, they don't have any clue who we are."

Christman broke in. "We're all cleared for Lake Mead. We've got the copter for as long as we need it."

Phillips interjected, "Backersley just found out about his guys we took out. He is not happy."

Bernard Backersley slammed the top of his desk. "What the hell happened?" He saw two of his agents on the ground. One was screaming with pain, while the other was unconscious.

"Don't know, sir," the agent in the field reported. "We've got one man shot through the knee, from the rear, and Team Leader Randall is out cold. No wounds visible, other than he looks like he got the living hell beat out of him."

"Hell beat out of him? Randall is a fucking animal! Who could do that?" screamed Backersley.

"Don't know, sir. We heard one shot and came out of the house. This is what we found. We are already in pursuit through the woods. One of our agents got a glimpse of someone running away. No contact as of yet."

"Keep me updated constantly." Backersley shut off the monitor. Turning to Myra Banks, he fumed, "Find out who the fuck was in ahead of us. I want answers *now*!"

T-Minus 2 Hours

After pulling ahead and scouting the interstate ahead, Christman, via the comm set, said to Starr, "Hey, about ten miles ahead of you, there is an off-ramp. Get off and take a right. About a mile ahead, there is a tree line with a large field next to the road. We can land there without drawing too much attention. Phillips and Styles are going to join you while I return and get the jet. Then I'll figure out how join you when I get back."

"Roger that, J. C."

"We'll be on the ground in ten minutes."

Fourteen minutes later, Starr came wheeling in, finding Styles and Phillips standing out by the road. Four large duffel bags were with them. Styles turned and signaled Christman, who immediately took off. Starr pulled up next to them, immediately opened the trunk, and jumped out and helped load the duffel bags. Then Styles jumped into the front passenger seat, with Phillips in the back. Before Styles got his door closed and seat belt latched, Phillips had three laptops open with fingers flying.

Starr spun the sedan around and sped back toward the interstate.

"I'm glad you got a big sedan; I was worried the gear wouldn't fit. How far ahead of us is he?" Styles asked. Calculating in his mind, Starr answered, "Maybe four miles, five at the most."

"Don't get pulled over for speeding. I don't want to explain the duffel bags."

"Under control, Marv."

Turning back to Phillips, Styles asked, "You onto anything?"

"Nothing threatening. Langley is trying to find out from the FAA who took off from the woods we just left. They don't appear to be able to identify the aircraft; J. C. was doing some of his transponder magic. Must've worked, whatever it was."

"Can they track J. C. by radar?"

"Not sure."

Styles radioed Christman. "Can they track the copter by radar?"

"Usually, yes, but not this time. I'll land at a couple of small airports, change the transponder ID number, and take off. They won't be able to tell who's who."

"What about the towers?" Styles quizzed.

"No problem. I'm landing at uncontrolled airports. I'll take off in the manner to mimic a small airplane. No way to track us."

"Good thinking, J. C."

Looking at Starr, he noticed he held a steady seventy miles per hour. "How fast did you say Ellhad was going?"

"'Bout sixty-five."

Styles thought quickly. "So it's going to take us an hour to catch up?"

"Yeah. I can go faster if you want."

"I'd like to, but I don't want to chance getting pulled over. Long as you're comfortable that we're not going to lose him, you handle it."

Starr looked over at Styles and grinned. "I'm comfy."

A chuckle could be heard from the backseat.

Bernard Backersley was sitting in the Roosevelt Room, straining to maintain his poker face, with the other major directors waiting on President Herbert Lamar. When he entered, all stood, received a nod, and sat when motioned to do so. The president looked visibly tired.

"Short and sweet, gentlemen! Where do we stand? Info on President Williams first."

Everyone looked around, and NSA Director Elliott Ragar stood. "We've ID'd the body pulled from Curtis Bay, at least I think that's what it's called. We're running every available search on him to see who he's connected with. We have some leads, but nothing that can be confirmed yet. Hopefully, within the next couple of hours. We've had satellite video and photos downloaded on all boat traffic within a forty-mile radius, double the distance we figure those scooters could have achieved. There are half a dozen that are now under constant surveillance."

"Exactly what does that mean?"

"Should someone step out onto the deck and into view of our cameras, we can get a clear enough picture to easily run them through facial recognition. Every face on those yachts is being run. If anybody on any of those vessels is in the system, we'll find them."

President Lamar nodded his approval. "Where are we on this bioagent?"

Matt Sanderson of the FBI stood. "First, I'd like to thank

Elliott for all his help on this. We've tracked it to Seattle. A team is converging on the suspected site as we speak. I expect to hear from them in a half hour or less."

CIA Director Bernard Backersley struggled to remain calm. He knew what Sanderson's team was going to find. He was also fully aware of what the FBI would not find—any trace of the CIA's little visit. He almost jumped in his chair when President Lamar addressed him.

"Backersley, have you been able to establish anything on an overseas connection?"

"To which issue do you refer, sir?"

"To any of the issues at hand," the president snapped.

"We are following several paths, sir, but like Matt, nothing that can be confirmed at this time. I will notify you the minute any confirmation occurs."

"See that you do," the president replied icily. "Anyone else?"

No one spoke.

"This is unacceptable. I want answers, confirmed answers. Now go do your damned jobs." He stormed out of the room.

John Clayton, chairman of the Joint Chiefs, muttered, "Took us over ten years to find Bin Laden. You'd think he'd know this isn't particularly easy."

32.

T-Minus 1 Hour

Asobe Sydar stood on the bridge of his yacht, hands on his hips. Looking over the bow, the west shore of the Chesapeake Bay was visible. The water was shimmering in the bright afternoon sunlight. The trees beyond created a dense green backdrop. A few homes and magnificent estates were visible perched among the sea of green leaves.

Nazir al-Hadid, standing a few feet away, looked very uncomfortable.

Sydar turned to his captain and ordered, "Find us an appropriate anchorage for two days."

Al-Hadid, in near panic, asked, "Are you sure about that? I mean, is this wise? The Americans will be watching every boat."

"Exactly, Nazir. The Americans will not believe that any vessel involved would come back. It will demonstrate that we have nothing to hide."

Al-Hadid was not convinced. "What if they board your vessel again?"

"Then they will find everything in perfect order. There is nothing that can possibly tie us to anything questionable. We have the same number of people on board, and your photo is now affixed to all the legal paperwork. We are just people on holiday."

"I pray you are correct, Asobe."

❋ ❋ ❋

Christman was hopping his way back to Portland to retrieve the jet. He had no direct knowledge but knew that somewhere he was driving someone nuts with his constant changing of the rental helicopter's transponder numbers. *Go ahead, boys, try to track me.* He was hoping to be back in Las Vegas by ten at night. He would check in with the group when he was on the trip back to check for instructions.

It was approaching five in the evening when J. C. finally made it back to the waiting jet. He arrived transmitting the original transponder numbers. *Something tells me I'd better be damned careful.* As soon as he landed, he dashed into the nearest hangar. There were two workmen at the far end servicing a prop plane, an older Bonanza V-Tail, an airplane considered far ahead of its time. They paid him no attention. He spotted a maintenance uniform indicating Graham's Flight Service and slipped it over his own clothes. He also grabbed a shabby-looking baseball cap with a large Seattle Seahawks embroidered patch in front. He pulled it down in front, but not so much as to be conspicuous. He made a roundabout approach to the hangar housing his group's jet aircraft. As he'd feared, he could make out a black Ford Crown Victoria parked off to the side. *There they are.* He held up out of sight to think. He was certain that if whoever in the car associated him with the jet, he'd undoubtedly be detained. He had to plan an escape. After several minutes, a grin came over his face. "When in Rome," he said aloud.

He retrieved his cell phone and with directory assistance called airport security.

"There is a dark Ford Crown Vic parked next to the tan-colored hangar just down from Graham's. I've seen someone get out twice, take some kind of package from the trunk, and walk away with it. He comes back in ten or fifteen minutes without the package. Just seems very strange, so I thought I'd better call it in."

"Yes, sir, absolutely. We'll check it out immediately, and thank you. What's your name?"

"Langley," he replied, chuckling to himself. "Rob Langley."

Within sixty seconds, five vehicles came screaming up and surrounded the Crown Vic. The airport security personnel poured out with guns drawn and ordered the occupants out of the car. In the confusion, Christman made his way unnoticed inside the hangar and boarded the jet. In five minutes, he'd filed a flight plan to Houston, Texas, while the ground crew was wheeling his plane out onto the tarmac. Looking over, he saw two men screaming at the airport security officers. He saw three take down the men and cuff them and then throw them into the backseat of separate vehicles. As he watched the security teams drive away with haste, he fired up the powerful jet engines. In his best Arnold imitation, he said aloud, "I won't be back." The last thing he did was ditch his cell phone after taking it apart and wiping everything for prints.

❈   ❈   ❈

CIA Team Leader Marty Larrow was sitting in his motel room on the phone with Bernard Backersley.

"Honest, Director, if I hadn't seen him with my own eyes, I wouldn't have believed it. Randall is really beat up."

"How bad? How long will he be out of action?"

"I have no idea on time. His injuries that I know of are a badly broken knee, shattered nose and orbital bone, and a broken jaw that apparently was caused by some kind of uppercut or something because he bit his own tongue in half. Surgeons were able to reattach it, but it's going to take rehab before he can speak decently. He also has a badly bruised sternum, partially collapsed lung, and two cracked ribs. He's a fucking mess. It looks like he got run over by a train."

"Have you been able to talk to him at all?"

"Sir, the man *can't* talk. He bit off his own tongue. They are keeping him heavily sedated, which is probably as much for their own safety as his. Apparently, he was a rather difficult patient when he woke up. He cracked his ribs when he fell trying to leave. That's when they knocked him out."

"So you have nothing."

"Not quite. The agent that was shot gave a description of Randall's attacker, but it wasn't much. He was dressed in full camo, including face paint. Stevenson thought the guy was about six feet tall, guessed his weight around two hundred pounds. He saw the tail end of the fight when he came out of the woods and said he'd never seen anyone move like this guy; he just owned Randall. He was getting ready to take the guy out when someone put a round through his kneecap from behind. That put him out of action. By the time the rest of the team got out of the house, the guy had disappeared into the woods. One agent said they thought they got a glimpse of him but was unable to provide any specifics. We got everybody out of there immediately. The FBI is on the scene now, including a forensics team. They're taking the place apart. We got a couple of shots off, but it's doubtful if we hit anything. We used AK-47s, so that should help displace blame."

Backersley was silent. "Larrow, this is a complete clusterfuck, but I can't fault you. Get your team, and get the hell out of there as quickly as possible, and try not to be noticed."

"On it, sir. I apologize for not having more defined information for you."

"So am I."

Starr, Styles, and Phillips were closing the distance on Rijah Ellhad.

Phillips had opened up a Google Earth program, zoomed in on the route they were traveling, and was able to spot two state troopers hidden in medians, using their radar to try to pick up speeders. Both times, Starr had slowed just a bit.

Styles could feel the tension starting to build. He knew what he had to do but just wasn't sure how he was going to do it. In his mind, securing the package and eliminating Ellhad had equal priority.

"You have a plan in mind?" Starr asked Styles.

"Sort of. Figure we'd follow him into whatever RV park he's headed for. You'll go in and reserve us a spot. Without being obvious, try to determine where he'll be located. If you can get close to him, that'd be good. From there, we're going to have to wing it. I wish we'd had time to lease an RV ourselves, but there just wasn't time."

"Maybe I can help with that," Phillips spoke up.

"How?"

"I'll see if I can lease us one and have it delivered. By the time it gets to the park, hopefully we'll just be able to point and have them set it up."

"Won't that look strange?" inquired Starr.

"How do I know? I'm just trying to come up with a plan," replied Phillips.

"I've got one better. Lease a tow vehicle along with the camper. That way, it'll stay and it might not look so weird—that is, if it would, anyway. Better be safe, though," Styles offered.

"Makes sense to me," agreed Phillips. "I'll get on it. By the way, Backersley knows what you did to Randall. Only description of you, which was given by the guy I shot in the knee, is that you were dressed out in camo, but he was pretty much spot on with your height and weight."

"I'm not worried."

"Knew you wouldn't be, and one other thing. I guess the CIA just barely got their asses outta there before the FBI joined the party. They don't know what the hell is up. I almost feel sorry for them. Matt Sanderson is going to have to do a lot of explaining to the new guy. They have a full forensics team on-site now."

"What about Ali's computer?"

"No need to worry. It's fried. I'm getting started on that intel now. Wish we had time to grab something to eat. I'm hungry."

Starr tossed a sack into the backseat. "There's a breakfast sandwich in there I picked up this morning. That should help until we get some time. I don't want to take the time to stop right now."

"That'll do, thanks." She ripped the bag open and devoured the sandwich. "Not bad, even cold."

Styles noticed that Starr was getting a grim look on his face. "You all right?"

"Yeah, just want this to come out okay."

"It will."

Ten miles behind Starr and company, two Middle Eastern men were traveling in a dark blue BMW, with windows tinted as dark as state law would allow, making it next to impossible to see the vehicle's occupants except through the windshield.

Imad al-Bin looked at his companion, another refugee from the Iraqi Republican Guard. "Assad, how far in front of us is Ellhad?"

"I'm not sure. I don't understand these damn things," Assad Bassir snarled, referring to a GPS tracker. "I think ten, maybe twelve miles."

The two men had been sent by Ryyaki Ali as hidden backup for Rijah Ellhad. They were under strict orders not to reveal themselves to Ellhad unless he ran into trouble. Ali respected Ellhad and did not want to insult him.

"Use the scale on the bottom of the screen if you are having problems," al-Bin suggested.

"That's what I'm doing," the big Iraqi snapped.

"Calm down, Assad. We are only babysitters."

"I do not like babysitting. I like action."

"We have our job. We will do that job."

"As you say."

Ten miles behind Starr and company, two Middle Eastern men were

"Rijah, come play with me."

"Sahleea, we will be at the campground in two hours. Can you not wait?"

"I want to play now. If you want to drive, fine; I will play alone right here in this truck." She started to slip her shorts down.

"Sahleea, someone may see you. We cannot draw attention to ourselves."

"Then you'd better find somewhere to pull over so we can go back in the camper. I want to play."

Relenting, he said, "There is a rest stop ahead. I will pull over." He wouldn't admit it, but just the sight of her slipping her shorts down had gotten his hormones raging, plus the prospect of having to kill her was tormenting him. He was not on any exact timetable, so he saw no reason not to indulge her one last time—for himself as well. Ten minutes later, he turned his turn signal on and pulled into the exit ramp for the rest area. A combination of cars, trucks, and large tractor-trailer rigs were in the parking area, which was surprisingly large. He spotted an area away from the other vehicles and found a spot. He hadn't shut the truck off before Sahleea was out the door. With a large grin on his own face, he followed her and unlocked the door of the camper, and both were instantly inside, tearing at each other's clothing.

"Hey, guys, looks like our friends have stopped. They're about twelve miles up the road. According to my map overlay, it appears they are in a rest stop," Phillips stated. "Gotta love Google Earth."

Styles asked, "Why did they do that? Shit, what if they're arming some type of device? Starr, get us there as fast as possible!"

Nine minutes later, the silver sedan was pulling into the rest area, and they spotted the camper they'd been following off to one side.

"Pull over between those two cars," he directed. He handed out three pairs of binoculars. "Starr, watch out for any cops. Phillips, check the rig with me." Ninety seconds went by with no one speaking. A chuckle came from Styles.

"What's so damned funny?" grumbled Starr.

"We clear?" asked Styles.

"Far as I can tell," answered Starr.

"Check the camper; look carefully."

"I don't see anything!" exclaimed Phillips.

"Look close, guys."

Finally, Phillips laughed. "I see what you mean. He's arming something, but it's not a weapon."

"What in the hell are you two talking about?" fumed Starr.

"They're doing the horizontal bop. The camper is rocking a bit. Looks like someone couldn't wait until the campground."

"You mean this guy is trying to poison Lake Mead, and he pulls off to snag some?" Starr asked incredulously.

"Looks that way. Starr, drive around and come up behind them. Shut the engine off and coast; I don't want to take a chance on them hearing us," instructed Styles as he reached behind his back, removing his suppressed Beretta. "We're taking these bastards right here."

"Nothing like catching them with their pants down, no pun intended," deadpanned Starr, who was already beginning to pull back out into the parking area. "Starr, after I jump out, give me about sixty seconds and then pull up alongside the camper, door side, as though we're supposed to be meeting them. Join me inside."

Forty-five seconds later, Starr cut the engine on the car and coasted up to within twenty feet of the back of the camper. Styles immediately dove out the passenger-door window, rolled, and then was immediately at the door of the camper. Up close, the large camper's rocking was even more evident, and muffled sounds of pleasure could be heard. He turned the doorknob and was surprised it was unlocked. A trap? He was certain it wasn't. Just two people who couldn't wait to get their hands on each other.

Cautiously, he opened the door slightly. The sounds were coming from the bedroom in the rear of the camper. The sounds were uninterrupted, and Styles slipped inside, the residue of the camo paint still on him. The door to the sleeping quarters was open, and Styles could clearly see the bottom half of a man's and woman's legs, entwined. Silently, he moved through the small living area and kitchen, down the hall, and past the surprisingly large bathroom on the right. It was opposite the bathroom wall where the head of the bed was located. The woman was positioning herself atop the man, sideways on the bed. Standing in the open doorway, each was oblivious of Styles's presence. Styles fired two suppressed rounds inches away from the man's ears. Both of them froze. *"Don't move."*

33.

"Very slowly get off him," Styles directed the young woman straddled across Rijah Ellhad.

"Do as he says," snarled Ellhad.

With great deliberation, the woman moved into the left back corner of the bed, tucked her knees to her chest with her arms folded, and buried her head in an attempt to cover herself.

"Who the fuck are you?" growled Ellhad.

Styles merely put his finger to his lips, motioning for Ellhad to be silent, rage pouring from Ellhad's eyes.

Moments later, the door opened, and Starr and Phillips entered, joining Styles in the bedroom.

"Did you bring your little satchel?" Styles asked Phillips.

"Yes."

Right then, Ellhad tried to leap from the bed, but Styles cracked him across his forehead with the butt of his pistol, sending Ellhad backward against the headboard.

"Do that again, and I shoot you in both shoulders," Styles said quite calmly, his voice chilling the room. The girl hadn't stirred. "Secure his hands to the bed frame," Styles instructed Starr while aiming the gun barrel directly at Ellhad's forehead.

Starr pulled two large plastic wire ties, and in seconds, the man was bound securely.

Styles nodded at Phillips, who inserted a needle into the man's neck and pushed the plunger on the syringe. Within half a minute, his eyes started to glaze slightly.

"Everything outside is clear. What about her?" Starr queried as he'd gone back on watch detail.

"This is war," Phillips asserted. In one motion, she retrieved her own silenced pistol she'd had in the middle of her back, aimed, and fired a single round down through the woman's head. The hollow-point bullet had more than done its job, blowing a large hole out of the base of the woman's neck. Her body slammed against the wall and then crumpled to the floor. Ellhad didn't even take notice. "He's ready; try questioning him," Phillips stated.

Styles nodded at Starr, who turned and without a word went back to the living area to keep watch from there.

Phillips looked at Styles. "You said yourself this is war. You are the one who made the decision to expand my role by placing me in the field. That trust brings responsibility, and I need you to know that I can handle that. I also know that although you would have done that without hesitation, you wouldn't have liked shooting an unarmed woman. I just did what we both knew had to be done. I didn't like or not like doing it. It's just part of the job."

Styles just nodded.

"Marv, might want to check this out!" hollered Starr from the living area.

"Watch him," Styles instructed Phillips, and then he looked in the direction Starr was pointing. Under the built-in table, strapped to its framework, was a wooden crate.

"I'd say that is what we are looking for!" exclaimed Starr. "Should we open it?"

"Not yet," determined Styles. "Let's question Ellhad first."

Returning to the bedroom, Styles leaned over him. He could see that Ellhad was having difficulty focusing on him.

"Let's start with an easy question. Is that wooden crate under the table the synthetic agent you were planning on releasing?"

Ellhad just mumbled in return.

Styles gave him a firm slap across his cheek. "Listen. Is that the agent?"

Still mumbling, he managed a slight nod, indicating yes.

"Is it safe to open?"

"Doo ... Doon't ... near water. Di ... soves."

"Is this *all* there is?"

Ellhad mumbled, "Ye ... yessss ..."

"Do you know anything about the death of the president?"

Ellhad attempted to struggle against the chemicals but lost. "Na, no."

Styles straightened up. "We're finished here. Go join Starr."

"I'd just as soon stay if that's all right with you."

"Suit yourself." He took out his silenced Beretta and shot Ellhad twice in the heart. He proceeded to remove a Benchmade Infidel, a razor-edged switchblade, from his pocket and thumbed the button upward, allowing the blade to spring straight out from its handle. He carved *terrorist* deeply into Ellhad's forehead, with little blood flowing due to his heart not beating. "Starr, grab that crate. Let's go."

"We've got company," alerted Starr as a dark blue BMW came pulling up quickly.

Styles thought quickly. "Phillips, grab that crate and climb into the bathtub. Keep low." He knew that the RV would not stop bullets very well. "Anybody but us comes through the door, shoot."

"You think—" Star interjected.

"Yeah, backup. We're going out the windshield." Moving quickly to the front, Styles kicked the large section of glass out, hearing it shatter against the pavement. "You go out, and get under the RV. Try to get to the back dual wheels. Shoot at whatever you can. I'm going up on top."

Both men climbed out of the opening, Styles high, Starr low. They heard two doors open and close and then footsteps advancing carefully.

While Starr was belly-crawling under the RV, Styles had jumped up on the roof and was crawling down the middle, staying as low as possible. He heard one of the men shout out, "Rijah!" and then Arabic jabbering. Styles could tell both men were advancing on the door side of the RV. He had made it halfway between the entrance door and the rear of the recreational vehicle. He could hear the men approaching his position and then slowly moving past him, toward the door. He crawled over to the side and looked over, making the decision to try to take them alive. He holstered his Beretta behind his back, snapping it in place. In one motion, he pivoted on the roof and then launched himself at the two men, both of whom brandished silenced handguns. He landed one foot on each man's shoulder and then rolled when he hit the pavement. The impact knocked both adversaries to the ground, and their pistols went skittering across the pavement. Styles jumped to his feet and kicked the closest one in the side of his head. This man was the smaller of the two. The larger man had managed to get to his feet, a look of pure rage on his face. He advanced toward Styles and tried to kick him in the balls. Styles moved aside, and the large man's foot swept past him. Styles circled the big man. Again, the man tried to kick him, this time catching a fist in the side of his knee for his trouble. He grunted but kept coming, drawing a knife in the process.

Republican Guard. Styles changed his stance, a bit more angled.

The man's hand thrust straight out with Styles first catching the man's wrist and pulling him forward while stepping into him, catching him with his hip. In a nonstop move, Styles flipped the man onto the pavement, never letting go of the wrist. Now he turned it completely over in one quick jerk, snapping it, sending the knife to the ground. The man gave a large grunt and flailed at Styles with his other hand. Styles raised his leg and brought it down square in the man's chest, knocking all the breath out of him. The man was done.

Styles turned at the sound of scuffling on the pavement. The second man had been able to regain his feet, only to find himself facing Starr. The man tried to gouge at Starr's eyes, only to receive two straight left jabs that backed him up and a solid right cross that connected perfectly with the man's liver. As he doubled over, Starr grabbed him by his long hair and brought his knee up into the man's face three times. He then threw the man to the ground. While the man was not out cold, Starr had driven the fight from him.

"Get them inside," Styles directed. He opened the door, grabbed the big man by his feet, and unceremoniously dragged him into the RV. Starr grabbed the second man under his arms and followed.

Styles yelled, "Phillips, come on out!" Looking at Starr, he said, "Nice job."

Starr nodded.

"Phillips, juice these guys."

Retrieving her small leather satchel, Phillips injected both men with her special sauce. Within minutes, both men sat tied on the couch, eyes glazed.

Styles walked over and slapped the smaller man across the face. The man barely stirred. He slapped him three more time, hard. This brought a reaction, slurred words of protest.

"What are you doing here?" demanded Styles.

Gibberish.

Styles slapped him twice more.

"Hold up a second," said Phillips. She gave him a second injection—Adrenalin. "That should help."

"*What are you doing here?*" demanded Styles.

"Pro ... Protct, Ellhad."

"Protect Ellhad from what?"

"Amerkans."

"Are there any other attacks planned?"

"Nooo."

"Who is the man with you?"

"Bu ... Butchr ..."

Styles turned and looked at Starr and Phillips. "I don't think Ellhad even knew these two were following him."

"How do you figure that?" Starr asked.

"If he'd known he had backup, he'd never have stopped in here just to get laid. I mean, think about it. You're on your way to perform one horrific terrorist act, and you stop to get laid? How stupid is that?"

"Pretty stupid," agreed Phillips.

"Stupidity caused by arrogance. I told you about these Republican Guard assholes. They think they're invincible. Starr, take the crate and put it in the backseat. See if you can secure it with the seat belt somehow. Phillips, check to see if the keys are in their car. If they are, go park it. When you get out, assume there are cameras watching; try to hide your face, and don't leave prints. I'll be right out."

Starr and Phillips left.

Styles took out his Beretta and shot both men right at the bridge of the nose. Then he took out his knife and carved up their foreheads. Then he was out the door.

Back on the road in their own sedan, Styles directed Starr to drive to Vegas. "Phillips, get hold of J. C., and tell him to pick us up in Vegas."

"Got it."

Styles, who was looking out the window at the passing landscape and seeing little, was deep in thought trying to plan their next move.

※　　※　　※

Myra Banks sat at her desk, her brain trying to comprehend what her eyes were reading. *You should have known better!* was the simple message she was staring at. At first, the scripture was large and bold, and then gradually it began to shrink and slowly disappeared altogether. The page was blank and after about three seconds went totally dark. Suddenly, a new page came up, which read: *Next time, I take out everything outside the country, as well. Consider yourself lucky.* Then that page followed the action of the preceding page. She frantically clicked her mouse and ran her fingers all over the keyboard. Her entire computer was down. She rolled her desk chair across to another desk and looked at another screen. Nothing. Her phone started ringing. Picking it up, she yelled, "I know!" and slammed the receiver down. For a minute, she put her head in her hands. *I knew it. You wouldn't let me leave her alone.* Possibly madder than she had ever been in her life, she stormed toward her director's office. She blew past his secretary and entered his office in a fury.

"Damn you, Bernie. I tried to tell you to stay away from Phillips, but no, you wouldn't listen. I all but begged you to leave her alone, but your damned arrogance just wouldn't let you. Now we're fucked."

Bernard Backersley was furious. "What's wrong with the computers? What do you mean we're fucked, and what's Phillips have to do with it?"

Myra Banks wouldn't even sit down. Standing across from him, she yelled, "What do you think I mean? She's hacked our system and wiped out everything. Hard drives, mainframes, I mean everything. It's gone. The only backup we have is what wasn't connected. Otherwise, it's all gone. Everything."

"What the hell are you talking about?"

Myra Banks rolled her eyes as she sat. "Okay, I'll use little words to try to make you understand," she said, purposely chastising her boss. "Against my better judgment, which I made *perfectly* clear to you, I continued investigating Darlene Phillips. She found out and set a trap, which I walked right into. She baited me into hacking into one of her e-mail accounts, and I fell for it. I opened up an e-mail that I shouldn't have. When I did, somehow something got into our system. A Trojan horse containing a virus like nothing I've ever seen infiltrated our entire computer network. Don't ask me how because I don't know. What I do know is this: right now, the CIA does not have one damned computer in this *entire* country that is up and running, at least not one that is hooked into our mainframe. She left me a message that said the next time she'd take out everything outside our borders too."

"Message? What are you talking about?"

"Christ, Bernie, are you that fucking dense? I can't show it to you because it's gone. Right now, I can't use one of our computers to log on to Facebook. We are going to have to rebuild our entire system. Everything. We're going to have to depend on backups that were not wired in, what we have in our foreign systems, and our own memory. She has virtually left us blind."

"How in the hell could she have done that? Myra, that's impossible. You have to be mistaken."

The anger had subsided, taken over by sheer resignation. "Bernie, you don't know how much I wish you were right. I don't know how she did it; it doesn't matter. I warned you about this woman, and you chose to ignore me. Now we have paid the piper, and there's not one damn thing we can do about it. We can't even prove she's the one who did it."

Bernard Backersley was refusing to accept this information. "Myra, no one could have done that kind of damage."

"Bernie, is your computer working?"

"*No!*"

"*Now* do you get it? And it's not going to work until I've rebuilt our entire network, and until I get that done, we are completely out of the game. We can't send an e-mail from here. We're going to have to rely on our personal laptops or whatever to contact anyone electronically. We have a backup mainframe that, thank the good Lord, was not wired into the system, so I'll have to go down and supervise the swapping out of the systems. That is only the beginning. It'll take at least twenty-four hours before we are operational, and that will only be limited. It'll take the better part of a week to get everything back. The important thing for you is to figure out how to keep this from getting out. Good luck with that. If it does, we're going to have our asses hauled up to the Hill answering some extremely difficult questions by the Senate that we do not want asked."

Backersley slammed both fists down on the top of his desk. "How could you let this happen?"

"Don't you *dare* try to put this on me! How many times did I tell you not to go nosing around Darlene Phillips? How many? This whole mess is square on you and you alone. And if I get hauled up in front of some subcommittee, you can bet your ass that's what I'm going to say. I'm not going to jail over your damned ego. You'll have to excuse me; I have to go try to clean up *your* clusterfuck." She stood up, grabbed Backersley's favorite coffee mug, and threw it across the room, shattering it against the wall. "Damn you, Bernie. *Damn you.* I suggest you'd better start making some phone calls to let our people know what the hell is going on. Don't call me; I'll call you. I have a shitload of work to do. *Thanks.*" She thundered out of his office, slamming the door so hard two framed photographs fell off the wall. She could hear telephones ringing off their hooks.

By the time she returned to her office, several members of her team were waiting for her. Approaching them, she merely held up her hand to stop any questions. "Everybody downstairs, and someone call maintenance; we're going to need some help. We have to swap out the mainframes. We've got a shitload of work to do and no time to do it, so everybody let's get going."

❈　　❈　　❈

Hidden inside a hangar at the McCarran International Airport in Las Vegas, Phillips was tapping a pencil at the conference table while Styles, Starr, and Christman were seated around opposing sofas.

"Well, the obvious question is what the hell do we do with this?" Starr asked, referencing the wooden crate strapped in place to the floor.

Phillips asked, "How much do we want to deal with this? Do we risk traveling with it? What if the plane crashes into a lake or river? Guys, I don't mind saying this thing scares the hell out of me."

"Good point," agreed Starr. "Marv, what are your thoughts?"

"I think I'll defer to J. C. for that. J. C.?"

Christman was quiet before he answered. "Well, obviously, we take it to somebody, or somebody comes to us. Who is that going to be? The chances of us crashing are extremely negligible, but there is always the possibility. Weigh that against what could happen to it if someone else becomes responsible for transporting it. How are they going to do that? My gut says it'll be flown; might end up having a military escort of some kind. I'm not sure. I think it would be as safe with us as anyone. To me, the bigger question is who do we give it to? FBI? CDC? NSA?"

"Good question," Styles agreed.

Phillips spoke up. "I've worked previously with Olivia Watson; she's the assistant director of the CDC in Atlanta. I think I could hand it off to her without a lot of questions."

"How would she explain how she got it?" Starr wanted to know.

"I'm not really sure. I'll just vaguely explain the circumstances and see what she comes up with. She's pretty sharp. Like I said, I've worked with her before."

"Darlene, if you trust her, that's good enough for me," Styles asserted, with everyone noticing that Styles was calling her by her first name more and more.

"Yes, I do. A couple of years ago, the CIA had a, uh, let's just say a delicate problem, and she proved herself. She's not afraid to act on her own. If we all agree, I'll give her a call."

"Well?" Styles asked, looking at Starr and Christman.

"Fine by me," agreed Starr with Christman nodding his agreement.

"Make the call."

Phillips retreated to the workstation she'd set up on the jet and opened up one of her laptops, retrieving a phone number. Using a secure line, she placed the call. After three rings, the call was picked up.

"Olivia Watson," announced the voice over the phone.

"Olivia, Darlene Phillips here. I'm going to give you a number. I want you to get a burn phone and call me back on it ASAP. It is critically important, and keep this between us. Here's the number," she continued, reciting it to her.

"I have one already that's never been used. I'll call you back in ten minutes. It's in my car."

"Great. I'll be waiting."

Returning to the group, Phillips announced, "She's calling me back on a burn phone. No need to advertise this conversation. I'd suggest we head for Atlanta."

"I'll get the tanks topped off, and we'll be on our way," Christman said, getting up and heading for the cockpit.

Phillips started to grin.

"What's with the smile?" Styles asked.

"Just thinking about how this is going to absolutely just burn Backersley's ass. I wish I could be a fly on the wall when the CDC comes up with this."

"Why would that piss him off?" Starr inquired.

"Because he wants to be top dog and hates it when he thinks that anyone is upstaging him. It doesn't matter one bit if it falls within his jurisdiction or operational assignment. With him, it all comes back to his ego. That's his shortcoming, and it's a big one. It makes him predictable."

"Not our problem," observed Styles.

"No, it's not."

Right then, Phillips's phone that she'd designated to Olivia Watson started ringing. Answering it, she said, "Thanks for getting back to me this quickly. Olivia, I have some news that absolutely has to stay between us. I know I can count on that. Please don't ask me any questions. Just take what I say as gospel. I need your word before I continue."

"You have it, Darlene. No questions asked."

"Good. Long story short, this new synthetic toxin that everybody is concerned about is no longer a threat—at least this particular batch. It has been secured, and I want to give it to you so CDC can take possession of it. No one can know about how you acquired it. I mean no one. You'll have to come up with a story on how you got it, but it *absolutely* cannot involve me. Do you understand?"

"Yes."

"I'll be on my way to Atlanta shortly. I'll call you back at this number, and we can make arrangements for you to pick it up. I want to meet only with you, but I suggest you have a heavily armed escort waiting for you. This is much too dangerous for you to try handling alone. However, I don't want anyone in your security detail to know that you are meeting with me. You'll have to handle the logistics for that."

"Understood. It won't be a problem."

"How much time do you need to make your arrangements?"

"An hour tops."

"I'll call you when I'm an hour out of Atlanta. Talk to you soon." Phillips hung up. "Everything is being set in place with the CDC to take this," she told Styles, Starr, and J. C. upon returning to the table.

"Good. I don't really like being around this thing," grumbled Starr.

Looking out the windows, they saw the fuel truck pulling up. "We should be on our way within fifteen minutes. I don't want to draw attention, so I'm not going to speed getting there. Figure about three hours and fifteen minutes' flight time," offered J. C.

"What about anyone watching us?" Starr asked with concern.

"No need to worry."

34.

FBI Director Matt Sanderson was on the phone with Special Agent Paul Hedges, who was leading the investigation on both the deaths of the CIA agent at the motel and the massacre at Ryyaki Ali's property. "So what is your take on this, Paul?"

"Director, I'm not quite sure. My gut is telling me if the CIA was involved at the motel, I'm betting they were at Ali's property, as well. As I've said before, there's no such thing as coincidence with the CIA."

"Are you saying you think the CIA killed Ali and the rest?"

"I can't answer that with certainty, sir. It's definitely a strong possibility. I have a contact I'm going to get in touch with who might be able to shed some light on the matter."

"For argument's sake, if it wasn't the CIA who was responsible for Ali, then who was?"

"That is the sixty-four-thousand-dollar question, sir. At first glance, certainly the CIA jumps to the head of the list, but I've got a feeling there might have been someone else involved."

"And that would be?"

"Again, don't know, sir. We're working 24-7 on this. I've had the forensics team out there nonstop. We've recovered brass in 5.56 from an AR-15, 7.62×39 from an AK-47, by far the most, and some .40-caliber Smith & Wesson found inside the house. The bodies inside the house were killed with the handgun; the guards outside and in the campground were all shot with 5.56. Someone carved the word *terrorist* in Ali's forehead."

"*What?*"

"It appears whoever killed Ali carved the word *terrorist* into his forehead. Does that mean something I don't know about?"

"Yes, but I can't get into it now. How much longer will you be on-site?"

"I'm planning on returning tomorrow. I'll leave the team in place. I want that place gone over with a microscope."

"When you get back, I'll explain the *terrorist* in the forehead."

"Yes, sir. I'll be in touch."

Sanderson ended the phone call and sat at his desk thinking. He'd heard rumors about similar occurrences that had taken place over in the Middle East. He decided to call Elliott Ragar of the NSA. After Sanderson had waited on hold for two minutes, Ragar's voice came on.

"Matt, what can I do for you?"

"Elliott, I have a question. Have you ever heard of the word *terrorist* being carved into the foreheads of terrorists killed over in the Middle East?"

Silence.

"Actually, I have. At least, I've heard the rumors, though I've never actually seen it myself or talked to someone who has."

"What else can you tell me about that? My guy in charge of the Ryyaki Ali assassination just told me that's what he found. I've heard rumors too, but I wanted to double-check."

"Matt, that makes me believe we've got a new player in the mix."

"That's what I think too. Any idea of who it might be?"

"No. The closest thing I know is it might have been a sniper who was referred to as the Ghost. I've never heard a name put to it. Again, this is only what I've heard, and it's all unconfirmed."

"I think it's time we start doing some digging. I have someone over at the Department of Defense who might be able to help."

"So do I. I'll get hold of my guy and get back with you. We can compare notes."

"Do we let the others in on this?"

"Hell no. Especially that damned Backersley. Until we have some solid evidence, let's keep this between us."

"My thought exactly. I'll be in touch."

❈ ❈ ❈

"Hey, guys, we're about an hour out of Atlanta," Christman announced.

"Thanks, J. C. I'll give Olivia Watson a call and set up a meeting!" Phillips hollered back.

Styles walked up to Phillips and asked, "Can you give me a report on everything you've been able to find out about the assassination of President Williams? Sometimes I think better reading information off paper than listening to it."

Phillips opened up a desk drawer and handed him a blue folder. "This about covers it. I had a feeling you might want it," she replied, trying to hide the fact that she was close to choking up.

Styles reached down and gently held her shoulder.

"You're not the only one in pain over this, Darlene. I'm hurting too. He was a good man in a world full of lying assholes."

Phillips reached up and cautiously squeezed his hand. "Thanks."

"Anytime, Darlene, anytime." He took the folder and stretched out on a sofa with a coffee table in front of it. He'd been working out on the plane for almost three hours and was ready to tackle the information that he would use to formulate his next move.

Starr, who had witnessed the exchange but had stayed silent, sat down across from Styles. "Want any help?"

"Sure," Styles tossed half the paperwork on the coffee table. "When we're through, we'll compare notes."

"Can I get a friggin' water?" Christman yelled.

Six seconds later, a bottled water came flying into the cockpit. "Hey, careful. You might hurt something up here."

"Next time, catch it," Starr replied, laughing.

"Starr, there's something bothering me a bit," admitted Styles.

"What's that?"

"Carving into Ali's and Ellhad's foreheads. The more I think about it, the more I think it was a major fuckup."

"Why? President Williams wanted us to send a message."

"Yeah, he did, but that is going to be a link to what happened in Europe, over in the sand, and eventually traced back to the marines if someone wants to dig deep enough."

"I didn't think about that," agreed Starr.

"Obviously, I didn't either."

Both looked up as Phillips joined them. "The digging has already begun. Sanderson of the FBI is asking questions over at the DOD. He has a contact there—don't have a name yet—but I intercepted an e-mail. The name *Ghost* has surfaced, tracing back over twelve years. I take it that is what the enemy called you?"

Styles looked up at the ceiling and muttered, "How could I have been so damned stupid?"

Starr, trying to reassure him, said, "Marv, no one can foresee everything."

"I know, but that was one major dumb-ass mistake."

Phillips interjected, "I don't mean to keep bringing this up, but the obvious is that we have to go dark like we've talked about. I mean completely. If we agree, then I'm going to start eliminating all digital footprints of us anywhere I can. I'm pretty sure I can make it appear as though we disappeared."

"What about people who know us?" Starr asked.

"I can't do anything about that, but as I've already been doing, I can change all photographs of us anywhere I find one. That will disrupt any facial recognition programs. If someone possesses a photograph of us, that could be a problem, but it's one we'll have to deal with as it comes up."

"All right," stated Styles. "Let's take care of getting rid of this damned toxin, and then we go after the president's killer and talk. Glad we don't have much to do!" he exclaimed sarcastically.

"I'll go fill J. C. in," Starr said, walking toward the cockpit.

"How many photographs are there of you?" Phillips asked Styles. "Any idea?"

"Actually, not very many. My father has a few, probably a couple from high school, military ID, that's about it."

"Same for me. I've never liked having my picture taken. As far as this disappearing issue, I have to visit my mother first. After that, I'm all for it."

"Yeah, I have to see my dad. As far as I know, I don't believe Starr has any close family left. No clue as far as J. C. goes except for his sister."

"I already have a program in place to find all photographs of us anywhere. I won't delete until we officially decide."

"Go ahead and start with me."

Phillips smiled at him. "Already have. Started that a while ago, but now I'm really getting on it. I knew you would want me to. Even the Marine Corps no longer has a photograph of you."

Styles looked at her. "You are getting to know me pretty well."

"Yes, I am, and I have to admit I am enjoying that."

Styles just nodded at her.

Phillips got up and started to return to her workstation but stopped and said, "That was smart taking out Ellhad back there. It saved time and any possible manner of him contaminating anything. In my opinion, that far outweighs the carving issue."

Styles just nodded at her again. "Hold up a second. When you contact Watson, give us an hour to survey the area and maybe set up surveillance. We don't need any surprises."

"Good idea."

Styles then went forward to apprise Starr and J. C. of the plan change.

❖ ❖ ❖

J. C. Christman had parked the team's aircraft beside the Jones-Spalding Aircraft Services hangar. Luckily, he had solid knowledge of the layout of the Hartsfield-Jackson Atlanta International Airport. He had drawn a quick layout to devise the best place for Phillips to hand off the crate to Olivia Watson of the CDC, which was scheduled to take place in approximately forty-five minutes.

"Are you sure that you can trust this woman to keep her word and come alone?" Starr asked.

"She'll have an escort close by, but she'll meet me alone. I know her; she'll keep her word," Phillips answered.

"J. C., be sure to have the plane ready to leave immediately. I mean I want the engines running," Styles directed. "I'll cover Phillips just in case, but make sure everything that needs to be done to get us the hell out of here is done. If for any reason this goes south, we could have a shitload of federal agents on our asses."

"I'll be ready. I've already got our flight plan filed for North Carolina. Fuel truck is on the way. We'll be set to go."

"I'm going to scout the perimeter and set up a place for cover. Starr, I want you to be just outside the plane near the access door to the storage area. Have an AR ready. Don't use it unless you have to."

"Hey, guys," Christman interrupted. "Hold on a second. I've got an idea. Why don't we just leave that crate where she can find it? Why put ourselves at risk? Think about this. The last thing we need is to risk a damned firefight here. Where are we gonna go? I can get us around pretty good, but not against the whole military. We could leave it in a spot where we can keep an eye on it. Doesn't that make more sense?"

Styles and Starr looked at each other.

"You're right; I'm way overthinking this," Styles replied.

"There's a bunch of boxes and crap right next to the hangar. Put it there. We can watch it from the plane. Keep the engines off, and we're just another one parked."

Phillips grabbed a Sharpie and strode over to the wooden crate. She wrote "this one" on its side. "That ought to do it."

Without a word, Christman grabbed the wooden crate, hoisted it to his shoulder, and departed the plane without speaking. The other three watched as he casually walked over to the building and stacked the crate on top of the pile. Turning around, he returned to the plane.

"Glad one of us is still keeping his head," Styles muttered as the fuel truck pulled up, with J. C. instructing the driver to top off the aircraft.

Phillips called Olivia Watson. "Olivia, there's a hangar on the west side of the airport, Jones-Spalding. You'll see a stack of boxes.

On top, there's a wooden crated marked with a Sharpie. You're on your own." She hung up. "Now we just wait and watch."

"Thanks, guys. I'm going to pull over there and park. I'm expecting company," Christman offered the fuel truck drivers.

"Sure, no problem. If you stay the night, you'd better check in with Jones."

"We should be gone before dark, but appreciate the heads-up," he answered, offering him one of the many credit cards he carried.

"Thanks for the business. Fly safely." He left after giving Christman the receipt.

Forty minutes later, a black SUV drove straight up to the debris pile next to Jones-Spalding Aviation Services. A blonde woman dressed in a black business suit got out and looked around carefully. Styles and company watched as she spoke over a small handheld radio.

"Look to the right, two hundred yards," Styles said.

All three, looking through binoculars, turned their attention to where Styles had directed. All of them saw two more black SUVs parked side by side.

"You think they have orders to intercept?" Starr asked.

"No. It looks more like a security detail. Phillips was right," Styles answered.

The woman walked over to the pile and immediately picked up the crate. Holding it in front of her, she motioned with her head, and the two other black SUVs immediately headed toward her, squealing their tires. Both pulled up directly in front of her, with four men getting out with guns drawn keeping a hard watch as a fifth man got out and took the crate from the woman and then carefully placed it in the rear of one of the two SUVs parked next to her. She walked back to her own vehicle, and all three drove away.

"That went smooth. Guess we got lucky for once," J. C. commented.

"Luck had nothing to do with it. You had your head in the game and made the right call," Styles insisted.

Phillips had returned to her computers. "Hey, guys, I've got something. I've been monitoring the boat traffic in the harbor around Baltimore. I've tracked twelve large yachts that have left the area since President Williams was killed." It was the first time she had been able to speak about the event out loud. "Eleven left, one came back. That one had been anchored but then went out about twenty miles and anchored again. They were there for about twelve hours before returning close to their original spot. While they were out, something very interesting happened."

"What was that?" Styles asked.

"Come see for yourselves."

All three men gathered around Phillips as she showcased a video. They were looking at a large yacht. Two people could be seen fishing. Then a cloud passed across the view, obscuring it somewhat. Phillips hit a couple of keys on her keyboard, and the screen split into two views—the original and infrared.

"See? On the left, before the cloud hits, we clearly see two figures. Now watch. On the infrared, you see the two figures. Now a third comes into view, *but he's in the water.*" All four observed the two men on the boat bringing the third aboard. The cloud passed over in time to see three men now standing at the rear of the yacht closing a large enclosure.

"What was that?" Starr queried.

"Large boats have water garages in the rear. They keep jet skis, small boats to shuttle back and forth to land, while the larger one stays at anchor. Something was just stashed there."

"Maybe an underwater scooter," growled Styles. Good job, Phillips. We have our target. J. C., get us the hell outta here."

"Baltimore?"

"Baltimore!"

"There is one more thing we need to be aware of," stated Phillips emphatically.

"What's that?"

"The guy who originally made up this synthetic agent; we don't know how much more might be out there. I've got bank accounts from Ryyaki Ali, and as soon as I can, I'm going to thoroughly research his financial transactions and see what I might be able to come up with."

"Damn, you're right about that," growled Styles. "Hell, no wonder we've got so many security agencies. There isn't enough time to track all these bastards."

"Welcome to my world," said Phillips.

35.

Olivia Watson was sitting in Michael Lang's office. The director of the CDC was reaming her a new one. Sitting across from him at his desk, she wasn't budging an inch. Lawrence Larkin was also in attendance, sitting off to one side in a leather chair.

"Olivia, do you honestly expect me to believe that you just happened on what might be the most dangerous toxin ever produced from the result of an anonymous phone tip?"

"I didn't say that, sir. I told you that I received the tip over the phone from someone I trust, and that is how I came to possess it. I immediately called Lawrence here, he met me, and I handed it over to him." Larkin nodded in agreement, supporting the latter part of her statement.

"Don't you think that the president is going to ask how in the hell *we* came up with this, when half of our intelligence force is looking for it?"

"I'm sure he will, sir, and I'm just as sure that you will provide a satisfactory answer. However, you will not get any more information from me. I gave my word, and I will keep my word. If you can't respect that, you can fire me!"

"Don't think I won't."

"Don't think I'm scared," she snapped back, eyes blazing. "Michael, we have the damned thing. The threat was stopped. You will get the credit. Get off my ass."

The phone on the director's desk rang. Lang picked it up to hear his secretary inform him that the president was on the phone.

"Put him through. Yes, Mr. President. You have heard correctly. We are in possession of what we believe was the synthetic agent that was responsible for the devastation in Alaska. There is no way to know if this is all of it, but we believe the amount we have would most certainly have been used as a terrorist act. We are just starting to study it. It's under the strongest CDC security available."

"I am very interested in learning how you obtained this, Michael," President Lamar demanded.

"Assistant Director Watson has a contact that led her to it."

"Michael, you have no idea of the resources I have put forth to locate this. Then Irving Vickers gets a phone call that you have it. I would like the rest of the story."

"Sir, that's a little difficult at the moment."

"*Difficult?*"

"Yes, sir. Watson is not willing to share any further information."

"Get Watson. I want to speak to her direct."

"She's sitting across from me. With your permission, I will put this call on speaker."

"Do it."

"Mr. President, you are now on speaker with me, Olivia Watson, and Lawrence Larkin. He's my most valuable team leader."

"Have Larkin leave. He's not to be part of this conversation."

Without a word and without looking at anyone, Larkin left the room.

"Larkin has left, sir. It's only Watson and me."

"Ms. Watson, I want to know, right now, all the specifics involved in how you obtained this toxin."

Olivia Watson gritted her teeth and responded, "I'm sorry, Mr. President, I can't do that. I was directed to it by someone I trust, and it was insisted that this person remain anonymous. I will not betray that trust. I believe the bigger picture is the fact we have it, not how I got it."

"Ms. Watson, I am the president of the United States, and I am ordering you to reveal any and all information you have pertinent to this discussion. Do I make myself clear?"

"Yes, sir; however, you have to understand that my word is more important to me than losing my job."

"Listen to me very carefully, Ms. Watson. I'm not talking about your job. You either start explaining, or you will go to jail for a very long time. I will throw every charge at you that the Department of Justice can possibly come up with, and I will make them stick, including aiding and abetting a terrorist organization. Do you understand what I am saying?"

"Yes, sir. Perfectly. I also understand our country was formed and built on principal. I am doing nothing different."

"Yes, you are, Ms. Watson. You are going to jail. Michael, hold Ms. Watson under lock and key until an FBI team arrives to take her into custody. If she is not there when the team gets there, I will hold you directly responsible." The call ended.

"Olivia, wake up. The man is serious. Hell, you could end up in GTMO. I mean fake a name, make up a story, but do something. I don't agree with what you're doing, but I don't want to see you go to jail either."

"Michael, anything I say I'm going to have to back up with proof. I can't—I won't—concoct some story. I gave my word, and I will keep my word, no matter what the consequences. If the president can't respect that, well, that is his problem. I don't want to talk about it. I'll wait in my office for the FBI. You have my word I won't run." She got up to leave.

Michael Lang stopped her. "Olivia, if you want to slip out the back, I won't stop you. I don't agree with you in the manner you have decided to take, but I also think it's wrong for you to be jailed."

"Thank you, Michael, but it's my decision, and I will live with it." With a nod, she walked out of his office headed for her own.

After a few moments, Lang instructed his secretary to connect him with the president. A few moments later, his phone rang, and answering it, he heard, "Please wait for the president."

"Yes, Michael. I take it that Ms. Watson has decided to cooperate?"

"Not exactly, sir. In fact, I am placing this call in defense of Ms. Watson." He swallowed hard. "Sir, she has some valid points. I am asking you to go easy on her."

"Michael, I have no wish to incarcerate Ms. Watson. However, it is imperative that everyone get on board with the expectations of my administration. When I ask questions, I want answers. When I don't get them, there will be consequences. Ms. Watson is willfully withholding information that I deem extremely important. It's my call. It's not just about how she came to find this toxin; it is what might domino from that action. Unless she is willing to cooperate, she will be charged with some extremely serious criminal charges."

"Mr. President, Olivia Watson is one of the most valuable assets in this agency. To lose her would damage the CDC's abilities."

"Nonetheless, Michael, it is what it is. Either she discloses the information she has, or else."

"Mr. President, please indulge me one more point."

"Go on."

"All of this ultimately comes back to the matter of trust, of which there is damned little these days. It was trust that allowed Olivia to obtain this agent. *Trust and only trust.* Hell, our own security agencies don't trust each other. I fully understand your need to know information, as that enables you to make the best decisions. However, I can also see that under extraordinary extenuating circumstances, it is just as important to keep a trust in place. Remember, if that had not been in play, we would *not* have this agent. Looking at the big picture, I strongly implore you to respect Ms. Watson's contact and just be thankful that she *had* that contact, for who knows when that might help us out at some point in the future."

Silence. Then, "I don't like it, Michael, but I do see your point. I'll have to think about it. I make no promises, but for the moment, I will hold off having her picked up. That does not mean I won't change my mind and have her picked up tomorrow. I'll have to think about it, strongly."

"Thank you, Mr. President. That's all I ask." Director Lang then called Olivia Watson. "You're off the hook for the moment, but it could only be temporary."

Elliott Ragar was in a quiet conversation with Matt Sanderson in the Situation Room. The directors of the major agencies were also present, milling about waiting on the arrival of President Lamar. It was surprisingly quiet.

"Any idea what this is about?" asked Sanderson.

"None. Have you found out any info on what we talked about before?"

"A little. Seems like a sniper who worked as a loner was responsible. If he's out, I'd say he's brought his show back home."

"Did you get an ID on him?"

With a frown, Sanderson answered, "No. I've had my people working on it, but it appears that records on this particular individual have been erased. Quite thoroughly, I might add. I can't get a name, a photo, not anything. I've got people over in the Middle East asking questions, but they aren't getting anywhere either. It's all very strange. The military is cooperating, barely, but they aren't going out of their way to help either—a code-of-silence thing."

Right then, President Lamar entered the room, with everybody rising to their feet.

"Please be seated," he instructed. "I want you all up to speed on information that was given to me a short while ago. The CDC is in possession of what they say is the toxin that was used in the Alaska incident. Director Lang has assured me of this. What we don't know is who was responsible for manufacturing it. Therefore, we need to continue our efforts in finding this individual before he can make more. I am not going to answer questions on how the CDC found it; at the moment, that is not important. Finding the individuals behind the assassination of President Williams and the individual for this toxic agent is—along with our other responsibilities, of course. I applaud the efforts of the CDC, as should you all. Let's get back to work." The president turned and left the room.

Everyone in the room was stunned, especially Bernard Backersley of the CIA. *How in the hell?*

Styles and Starr were up front in the cockpit of the jet, headed for Baltimore and talking with Christman. Styles left the group and walked rearward.

"Care to join us up front?" Styles asked Phillips.

"Be right there." Thirty seconds later, she joined the three men in the cockpit of their jet.

"Okay, guys, here's the deal. I think I made a mistake that may leave a door ajar for someone to find me, which would lead to us. I thought this could wait, but now I'm not so sure," Styles asserted.

"I vote we go dark," stated Christman emphatically.

"So do I," agreed Starr.

"I need to see my mother, but you know where I stand," offered Phillips.

"You guys know what this means, right? We lose contact with everyone we know, probably for the rest of our lives. We'd lose pensions, medical benefits, the whole deal."

"Unless they agree to go dark with us," interjected Phillips.

Styles looked at her. "You sure you can do that?"

"I could create our own little witness protection program: my mother, your father, and anyone else Starr or J. C. might want to bring along."

"No one on my end," Starr said flatly.

Christman was thoughtful for a few moments. "There's someone I need to speak with, but after that, no."

"I need to speak with my dad," asserted Styles. "I'm sorry to spring this on you like this, but we can't afford to take chances. Phillips, you said you could make us disappear? Make us disappear. Start ASAP."

"As you know, I already started with you. I've already deleted everything from military records to social security. People who know you will just wonder what happened. The smart ones might guess, but it won't matter; they won't find us."

"For what it's worth, I wish it hadn't come to this," Styles said in an almost apologetic tone.

Starr looked at him and declared, "We agreed to wage this war. If this is where it takes us, then this is where we all decided to go. As the three musketeers said—"

"Not to keep being repetitive, but you three have thought this through carefully and understand just how it will affect us, right?"

"Marv, chill. We know. We three have talked about it. We're in with no regrets," Starr affirmed.

"J. C., how fast can you get me to Sarasota?" Styles questioned.

"From here, hour and ten minutes, give or take."

"Do it. Thanks." He retreated to the rear of the plane and called his father.

"Hi, Dad, it's me. I need you to meet me at the Sarasota-Bradenton airport in about an hour and fifteen minutes. It's critical. Sorry for the short notice, but it's necessary." After a short pause, Styles replied, "Yeah, meet me in the main bar. If you get there first, grab a table off to the side. Keep this to yourself. See you soon."

Phillips called him over to her workstation and motioned for Starr to join them. "I've been working on the video of the yacht I've been watching. I went back over it with the same program that I used on the Alaska lake video—you know, the one that was able to distinguish heat signatures? Something interesting happened the night before the attack. Watch this." She played the program on the large LED screen. It showed three orange figures very close to one another. After a few moments, one of them seemed to break away from the other two, and then the color of the object dimmed before disappearing altogether.

Starr asked, "What do you make of that?"

Styles answered, "Well, something eliminated that third heat source."

"Correct," agreed Phillips. "I've watched it about ten times, and with the hour involved, three fifteen in the morning, I think that two people threw a third overboard, and sinking in the water caused the loss of the heat signature. It's only a guess, but it's an educated guess based on a theory I came up with. For argument's sake, let's say that is the boat, which I think it is, that picked up the diver that killed President Williams. If the boat is registered outside of this country, at some point it would have had to go through customs. There would be a record of everyone on board. Now all of a sudden there is an extra person. If the boat is rechecked, how would they explain that? The answer is to keep the number the same, which involves eliminating one, thus tossing somebody into the water. It would be easy enough to just switch the photograph on the paperwork. If they're checked now, everything matches."

Styles whistled softly. "That's a hell of a deduction, Darlene. It explains a lot, answers a lot of questions. I think you've hit it."

"I think you're right. It makes good common, logical sense," Starr inserted.

"As soon as I'm done talking to my father, we'll head for Baltimore and come up with a plan," Styles added.

"Hey, guys, we're about twenty minutes out of Sarasota!" J. C. hollered back at them.

36.

Back in the Oval Office and still drinking coffee, President Lamar demanded, "Okay, Irving. Just how did the CDC end up with that horrid toxin with their people when the people who are supposed to find it can't?"

"I have no clue. This Watson woman is sticking to her guns about not revealing information. I talked with Director Lang, and he believes that she will continue to do so, no matter what we threaten her with. She apparently is very strong on conviction. He threatened her with her job, and she told him point-blank that she didn't care. You, yourself, threatened her with jail. Her stance is that we possess it, and that should suffice."

"Nothing suffices until I say so."

"Yes, Mr. President. I agree with you; unfortunately, Ms. Watson does not."

"There are ways."

"Do you seriously want to go down that road? Ms. Watson has a lot of friends. If you try anything that is not completely above board, it will bite us in the ass." He regretted the last word immediately, as his boss did not approve whatsoever of swearing, though on the rare occasion he had done so himself. Luckily, he received only a hard glare. "Sorry."

"How do we know that the entire batch has indeed been recovered? Are we supposed to just take her word for it?"

"Sir, that was discussed with Director Lang. He believes, with certainty, that Ms. Watson is correct in this assessment."

"But how do we know?"

"In truth, I guess we don't. If you think it's appropriate, we can continue looking."

"That makes me rest a bit easier, Irving. Keep it low-key, though."

"In other words, don't let Lang know?"

"Exactly."

"Sir, I have one more thought on this subject."

"By all means, let me hear it."

"Invoking the KISS concept—*Keep It Simple, Stupid*—my feeling is that Ms. Watson was given this toxin by the people who recovered it. That's a gimme. If that's the case, and I'm sure it is, this new group does not want to be found. Looking down the road, this just might play well into our hands. Plainly speaking, the fact this new group found it speaks volumes of their ability. Sometimes it's just best to let a sleeping dog lie."

"So you are suggesting just letting this go?"

"I'm saying it is strongly worthy of your consideration. All things considered, we got lucky. Why kick that?"

President Lamar was silent for a few moments. "I'll consider what you've suggested."

"I'm only stating my honest opinion, sir."

"You always do; that's why you are my chief of staff."

❈   ❈   ❈

Styles walked into the Terminal Bar and immediately spotted his father sitting at a table off in a corner. He walked over with his father rising to his feet, and they gave each other a strong hug.

"Hi, Dad."

"Hello, Marvin. What's so important?" he asked, sitting back down.

Styles, sitting down opposite him, said, "Let's order a beer, and then we'll talk."

After two cold Sam Adams drafts had been placed in front of them by their server, Styles began.

"I'm going to give you the short version because the long would simply take too damned long. I've never spoken much about what I do or have done. For the last fifteen years, I've been a sniper in various areas of the Middle East. I always worked alone. Kind of a lone wolf, I suppose. I had a private handler. My task was simple. Kill the enemy. Leaving the military wasn't my choice."

Styles paused and sipped his beer and then continued, "I smacked some asshole captain who ordered soldiers into an area where I had just observed enemy occupation. He insisted that drones showed the area clear, ignored me, and we lost many men. I lost my temper and slapped the shit out of him. One thing led to another, and I was offered a full pension if I left voluntarily. I had my twenty in. I was disgusted with the way things were being run over there, so I thought it best to just walk away."

His father nodded. "It sounds like you did the right thing—walking away, that is."

Styles was impressed on how fixated his dad was. "When I arrived back in the States, I immediately got picked up by two secret service agents who took me to Washington."

He paused to take a long drink from his glass of beer.

"The man who commanded me the most met me and took me to see the president, President Williams. I didn't know that he and Starr—that's my commander—went back as far as they did friendship-wise. President Williams had made a decision, along with Starr's input, to try a different approach to fighting terrorism. He wanted his own personal assassin. Starr, who had found out about me getting bounced out of the marines, thought I would make a good fit."

Styles noticed his father nodding again. "We had a meeting, and I agreed. What started out as just Starr and me has turned into a four-man team, and I admit it is working well. It was hard for me; I've never been a team player, and it took a lot of adjusting on my part, and I'm sure the others, as well, and we have jelled. We make a good unit. The team consists of a pilot, Starr, a woman who can do magic with a computer—honestly, Dad, I've never seen anything like it—and me. Remember the terrorists who got taken out in Indianapolis over Memorial Day? That was us. We've also taken out targets, all at the direction of President Williams, in Europe and the Middle East."

He paused again and took another sip of beer.

"With the death of President Williams, everything has changed. Our team has been hidden under the DPO, the Department of the Presidential Office. President Lamar is going to eliminate that group. President Williams had written us a letter that was only to be read if he became incapable of fulfilling his duties as president. He thought it was imperative that we continue as a group, to continue with what he had us doing, and he thought that Lamar wouldn't go along with it. He felt we would have to go dark, do this completely on our own. We've talked about it and agreed that is what we are going to do. We believe strongly in what we are doing, and I can tell you that we have prevented serious damage from being done to our country." Styles was impressed at how intently he could see his father listening to every word.

"Where this involves you is this. Once we go dark, I can never have contact with you again. Ever. It would put you in danger. I won't do that. There is one option. You can choose to go dark too. Phillips—she's the hacker—can set up a sort of witness protection thing for you. She would give you a new identity that could never be compromised. That way we can keep in contact. You would have to leave everything you know, are connected with, *everything*, behind. No pension, no insurance, no nothing. Of course we would replace that, but still, walk away and never look back. You would be relocated any place you choose. I know you are enjoying a relationship with your girlfriend; I'm not sure about that. I haven't talked to Phillips, but if this ends up being a joint decision between the two of you, I'm sure she could go with you. I don't need an answer right now; you have a few days to think about it. I wish my situation hadn't come to this, but it has, and I have to accept it."

David Styles looked at his son, his eyes wet. "Marvin, we both know that until recently, we were never close. I've always loved you, make no mistake about that. It's just after the loss of your mother, I just, I guess I was just afraid to show love again. That is why it took me so many years to even consider letting another woman into my life. Your mother is irreplaceable, but I've finally learned to live with it. I'm finally able to enjoy the company of a woman without feeling that somehow I'm disrespecting your mother."

"Dad, Mom would want that."

"I know. It just took a very long time for me to realize that. Marvin, I'm not going to risk losing what took us way too long to establish. I need to talk to Sara, and make no mistake; I have grown extremely fond of her. To the point of I'm thinking about asking her to marry me. I need to explain the situation to her. You say you think she could join me?"

"I'll make it happen. Count on it."

"Regardless of anything else, I'm not losing you, so count me in. I only hope I can convince Sara. I don't like having to make a choice, but if I have to, you are my son." For the first time since the death of his wife over three decades earlier, David Styles saw tears in his son's eyes.

Bernard Backersley was about to tear his remaining hair out. In thirty-six hours, his response team had been bested by an unknown entity. His team leader, a man who Backersley considered all but invincible, was lying in a hospital and not going anywhere anytime soon. His cyber unit had been attacked and rendered all but useless, though Myra Banks was working virtually nonstop to get them back up and running. She had spoken very little to him since the computer attack. He had asked her once about Darlene Phillips and had only gotten a "Fuck off" in return. He knew better than to push it.

Martin Larrow, his team leader in Oregon, was on his way to his office. Two minutes later, Backersley's secretary had announced Larrow's arrival, with Backersley instructing her to usher him into his office.

"Sir," Larrow stated upon entering.

"Sit down, Marty."

Larrow made himself comfortable in one of the overstuffed leather chairs in Backersley's office.

"Tell me about the event at Ryyaki Ali's estate," ordered Backersley.

"You know most if it already."

"What is Randall's condition?"

"Pretty bad. He's looking at probably six weeks in the hospital, at least two months' healing time, and rehab after that. He took a pounding. I doubt most men could have survived."

"Do you think whoever attacked him was trying to kill him?"

"Actually, no. I think if that were the case, he'd be dead. I think because Randall is Randall, it took that much to put him down. If I may ask, how are we doing on getting our cyber unit up and running?"

"Soon, but not soon enough," Backersley answered testily.

"Where do I go from here?"

"Keep on your FBI contact. Find out everything you can. I want to know who beat us to Ali's estate."

"Yes, sir. I'll be in touch the moment I learn anything."

"Do that."

37.

"So no one else has this video?" Styles asked Phillips.

"Somebody has something, but no one has this infrared version. The only reason President Williams had it was because we gave it to them. I'm not giving this to anyone."

From all appearances, the people on the yacht *Oceaneer* were relaxing on holiday. Two men could be seen fishing. Three women were sunbathing. Other individuals could occasionally be seen going about yacht business. Anchored within fifteen miles of the spot where the American president had just been killed, there weren't the emotional feelings that might have been expected. It was this observation that had roused Darlene Phillips's suspicion.

J. C. had piloted the group back to their home airbase, where the group transferred to their chopper. While on the ground. they had been able to pick up five hours of much-needed sleep.

"We need to come up with an idea on how to get aboard that yacht," Starr declared.

"Without drawing a lot of unwanted attention, either from the yacht or any onlookers," Phillips added.

"You know the adage about how sometimes the best place to hide is out in the open?" Styles queried. "Maybe an open approach

272

is our answer. I've thought about going in after dark and other scenarios, but this idea has me intrigued."

"That being …?" responded Starr.

"What if we faked being the Coast Guard? Somehow we come up with a small Coast Guard boat; under that guise, we board them, and the rest is history."

"Who would go?" Phillips probed.

"Starr, you, and me. We'd have J. C. monitoring all radio communications with interested parties."

Nodding, Starr remarked, "You know, that's not half-bad. Anyone watching might show a curious interest, but I wouldn't think much more. Assholes on the yacht aren't going to start any shit with the Coast Guard. Yeah, it gets us on board where we can take control. I like it."

Phillips added, "I should be able to finagle any paperwork making us appear legitimate. I second the idea."

"That's it, then. Phillips, start doing your magic and see where we might borrow a Coast Guard boat. Since it's an international port, it shouldn't be too much of a problem," Styles directed. "Okay, let's go inform J. C.!"

❂　❂　❂

Phillips had researched the activities of the Coast Guard and was well versed on their plan of action. They were conducting a second stringent investigation of the boats in the area but were behind the curve on information regarding the *Oceaneer*.

Starr had gone to a local army/navy surplus store and bought clothing that would pass for Coast Guard attire.

"I've got the perfect boat, guys. It went in for repairs at a local service yard and is scheduled to be picked up tomorrow. We'll grab it early. I've already got the paperwork ready, including a full set of orders to carry with us."

"I'll retrieve the boat myself. Marv, you don't look military enough," Starr said, chiding him about his appearance.

"Fine by me," he said without looking up. "We'll be decked out and waiting for you at the dock. I'm glad this is a civilian facility. We shouldn't be bothered."

Christman had landed the team's helicopter after swapping over from their jet near the service yard in an area where they were unobserved.

Starr walked straight toward the office while the other three offloaded the gear they intended to bring. All of it was contained in duffel bags, with Styles, Phillips, and Christman shouldering AR-15s. Phillips was also carrying two medium-size metal briefcases containing three of her laptops. They were on the dock less than ten minutes when service yard employees brought the twenty-six-foot center console equipped with twin Yamaha two-hundred-horsepower outboard engines and tied it off twenty feet away from where the group was standing. Without giving them a second look, they hurried away as the three started loading the boat. Four minutes later, Starr joined them.

"Who's running the boat? Probably look weird if 'White'," Christman said, referencing the officer in command, "pilots the craft."

Styles agreed. "I'll run it, or J. C., you can. Doesn't matter to me."

"I'll take it. I'd feel better with your attention on everything else."

Six minutes later at exactly eight in the morning, the foursome was heading out into the harbor.

Phillips had inserted all the proper requirements into the local Coast Guard computers if anyone might happen to check. Unless delved into deeply, their cover would hold.

Styles, using binoculars to scout the area, saw one other Coast Guard boat heading off in the opposite direction. "We don't seem to have a lot of company other than where the helicopters went down, which was on the opposite side of the bay. Lot of activity over there."

"That area will be closed off for a while," remarked Starr.

Within fifteen minutes, they were in sight of the *Oceaneer*.

"Okay, guys, game faces on," Styles directed.

Rather than use the radio that would be overheard, the decision had been made to hail the large yacht by bullhorn.

"*Oceaneer*, this is the United States Coast Guard. Prepare to be boarded," Starr instructed in a no-nonsense tone.

Two crew members appeared from the rear of the main salon, located middeck on the triple-decked craft. Both walked over to the rail.

"What do you want?" the older of the two men yelled back.

"General inspection of craft and documentation," answered Starr.

"That has already been done."

"It's going to be done again. We are boarding your vessel."

In emphasis, Styles and Phillips unslung their AR-15s, holding them across their chests.

"I will get the captain."

"You do that. Make it quick."

J. C. brought the boat to the rear landing platform and expertly guided it right next to it. Styles, with two lines in hand, jumped off and tied up the boat, with Phillips still holding her assault rifle at the ready. The boat secured, Starr and Phillips joined Styles on the landing deck. Styles had his rifle back in hand. Starr was standing between them with a large clipboard in hand. All three had cross looks upon their faces. Christman, with the motors shut down, was busy checking radio traffic.

The man who had met them at the rail returned with the captain of the boat, a man in his midforties and of heavy build. Two blonde women had come out on the deck above to observe the scene.

Styles muttered low, "The women are European, the men Middle Eastern."

The captain came down to greet them. "What is this about? We have been thoroughly checked out, and there are no problems. Why must we go through this again?"

"Because I said so," snapped Starr. "I want to see your ship's documents, passports of everyone on board, and I want everyone in your salon in ten minutes. Anyone who is not there is leaving with us. *Now!*"

"Follow me," the captain retorted, grumbling.

"What is your name, Captain?"

"Madid."

"Unusual name for a boat registered in Greece."

Captain Madid turned and faced Starr. "I'm not aware that a captain has to be from the country that his vessel is registered."

"I didn't say he did. I just made an observation. Is there a problem here?"

"No. No problem."

"Captain, the sooner we complete our task, the sooner we'll be off your boat."

"That is fine with me."

Starr, Styles, and Phillips stood impatiently in the large, lavishly decorated salon as Captain Madid ordered his first officer to immediately have everyone join them.

"Be sure they bring their passports."

"Yes, sir," the first officer said as he left to find everyone.

"How many people are aboard, Captain?" probed Starr.

"Eleven. Five are crew members, and six are guests."

"Is the owner of this vessel aboard?"

"No. He was kind enough to give this cruise as a wedding present."

"Wow. That is one hell of a wedding present."

"I agree."

"If I might inquire, what is the relationship between the owner and who he gave the boat to?"

"His brother-in-law; he was married two weeks ago."

"How long is this cruise to last?"

"I've been instructed to take up to two months. They have a list of locations they would like to visit."

"Where have you been prior?"

"We spent five days in the Bahamas. This is our second stop. From here, we are to depart for Miami."

Two couples entered the salon holding passports. The captain directed them to sit on one of the three large leather sofas. With three glass walls encompassing the salon, the view was magnificent.

A wet bar, large flat-screen television mounted on the front wall, a computer station: it was lacking for nothing.

"Have everyone hold on to their passports until everyone arrives. We'll check them one at a time," Starr ordered.

"As you wish."

Over the next fifteen minutes, all but one arrived.

"Captain, Roberto is down in the engine room performing some maintenance task. He said he would be up in twenty minutes," the first officer reported.

Starr looked at Styles and nodded and then looked at the first officer and stated, "Take him to this Roberto. Get his ass up here right now!"

"Yes, sir," Styles responded with Phillips hiding a grin. Styles followed the first officer out of the room.

"I apologize for the inconvenience; however, under the present circumstances, all foreign-registered vessels are being double-checked. We'll get this over with as quickly as possible," Starr stated.

Walking over to the far-left person sitting on the left side sofa, Phillips stared hard at the woman and commanded, "Passport." The woman handed it over. Phillips studied it intently, particularly the photograph, made some notes on the clipboard she was carrying, and then returned it. One at a time, she went to each individual and repeated the process. She had slung her AR-15 across her back.

Phillips, after studying the passport of one man, walked over to Starr. "Remember the video we captured of two guys helping a third out of the water?"

"Yeah."

"This is definitely one of the two guys."

Starr grabbed the passport and walked over to him. Looking intently at the passport and then back at the man it belonged to, Starr ordered, "Stand up and turn around."

The man pretended not to understand.

"Rifles at ready," Starr ordered, and in an instant, he and Phillips had their ARs at the ready. "Captain, tell this man to stand up and turn around, or I'll shoot him where he sits. Do it."

Captain Madid spoke to the man in an Arabic language.

Slowly, the sitting man stood, glaring angrily at Starr, and turned around.

Starr took a long wire tie and secured the man's hands behind his back, turned him around, and pushed him back on the sofa. "Don't move!" Starr ordered.

Captain Madid spoke to the man in Arabic.

Phillips drew down on Captain Madid. "Starr, there's a knife under the cushion behind him."

Starr cracked the man in the side of the head with the butt of his rifle, grabbed him by his shirt, and threw him on the floor. He reached in between the cushions and came out with a sheathed knife. He turned to Captain Madid.

"Turn around." Starr immediately secured him, as well.

Christman, still on the Coast Guard boat, spotted another one headed toward him. He picked up his binoculars and was able to clearly make out yet another CG vessel.

"Starr," he said over the comm set they were all wearing. "We've got company—more Coast Guard guys."

"Roger," he replied to J. C. Addressing Phillips, he instructed, "Hold up at the ready." She placed the clipboard aside and unslung her AR, holding it across her chest, finger on the trigger. She didn't bother to look at him. Starr proceeded outside and walked to the rail as the second vessel was coming up to Christman. This boat contained two seamen, an obvious commanding officer, and two men dressed in civilian clothing, which Christman thought odd.

The commanding officer on board yelled over to Christman, "Surprised to see you! This boat is on our list to check!"

Thinking fast, Christman responded, "We have a computer guru with us. Someone wants this boat's computers checked. We just got word about three hours ago. Guess the paperwork didn't catch up with you yet."

"My, what a surprise," the second boat's commander joked. "Well, no sense in both of us here, so have fun; we'll be on our way to the next one." Looking up at the rail, he saw Starr and saluted, receiving one in return. The second vessel turned and headed away with the two civilians looking hard at him.

"Good answer, J. C.," Starr said, and he returned to the salon. "We're all set; keep going," he instructed Phillips.

"Starr, who do you think the two guys in street clothes were?" asked J. C.

Phillips cut in. "I can answer that. The feds are going to have their people on board to try to find something that the Coast Guard guys might have overlooked the first time. No doubt that's who they were."

"Guess that explains why they were staring daggers at me as they left," Christman retorted.

"J. C., keep a sharp eye out for them. If they return, we don't want to be surprised," instructed Starr.

"Copy that."

❖   ❖   ❖

Styles was following the first officer down to the engine room. He was impressed with the cleanliness of the yacht. There did not appear to be a spot anywhere on anything. The bright work of chrome and brass absolutely shimmered. He was led down some stairs and to a large metal door.

"In there," pointed the first officer.

"After you," instructed Styles.

With a shrug, the man opened the door and stepped inside. There was no obvious response to his entrance.

"Now down on the floor, face-first, legs spread, and interlock your fingers behind your head," commanded Styles.

The man was reluctant to do so.

Styles, who had not yet entered the room, stated calmly, "I have no problem whatsoever shooting you. Down on the floor."

The first officer complied quickly.

Styles quickly stood over the man and secured him with plastic wire ties, binding his arms and feet. He stuffed a rag in his mouth to silence him.

Styles moved quickly throughout the entire engine compartment. Checking everywhere, Roberto was not to be found. Then a thought hit him, hard.

Over their earbuds, Styles warned, "Starr, nobody's home. I think he might be headed for the fuel tanks. Put Phillips on guard, and you start making your way downstairs. The tanks should be on the lowest level, amidships or slightly rearward. If you spot him, unless he's actively trying to blow us up, let me know where he is. If you have to shoot, try not to kill him, and don't hit the damn tanks."

"Gotcha."

Styles moved as quickly as he dared to where he thought the tanks would be without putting himself at risk. There was no doubt in his mind that the man he sought was none other than Nazir al-Hadid, who would be more than willing to blow himself and everyone else up. He also knew he probably had very little time. Up ahead, he saw a trapdoor. That should be it.

"Starr, there's a trapdoor in a hallway, probably directly below you, two flights down. I'm going in." Styles had developed a knack for walking in virtual silence, which he employed now. Reaching the entrance in the floor, he put his ear to the steel floor and could make out noises below him. In a low voice, he told Starr, "I'm leaving my AR on the floor. Make sure it's secure." He had his Beretta in one hand as he slowly opened the door in the floor. No response. He looked inside and did not see anyone within a fifteen-foot circle. There were two large metal cabinets just to his right with a four-foot space between them, both full of gauges. In one motion, he dropped through the opening to the floor seven feet below and then tucked and rolled between the two cabinets.

Immediately, two shots rang out at him, each missing by more than three feet. *Stupid, now I know where you are.* Styles holstered his Beretta and retrieved two of his throwing knives. Like a snake, he inched along the floor until he could see a shadow moving from light that was thrown by the fluorescent fixtures above. Another shot rang out, directed toward the place that Styles no longer occupied. He guessed he was about twelve feet from his quarry. In one motion, Styles stood and cocked his throwing arm. A single glance told him that Nazir al-Hadid was just finishing affixing a bomb to the fuel tanks. A flash split the air and impaled al-Hadid in the right shoulder, causing him to scream. A second followed, hitting him just above the left elbow, and he collapsed onto the corrugated steel floor. The wounds were not life threatening, but certainly disabling. Looking around cautiously as he approached al-Hadid, he was certain that only the two of them were in the room. The fuel tanks were enormous. He couldn't even begin to guess their capacity. Standing over al-Hadid, he kicked the Glock nine-millimeter pistol away that had been dropped.

"Unlike you, I don't want to blow us up." He reached down and yanked both knives out of his victim. Wiping the blood on al-Hadid's shirt, he told Starr, "Al-Hadid is secure." He holstered his knives.

Through his pain, sheer rage glowered from Nazir al-Hadid's eyes. "How do you know my name?" he snarled before realizing the mistake of admission.

Styles squatted down beside him. "Good. You like to talk. You'll talk more."

"I will tell you nothing."

"You won't have a choice," growled Styles.

Styles turned him over and thoroughly checked him for weapons. Finding none, he secured both his arms and legs with wire ties. He then hoisted him over his shoulder and managed to get him up out of the engine bay and into the corridor. He started making his way back, found a stateroom close to the main salon, and dumped al-Hadid onto the bed. He double-checked the ties and then went to rejoin his group.

"The first officer is secure in the engine room. Al-Hadid is wounded and secure in a stateroom just down the hall."

"What about the others?" asked Starr.

"I think it's safe to assume the entire crew is part of the terrorist plot, but I'm not sure about the passengers."

"I've been running the passports, and by all accounts, the

wedding party is just that. I think they're being used as a cover," offered Phillips.

"So what do we do with them? They've seen us," stated Christman.

"No innocents; that's what he said. We can't ignore that!" exclaimed Starr.

"I agree," stated Phillips.

"Take them back to their staterooms, be damn sure they are secure, and we'll leave the rest of the crew here," Styles directed.

As Phillips and Christman led the wedding party away, Starr and Styles bound the crew members with the plastic wire ties and then went and retrieved the first officer.

Styles walked back in with the first officer slung over his shoulder just as Phillips and J. C. returned. "Those people all set?"

"Yeah, they're not going anywhere," Phillips asserted emphatically.

Styles turned and started to leave.

"Where are you going?" Starr asked.

"To find an empty state room or something. Phillips, you're with me." The second door on the left was exactly what Styles was looking for, a small conference room. He tossed al-Hadid into a blue overstuffed leather lounger. "Give him something for the pain."

Looking a little confused, Phillips went to her small leather case and retrieved a syringe and then drew morphine into it from a small vial. Finding a vein in al-Hadid's right forearm, she injected the painkiller. Almost immediately, the man appeared more comfortable.

Styles peered hard into al-Hadid's eyes. "I gave you that to show you that if you answer my questions, this will go well for you. If you don't answer, it won't."

"I have nothing to say."

"Load that thing up with your special sauce," addressing Phillips.

Picking up another vial, she extracted the liquid it contained into the syringe. She nodded.

"Give it to him."

Finding the same vein, she injected approximately one-third of the contents into al-Hadid. His eyes immediately started to glaze over slightly.

"What is your name?" Styles demanded.

"I tell you nothing."

Styles nodded at Phillips, who injected half the remaining serum into al-Hadid.

They watched as his head started to fall to his chest. Styles grabbed him by his hair and yanked his head upright.

"What is your name?"

"A ... a ... Hadeddd ..."

"He's under pretty far," Phillips offered.

"Who ordered the death of the American president?"

"All of us," al-Hadid stammered, managing a smirk, and then he reeled as Styles slapped him hard across his face. Styles knew that the blow wouldn't hurt due to the morphine; it was the shock value he wanted. Al-Hadid continued, "I shot down."

"Who planned it? Give me a name."

Al-Hadid was struggling valiantly against the drugs but was losing the battle. "I do not know."

Styles nodded again, but Phillips cautioned him.

"He's pretty close to the limit now."

"Take it to the limit—past if need be. We need answers."

Phillips injected the remaining portion in the syringe into al-Hadid. His eyes now were closed. Styles slapped him hard across his cheeks three times, causing his eyes to open slightly.

"Who planned the assassination of the American president?" Styles snarled at him.

"Al ... Ali ... Ryki Ali ... and his brother." With that, his head collapsed on his chest. He jerked violently twice and died.

Over their earpieces, Starr informed them that they had company.

"Looks like the same bunch."

Looking at Phillips, Styles said, "We don't have much time. Find the computers and do whatever you do. We need the intel. Don't stop no matter what you hear." With that, he was running back toward Starr.

"Where's Phillips?" Starr asked.

"Getting the intel off their computers. We need to buy her time."

"What's the plan?"

"Wing it, what else? J. C., you copy that?"

"Copy that. What do you want from me?"

"Stand ready and look mad."

38.

At six in the morning in the Oval Office, President Lamar was having a meeting with only three of his directors; Elliott Ragar of the NSA, Charles Rockford of Homeland Security, and Matt Sanderson of the FBI were in attendance.

"Gentlemen, where do we stand with regard to President Williams?"

Sanderson answered, "Sir, we have fifteen yachts under observance where the recovered scuba diver could have retreated to. They are being watched 24-7. The Coast Guard is going to board them again to double-check all their paperwork. Four of them are foreign registry. They'll be gone over with an even finer-tooth comb. We are confident we will find something linking one of them to the assassination."

President Lamar did not hide his contempt. "So, Matt, you're telling me that you think that a group capable of killing the president of the United States is going to leave something on board their boat connecting them to that? I find that highly implausible."

Ragar spoke up. "Sir, sometimes it's the smallest item that may be overlooked. When the vessels are boarded, we will have at least two of our people along, people who are extremely experienced in picking up on information that the Coast Guard may not spot."

"And that information might be …?"

"We won't know until we find it, sir."

"I honestly wish I could share your faith. When I think about how they were able to bring three helicopters down with such ease, it sends ice-cold shivers up and down my spine. My God, man, their plan was brilliant. I'm only surprised it hasn't happened sooner. I'm having my secret service detail work out different travel scenarios for me. I have no wish to have a missile explode in my face."

"Yes, sir," all three echoed.

"When will you start these Coast Guard inspections?"

"We are assembling the secondary teams now as a follow-up to the primary inspections," answered Rockford. "We are bringing in personnel from all three of our agencies to assist in the operation. We also have the Coast Guard checking any yachts capable of long-range cruises within a two-hundred-mile radius."

"Let me know what you find, and gentleman, *find something*!"

"We will, sir. You can count on it."

The president gave a halfhearted nod and dismissed the three with a wave of his hand. The door had no more closed when a second one opened, and Irving Vickers entered.

"What do you think, Irving?"

"The plan seems sound, sir. I also agree with your assessment that I doubt anything will be found linking a group to this horrific act."

"I know that those three are doing everything that they can, but I can't help but worry it's simply not enough."

❋   ❋   ❋

CIA agent Martin Larrow had stopped by the hospital to check in on Robert Randall, who was lying in a hospital bed. He was awake, semialert, and sedated, but inside, he was in a rage. He could not get the face of the man who had put him where he was out of his mind. With great effort, he could speak slowly between his teeth, a fact that bothered him even more. The overall team leader, Marty Larrow, was attempting to question him.

"I'm not going to waste time asking you how you are. I can see that for myself. I want to know if you can give a description of the man who attacked you. One of your group got a glimpse of him but because of face paint could only give a very general description. Can you do any better?"

Randall only grunted in rage.

"Look, right now we've actually got more important items to deal with besides how pissed off you are. Look at it this way. If you can help ID this guy, you're closer to getting back at him." Larrow was trying to use Randall's arrogance to his advantage.

Randall glared fire at Larrow before responding painfully, "Trained. Good. Military or better. Scar on left side of face. Hard to see. Real fast. Accurate."

"That's good. Anything else you can think of?"

"Both hands."

"You mean he was ambidextrous?"

Randall nodded slightly. "When do I get out?"

"Not for a while. We'll fly you back home when you can travel. Probably be at least six more weeks."

Randall only stared daggers at him.

"Sorry, but it's the doctor's call. I'll check on you again."

"Don't bother."

"Your choice," Larrow replied as he got up to leave.

"Yes," Randall said as loud as possible.

Larrow only nodded and left. Walking down the hall toward the parking lot, he called Backersley.

"Sir, I just spoke with Randall. The only information he could provide was the guy was six feet tall, about two hundred pounds, and has a scar on the left side of his face. He had a tough time talking. He did mention that possibly the guy was top military trained."

"Not much more to go on. I'll start running a facial against anyone who might fill the bill," he responded.

"I'm on my way back to Langley."

"Report to me as soon as you get here."

"Absolutely."

After the conversation with Larrow, Backersley called Myra Banks.

"Where do we stand?"

"We're about 80 percent. The new servers are up; now it's a matter of loading programs and intel. I'm going back to my office and sleep. Bernie, I don't care if the damned world comes to an end, do not wake me up." She was still incredibly angry with him.

"Thanks, Myra. I won't." He wasn't quite sure what to do, which was rare. He knew he could use some help, but his options were limited. Since he was in the middle of something he'd been ordered out of, he had to do everything on the sly. He finally decided to try to utilize his unknown cyber contact. *Trying to find info on an unknown operative with highest skill in hand-to-hand combat. Scar on side of face. Six feet tall, two hundred pounds. Probably military. Any help appreciated.*

Just under an hour later, he received an answer. *Will take time.*

Despite everything in the world that the CIA was involved with, at that particular moment, Bernard Backersley felt like he was standing still.

❈ ❈ ❈

Aboard the second Coast Guard boat that had approached the *Oceaneer*, two members from the FBI were huddled together. Albert Haines had been specifically assigned to head up a six-man team to assist the Coast Guard in the search for any clues regarding the assassination of President Robert Williams. He held a PhD in criminal psychology and was blessed with a near photographic memory. He had personally chosen the team and had assigned Del Forbanks as his partner.

Forbanks excelled in cyberwarfare, and Haines thought it prudent to have a computer expert as half of each team.

"Anything about that team we just ran across bother you?" Haines asked Forbanks.

"Nothing stood out. Why? Did you pick up on something?"

"The clothes the guy in the boat was wearing. It wasn't the latest CG issue."

"Do you think that is pertinent? Maybe the guy just has old stuff left. The Guard is a little more relaxed in their dress code."

"True. It just stood out, and that's what we are here to find, anything that might stand out."

"So you want to go back and ask that guy about his clothes? Al, I'm not sure what a shirt might have to do with shooting down the president."

"That wasn't the only thing. The AR the guy had. It was equipped with an EOTech holographic sight system. That is definitely not standard Coast Guard issue. I think we should follow up on anything that is out of the ordinary, and those two items were."

"So what is your thought process here?"

"What if that bunch isn't Coast Guard?"

"Then who the hell are they? It looked like they were doing exactly what we're supposed to be doing. They were in a Coast Guard boat. It's your call, but I think it's a waste of time."

"I'd rather waste a little time than to be wrong about something."

"I can't argue that."

Agent Haines got up and approached the Coast Guard commander of the small craft.

"Sir, I want to go back and check out that other team on the large yacht we just left."

"Any particular reason?"

"No, just a hunch, I guess."

"You are aware we have other boats to check."

"I know, but it will only take a short time. I'm just doing my job."

"As you wish," and ordered the boat's return.

❈   ❈   ❈

The second Coast Guard boat containing the two FBI agents tied off against the craft that Styles and crew had used, which was tied off against the rear of the *Oceaneer*. Styles and Christman were each standing off to one side of Starr, flanking him.

"I'll handle this," he had emphasized.

One of the FBI agents looked at Starr and requested, "Permission to come aboard?"

Testily, Starr replied, "Permission denied."

"Huh?"

"Permission denied. We are conducting an authorized military operation. Permission denied."

Holding up his credentials, the agent said, "We're the FBI, here on probably the same mission. We need to come aboard."

"I don't care if your Santa's helpers. You are not in my chain of command." Looking at the commander of the second CG vessel, Starr demanded, "Where do you stand on this?"

The commander was obviously uncomfortable. "I was ordered to bring these two agents with us to assist in secondary reconnaissance of foreign-registered vessels and work with them, but I am in command of this boat. Give me a second." He immediately got on his own radio. A short conversation ensued; then he looked at the two FBI agents. "According to my commander, this is an ongoing operation."

Starr nodded. Looking back at the two FBI agents, he continued, "You will not come aboard this vessel while we are conducting our operation. Any attempt will be met with deadly force. Do you understand?" Styles and Christman brought their assault rifles to the ready.

"Are you serious? We're the FBI!" Agent Haines looked as though he was about to go into cardiac arrest he was so red in the face. "We have to board that boat."

"The discussion is over. Commander, get these men out of here before there is real trouble."

"Yes, sir," he said, saluting Starr and receiving one in return. "Proceed back to where we were going," he told the seaman at the wheel.

"We're not going anywhere," ordered Haines in complete frustration.

The commander of the second boat walked straight up to Agent Haines and stood face-to-face with him less than ten inches apart.

"Apparently, you don't hear real well. Make no mistake, these men will shoot you. You have no authority whatsoever over them, and if you compromise a military operation, they do have standing protocol to use lethal force, and I don't want the paperwork of trying to explain your stupidity. You are not going on that boat, and that's final. One more word from you, and I'll take you both back to the dock. Are we clear on this?"

"You're making a big mistake, Commander."

"Maybe, maybe not. That's my choice. Holloway!" he called to the seaman at the helm. "Get us the hell out of here!"

"Just a second, Commander," said Agent Forbanks as he was holding his cell phone. "I want confirmation of this."

In a flash, Styles had leaped across his own boat and jumped into the second craft, brushing past the shocked Coast Guardsman, almost knocking down Special Agent Haines, and snatching Agent Forbanks's cell phone from his hand and tossed it overboard. "As my commander stated clearly, this is a military operation, and you civilian clowns are not going to interfere." He whirled around and advanced toward Agent Haines.

"Give me your cell phone!"

"I will not."

Styles grabbed the man's hand, turning it over and then up and backward. "Give me your cell phone, or I snap your wrist."

The commander of the second boat was totally perplexed. He had a hard time believing what he was witnessing.

"I won't say it again," snarled Styles.

Agent Haines fumbled in his sport coat pocket and came out with his cell phone. Handing it over, he growled, "You are going to regret this."

"Not as long as I'm doing *my* job, I won't."

The splash indicated where the second cell phone had landed and then sunk.

Styles was immediately back, flanking Starr.

"You're good to go, Commander," Starr verified.

"I don't know what the hell is going on here, but I know I want no part of it!" exclaimed the commander of the second boat.

Starr, Styles, and Christman watched as the boat turned and sped away from the scene.

"You handled that with the aplomb that I remember so well," Styles said with more than a hint of sarcasm.

"It worked, didn't it? I noticed it didn't take you long to get rid of those cell phones."

"Everybody gets lucky once in a while," he said with a grin.

With the second vessel gone, they returned to the salon. "J. C., keep an eye out just in case," instructed Styles.

"What do we do with the rest of these guys?" asked Phillips, who had just come up from the ship's office. "I uploaded everything onto a portable hard drive. They only had one computer. I did secure this satellite phone, though. I should be able to retrieve some numbers from it."

Starr offered up a suggestion. "Let's do something different. We have the info we came for. We could notify proper channels these people are here and let them sort it out. Plus, it just might be good to let the government look like they actually know what they're doing for a change."

Styles just looked at him.

"Marv, we have the intel that al-Hadid obviously isn't going to give them. It'll take a while for us to interrogate the other crew members. I'm sure they're in on what happened, but I'd bet they don't know what al-Hadid knew. That's how they work. You know that. Everybody is a spoke in the wheel."

Styles looked at Phillips and Christman. "What do you guys think?"

Christman offered, "I can see both sides of the fence. I know that's not much help."

"I say leave a note explaining the basics and shoot the crew. Why waste taxpayer money? I'm with Starr; I think they knew what was going on. We're supposed to kill terrorists. This bunch killed the president; why are we even talking about this?" Phillips stated emphatically.

"I agree with Phillips," said Styles. "Leave a note."

"Marv, you sure about this?" quizzed Starr.

"Discussion's over." He screwed the suppressor onto the barrel of his Beretta, walked over to each man, and told them in Arabic,

292

"This is for killing the president." He fired two rounds into the middle of each man's forehead. He asked Phillips, "What did you write?"

"Nazir al-Hadid was one of two men who shot down the president's helicopters, the crew members were part of the scheme, and the wedding party is believed to be uninvolved."

"That'll work. Let's get the hell out of here. J. C., once we're away, contact that other boat and request assistance at the *Oceaneer*. Don't say anything else."

Five minutes later, the *Oceaneer* was a distant view. Forty minutes later, after securing the Coast Guard boat to a dock, the group was airborne in their own helicopter flying over the bay. Boats could be seen speeding toward the *Oceaneer* with several already tied up to her.

"Gonna be a hornets' nest down there," quipped Starr.

EPILOGUE

It seemed like forever since the group had relaxed around the dining room table at the Ranch, yet it had only been four days.

"Ryyaki Ali had two brothers. One was killed six years ago in a military air strike perpetuated by us. Zabakkar Ali is the surviving brother. He is the one that Nazir al-Hadid referenced. I'm running a search on him, but so far no luck," Phillips reported.

Styles looked at her and asked, "Just what is in that concoction of yours? I've seen quite a few chemicals used in my time, but nothing that works with that kind of speed."

She answered, "The basic formula is actually Russian. I've just added a few, shall we say, spices to the mixture. The one drawback is it does often lead to cardiac arrest. I didn't think any of us would be overly concerned about that particular side effect under the circumstances. With the amount I gave him, he would be good for five, maybe six answers before either we stopped or, well, you saw what happened. It is not something I'd use on someone we were concerned about keeping alive. Speaking of chemicals, I've started researching the Chemist that I picked up in chatter couple of days ago. I think I have it narrowed down to three possibilities, but it will take more time."

"You were right on both counts. Anyone had second thoughts about going totally dark?" Styles asked.

Christman and Starr both shook their heads.

Phillips spoke up. "I've been thinking about whether it is absolutely necessary for us to involve family."

Styles answered, "That's crossed my mind half a dozen times, and it always comes back to that if we guess wrong, we guess real wrong. Darlene, I have no doubt whatsoever that no one can make us disappear as well as you, but if we don't go dark, somehow, somewhere, if someone digs deep enough, somebody is going to find something on one of us. Then it would only be a matter of time before they could trace it back to either your mother or my father. We can't put them in harm's way. My dad is okay with it. He's going to talk to his friend, and I believe invite her to join him, which, if that is what he wants, that's what we'll do. J. C. and Starr both state they don't really have anyone, which leaves just us. It's completely your call as to whether you involve your mother or not."

"I know her. She won't join us. I'll just have to make arrangements to pursue another route to maintain contact with her. We're not that close, anyway. Like I said before, we don't share the same last name. I've never said this out loud before, but she and my father were never married. She has never married. Of my brothers, only two of us share the same father, so no one is going to be able to track anything from me back to him. I've gone by Phillips since the day I left home at seventeen. No one else in my family uses that surname."

"We need to get started, then."

"I've already sent my retirement papers to all the channels," said Christman. "I'll be processed out within ten days. I've given them a PO box in Delaware as a mailing address. It's where I was born. The box is a fake. All mail sent there will simply sit. I do have a question, though. Since we are all giving up our retirement pensions, I figure that somehow we should get paid something?"

Everyone started to laugh. "I forgot all about that," admitted Styles.

"Starr, you're the bookkeeper. How about that?"

"I thought I'd start everyone at eighteen thousand per year," he said and ducked as Christman threw a magazine at him.

"Seriously, I'll have Phillips set us all up with accounts under our new names. We will all earn the same amount. I'm not exactly sure what the amount will be, but it will be sufficient for what we do."

Christman asked, "Is it permitted to ask how much money we actually have at our disposal?"

"The president set us up with a total of about three billion dollars. It's widely diversified, and I want Phillips to take a look at it and see what she can do with it," answered Starr.

Phillips added, "Plus, I have access to certain CIA accounts that I can close without anyone knowing. That would probably be worth another thirty to fifty million," Phillips added.

"Well, it's nice to know at least we'll be able to eat," joked Christman.

"As long as Styles doesn't do the cooking," emphasized Phillips. "If it's okay, I'd like to rehash something."

"Sure," said Starr.

"This going-dark thing. I might have a way to do that, not involve families, and keep everyone safe."

Styles looked up, interested. "How is that?"

"I'm using the KISS approach. The less the better."

"Can't argue with that. What's the less?"

"Family. The more I have to cover up, the greater the chance somehow something might be uncovered. I've got another idea."

"Which is?"

"The four of us fake our deaths. Plus, we officially sever all ties to our families. I'm talking about birth records, the works. They will know, but no one else."

"I'm not sure about that, Darlene. I don't want my dad in any danger because of us."

"Nor do I. Look, I'm just presenting an alternative plan. Final decision about your father is entirely your call. I'm just saying that I can make it appear as though your father never had any children. We fake our own deaths and that takes relatives off the table. I've thought this through very carefully, and it's how I'm going to protect my mother. If I wasn't sure that it would work, I wouldn't bring it up."

Styles was quiet. He got up and walked over to the window looking out over the fields. He smiled as he caught sight of a doe and two fawns grazing in the clover. Turning around, he addressed

Phillips. "If you're sure about this, that's good enough for me. I'll need to talk with Dad, let him in on the new plan. This approach does seem easier."

"It is, and easy is often the best," she replied, nodding at him. "Bear in mind he does have the choice."

"Anyone got anything else to say?"

"I can fake a plane crash pretty easy. We'll have to purchase another jet, substitute it for ours, and put it into the sea where they can't find it."

"How do we get you?" asked Starr.

"Get me? Hell, I'll be relaxing here with a cold beer."

Phillips said, "We've got two more subjects to decide about."

"Ryyaki Ali's brother," replied Starr.

"And the bastard that came up with that synthetic toxin," added Styles. "The Chemist, as Phillips calls him."

"Exactly," agreed Phillips. "So what do you guys think?"

"My vote is we go after the Chemist first. Put him out of business, permanently," suggested Starr.

"Then go after what's-his-name, the brother," stated Christman.

"My idea exactly," confirmed Phillips. "I'm getting the intel together on Zabakkar Ali; that should be finished by the end of the day. I'm running both facial and vocal recognition programs on the man that Ryyaki Ali referred to as Smith. Those will probably take longer to put together. I'm tapped into worldwide programs, but he's kept a very low profile. We got lucky that Ali had video set up in his office. That's where I found him. No one else has that info either."

"Are you going to be able to find him?" asked Starr.

"If he's on record anywhere, I'll find him. It's just a matter of when."

"So, for the moment, I take it we're on standby?" questioned Styles.

"Sounds like that to me."

"Okay. I'm going to phone my father and tell him of the game plan change. I think it would be a good idea for him to move, although he probably won't like that. The security guards there can put us together. I thought that our group could purchase his place, maybe use it as a safe house. Any objections?"

Starr nodded his approval. "That sounds like a reasonable plan. We could set it up as a rental at other times to explain different people going in and out."

"When I'm done with my dad, I'm going for a long run. If you need me, fire the shots."

"Got it. J. C., what are you up to?" inquired Starr.

"Going to work out in the gym for a while."

"Mind if I join you?" asked Phillips.

"Not at all. Be fun to have company that doesn't beat the hell outta me."

"Says who?" Phillips retorted with a grin.

※　※　※

Zabakkar Ali was sitting on the fantail of his ship, thinking of the three nude women in the hot tub one deck above him, three blonde Scandinavian women. He was cruising in the Mediterranean toward Greece aboard his opulent 246-foot custom-built yacht. It took more than four years to manufacture at a cost of just shy of half a billion dollars. It featured state-of-the-art everything, from navigation to the latest in the four turbo diesel engines that powered it. So powerful the vessel was capable of a thirty-knot cruise speed, unheard of for a craft its size. A statement of pure overkill, it featured everything from a two-lane bowling alley to a batting cage located on one of the decks of the bow. The interior was primarily comprised of rosewood, which was overly lavish throughout. The fixtures in all fourteen bathrooms aboard were solid gold. It had a galley that would be the envy of a five-star restaurant, featuring three chefs capable of serving any meal that anyone could possibly desire. The wine cellar was worth approximately $3 million, contents only.

When Zabakkar Ali commissioned the build, he demanded only one thing. "I do not want to be overshadowed by anyone, anywhere. I want to be the sheer envy of every man that looks at this craft. I want every woman to want to be aboard her, aboard me."

Five years later, his dream had been realized. He was seven months into the maiden cruise, and every whim had been more than satisfied. No matter what port he pulled into, eyes were cast in his direction. He still had no clear-cut figure for the final amount of money he'd spent, and he didn't care, as it was no object. Only his ego mattered.

His personal fortune was north of $5 billion courtesy of Saddam Hussein. Of course, Hussein never knew.

All the women around him had to be blonde. That was a prerequisite. Looking back at the sapphire-blue water, he finished his third mimosa of the afternoon. Thinking of his brother, he said aloud, "Ryyaki, if you only knew what you were missing!" He then arose and motioned for his chief steward.

"Bring two bottles of Dom to the hot tub; be sure to avert your eyes."

He received only a curt nod in return. Zabakkar Ali did not allow eye contact with himself by any of his crew, unless directed otherwise with a certain gesture of his hand. Failure to observe this protocol was certain death, which he'd proved on more than one occasion, enjoying it a little too much.

Before retreating upstairs to join his women, he allowed himself a silent toast to his brother, who had martyred himself in the greatest attack on America yet. *There will be more to follow, my brother. Allahu Akbar…*

Lightning Source UK Ltd.
Milton Keynes UK
UKOW04n1526050917

308635UK00002B/31/P